Farrow, John,
1947-

The storm murders.

The STORM MURDERS

NOVELS (AS JOHN FARROW)

River City

Ice Lake

City of Ice

NOVELS (AS TREVOR FERGUSON)

The River Burns

The Timekeeper

The Fire Line

The True Life Adventures of Sparrow Drinkwater

The Kinkajou

Onyx John

High Water Chants

DRAMA

Long, Long, Short, Long

Beach House, Burnt Sienna

Barnacle Wood

Zarathustra Said Some Things, No?

FILM

The Timekeeper

The STORM MURDERS

JOHN FARROW

MINOTAUR BOOKS
A Thomas Dunne Book
New York

This is a work of fiction. All of the characters, organizations, and events portrayed in this novel are either products of the author's imagination or are used fictitiously.

A THOMAS DUNNE BOOK FOR MINOTAUR BOOKS.
An imprint of St. Martin's Publishing Group.

www.thomasdunnebooks.com
www.minotaurbooks.com

The Library of Congress Cataloging-in-Publication Data is available upon request.

ISBN 978-1-250-05768-6 (hardcover)
ISBN 978-1-4668-7383-4 (e-book)

Minotaur books may be purchased for educational, business, or promotional use. For information on bulk purchases, please contact the Macmillan Corporate and Premium Sales Department at 1-800-221-7945, extension 5442, or write to specialmarkets@macmillan.com.

First Edition: May 2015

10 9 8 7 6 5 4 3 2 1

In memoriam,

for P.A. and Jo

and my kid brother, Jamie

ACKNOWLEDGMENTS

The author thanks his agents, Carolyn Forde and Bruce Westwood,
his current editor at Thomas Dunne Books, Marcia Markland,
all past editors and publishers,
readers who kept agitating for more of Cinq-Mars,
and the poker boys for not taking too much off the table.

PART 1

ONE

Sudden on the windshield, the sunlight was blinding. As the squad car emerged from a canyon formed by towering dense spruce onto a broad plateau of farmland, the officers inside the vehicle snapped down their visors. Wild gusts sculpted fields of fresh powder into rhythmic waves overnight, but as the storm passed the wind ceased. No trace of movement disturbed the distant view to the horizon, a seamless ocean of white lying perfectly still as though arrested at the moment of a tidal shift. Plows made a pass, yet the road remained slick with a glimmer of snow. The two cops fumbled for their sunglasses, neither for effect nor from any sense of police propriety, but the reflection off snow on a clear day under a cold snap in February created a brilliance more luminous than any summer's noon.

The man riding shotgun scanned the horizon. He daydreamed of distant destinations, all south. His driver, silent also, remained intent on the soft shoulders as he slowed for a turn and steered up a long drive last cleared before the storm's advent. Uniformly white, the road proved difficult to distinguish from its ditches. No tire tracks guided them to the farmhouse a half-mile in from the county highway.

A pale green two-story cottage ascended into view, its peaked roof adorned by gables. Nary a cloud in sight. White furnace smoke slipped from the chimney into a cerulean sky. Window frames were outlined in black trim, in contrast to the frilly lace curtains inside. The color of rust, the front door stood out.

A serene, innate peacefulness personified the dwelling.

The car pulled up behind a battered blue pickup that, half-buried by snow, was not readily identifiable. The men experienced the rapt peace of the place and braced themselves to feel a bone-brutal cold the second they bullied the doors open.

"The road to hell," postulated the uniformed officer in the passenger seat, "is paved—well, why don't you tell me with what?"

"Asphalt?" The driver raised his voice above the blast of the car's heater.

"Dude, it's a real serious question."

The rookie sighed, then obliged his partner. "Good intentions." He knew he'd be wrong. Even when he was right his partner would change the premise of the question to make sure that he was wrong. His way of trying to be a useful instructor.

"In the real world," the more senior cop remarked, "maybe. In our world—"

"Our world's not real?" The rookie shut the motor off. Dead silence.

"Hyperreal," the veteran said.

"What's that supposed to mean?" He left the keys in the ignition.

"More real than real. Beyond reality."

"So it's not good intentions, in our world, that buys you a ticket to hell?"

"Good intentions will fuck a cop over, that's true, but it's not the worst thing. Dude, the worst thing is *hesitations*. In our world, the road to hell is paved with a long series of *gee whiz, let-me-think-about-this-for-a-second* hesitations."

"So we should get out now," the junior cop concluded. He was a smartass.

Thirty-one, the elder of the two was a five-year vet. The driver was twenty-three and confident, not only a rookie but as keen as a razor and possessed of sharpened ideals to match. The men stood in the frigid air. The car doors remained ajar, as if frozen in place by the shock of the cold.

Nothing moved. Even the smoke seemed still, painted onto this pristine canvas. Usually they worked in the countryside, but both cops were city boys who commuted to the job. The depth of this unrelenting stillness unnerved them.

"Fucking quiet," the older one whispered, his voice scratchy in the dry air.

"Fucking cold," the younger remarked. He could deal with the quiet.

Their breath was visible. Against the side of the barn stood a tractor, the steel blade of its plow gleaming in the sunlight. The reflection blinked on their dark green glasses.

"Yeah," the senior officer concurred, and tacked on a grunt.

They slammed their doors simultaneously, a joint *kahjunk!* that wandered across the waves of snow and echoed in the distance against a stand of hardwood. The two men glanced around, but really there wasn't much to see. The yard and the small barn's exterior of bare wood appeared well-kempt. A farm without animals in winter. No place at all. Not a place where anything ever happened.

Except, they'd received a call.

The youngest took three steps toward the house.

"Where're you going?" his partner demanded, coming around the car.

"Where do you think? To the house. I'm trying to not hesitate."

Fifteen feet from the first stair the senior officer pressed his hand briefly against his partner's near elbow, stopping him. "Ron," he cautioned.

"What?"

"Look first."

"At what?"

"The snow."

Swirls lay undisturbed up the stairs and across the windblown porch. No one had come out that day. No one had gone in.

"Remember that for your report. Ours are the only footprints visible."

"You're planning to make detective?" Ron chided him.

"It's in the cards, kid. Why not? Bound to happen someday."

"Kid." The younger man repeated that one word as a scoff.

"What?"

"I don't think you're old enough to call me kid."

Up the steps, the more junior officer rapped on the door.

No buzzer. No doorknocker.

They waited.

"So you believe in fate, crap like that?" needled the rookie.

"Don't talk your shit to me, Ron."

"It's in the cards, you said. The cards. That means fate."

No answer from inside. Ron the rookie knocked again. That pervasive silence.

"Figures," the veteran officer decided. He crossed the porch to look in the window and put both hands on the glass to shield his eyes from the sunlight's glare. Then he took his sunglasses off and tried again. Still difficult to see inside, to go from brightness into what's dim. He stood there, awhile, searching.

"What do you see?"

"Fuck's sake," the senior cop said quietly, with some urgency. He unsnapped his holster cover and withdrew his pistol. "Call it in."

"And say what?" Ron tapped the transmitter on his collar that relayed through the car's two-way radio and requested a reply.

"We're entering. Let them know. Possible medical. Ask them to stand by."

Ron called it in, unbuckled his holster, and slipped his own weapon into his palm. He adjusted the unfamiliar weight in his hand.

For now, the steel felt warmer than the air. Strange, that.

The door was locked. A dead bolt. Smart, out here alone, and yet unusual for a farmhouse. Most folks never bothered. The older of the two raised his right boot and kicked the door hard. Then again. Nothing much happened. He'd never kicked down a door before. He began ramming it with his body, putting his shoulder into the task until the old wood started to splinter. Then another big kick.

They stumbled inside, weapons raised.

"This way."

The two officers crept into the living room. Ron removed his sunglasses, wishing he was privy to whatever his partner had seen, so he'd have a clue what to expect. He never imagined that in his first year on the job, in only his third month with this detachment, merely his second career posting, he'd be stepping around a hefty dog-eared brown sofa to view a man lying dead on a farmhouse floor. Relatively fresh-looking blood pooled out from the hefty man's skull. He lay faceup staring at the ceiling, his mouth and eyelids agape. Even as his partner crept closer to the man and knelt down Ron knew that he was dead.

Had to be. All that blood. That vacant stare.

The stillness. The thrum of the furnace came on, the sound a blessing. A little white noise to fill the hollows in his head that felt cavernous now, as if his brain was being stretched wide. Ron consciously tightened his sphincter before the whole of his body loosened and disassembled. Talk about hyperreal, all right.

His partner continued checking around the corpse. He shouldn't be touching it, but he knew that. "Marc?" Speaking quietly. "What're you doing?"

"I can't see his hands."

The dead man looked armless. But he wasn't.

"Don't touch him."

He touched him. "He's tied up. His wrists."

"What?"

His arms lay behind his back. More blood swam under him.

Marc rose from his crouch. "Tied up and shot. I think he's missing a fucking finger. This is not just a murder. It's a fucking assassination. Call it in."

Ron did so. Glad for the task, and to hear back that help was on the way.

"He must've come and gone by the back door, in and out."

"Who? What?"

"The killer, Ron. He must've come and gone by the back way. You saw the road, the snow. No footprints. Nobody's moved. Let's check it out. Stay alert."

"Alert?"

As an answer, Marc raised his pistol, aimed at the ceiling. Ron caught on and did the same. He'd never drawn his weapon on duty before. All he'd ever pulled out on the job was a booklet of tickets to nail a speeder.

The downstairs level was a warren, a contagion of cramped rooms and closets and a bare-bones, yet charming kitchen, so it took a few seconds to find the route to the rear of the house to manage a clear view outside.

They scanned the yard, the field beyond and the gently rolling hills. Not even a coyote track. A few distant fences, but nothing disturbed the beauty of the storm's overnight snowfall.

The furnace cut off, and they were returned to dead silence again.

"Check the side," Marc ordered. The rookie crossed the room and took in the view from the window there. Not so much as a snowshoe print. If Ski-Doo trails existed out there, and they probably did, they lay buried.

"Nothing," Ron reported. "The killer took off during the storm. Or before it."

"The guy's not been dead long enough." Marc was whispering. "He's warm. His blood—"

Without knowing the reason for it, the younger cop also lowered his voice to a hush. "How's that possible?"

Marc's voice was scarcely audible. "The killer's still in the house."

The rookie wanted to say, "What?" but swallowed the word. He got it. Adrenaline jumped through him even as he stood stock-still. He snapped out of it. He moved next to his partner. This time, he didn't have to be told to keep his pistol raised.

"Downstairs rooms first. One at a time."

"We don't wait for backup?" Whispering still.

"With a killer lurking around maybe? You want to sit still, wait to get shot?"

Ron was not sure. Neither choice seemed grand. The options might be equally dangerous, but he didn't think that that was the point. Weren't they *supposed* to wait for backup?

"Here's the thing," Marc determined. "That guy in the living room? He doesn't live alone. Somebody's life could be in danger here. Where's his wife?"

"Maybe she killed him."

"Maybe. Probably. Who else? Or—she's a victim, too. We don't know."

Photographs of her smiled up at them from the coffee table. A middle-aged, matronly sort. Not your average assassin. Not one to tie up her husband before she shot him. Ron nodded. Yes. This is why he became a cop. He was onside with this. They proceeded to the nearest room, a kind of home office, small, where he waited at the doorway as Marc went in and checked the large closet. Empty.

Marc returned to the doorway. Tall. An angular face. If he was an actor, he'd more likely be cast as an academic, or as an accountant, than as a cop. He'd never find work as an actor trying to play a cop. "Clear," he whispered.

"Do we announce?" Ron asked. The more powerful of the two, a solidness was reflected in his squared-off cheekbones and chin. "We should announce."

Marc didn't like to be corrected by a protégé. "Okay. Whatever. Whoever's here already knows we're here." To maintain his status, he said, "You announce."

Scared, Ron shouted out, "Police! Sûreté du Québec! This is the police! Identify yourself!" In French only. He repeated, "Police!" which worked in either language.

That silence.

"Happy now?" Marc asked him. Ron considered it an unwarranted comment and didn't forgive his partner's sarcasm. He felt that he didn't really like this guy anymore but that was no big concern. They were bound together. In fear, and, as it happened, in mutual trust.

Next was a sewing room, which doubled perhaps as a guest bedroom. Ron slipped in, his heart thumping through his brains. He came back out and muttered, "Clear." The word caught in his throat. He hoped his high anxiety wasn't showing.

But it was okay. Marc looked frightened, too. Fear, Ron reminded himself, was never the point. What counts is not how scared you are or how brave you claim to be or even how calm you are. All that matters is what you do.

More small rooms. Definitely, a woman lived there with a man. The furnace came on again, giving them a start. With the front door smashed, the inrush of cold air was causing it to frequently cycle on. They glanced at one another. *The furnace.* So there's a basement. Of course. And an upstairs. They were caught between the two. The door down was in the kitchen. Marc made the decision and Ron went down the stairs partway and swept his eyes around. Washing machine and dryer. A work bench. A radial-arm saw. Tools. Various ladders. Farm and garden implements, shovels, rakes, and a pitchfork. The furnace. The oil tank. A hot-water heater. Storage boxes on a rack. Kitty litter. Everything was up off the floor as if the space flooded on occasion. A sump pump. A tidy basement. But no one with a gun, and no dead people with their blood on the floor. No hiding places. He went back up.

They checked more small rooms.

A powder room. A TV room. A large hall closet. What looked like a music room. Now that was a luxury.

Time to go upstairs.

On the balls of their feet they moved slowly, but the old wood underfoot announced their trespass. Creaking.

A heating pipe banged and Ron shouted back, "Police! SQ! Identify yourself!"

"Shut up, for Christ's sake," hissed Marc.

Ron really didn't like the guy. Why did he ever tell his girlfriend that his partner was okay, a tad full of himself maybe? He was a whole lot more than full of himself. He let him go first. He'd rather not take a bullet for him if he could help it.

"Fucking procedure," attested Ron, mumbling really. "You got to identify yourself before you go shooting anybody. That's so basic."

Marc decided that he might as well bellow, too. "Missus? Are you here? Lady?"

Furnace thrum, a clanging radiator, and under all that a gawking silence.

They made it to the top of the stairs and their legs and breathing felt as though they'd just climbed Everest. Marc signaled his partner to check the room on their left. Ron preferred not to do so but he was given no choice. The door stood open. He flashed his head in the doorway, pulled it back instantly, then processed what he saw in that moment. Nothing. He looked in again and held his gaze. He entered as he'd been taught to do, weight and pistol forward. Recruits were taught to do it that way. If shot, the officer falls forward, which might allow him to get off a few rounds of his own. Maybe save his life that way, at least in theory. *Yeah, right.* Ron figured it really meant that he'd hit the floor face-first. Bust his nose. Mess up his corpse for the coffin. No one in the room, no one in the closet, no sign of any disturbance. The ceilings were low and the slope of the roofline evident. The room occupied half the upper floor, a bedroom, yet without the look of a master suite. It appeared to be infrequently used. Pillowcases did not adorn the pillows.

He held his breath and checked under the bed. No one. No shooter, no second vic.

Ron came back out.

Marc led the way down the hall. A bathroom was nearly opposite the top of the stairs. He crossed to the far side of the door. Ron glanced in. On his second look, he could see more of the room by checking the mirror on the face of the medicine cabinet. Then he went in and confirmed that the space was empty. He mouthed the word, *"Secure,"* and followed Marc farther along. The door to the last room on the floor was also open. Marc's turn. He glanced in and jerked his head back. He looked at Ron, which was not procedure. He took a breath. Whispered, "Woman on the floor. We got another one."

"Suicide?"

"How the fuck do I know? Looks like it anyway."

He risked a longer glance in, not looking at the woman so much but at the far corners, at the edge of the bed, searching for anything that might move. Not even a cat. A farmhouse, and not even a cat. He went in weapon raised and checked behind the door, in the open closet, over the far side of the bed. He signaled Ron to check under the bed. Ron wanted to puke. He'd been looking at the woman. On his knees, he lifted up the bed ruffle and checked that space. A few small storage items, but no killer.

Ron rose, relieved that his head hadn't been blown off. Marc entered the room first but left him the scariest task. Now they both looked at the woman. A dismal view, more so because she was naked. The indignity. Legs akimbo. Blood smudged. Marc had seen dead people on the job mangled in their cars. Gruesome enough. He went closer. He touched her. He was not supposed to do that. "Fuck," he said, but in a way that sounded amazed. "Still breathing."

"Really? No way." So much blood, from her head wound and also her hand. Blood from the hand had splashed around.

"Call it in."

Ron did so. He reported that one victim was alive and requested an ambulance. He was told that one was on the way, that it had been on the way for a while, just in case.

In case of what? he wondered.

Then an impression gnawing at him struck home. "Marc," he said.

"What?"

"There's no gun. No weapon."

They looked around. If this was a suicide then she shot herself through the back of the head without a weapon. The dead man downstairs had his hands tied behind his back. He didn't do it. And no footprints left the house.

Under his breath, Marc said aloud what Ron already knew. "Still here."

Yet they'd searched everywhere.

They stuck close to each other near the door, their backs against the wall for additional protection, listening.

"Wait for backup?" Ron suggested. He was afraid he might piss himself. He felt that he was all right overall, he could handle this, but he might piss himself.

"Yeah. We wait for backup." Marc didn't know what else to do. He looked at the woman. He was pretty sure that the man downstairs had a finger cut off. That was certainly true for the woman.

Marc glanced out to the hallway, just to check there. When reinforcements arrived he wouldn't let them see him like this, cowering. He'd tell them that they stayed in the room to protect the woman and because waiting for backup was fucking procedure. Fuck this shit. He wanted to be a detective, he joined to become a detective, not some uniform risking his life in some godforsaken farmhouse in what was not only the middle of nowhere but the worthless *center* of the middle of nowhere in the freezing fucking cold. But *shit* it was exciting, too. A double murder! Unless the woman makes it, but still, a double *shooting* on his watch and the killer might still be around if he hadn't left by helicopter or by Santa's bright red sleigh.

Marc glanced out the door again to make sure that no one was creeping up on them. He didn't see a thing and drew a deeper breath to release his tension and before he got to fully exhale he dropped to the floor, landing awkwardly, and toppled over. Ron saw him fall and the shock of the blast turned his blood to glue. He didn't think *don't hesitate*, although he wanted to think that way, but he couldn't think anything and yet he hardly hesitated at all and bent his arm around the doorjamb with his pistol ready to fire and his hand shaking and his heart bursting out the top of his head and his eyeballs out his skull and yet he had no one to shoot at. He only had walls in his line of sight and the shooter, he figured, must be behind the wall at the top of the stairs and he aimed at the spot waiting for the shooter to show himself and yet he never did and he yelled into his collar transmitter, breathless, "Officer down! Officer down!" because he couldn't remember the code, he'd never needed to remember that code, then he yelled like a crazy man, "Police! Come out—" and although no one was there he never discerned that fact as he heard a sound, a small sound, like a shuffling, and then his brain imploded and he fell upon his partner, and as he bled his blood commingled with his partner's. Nor was he aware that all there was before him now and under him and around him was that silence, that perfect stillness which he experienced initially as an unfathomable dread, but now became the perfect silence of a swift death.

Silence throughout the countryside, interrupted for those moments, ensued for a spell, then broke again. Across the snowy fields, echoing off the hardwoods, came the bark of yet another gunshot, so the quiet that returned, contrasted by the shot, felt immense, sustained, eternal, as brilliant as the sunshine, until there occurred a rising bedlam, a raring noise, distant at first then drawing closer, as sirens raced to that snowbound cottage, police and ambulance and more police, and something in the wailing, something in the plaintiveness over the waves of fresh snow on the serene fields, suggested that their speed was insufficient, that their urgency, both provoked and necessary, was too little and could only arrive too late.

TWO

Retirement was not serving former Sergeant-Detective Émile Cinq-Mars as well as desired. He had much to do, especially with his wife's horse business, and a variety of interests engaged his attention. So he did not suffer from any lack of activity and contrary to his prior speculations hardly missed the job at all. But he was wickedly unlucky. He fell, not *off* a horse, which he might have expected and carried with a certain honor—what horseman did not brave more than one nasty fall?—but he tripped over a bucket and tumbled *into* a horse who, startled, gave a kick, catching him right below the heart. The near-miss might have been his salvation although, for about six seconds, Cinq-Mars thought he was dead, then for the next six hours wished that he was. Notwithstanding the evidence of his survival, the broken ribs took their own sweet time to heal, a painful and lethargic process.

His first stroke of bad luck proved not to be his last.

Amid the fanfare concerning his retirement, during which time he was feted and anointed by colleagues both respected and despised, pumped for knowledge and contacts, equally praised and excoriated in the press so that a public debate ensued over whether citizens ought to be dancing in the streets or wearing sackcloth—somewhere within that repetitive munificence of sentiment and gift-giving he was handed the de rigueur gold watch. Initially, Cinq-Mars felt disrespected that a superior would stoop to such a banal gift when a halfhearted handshake would do, and irritate him less, but then he checked the watch. Hey. A nice watch. He liked it. He had never possessed an object of such obvious value before and grudgingly made peace with the symbolism. *Time's up.* Or, *All you got left is time now.* Or, *About time you got the hell out of here.* Or even, *We couldn't think of anything else but it's the thought that counts, right?* He was the recipient of retirement cards that humorously underscored such sentiments. But he liked the watch and enjoyed putting it on in the morning, at least until the day that he strapped it onto his wrist and discovered that for all its value and beauty and artful weight it offered back the wrong hour.

Still ticking, but 247 minutes behind.

To effect the repair under warranty required that he return it to the jeweler where the watch was initially purchased. Which is when he discovered that it was worth over two grand. Police department money wasn't tapped to purchase the timepiece, not at that price, the cash raised instead among colleagues, from among those both favored and despised. Indeed, from among those who exhorted him to stay and from those who were counting down the minutes, perhaps using the pricy watch, to his departure. Cinq-Mars felt a pang. Of affection. Of loss. For the old camaraderie. Even for the old daily frictions. In returning to retrieve the repaired Rolex he took note that this was only the fourth time in his life that he found himself inside an upscale jewelry boutique as a paying customer rather than as an officer of the law. Once to buy a ring for a girlfriend as a young man, once to choose an engagement ring and wedding bands for himself and his future wife—she went back to pick them up—once to return his broken watch and now, a fourth time, to pick it up. On his first two trips he wasn't retired, and went in on his lunch break, wearing a regulation pistol. So bringing the watch in, and now to pick it up, constituted his only times in a jewelry store unarmed, which struck him as both ironic and unfortunate given that he was interrupting a robbery-in-progress.

He could try a well-aimed punch to the thief's prominent jaw, except that his ribs remained sore from the horse kick and the punch undoubtedly would hurt him more. Besides, he'd not swung at anybody in decades and who knew if he could still put much behind the blow. And the guy was showing off his gun, so he might be shot for his trouble, which his wife, for one, would not appreciate. After all, it was only a bloody watch. Albeit a Rolex. So he tried something else. He stood in the doorway and didn't let the crook out without first having a word.

"Hi, there," he said.

"You old fuck, get out of my way," sneered the thief, a belligerent, unwary lad.

Old. Cinq-Mars hoped the guy didn't recognize him and therefore wasn't submitting a comment on his retirement. Standing in the doorway of the slightly subterranean shop, a step up from the miscreant, his six-foot-three-inch frame towered above the imp who stood at a chubby five-seven. He could stare down the immensity of his impressive nose and assume that that would have an intimidating effect upon the man nervously, if defiantly, gazing up at him.

"How're you doing?" he asked. From his pocket he withdrew a stick of gum—the miscreant flinched—casually unwrapped it, folded the stick in half to more easily drop it into his mouth, and did so. "My name's Émile Cinq-Mars. What's yours?"

Although unwilling to tell him, the jewel thief no longer insisted that he get out of his way. Cinq-Mars noticed that the man's glance seemed to trip over his nose. His massive honker was always his particular identifier, both because it deserved to be, but also because the city's cartoonists loved drawing his beak with comic exaggeration. In any case, the thief was undergoing a change of heart and seemed willing to talk.

"Heard you retired, I heard."

"It's no secret. Is that why you're here? You think it's safe to steal now?"

"No, but—"

"But what?"

"I got a gun. Like you can see. Do you? No, you're retired. You done your part. So maybe you should get out of my way and go play *bocce* or something."

He liked this jewel thief. His argument revealed a certain innate consideration for another person. "Maybe I should. Get out of your way, at least, but maybe you might want to consider a few things first. Such as, friendly advice, if you shoot me with that thing—I mean, how many cops do you know just by their names? I never showed you my shield, because you're right, I don't have one, I'm retired. But shoot me? Oh man. Do you have any idea the grief that falls on your head for that? Brought on by cops. By prosecutors and judges. By the man in the street, even. Your own family might not forgive you. With so many cops in jail now, you might not get a break on the inside. Don't count on it. Cop killer? You want that on your sheet, do you?"

The thief's posture and expression indicated that he didn't, not really. But he came up with an idea. "I could just wound you, like. Like maybe in the leg."

"Are you telling me that I won't find your mug shot in a stack of jewel-thief portraits? Sure I will. No, if you're going to shoot me, you want me dead."

Cinq-Mars won that argument as well.

"So, you know, this is like none of your business," the thief maintained, as if to appeal to his sense of fairness, if not of justice.

"That's where you're wrong. I know it's unfortunate, this is bad luck for you, but I saw you put my watch in your bag. It's in for repairs. I'm here to pick it up. I could tell you that it has sentimental value, but that would be a lie. Still. It's my watch. Not yours."

Barely into his thirties, the man's hair was noticeably thinning. As an adolescent he'd had bad skin and coming of age he did some time, Cinq-Mars could tell, just by the look of his face, the pallor and texture. Twin gold rings graced an earlobe—enough of an identifier to get him back into prison for a future crime, if the guy proved smart enough to abandon this heist.

The owner of the store, bent behind a counter, seemed baffled by the exchange, but acquiesced to allowing it to play out.

"So. Why don't I just give you back your watch then? We forget about it."

A relatively generous offer. Cinq-Mars weighed it quickly. "At my age? I'm not going to start taking bribes now. Not after all these years. Just leave everything behind and we'll let this one pass."

"All of it? You want me to give back—"

"You might be holding the bag, friend, but the contents don't belong to you."

The crook seemed to consider his circumstances. "Then what?"

"Then walk out of here."

"I get to walk?"

"Run, even. That's up to you. I don't have a gun. Or a badge. I can't arrest you. Put the bag down and none of this ever happened. If you don't put it down—do you think I don't have connections? Do you think the whole police department, or any police department anywhere in the world, won't come down on you like a ton of bricks?" He didn't like that analogy so took a second stab at it. "Like a stampede of wild horses?" He didn't like that one either but gave up. "Cops gave me that watch. They won't be impressed with you. I know you're not too bright but you can still make a half-assed smart decision, can't you?"

The man agreed that he could do that. He also wanted to argue the issue of his intelligence, and Cinq-Mars was thinking that that was a low blow, one quite possibly untrue, but in the end the crook let it go and put the bag down.

Cinq-Mars stepped aside.

The thief couldn't believe it and, not fully believing it, when he got outside, he ran, kicking up his heels with something akin to glee, as if he was stealing the Crown Jewels when really he wasn't swiping a thing. In terms of his profession he was having a bad day at work, but that perception hadn't dawned on him as yet.

More joyful still was the jeweler. Five-two, he was barely visible above the countertops. He came out from behind their shelter and embraced the towering ex-cop, his head merely halfway up his midriff. Then he held him by the biceps at arm's length. Gazing up at him with supreme happiness and an abject adoration, he offered him dinner. Hockey tickets in the reds. Italian wine, but more importantly, the finest olive oils. "Stuff you don't get in stores." Cinq-Mars declined. After all, he explained, he didn't do anything. The jeweler hugged him again, then sneezed, then got up on his tiptoes and the ex-cop politely leaned down to be kissed on both cheeks. Cinq-Mars thanked him and the jeweler kissed both his cheeks again, then coughed, then sneezed once more and apologized for having the flu, which was transmitted to Cinq-Mars as part of his current run of bad luck and developed soon enough into a cocktail of flu, sore ribs, and finally, in a week's time, pneumonia.

The pneumonia took longer to be gone than the ribs did to heal, although the ribs hurt like hell whenever he sneezed, coughed, blew his nose, or even evacuated his bowels.

At least he was retired. Going to work would have been a killer.

If bad things came in threes then one more turn of nasty luck lay ahead of him, yet when it arrived he could scarcely comprehend his misfortune. His wife, who was much younger than him and the guiding principal behind his retirement because she really didn't want him getting himself killed on the job, now let him know that she was thinking about leaving. A head's up. At least she'd not made a definitive decision to decamp.

Thank goodness for small mercies—he was counting on bad luck to come only in threes. He'd swallowed his full dose. He didn't want the breakup to occur.

To that end he was staying around the house a lot, so that when the phone rang on a mild and cloudy day, a few flurries in the morning, just an inch predicted for later that afternoon, he was home to answer. He put down a crossword puzzle which wasn't going well either. He'd never attempted one prior to retiring, and had yet to complete one. "I got it," he called through the house.

Sandra didn't respond. She was taking it upon herself to scrub every pot in the kitchen. Her husband chose not to question why.

"Cinq-Mars," he said into the receiver. Sandra frequently admonished him but old habits were difficult to scuttle. She suggested that a simple hello would suffice, but in any case, if he really did feel the need to announce himself, he might include his first name, as only friends were likely to be calling now.

"And telemarketers," he pointed out.

"Why reveal your identity to them?"

He didn't see why not but that was another argument not worth the trouble.

"Hi there, Émile, it's Bill."

"Bill!" Mathers. His longtime partner, who inherited his rank after Cinq-Mars left the force. "How are you?"

Pot in hand, Sandra wandered through to the living room, curious about the call. Pleasantries went on as the two men caught up on department scuttlebutt, but her intuition kept her nearby. As the small-talk concluded, Cinq-Mars kept listening with the phone to his ear while Bill Mathers prattled on. She heard her husband say, "I don't know how I can help with that," and then he listened some more. He was growing impatient with the call, rather than intrigued, which she counted as a good thing. Finally, he conceded, "All right. Sure. Come over. . . . Actually, I muck out stalls at that hour. Can you make it for three? . . . Okay. See you then. . . . Yeah. It'll be good to see you, too. Bye, now."

He hung up.

Cinq-Mars returned to his crossword, though he knew she was watching.

"I have a very heavy pot in my hands," Sandra mentioned. "Do I really need to bong you over the head with it?"

"That was Bill. Mathers."

"I know who it was. What does he want?"

Cinq-Mars folded up the paper neatly and put it down at his hip. No easy way out of this. "He's coming over at three. He wants to consult with me, but he's vague about the details. Needs to talk to me in person, apparently. So I said fine. It's not likely that I'll be going in to the office or anything like that."

Sandra continued to dry the heavy pot in her hands. "Okay. Consult. I'll put something out for you." She turned back to the kitchen.

"Ah." Cinq-Mars started to say something, then stopped.

Sandra also stopped, and faced him again. "What now?"

"He's not coming alone. Another man will be with him."

"Who?" she asked.

"No one I know."

"Who?" she asked again.

Cinq-Mars pursed his lips. "Sandra, it's only a consultation."

"Who, Émile?" she insisted.

He sighed. "Some FBI agent, apparently. I don't know what's going on."

Sandra seemed to receive the news as if she expected it. "Lovely," she said.

"Sandra—"

"Émile."

"It's a consultation!"

"It's fine. I'll put something out for the three of you. Unless the FBI is bringing in the marines?"

She returned to the kitchen, and Cinq-Mars, eventually, to the crossword. He didn't know how people got through these things. He was smart, he was well-read, adept at the language even though he was working in English and not his mother tongue. How did people get their heads around these infernal things? He was stumped by the next word and put his pencil down. *What's a five-letter word for nincompoop*, he wanted to ask, but he was really thinking that whatever it was that Bill wanted, he was going to have to turn him down flat.

Anyway, Sandra would probably suggest an answer: *Émile.*

THREE

The former Montreal city detective weighed more than his wife's concerns about his imminent and violent death before choosing to retire. He sharpened a pencil and composed a pair of lists. A "Why Not Stay On Forever?" list and a "Get Out of Dodge While You Can!" list. On the latter he wrote:

1. Most of the time, Sandra wants me more alive than dead.

Émile Cinq-Mars put a star beside his first selection, which remained his singular choice for quite a few days before he got into the swing of things and added further items. In time, he erased the star. He also decided that a numerical system was not indicative of the order of importance, only the order in which his thoughts occurred to him, for although his first choice was probably the most important reason to quit, he failed to differentiate among the other entries as to which ones were more, or less, vital than the next.

2. The long commute.

He considered adding subcategories, such as the long commute in winter, but realized that hot summer days, the traffic made worse by highway, overpass, and bridge construction, were more tedious and no less dangerous, and the drives in winter were sometimes so magical he wanted those trips to never end.

3. The new idiots at the top.

Dwelling on that one, he thought it might become his most emphatic and irrefutable motivation to retire, except that it soon got into a toss-up with another competing issue regarding police personnel.

4. The new idiots at the bottom.

New recruits were not necessarily dumber than they used to be, and in fact they seemed generally brighter, but they also carried a greater sense of entitlement and were far less malleable. They were less willing to be taught a damn thing, and he no longer possessed the patience to come up against that hurdle when dealing with them.

5. I no longer have the patience.
6. I can spend more time with the horses.
7. I can spend more time with Sandra.

This is when he decided that the numerical order was merely random and he erased the star from Item 1 and made a mental note to himself not to show the list to his wife in its current state.

8. Quit now and avoid a possible promotion.
9. Quit now and avoid a possible demotion.
10. If my brain or my eyesight don't fail me first, my back might.

A compelling argument. His brain and his eyesight were fine, and even his long-standing arthritis wasn't so bad, but his back was becoming a chronic, growing and cantankerous issue. During any flare-up on the job he was incapacitated, and he hated that. Which is why, when

Sergeant-Detective William "Bill" Mathers arrived on his doorstep in the company of an unknown FBI agent from south of the border, Cinq-Mars was down on his living room carpet faithfully performing gyrations taught to him by an osteopath. Sandra answered the bell while he remained stationary, one leg straight out behind him, the arm on his opposite side straight out before him, his weight on the other hand and on one knee, eyes front like a pointer with a duck dead in its sights. Sphincter and tummy muscles tucked and taut, he sustained the position for a requisite ten-count, then relaxed and remembered to breathe.

He was still down on the floor when his guests came into the room. In preparing his "Why Not Stay On Forever?" list, he had come up with only one good reason, which he had also numbered.

1. Seriously, what will I do with myself if I quit?

Do weird exercises on the living room carpet between crosswords, apparently.

Mathers, of course, seized the opportunity to rub that in. "So this is what retirement is like. You finally hit the gym. I always said you should."

"No, *I* always said *you* should. Good afternoon." Cinq-Mars greeted the man he didn't know as he tightened his stomach muscles again to assist his progress to an upright position. "Émile Cinq-Mars, as you may have guessed. I'm not at my best. You've met Sandra?"

"Indeed, we were introduced." The new arrival turned his shoulders to more formally include her. "What a charming home, Mrs. Cinq-Mars."

The older man with the younger wife wondered if the visiting American with the firm handshake was not flirting. You could never tell with them. Yanks had a way of being effusive that in many cultures came across as flirtatious, but really demonstrated nothing more than an excessive insecurity. Formulaic, somehow. He enjoyed the way that Sandra, an American herself and comfortable with the style, received the compliment, acknowledged it with a smile, yet declined to rise to the bait. She'd been living in Canada too long, perhaps. "Thank you very much, Mr. Dreher. We're comfortable here." A glance at her husband acknowledged the irony, for lately she was not comfortable at all.

Cinq-Mars shook Mathers's hand as well and they exchanged a grin.

Having seen to their coats, Sandra advised the men that she'd leave them to chat momentarily, but first she'd be back in a jiff with something to munch on, and did they prefer coffee or tea?

"Oh, please, don't let us be any trouble," Bill implored her in the Canadian style, which demanded that any proffered act of hospitality must at first be politely declined.

"You've come a distance. You may need the nourishment to get home."

A routine joke for this household, and the visitors chuckled lightly. They were not going to protest any further, as it had been well over an hour's drive out and they could both use a nosh. Each man, including their host, chose coffee.

A ring of shrimp with a red dipping sauce went first, but once the guests sampled Sandra's coconut squares they became a big hit. The cookies were also a favorite, and even the celery and carrot sticks with a dip were consumed. Coffee arrived served in mugs and a thermos was set before them for refills, so that they were left in a position to talk at length without further interruption. Cinq-Mars wondered what his wife knew that he didn't, but she'd probably answer: *you*.

Not that he was chatty. Hardly. But in being introduced to a professional whom he'd not met his tendency was to be oblique and circuitous, to circle the man's position and intelligence as he assessed his words under a microscope. All that usually took time.

Mathers was the one to get down to it. "So we're here, as I said, about the police shootings."

Cinq-Mars grunted.

"You've followed the investigation on the news?" Agent Rand Dreher inquired. He explained at the outset that he preferred to be called Rand, not Randolph, which seemed an utterly preposterous name, he espoused, and, of course, not Randy, which as he tried to joke sounded too—he hesitated for comic effect—*randy.*

Cinq-Mars grunted a second time.

"So you haven't been following it?" Mathers asked. "Are you *that* retired?"

He put his cup down and made a decision to be more accommodating, or at least less distant. "The papers—the media—haven't reported on much, Bill, except to say that they have nothing new to report on.

So I suppose I know the details of the crime—may I point out that not only policemen were killed—but I really don't know much else." He studied Dreher. Tall and broad, he was about 220 pounds and carried it well. He had probably played football in college, or some other team sport, and the fitness regimen necessary at that time still held him in good stead. In the FBI style, he was well dressed and superbly coiffed, and struck a conservative style. The only discernible flaw which would not favor him as a *GQ* specimen was a bushiness—trimmed, but nonetheless a wildness—to his eyebrows. He was in his early forties, but when today's jet-black hair turned gray, those eyebrows would become a distinctive feature. For the time being, they were probably an embarrassment that required weekly attention to tame. "So, have I been following the crime in the media? There's been precious little to follow. That's not to say that I have no interest in being informed, to hear what transpired."

Dreher overcame his shyness about doing so to pinch the last square.

"Good. Of course." He brushed a few crumbs from his fingertips onto a plate.

What the man considered either good or obvious Cinq-Mars could not tell. "Where are you from?" he asked him.

The agent sounded unsure. "The U.S." He appeared dismayed that his host might not know the country where the Federal Bureau of Investigation was located.

"Where," Cinq-Mars coaxed him along, "in the U.S.? I'm curious."

"Oh. Sure. The Midwest."

He was not going to be more forthcoming than that. Cinq-Mars considered pressing him on where in the Midwest but suspected that that game could go on an indefinite time and he wasn't *that* curious. Clearly, the agent was a close-to-the-vest kind of guy, so at least he'd learned something.

"The papers aren't reporting much," Mathers enlightened him, "because there's nothing to report. Which is pretty much all that we know. Nothing."

"We?" Cinq-Mars asked. He smiled, and for old time's sake enjoyed his partner's mild consternation. Bill was reaching his mature years, in his late forties now. Cinq-Mars was pleased to see that apart from the inevitable plumpness, he appeared to be growing into himself, rather than out of whom he used to be. He looked fine, more handsome than ever. Lines in his face that might not have been in evidence a decade ago spoke to his experience and a well-earned self-confidence. Roundly baby-faced, though, after a fashion. He'd carry that look into his nineties.

"What do you mean?" Mathers asked.

As was his wont, Cinq-Mars chose to answer a question with more questions.

"Gentlemen, what is it that you know that I am having difficulty figuring out? If you have some personal or professional interest in this case, or special information, why aren't you talking to the Sûreté du Québec? The SQ are the ones who lost two officers. They're the ones investigating this case. Not—if I may be presumptuous here—you. I might be out of touch, Bill, but I'm pretty sure the Montreal Urban Community Police Department does not get to investigate murders that take place off-island. Not only are you off the reservation, you might as well be light-years away from your jurisdiction. Or has that changed? What's more, and I'll point this out to you because you used to freely point it out to me, you're not in Homicide. And the FBI? Seriously? You're not even in the same galaxy here. Why the hell would the FBI be even *remotely* interested in local murders, let alone send an agent all the way from—we don't know from where exactly, do we?—to check them out?"

"I was told that you were a tough nut," Dreher said, testing his American charm again.

"Not true. I'm retired. An old softy now. My wife will confirm it. But the fact of the matter is, Agent Dreher—"

"Call me Rand."

"Thank you. Rand. I don't know what you're doing here. By *here*, I mean, why are you investigating this case, or even talking about it, in a country where you are the foreigner, number one, and two, why are you talking specifically to me?"

"Fair enough. I was planning to keep that sort of thing to myself for now, until we determined your level of interest, but I'll answer you. The SQ has given us permission—"

"Us, meaning the FBI, or you and Bill?"

"Ah, the FBI, actually."

Cinq-Mars poured himself more coffee and offered to do the same for the other men. They declined with simple gestures.

"The SQ has given . . . *me* . . ." Dreher emphasized, growing accustomed to the older detective's legendary persnickety attention to the exact meanings of words, both the intentions of words, and their ability to obfuscate the truth, "license to have a look at the crime scene, to determine if these killings are connected in any way, shape, or form, to murders south of the border."

"Ah," Cinq-Mars acknowledged. Folding his arms over his chest appeared to indicate that he was growing more at ease with their discussion, as the parameters were beginning to make sense.

"I was hoping, Detective Cinq-Mars—"

"Please. Call me Émile. The detective thing doesn't fly anymore."

Dreher dipped his head to receive the invitation. "Émile. I was hoping that you might accompany us to the crime scene. Your expertise is legendary. This is your neck of the woods. Perhaps you might be of assistance."

He wanted to stand. His back problems flared up after he sat for too long. Yet this was not the moment to interrupt their exchange, so he remained in his chair. He recognized one incongruity right off the top. All that stuff about him being a legendary detective would not hold an ounce of spirits in a shot glass inside the FBI. A smoke-screen, but one that made him more curious.

"The crime scene's gone stale," Cinq-Mars reminded his visitors. "It's what, ten days old? Two cops dead, I'm sure the SQ picked over it with a fine-tooth comb. I doubt very much that I can help. What can you tell me about the other murders, the ones in your own country?"

Agent Dreher seemed to genuinely regret being unable to say more and indicated that his hands were tied. "Examine the scene with us. If you show an interest in helping us out, more can be explained. If you choose not to be involved, I'll have nothing further to add. I'm afraid that I can't offer much more at this time."

Involved. He was retired. Why would he be *involved*? Why would anyone ask?

"So far," he mused, "I have some idea of why you're here. But Bill, my friend, my old partner, how did you get dragged into this? Why are *you* here?"

Mathers seemed sheepish. He separated his hands, then knitted them together again, a gesture of pleading. His expression indicated embarrassment.

"What?" Cinq-Mars pressed him.

"I'm here," Bill Mathers admitted, "because I know you. I'm the one who's supposed to convince you to do this."

A silent few seconds passed between them, their eyes locked on one another's, before Cinq-Mars broke off that connection and commenced a guttural chuckling that worked its way up through his lips and cheeks. Mathers quietly joined in. They were obviously finding the circumstance, and Mathers's explanation, hilarious.

"What's so funny?" Dreher asked.

Cinq-Mars altered his seated posture and apologized. "Sorry. Inside joke. Look, if my wife is willing to let me out of the house—she'll probably jump at the prospect—I'll visit the crime scene with you. But if I help you out at all, which I sincerely doubt will happen, you have to agree to help me out in exchange."

"How?" Agent Dreher asked.

"By being more bloody forthcoming. I know it's part of your FBI pedigree, but if you can draw me, however briefly, out of retirement, then you should be able to shed the bullshit for a minute or two. No song. No dance. Agreed?"

Dreher glanced over at Mathers, but failed to find help there. He bobbed his head when he faced Cinq-Mars again.

"Let's go ask your wife if she'll let you out of the house," he suggested.

"That's okay," the former city cop told him. "I can do that on my own."

FOUR

Sergeant-Detective Bill Mathers had arrived on a day off. Otherwise, Cinq-Mars deduced, he'd be driving a department issue, given that he was the host officer with local knowledge. From the Quebec license plate to the wee sticker on a side window—even to the model of car, a Chevy Malibu—the obvious signs suggested that the black vehicle in which the men arrived was a rental. The agent, then, didn't drive north in his own vehicle from, say, Albany, in upstate New York, or Poughkeepsie, a modest distance farther south, but had flown into Montreal, picking up the car at the airport. Strange that he was here at all—that either man had been sanctioned by their respective forces to operate outside their jurisdictions. Émile was inclined to suspect the FBI guy of being a lone wolf, a renegade who was not on official assignment. At the very least, he was going to hold that thought in abeyance.

He tried again to pin him down, to scrape a nick from his shell.

"How was the weather when you left? So-so?"

Dreher looked over at him with evident caution.

"When you flew out? Cold?"

Agent Rand Dreher removed his gray leather gloves from a coat pocket.

He permitted a smile to touch the edges of his lips and considered whether or not to reply. He conceded, "Forty-five, give or take. Fahrenheit, of course. Cloudy. So yeah, so-so."

"Had to be Fahrenheit," Cinq-Mars noted, "down there at nine-three-five."

Fishing, he was referring to 935 Pennsylvania Avenue, Washington, D.C. The agent smiled broadly this time, if not altogether warmly. "Émile, does it make a difference? Yes. I've come up here from down there."

"Merely curious," Cinq-Mars demurred. "Pleasant flight?"

"Routine. When you fly as much as I do, nothing can be more pleasant than that. Have you been there?"

Cinq-Mars returned the look. "Washington? Or FBI Headquarters?"

"I meant the city. But either? Both?"

"The city, for cherry blossom time, and to your headquarters in other seasons."

"I didn't know."

"I'm sure the record exists. This isn't the first time you guys have tried to recruit me."

"Not recruit." In the cold, Dreher pulled on his gloves and deeply exhaled, his breath visible. "Just seeking your help and advice, Émile. Plain and simple. The good counsel of a famous detective. Shall we go in my car?"

"I'll drive my own." His guest, by lifting his abundant eyebrows, raised the obvious question, so he explained himself. "It's a bit of a hike. More or less back toward Montreal. If I take my car, then when we're done you can carry on, skip the long detour driving me home again."

That made sense, so Dreher and Mathers started off ahead of him and Cinq-Mars fell in behind in his Jeep. He had things to think about—Sandra's reaction, for one—and welcomed the solitude. "Go, Émile," she insisted. "Go." Almost shooing him out the door. Tacking on, "It's in your blood, there's no denying that."

He'd expected her to acquiesce, but her enthusiasm took him by surprise.

Émile wanted to argue the point, but as his guests were pulling on their boots in his vestibule it was neither the place nor the appropriate time. Was he really failing that badly as a retiree that she was willing to shove him right back into the line of fire after, for so long, extolling the virtues of quitting? He enjoyed many aspects of retirement, and if not for his bout with pneumonia and the time on his back with cracked ribs, he might have discovered more. He guessed what was being implied here, that she cottoned on to his own dismay. Sandra might disagree, but the old job was not something he needed. He didn't miss it. What he did miss was using his brain, and so much—too much, he'd say—of his work with horses was strictly physical. He didn't mind the activity, he reveled in it, actually, but the lack of intellectual stimulation was beginning to gnaw at him. He felt impoverished for real human puzzles, not the crossword variety, which he was lousy at anyway, and twice he caught himself carving patterns in straw to create some unfathomable maze that only he could then resolve. He wasn't sure at such a moment if he was searching for cosmic clues or suffering from early onset Alzheimer's. When they visited friends for an evening he covertly delved into their secret lives in ways that would have ended the meal abruptly had his wonderments surfaced. Knowing him so well, Sandra may have concluded that he needed the mental stimulus of the job, and perhaps she determined that this was a way for him to get his fix: to confer, to analyze and suggest, yet free from the stress, and particularly from the danger, that came with carrying a gold shield and a Glock.

Thinking that way, a suspicion roused in him. Had she herself contacted Bill Mathers? Was she behind this? Had Sandra suggested to his former police partner that if any out-of-the-loop dalliance came up he should consider including his old boss? The coincidence nagged him and the thought took hold, though he doubted that she ever intended for him to become involved in the investigation of a double-cop murder that was half a quadruple murder. That part came under the rubric of getting more than anyone ever imagined or bargained for.

Or, and the thought caused him to feel grim, did she think that getting him back to being a detective would assist her out the door, ease her conscience, should she choose to leave?

Cinq-Mars followed behind the odd couple of Dreher and Mathers, noticing the occasional drift of snow kicked up by their tires, the hardtop otherwise dry. To improve his mood he speculated on whether or not Bill smartened up about the shenanigans that occurred among various forces. The FBI agent would be pumping him for information on the SQ, on Montreal crime, on Cinq-Mars and his history in the Montreal Police Department, and if Bill remained as gullible as always—he'd not know to censor his tongue—words might cross forbidden frontiers. He didn't want to think ill of Bill, and was confident that his old partner took his new responsibilities seriously, but he probably remained inept when it came to trapdoors and secret codes and dirty tricks in the company of an intraforce colleague who wanted something out of him, especially when he didn't know that he had a thing to give. By the time Dreher had filched keys to a vault of knowledge from his hip pocket and siphoned the juiciest bits from the nether parts of his cranium, Mathers would probably still not know if he'd just made a new best friend for life or was suckered into a sinister duel in which he was doomed from the outset.

Poor guy. He should have driven with him maybe.

Dreher, though, would notice that he was protecting him and merely bide his time. So Cinq-Mars reminded himself that he was formally and officially retired, and none of it really mattered anymore.

Or, at least, it shouldn't.

He drove on.

He gauged the distance to the crime scene as being thirty kliks from his home, what the American would count as about twenty miles. Canadians were funny that way. In converting to the metric system, the populace had settled on its own hodgepodge system, part metric, part standard, part imperial, part hybrid, so the retired cop commonly judged distances in kilometers now, and would compare prices for a liter of gas, yet if he was buying a car he'd want to know how many *miles* it got to the *gallon.* A dichotomy that had become entrenched in the culture. He bought his beef by the kilogram, but he needed the weight of a perpetrator to be reported only in pounds. The distance between a murder victim and the murder weapon might be six meters, but the height of the victim had to be stated as six *feet,* or four foot ten, whatever it was, otherwise, who would know? Provide a person's height in centimeters and no one of his generation would have a clue how tall the individual might be. Every year when he received his driver's license renewal form he noticed his own height recorded in meters, then promptly forgot it. He was six foot three, still, in *feet* and *inches*, although these days he needed to consciously make an effort to straighten up to get close to that height. His driver's license now lied. He'd shrunk, although his osteopath's exercises were getting him to stretch himself out to his full length again. Partly because both miles and kilometers were provided by the speedometers of cars purchased in Canada, even though odometers registered kilometers only, he and his compatriots successfully negotiated miles into kliks and back again, but doing so with respect to temperature was always a non-starter. He, like everyone he knew, now understood Celsius and used it to communicate the temperature out-of-doors, while converting back to Fahrenheit, despite having grown up with it, seemed to require a degree in astrophysics. Unless, of course, he happened to be cooking, in which case the Fahrenheit scale prevailed.

All a perpetual muddle.

On the detective side of his mind, he calculated that if he ever wanted to discern if someone was really a Canadian or an impostor from, say, Delaware, the metric system might serve as a shibboleth. Sooner or later, the American would get it wrong, either by being too officially metric or too casually standard.

Twenty miles—thirty-two kilometers, according to his odometer—zipped by. Although close to home, Cinq-Mars was not familiar with this particular county road, which was just far enough out of the way that he rarely had reason to travel down it and had done so less than a dozen times over many years. Yet as he descended onto the plateau he was struck by how closely it shared the look and geography of the general area, and that's when the eeriness of such a vile crime occurring, essentially, in his own backyard and among his rural neighbors, overcame him. Those poor people, slaughtered in their quiet, isolated home. Those poor cops who had gone—or so the couple, if given the chance, might have surmised—to their rescue.

Millions of other homes enjoyed similar comforts around the world and an equivalent solitude, but a *more* serene, quieter, or relaxed setting for a country home could not be imagined. The distant white fields sweeping up to a rim of woodlots were as still as stone, yet in their own way as majestic as a sea.

Mathers and Dreher were waiting as Cinq-Mars stepped from his car.

"How'd you know how to get here?" he asked.

"GPS," Mathers said.

"Ah." As his former partner gave him a skeptical glance, he added, "Yes, Bill, I know what that is. Sandra takes one on horseback rides. She can explore new trails without worrying about getting lost."

"They are a marvel," Rand Dreher concurred and removed the instrument from his coat pocket, admired it, then put it back.

"Do you think he used one?" Cinq-Mars inquired.

"Excuse me?"

"Our killer. He arrived in a storm, I hear, then left on a cloud. Navigating through a winter storm without landmarks is not easy. Finding your way perfectly snow blind? Impossible. Even house lights won't guide you, not through a blizzard that intense. If he walked in under those conditions, he must have had a GPS to guide him."

"You're probably right," Dreher acknowledged.

"That's why I hate technology. For all the good they do, the bad guys use those gadgets for evil."

The agent seemed to be perpetually evaluating the man he'd brought along. "You seem to be a good-and-evil kind of guy," Dreher said.

He gave out a laugh. "Is that why you asked me here?" He knew that Dreher would never understand the question, so he explained himself right away. "It's become an American trait, don't you think? Breaking the world down into good and evil. Where else in the world do you have politicians willing to mention Satan?"

"Iran," Dreher answered.

"True enough. You got me there. But that's my point. Yes, I will mention good and evil. But no, I'm not like that. God has better things to do in my estimation than answer a quarterback's prayers for a tight spiral, and so does Satan have better things to do than attack American institutions."

"Santorum," Dreher muttered.

"Yeah. That guy."

"Me, too," Dreher admitted, but as Cinq-Mars didn't follow his thread, he explained himself. "He's driving me nuts, that one. Mind you, I have my issues with the man whose job he's after."

"I didn't think you guys were allowed to discuss politics."

"We're not supposed to," the agent agreed. "But—"

Cinq-Mars finished his sentence when Dreher did not. "You're out of the country. You're wandering around aimlessly. You're among friends."

"All that. Plus, I was baited."

Cinq-Mars acknowledged his culpability with a slight bob of his head. He took a breath. "So this is where it all transpired."

"You don't talk like a cop, do you?"

"I hate the lingo. You?"

Mathers, Cinq-Mars noted, was smirking.

The American tucked his hands under his armpits and hugged himself as a breach against the cold that, while not anywhere near extreme, had a bite today. "I'll try to watch my words, Émile. So. The premises, we know, were contaminated the moment more police and an ambulance showed up. So there's some leeway, but very little, in the exterior study of the grounds the day of the murders. Around three sides of the house, really through an arc of three hundred and thirty degrees, not a footprint could be found in the fresh snow. Obviously, the officers who were killed drove up to the house. The next vehicle was a cop car, and those officers swear that their car was only the second one to drive down that long road."

"How would they know for sure? Another car could have followed in the same ruts, no? They wouldn't be driving up to the farmhouse trying to notice that detail."

Dreher agreed with him, to a point, and jumped into the conversation. "True, Émile. But their report convinced me. In part because they were trying to follow the exact track themselves, simply because it was easier to drive through deep snow that way. They commented to each other, long before they knew that it mattered, that only one car had gone ahead of them. The other thing they noticed was that the tire tracks led straight to the dead officers' car. Had there been a second vehicle, it would have had a second destination, no? Or a separate point of departure."

Cinq-Mars conceded the strength of that argument. "Still, the original cop car could have followed a footpath, for instance, covering it up as it drove along."

Dreher looked to Mathers to pick this up. "Could have," Bill agreed. "Except the roadway was scoured from beginning to end. No footprint was detected. You'd expect to find at least one misstep. As well, not a single footprint was found once the investigators got to the highway. If due to some unfathomable fluke the squad car perfectly covered up prints on the driveway, that would still not be possible on the highway. So where were those prints? Even if they only show somebody getting into a car, where were they?"

"A mystery," Cinq-Mars concurred. He couldn't deny his old partner's point of view. His blood, the blood his wife had mentioned, was warming to this challenge.

"GPS in a snowstorm gets our guy here," Dreher summed up, "but how did he escape after the storm without leaving a trace?"

"That's what has the SQ—and me—stumped," Mathers acknowledged. He was saying one thing but looking at Cinq-Mars in an odd way. He seemed smug.

"What?" the older man asked.

The jacket he wore, which dropped just below the waist, was fluffy with a bright tan nylon shell. Mathers reached out and tugged on the sleeve.

"That's down. Is that down?"

"Sue me. I don't wear heavy wool topcoats anymore. *Cop* coats, I call them. Are you really surprised?"

"It's just that I've never seen you wear anything else in the winter. Sharp, Émile. I like the look."

"For one thing, I don't have a gun to hide anymore."

"I'm serious. It's spiffy."

"It's unbelievably light and warm. So take your spiffy and go to hell."

"Shall we go inside first?" Dreher interrupted, and proceeded to lead the way. He'd been loaned a key, which sprung open the back door. The entryway in front, he explained, was busted down by the policemen first on the scene, it was assumed, and only a crude repair effected since then kept the weather out. The door was no longer operable. They went in via the kitchen where the men removed their overshoes on a mat. For Cinq-Mars, that left him in socks, but he didn't mind as he surveyed the cosy home.

"Okay," he said.

"Okay what?" Mathers asked.

"It's not a grow-op." Indoor operations to grow marijuana were common in the area, but these rooms in his visual range were tidy.

"No indication, according to the SQ, that the victims were anything but legit. They weren't real farmers though. They didn't work the land themselves. They rented it out. They just lived on it."

"What about the victims' families?" Cinq-Mars inquired.

"Childless," Dreher told him. "As far as we know. Old enough in their fifties not to have parents who are still alive, that can be expected, but no siblings have shown up either. No family pictures were found on the premises. The thing is, not much is known about these two. They seem to have come from the Maritimes originally, according to neighbors, about four years ago. The SQ is trying to track down their histories. We don't know where they came from exactly."

"Or why," Cinq-Mars noted.

"Excuse me?"

"Why come here? Nobody—I mean nobody—leaves the Maritimes to live on a farm in Quebec. Not with our taxes. To go to the big city, sure, it's exciting. But here? When there's other places? Why would anyone do that?"

"Peace and quiet," Dreher suggested.

"Who wants that? Most people only think they want it until they get it. But the point is, they could have found peace and quiet in the Maritimes. Besides, look what it bought these two."

Glancing into small, main-level rooms, the three men slowly made their way to the front of the house. In the living room they came upon a chalk mark that outlined the position of one victim.

"This is a key to the killer's modus operandi south of the border. It's what caught the attention of my people," Dreher revealed.

Cinq-Mars silently studied the outline as though he wasn't listening, then asked, "What is? What's his MO?"

"The husband or the boyfriend is always shot or knifed to death downstairs. That happens first. Then the wife or the girlfriend is killed upstairs."

Cinq-Mars stared at the scene awhile. "What was his name?"

"Morris Lumen," Mathers told him.

"Morris. Like Maurice, but English?"

"That's right. His wife's name was Adele."

"Morris and Adele. That sounds quaint. So there's always a dead guy?" Cinq-Mars asked Agent Dreher.

"And a dead woman."

"Always two floors?"

"Every time. Male victim downstairs, the woman on the second floor."

"Sometimes shot. Sometimes knifed. That doesn't sound like the same MO."

"In certain circumstances, the killer may have needed to be quiet."

"How many murders?" Cinq-Mars looked directly at him. "On your side of the border?"

"Can't tell you that yet, Émile."

"Right. I haven't indicated if I'll be, as you say, *involved.* I find it curious."

"Excuse me?"

"Your reticence," Cinq-Mars told him. "It's curious."

"This is the way it has to be, that's all," Dreher confirmed.

Testy for the first time on this trip, Cinq-Mars replied, "Oh, I doubt that."

Dreher looked angry, but said nothing.

As if trying to break that rising tension, Mathers suggested they go upstairs.

"You go," Cinq-Mars directed them both. "I want to hang back a minute."

Both Mathers and Dreher thought that odd. The crime scene was cold, they couldn't imagine what might be gleaned from a chalk mark on the floor of an empty room, but dutifully they lumbered up the stairs to the second story.

Cinq-Mars kneeled over the outline of the dead body. More than anything, he wanted a moment in the quiet of this house. To soak in the atmosphere, to feel what that might tell him. He wasn't going to explain the method to anyone, as he could scarcely explain it to himself, but in his estimation investigating officers talked too much and thought too much and never allowed the environment to have its say.

Nor did they give the mind a chance to truly think.

He couldn't stay crouched for too long though. His knees and fragile back. Straightening, he stood still. The premises were astonishingly quiet, and somehow that felt significant. He gazed out the window at the snow, and at the adjacent barn. What was wrong with all this peacefulness? The loudest sound proved to be the footsteps of the two detectives overhead and their muffled voices, and even that was intermittent.

Cinq-Mars regarded the chalk mark again. Then the sofa took up his attention. He examined it up close, picking at the fabric. He returned to the kitchen and checked the cupboards and the pantry. Around about this time the heating system came on and he went down into the basement. He found what he was looking for beyond the oil tank, then climbed the stairs again to the first floor. He checked the TV room and another small alcove downstairs, then joined the two officers up above.

"So what did you discover?" Dreher inquired. If he had been hopeful of this partnership ahead of time, his confidence now appeared to be waning.

"Where are the animals?" Cinq-Mars asked.

"What do you mean? Horses, cows? They didn't have any."

"Cats, dogs. It's a farm. What farmhouse isn't overrun with mice without a cat or two? Where are they?"

"The reports don't mention animals," Mathers pointed out to him.

Dreher picked that up. "No cats. No dogs. No pigs. No hens. What does it matter? No nothing. There are no animals."

"Then why does the living room sofa have claw marks where it's been used as a scratching post? Why do the floors show nicks like those my dog makes when her nails have grown too long? Why do we find dog hairs and cat hairs or some kind of hair on the carpets? Why is there a full kitty-litter box in the basement, with some old droppings, if a cat hasn't lived here? And why keep a dog's cushion on the floor of the TV room if no dog lies on it? I suppose Morris and Adele kept cat and dog food, both, in the pantry for an occasional late-night snack on their own?"

"Holy shit," Mathers exclaimed. "Where are the animals?"

Cinq-Mars glanced at him. "That's *my* question," he said.

Mathers held up his hands.

Agent Rand Dreher, in the meantime, appeared to be consumed by thought.

Cinq-Mars examined the chalk lines that demarcated where the policemen and the woman of the house met their fate. He could tell which represented the officers as the artist had carefully drawn the pistols found in each man's hand. "Ask the SQ to bring in their canine squad, Bill."

"The trail's shit-cold, Émile. You know that."

"The animals, Bill. You'll find them dead in the snow somewhere nearby. If they were in the house, we'd be smelling them by now. I'm not counting on it, but their collars might relinquish a thumb print. Or something. Maybe they managed to get in a bite of flesh. Maybe a nail scratched our killer."

"How do you know for sure they're out there?"

"Where else would they be? The killer didn't dig them cute little graves in the frozen ground. If he tried he'd still be digging. He just dropped them in the snow. He doesn't expect them to be found until it melts. By then, Mother Nature will deal with the carcasses before anyone finds them in the tall spring grass. Whoever does, the assumption will be that wild animals did them in, or exposure. Nobody will care or think twice, and anyway there might be nothing left. Thinking that way, maybe our guy allowed himself to be careless. So, canine squad, Bill. Worth a shot."

"Okay, but if he dropped them in the snow," Mathers argued, "why can't we just follow his steps right to them? Oh. Right. His footprints are invisible somehow."

"He killed the animals first, Bill. That tells us that he was here awhile. Perhaps waiting for his victims to show up. He killed them during, or perhaps before, the storm."

Dreher was nodding. He finally seemed impressed. "What does this bedroom tell you?" he asked, and Mathers noticed that the man's tone now conveyed a smidgen of respect rather than mere guarded judgment.

Cinq-Mars was looking around the space. The silence, even with the heating system engaged, kept getting to him, speaking to him, in a way. As below, the floor was stained by the mopped-up blood of the victims.

"One man was shot through the back of his head," Mathers offered. "The other, straight through the top of his forehead."

"The woman," Cinq-Mars inquired. "Adele. Any signs of sexual assault?"

"Both victims had the ring fingers of their left hands severed," Dreher replied. "Both the rings and the fingers are missing. That's always true south of the border as well. The women, here and in the States, are found naked, but their ordeals do not include rape or any apparent sign of sexual transgression. Except, I guess, for the nudity."

The very strangeness of all that kept the three men quiet and studying the floor. Then Cinq-Mars asked, "Any surprises with the autopsies?"

No one said anything so he looked up.

Mathers seemed to be hesitating about something.

"What?" Cinq-Mars encouraged him.

"A discrepancy," Mathers said. "At least, it felt like that to me." By the way Dreher's head elevated, the senior cop assumed that this was coming as news to him also, which meant that the pair had not thoroughly debriefed one another.

"Go on."

"Something weird. The officers, the ones who got shot, they phoned in that the woman was still alive. They requested an ambulance. Yet the autopsy showed that the female victim had *two* gunshot wounds. Both to the head. One entered under the chin and exited out the top of her skull, which, the pathologist stated, did so much damage it could only have killed her instantly. If that is so, why did the cops call in to say that she was still breathing?"

The three men surrounded the lines on the floor in the shape of the woman's form. Dreher at her head, Mathers at the base of her spine, with Cinq-Mars on the opposite side of the body's outline standing by her knees and thighs. The retired cop was the first to do so, but then each man followed suit, tucking his hands into the front pockets of his trousers and dwelling on all this.

Cinq-Mars answered, "Because she was still alive then, Bill. The fatal bullet occurred after the officers called to say that she was still alive. That's why the officers were killed."

"Excuse me?" queried Dreher. "How the hell do you know that?"

"Isn't it obvious?" Cinq-Mars appeared to be speaking to the sketch of the woman's shape on the hardwood floor. "What other explanation is there? The officers radioed that she was still alive. The killer overheard that conversation. At that moment their fates were sealed. He could not allow the woman to remain alive and possibly recover and identify him—or for other reasons—but in order to kill her, he had to get to her, and that meant killing the officers first, and with some haste, since an ambulance and other police were on the way."

"Okay," Mathers allowed. He got that much. "But how?"

Cinq-Mars gazed between the two men a moment, then looked behind him. Next, he turned back and pulled his hands from his pockets as he stepped over behind Bill Mathers. Before him stood a pair of Queen Anne chairs and between them a sturdy table which held magazines in its base and a pair of coffee coasters on its mahogany surface. "There's your footprints in the snow," he pointed out. Both Dreher and Mathers leaned in closer. "Only they're in the rug." The pale, soft-pile, oval rug that covered the surface around the chairs showed indentations the table had made in its original location. The table's feet now stood slightly to the side of those twin marks.

"Okay, the table's been moved slightly," Mathers noted. "So? Are you saying that it got bumped during a struggle?"

Cinq-Mars ignored him. He returned to the hallway. Mathers followed closely behind but Dreher seemed to hold himself back. Cinq-Mars pointed up. To a trapdoor. "He stood on the table to get into the attic. He could push open the trapdoor standing on the table, and a strong man can pull himself up from there. Notice the hall runner." He pointed to spots between his feet. "It also has slight indentations which match the table legs from when he put his weight on it. Up he goes. When the first cop poked his head out, and when he happened to look down, he was shot through the back of his skull from above. When the second cop peeked around the corner, wondering where that shot had come from, he heard something—the trapdoor being opened ajar, perhaps—and glanced up. Either that or he figured out the first bullet's trajectory. His last split-second alive. Shot through the forehead. He jolts back, his head hits the doorjamb at this blood mark, then pitches forward."

Mathers's focus repeatedly swung between the chalk marks representing the two dead cops and the trapdoor in the hall ceiling. "Son of a bitch," he said.

Cinq-Mars maintained a deliberately blithe tone when he said, "Our killer could still be up there, Bill."

Mathers didn't bite, but he did catch on to what transpired next.

"That means—No shit."

"Exactly. He was up there the whole time the SQ was scouring the place looking for clues. He got to listen in to everything they said. But a word of caution, Bill, he could *still* be up there, listening in to us."

"You're not serious."

"I'm not, truth be told. But I'm not a cop anymore. You are. What does correct procedure require of you?" As Mathers was looking around for a prop and seemed to be considering the same table the killer had used, Cinq-Mars helped him out. "I saw a stepladder in the basement."

Mathers went down to fetch it, which made him feel somewhat like a junior detective again, a gofer, but in the company he was keeping his sergeant-detective status didn't carry much weight. On the upper landing, Dreher sidled up next to Cinq-Mars and spoke softly.

"So the killer pulls himself into the attic. Doesn't that leave the table underneath the trapdoor? Wouldn't the first responders discover it when they came on the scene?"

"He has his methods. But why don't you tell me what they are?"

"How do you suppose I can tell you that?" He wore a slight smile, and Cinq-Mars determined that he could get along with this guy if circumstances ever required him to do so. He sensed that he was no dummy, and not an FBI robot either.

"Isn't it part of his modus operandi? Which you know. You didn't bring me here to figure any of this out. You've known it all along."

The agent raised one of his bushy eyebrows and gave him a sharp look. "Our killer brings a rope with him," he began. "He pulls himself up, as you said, then he either lifts the chair or the table, whatever he uses, back up behind him, or he puts it back where he found it. By this point, he has tied the rope to beams in the attic—once he left rope fibers behind on the wood, scraping the wood a little—which he can then use to go up and down as he pleases. He arrives when his victims are out of the house and waits—in one case, for days—for his victims to return. In this case, I suppose he had to dispose of a dog and a cat, or cats. So he's in the house and is familiar with the layout by the time his victims come home. In one example, we believe that the victims arrived home with friends in tow, so he remained in the attic and waited for the guests to leave. He kills on his own time, then remains in the attic until after the police arrive and eventually vacate the house, and then, and only then, does he rob the place. Even taking clues away with him sometimes. In this case, he shot the officers, I'm guessing, for the reason you gave. After that, he didn't bother with a robbery as far as anyone can tell. That's what's different this time—dead cops and no theft. After killing the police officers, he knew that more were on the way. He hid in the attic, but with dead cops, he knew the crime scene would get more attention than usual. He got out while the getting was good, I'm guessing. No time for theft."

"Or what he stole remains secret," Cinq-Mars added.

"So now you know what I know," Dreher said as Mathers returned up the stairs and erected the ladder under the trapdoor. He had been climbing the steps slowly, catching the tail end of the agent's remarks.

"So why didn't you tell us all this when we first got here?" Mathers sounded petulant.

Cinq-Mars chose to answer when Agent Dreher did not. "He's testing me, Bill. He wants to know if I live up to my reputation."

With a slight nod, Dreher concurred.

"I hate being tested," Cinq-Mars declared, in a tone that conveyed exactly that sentiment. "Were you aware of that?"

"I might have guessed."

"So, mystery solved," Mathers enthused.

His mentor cautioned him. "No, Bill. A much larger one has opened up."

"What's that?"

"Who called the cops to come out here in the first place?"

Surprised by the query, the two policemen currently on the job looked questioningly at one another. Neither man proposed an answer.

"Come on, guys," Cinq-Mars chided them. "Two police officers didn't drive out here on a whim. Somebody set them up. Or intended to set the killer up, before it all went south."

FIVE

As they tramped through snow across the wide yard to the barn, at Cinq-Mars's suggestion, the three men remained mute. A simple latch on the gate gave them entry and they flicked on a light. Again they found a premises properly cared for, tidy, likely underused. Once inside, with the door shut behind them against wind from that direction, Mathers was first to speak, citing a report that claimed that the barn had been thoroughly scoured by the SQ. Nothing suggested that any aspect of the crime had extended to the dull gray building.

Cinq-Mars did not seem to care, off on a tangent, musing. "I could use a barn like this. Let me know if any relatives show up. I might take it off their hands."

Dreher gazed at him as if the man had just returned from a stint in an asylum, a look the older detective ignored. Instead he roamed around with his eyes fixed on the rafters. When he returned to where they stood, the agent noted, as if to mollify him, "Still no cats, huh?"

"This place must be infested with mice."

"So, no sale?"

Cinq-Mars offered the visitor his most agreeable smile yet. He liked his little quip. "For the barn, maybe not. Although if I bought it, I'd move it, and that might shake the rodents out. But I'll tell you what, Rand. Say why you asked me out here, and I'll let you know whether or not *you* have a sale."

A few feet away, Mathers positioned himself upon a bale of straw and stuck a stalk between his lips. He took it out when Cinq-Mars warned that it might be covered in mouse poop. For his part, Dreher relaxed against a sturdy post, his hands behind his back for support. Still smiling, Cinq-Mars faced the two men who were trying to conscript him and zipped his jacket higher. He was finding it not only cold in the barn but damp.

"Émile," explained Dreher, "it's simple. We want to get this guy. Obviously, I have no jurisdiction in your country, so I need someone who can be on the ground locally. Someone I can trust, and someone who's good, not a dumb-assed private eye who usually spends his days following housewives around. I need a pro who might actually get the job done. Your name came up. Since I'm from across the border, I need a Canadian. Obviously, the person has to speak French to work this territory. Given that you actually live out here, near the crime scene, well, that's a bonus."

"May I suggest the obvious?" Cinq-Mars inquired.

"The SQ?" The agent inhaled a deep breath and looked away to marshal his argument. "Émile, as I said, it's simple. I need someone who's independent, who may be free to come to the U.S. to retrace a couple of our cases, pick up some of background that way. Imagine the bureaucracy if my man is in the SQ. He'd spend two months getting clearance to work with me. Plus, it's not obvious why he'd bother, given that they're investigating the crime anyway. They have their priorities, and who can blame them for that, with two of their own cops dead? Even if I got the SQ interested in the bigger picture here, they'd spend another month to propose a budget which would then sit on their agenda for two more months waiting to be approved. Then, if it is approved, who's to say they'll send me their brightest light? I'm just being pragmatic here, and I would say, realistic. It's a question of efficiency, Émile, trust, and time."

Cinq-Mars drew a circle in the dust with the toe of his boot, then carved a line through it and circled that. Dreher seemed to be following the hieroglyphic. "What you really want," Cinq-Mars told him, "is a guy who'll answer to you."

Dreher thought through his objection. "Not answer to me, Émile, but keep me apprised, yes. This is important. We may, you see, have a break in the case here, after this episode."

"How so?"

Responding to Cinq-Mars's foot drawing, Dreher moved dirt around with the outside edge of a boot. Then stopped. "Every previous event, Émile, followed a natural disaster. A hurricane—Katrina, in New Orleans—a tornado in Alabama, a North Dakota flood. In California, a small earthquake, albeit with only mild property damage. In this instance, that's what's different. No disaster."

"So in the aftermath of a natural disaster, your killer strikes. How's that for a modus operandi, Bill?"

"Beats the hell out of me," Mathers agreed. "Last week, my eldest boy came home from school with a new phrase. *Pure weird*. This is pure weird, Émile."

"It's all of that. Out here, Rand, we had a snowstorm. A big one."

"Okay, but hardly a disaster. You always have snowstorms in winter. You guys can handle big snowstorms."

"So," Cinq-Mars postulated, "you believe an individual travels to disaster zones to perpetuate his crimes—maybe because in those situations law enforcement is already up to its earlobes—"

"That's right."

"But this time—"

"He became impatient. We think it's a possibility."

"What is?" Mathers asked, struggling to keep up. "How is he impatient?"

Dreher locked his gaze on Cinq-Mars and declined to answer. The retired detective met his challenge. "Am I being tested again?" Rather than answer, Dreher kept silent, and Cinq-Mars shot a glance over at Mathers. "Agent Dreher thinks his killer, the man responsible for murders all over the United States of America, might be from here. A Québécois."

"Exactly."

"So I passed another test. Whoopee."

"Why does he—? Why do you—why think that?" Mathers asked.

"Because the killer got impatient waiting for a natural disaster."

"He was waiting to kill. But natural disasters aren't reliable. He settled for a local storm. Which means he had to be nearby. Was he nearby because he lived here, or was he visiting and waiting for snow? We don't know. Will you take the case, Émile?"

He smiled. "Well, sir," he considered, "that depends."

"I'm sure we can come to an accommodation with respect to compensation."

"Good. Because I'm sure that I don't come cheap. But to be honest with you, I wasn't thinking of that. It's not the stickiest issue I have, although it might help with one of them."

"What's your stickiest issue?"

Resuming his inspection of the rafters again, Cinq-Mars took a moment to reply. "Partly it depends on what you're not telling me."

Recognizing that his former mentor was moving into battle mode, Bill Mathers crossed his legs and leaned back against a higher tier of straw, making himself comfortable.

"Come on, Émile, why do you think I'm not telling you something?"

He took his time, but lowered his gaze from the ceiling and looked directly at Dreher. "Because I've worked with the FBI in the past. Several times."

"I can't speak for those officers—"

"It's in your training. Becomes part of your DNA. It has to do with how you think of yourselves. You have a style. You can't seem to get out from under it."

"Aside from the details of the other murders, Émile, which I'll provide, what I know about this case is now what you know."

He smiled. He nearly laughed. "Okay. Look, I'm tempted to take the case if for no other reason than to see if that statement holds up. Tell you what, if it doesn't, if I work things through and show you later what you are deliberately holding back from me now—and why—then my *accommodation*, as you so elegantly phrased it, doubles. Not only do I want that in writing, I want my potential bonus for your malfeasance placed in an escrow account. And yes, I'm serious. I know that I can never get the FBI to admit to deliberately misleading a colleague, so I'll ask for the next best thing. I'll make the FBI *pay* for doing so."

To Mathers, it seemed clear that Dreher wanted to inquire if Cinq-Mars was serious, if not out on farmland howling at the moon, but he curtailed his own gut reactions. "On a matter of that nature," he stated, "I'll need to speak to my superiors."

"Do so." In raising his chin, he looked down his magisterial beak at him, his eyes as penetrating as an eagle's. "Now it's my turn to test you, Rand. Let's see if you can't get that done within two days. I have to think about it some more, pass it by my wife. She might be the stickiest issue of all. I can't predict how that might shake down. I am, after all, supposedly, retired. I'll also need to have a private word with Bill here, before you go. If I'm to be of any use to you, I'll need some help myself. That's where Bill comes in. After all, he's an officer of the law. Not much of a brain but he packs a weapon."

"Which I might indiscriminately use on an old retired kook like you," Mathers chimed in, straightening up on his bale now.

"Did you say kook or coot?"

Mathers thought about it. "Either applies. Take your pick."

Cinq-Mars enjoyed the joust, a refresher from the old days.

He continued, "While you're in with your superiors, Rand, bargaining for my substantial pay increase, why not advise them that they can save considerable expense, and time, and everyone a great deal of trouble, if you just tell me now what you don't want me to know ever. I'll give you that out, that chance to reform."

Agent Rand Dreher pulled his car keys from his pocket, his way of wrapping up their conversation. "I hope to disabuse you of your suspicions, Émile. Though I suppose it's an occupational hazard. I've kept nothing from you. What makes you think that I have secrets?"

Touching the man's shoulder briefly, Cinq-Mars smiled again, not without some obvious pleasure. He winked at Mathers. "Agent Dreher, you're FBI. Of course you have secrets."

SIX

Believing he'd made substantial progress in recruiting Émile Cinq-Mars, Rand Dreher was not put out to leave him alone in the barn with Sergeant-Detective Mathers while he returned outside to warm up the car. Cinq-Mars promised not to be long, although Dreher called over his shoulder to take his time.

With the barn door shut again, the former cop paced. Mathers stood still and observed him. He'd seen this contemplative visage before. The cold and the barn's dampness brought a spot of fluid to the tip of his mentor's nose, which he knocked away with a gloved hand, and went on thinking. Mathers waited beyond his point of impatience, but when the silence was just too much for him, he finally asked, "What's bugging you?"

He recognized that much. The wily retired detective was not flummoxed by some notion he did not understand, but he was visibly upset.

"He doesn't want the SQ involved for a reason."

"Would you?"

Cinq-Mars rocked his head gently, quizzically, from side to side. "Touché, Bill. But I know them. I have cause not to want to work with them. But why doesn't *he* want them around? He's an outsider. What does he know?"

"So, are you saying you're not buying his argument for an independent investigator? Made perfect sense to me." With his hands in his coat pockets, Mathers caused the bottom portion of the coat to flap a moment. Either that motion, or what he said, stopped his colleague's pacing.

"The man lies with confidence, doesn't he?" Cinq-Mars noted. "Man, what a crock of pig manure. That's one thing about a truckload of pig shit, Bill. You'd know this if you lived out here. Sure it has a purpose, but my God it stinks."

Mathers let his friend's anger settle a moment. "Why, then?" he asked. "What's the real reason he doesn't want the SQ to help investigate the earlier murders?"

"My hunch, you mean? I have no proof."

"I miss your hunches, Émile. When you left the force we were finally rid of them. I thought life would be enjoyable again. But I was wrong. I've missed them."

"Channels," Cinq-Mars said, ignoring the younger man's whimsy. "The FBI—or specifically our Agent Dreher—may not want to sift through SQ channels. I understand that, but still, whether it's convenient or necessary, if they must go through channels they will do so. But the problem for them is this: it becomes tit-for-tat. That's how the system works. The SQ will expect to work back through FBI channels, be in touch with other key officers, higher authorities."

Mathers let his eyes wander as he mulled this over. He tried to fathom what Cinq-Mars found so fascinating about the upper rafters. They looked like old beams to him. "Are you suggesting—you are, aren't you?—you're suggesting that Dreher is out here taking a flyer on his own? He doesn't want the SQ involved because he doesn't want the FBI involved. No tit-for-tat. Is that it? You think he's gone rogue, or he's doing all this on his own dime?"

"That's the new phrase now, isn't it?" Mathers might miss his partner's propensity for hunches, but he could still do without the sarcasm. "Gone rogue," Cinq-Mars repeated. "More infuriating cop lingo to make cops feel like cops. Isn't it?"

Mathers flapped his coat again. "I don't know," he demurred. "Just a phrase." He waited a moment, then tried again. "So has he? Gone rogue?"

The older man's interests drifted up into the rafters again, but there was nothing up there, Mathers was convinced, not a blessed thing.

"Possibly," Cinq-Mars finally indicated. "More likely, he has reasons to not want someone in the Bureau—superiors, peers, underlings, who knows?—to find out what he's up to. I know what that's like. Been there myself. You keep your nose clean, Bill, procedure-wise. I never did, as you know, and our agent out there might not either. We represent his way to investigate this case yet keep it under the radar *inside* the FBI. They probably don't even know he's in Canada. He's not packing a piece, did you notice?"

Rather than admit that he hadn't, Mathers said, "Packing a piece. Cop lingo."

"Bill, you should've noticed. I figure it's because he didn't want to announce himself as FBI leaving the U.S., or entering Canada, or re-entering the States. He's at least semi-incognito, is my bet."

Mathers caught on to something then. "So that's why you asked for the payment bonus. To test your theory. To see if he can pull that off."

"He's been testing me, Bill. I can do the same back, no? Why not?"

Mathers agreed that he could do that. "Émile, you told him that you wanted me to help you. I don't know if you were serious—"

"Why wouldn't I be?"

"Unlike you, I'm not retired. Unlike you, I answer to bosses, and unlike the way you used to be, I can't just go off on my own within the department."

"True," Cinq-Mars conceded, "and I should have asked first. Pardon my manners. But, like me, you're curious about the case and upset about dead cops. Besides, I'll need your help, precisely because you're not retired. First, get the SQ to bring out their dog squad. Their K-9. Most likely they'll turn up the dead animals but no evidence, but the SQ will feel involved that way, in the loop, and that might keep them onside and allow us to muddle in what is essentially their business. At the very least, the pets will get a decent grave. See, I can only ask for K-9 by going through my connections, and that'll piss people off inside the SQ. But you can ask, and that'll make folks happy inside the SQ. See the difference?"

“Okay.”

“Next,” Cinq-Mars pressed on, “after I get the information from Dreher on the previous murders, do your own inquiry into them. Use appropriate protocol for police networks. Ring no bells. Show me what local police and local journalists had to say about the killings. If you find out the names and numbers of the specific investigating officers, pass that along. See? I can’t get any of that without you.”

“Okay. I can do that. What are you going to do?”

“Talk to my wife, Bill. That’s the biggest hurdle here. Then, if she lets me, I’ll talk to the SQ. If I’m going to be the FBI’s man on the ground, then the SQ should know that and hear it in such a way that they don’t get their collective back up. Just because he doesn’t want relations with them doesn’t mean that I have to adhere to the policy. Besides, I can help them out. I know I can. That way, they might help me. If the Bureau wants to be in the shadows, that’s their choice. Or Dreher’s choice. The rest of us are still free to walk around in the light of day. But, Bill. Don’t tell Dreher that I’m willing to work with the SQ. Let that be our secret.”

Mathers took a moment to consider all this. “Émile, come on, what are you up to?”

That earned him a wide grin from his former partner. “Bill, did anyone ever tell you that you’re cute when you’re suspicious? I’m retired. Isn’t there a song? *Old men just wanna have fun*. There’s nothing more to it than that. But, Bill, Bill, here’s a head’s-up. A farm without farm animals and a bare minimum of domestic pets. The people who lived here did not farm. Whatever comes back about their histories, if anything, get that back to me. I can’t do that without you. This barn, for instance. It’s clean and well looked after because it’s empty and unused. All we know about our dead farmers is that they weren’t farmers. I really hate to cast aspersions about the victims, but that’s suspicious, don’t you think?”

Mathers waited a respectful half minute, then asked, “Are we done here?”

“Yeah. He’s cooled his jets long enough. His blood level’s been raised. He’ll be pumping you for information all the way home, but since you don’t have any, you won’t say peep. Right?”

“Right.”

“So let’s go. Good to see you, Bill.”

"First," Mathers said, failing to budge, "tell me what you see, Émile."

"What I see?"

"Up in the rafters."

Cinq-Mars gazed up there again. "I might want to buy this barn," he said.

"No, Émile. Seriously."

"Barns can be moved, Bill. Don't you know that?"

Mathers sighed. "All right. Keep me in the dark. See what that does for you."

They both turned to leave in unison this time.

"Don't worry, Bill," Cinq-Mars told him. "I will."

"That's how you know he has secrets. You keep so many of your own."

The older detective chuckled quite brightly. "That must be it," he concurred. "You might have something there. My God, you're finally starting to think like me!"

SEVEN

Émile and Sandra Cinq-Mars did not get into a lengthy discussion on his job offer—if he could call it that, it seemed strange to do so—upon his return home. She was busy in the barn securing water and feed for the horses, which took longer than usual as he had not been around to assist, and then it was her night to prepare the evening meal. She was well into her culinary creation as Émile slumped home. Over his iPod and through the living room speakers he played Chopin, and further fortified himself with a single malt. In a choice between two favorites, the Talisker and the Highland Park, he simply went for the easiest reach and safest bend for his back, which turned out to be the Talisker. Then he sat, sipped, closed his eyes, and opened his ears to the music.

If he was at all in the doghouse, his status was not borne out by the meal. A pasta in crème sauce, with shrimp, lobster bits, and scallop pieces, the edges of the bowl rimmed by mussels and small asparagus flowers under a drizzle of sauce. Nothing thrown together. Candlelight aided the ambiance and the white wine was pleasant, causing Cinq-Mars to regret that he had carried to the table a serious subject to broach.

Sandra beat him to it.

"So, Mr. Famous Detective, what do the dogs of war want now?"

He buttered a slice of focaccia. "It's the cop killings and that poor couple."

"Seriously? The FBI is involved with that?"

"Apparently it relates to something they've been looking at."

"I see." As a policeman's wife, a chill went over her at the mention of cops being killed. She didn't suppose that the feeling would ever dissipate merely because her husband had retired. "So, what, are you like a hired gun now?"

"Hired goon, maybe. Except I haven't been issued a weapon."

"East of Aldgate," she said.

He used to utter the phrase, lifted from a Sherlock Holmes teleplay, but he hadn't repeated it in some time and was surprised to hear it tossed back at him. Holmes, who did not commonly arm himself, had advised his good friend, "Always carry a firearm east of Aldgate, Watson." He'd been heading for that part of London, a notoriously violent neighborhood, at the time.

"Two policemen dead," he explained. "It's difficult to sit still for that."

"It's difficult for you to sit still." She was trying to make nice, but being anxious about the conversation, her husband failed to catch her tone.

"Sandra, if you don't want me to do this, say so. I haven't committed to anything. I told everyone that I need to discuss it with you."

"Oh, please, Émile, don't make it my burden. Do what you wish to do. Or need to do. You might have thought differently, but you were never a great candidate for retirement. I concede, I hoped otherwise. But you're more interested in horse-trading than in their day-to-day— Oh, don't deny it, you know it's true. And it's still true even though you're less interested in horse-trading than you used to be."

He took his time responding and chewed a shrimp. "It's a matter of looking into the situation to see if I can help. Nobody's asking me to head up a squad or anything like that."

"Do you have to sound so disappointed? I'm not fighting you. Seriously, Émile. I'm really not fighting. Look." She showed him her hands, upraised and flat on the table. "Open palms. No fists." Her smile was tentative, and he returned his own, as if agreeing to cool down. Sandra continued, "Tell you what. Since this is *apparently* a negotiation, at least *you* seem to be treating it that way, we'll negotiate. Say what it is you want, and I'll draw up my own demands."

"Demands," he repeated.

"If you want everything to go smoothly, expect demands. What's wrong with that?"

He was amenable, in theory.

They ate peaceably and Émile poured wine for both of them again. She said, "Okay. I've thought it through."

"So soon? You know your demands? Okay. Demand."

Placing her elbows on the table, Sandra knitted her fingers. She looked demure, rather pleased with herself. "Demand number one. Two policemen dead must never become three policemen dead, or two policemen and one retired cop who ought to know better."

The tension between them of late had dulled his sensitivities. He was finally getting the idea that she was not in a bad mood after all, nor was she mad at him. He cast his eyes over the meal again, the presentation, the candlelight, the fact that she had allowed the Chopin to stay on and filter through from the other room. He was off his game. He should have realized much sooner that things were going his way here.

"Okay," he consented, and smiled more openly.

"Okay is not good enough. Promise."

"All right. I promise."

"And here's the real kicker," Sandra proposed. "You're nobody's employee. So you're no longer bound to professional silence. This time around, keep me apprised of the investigation. As you never have before. If that means that from time to time you're obliged to tolerate my input, you will do so. Now. Promise me."

He had been drafting schemes to possibly place a salve on their marriage. Now he realized that, even though she had initiated the matter of splitting up, she might be doing exactly the same thing. She was saving them.

Émile told her, "I promise to tolerate you."

Which won a smile. "Not exactly how I would put it, but I'll accept that." She scooped the last of her main course, mostly sauce, onto her spoon. "Guess what?" Her mood seemed downright flirtatious. "I made dessert."

He was even allowed to kick his diet for an evening. Émile Cinq-Mars was counting this as a good day, with all the potential for a good night ahead of him.

EIGHT

Over the next few days, the region experienced dramatic fluctuations in temperature. Émile Cinq-Mars did little more than putter around the farm or study intermittent reports that Mathers sent over by courier. On a Thursday, the weather offered more of the same. A light rain fell through mid-morning and froze across the snowfields in the afternoon, creating a surface glaze by late evening as the thermometer seriously dipped. In the light of a waxing moon, pastures glistened and sparkled. Reminiscent of old times, the former detective waited just off the road on what served as a tractor path in summer, the car radio tuned to a classical music station. He was allowing a latent affection for music to grow in his retirement, and he was now fond of educating himself. The clear night, however, brought in distant stations crackling over top of the one he desired, and the first selection on the program, Brahms, did not inspire him, so in the end he opted for quiet.

Which instigated a level of inspiration all on its own.

A barren road, particularly in winter. He had written the directions verbatim, yet a subliminal anxiety warned that he and the other man might have gotten their signals crossed. His counterpart was seven minutes late, so far, with still no sign, way down the road in either direction, of anyone's headlights.

Émile restarted the car to generate warmth, blasting hot air for a minute, and turned on the coils under his posterior. In an idle mood, he wondered if heated car seats ever caught fire. He figured he'd smell the burn before his rump ignited. Closing his eyes, he made it a point not to fall asleep, sniffing the air for flaming upholstery to confirm that he hadn't yet asphyxiated. Distant chicken-barn stink wafted by.

He turned the engine off again.

And wondered if over the years he hadn't acquired a preference for discomfort on the job. At the very least, the chill kept him awake.

A car was sighted, seventeen minutes late. He guessed that only his guy was likely to be out there at this time of night, a presumption that proved correct as the vehicle first passed him, stopped, then backed up to pull in behind him. He was willing to get out, but the other fellow was quicker to emerge, coming around to the passenger side of his Jeep.

Captain Gabriel Borde, of the Sûreté du Québec, the SQ, rubbed his hands together, then slammed the door on their covert meeting.

"Fucking turn the heat on, Émile. I'm freezing my ass off in here."

The division of police forces in Canada followed its own logic. The Royal Canadian Mounted Police held geographic sway across the land, performing the work Scotland Yard did in the U.K. or the FBI in the U.S., and yet, unlike their counterparts, the Mounties also did a great deal of local policing. Everything from highways to small towns to mid-sized cities came under their aegis, yielding to local police departments only as cities grew to a certain size. Some crimes crossed borders, and so demanded their involvement even if they initially occurred within another jurisdiction—the importation and the movement of illicit drugs, the policing of airports, serial murders across provincial boundaries—but generally their presence in big cities was minimal. Two provinces, Quebec and Ontario, elected to have their own provincial police departments. Ontario did so out of hubris, essentially, as the province once saw itself as wealthy and superior—although time was demonstrating that that self-imposed prominence could not be sustained. In Quebec, the choice was political, as federal police, visible and preeminent in a nationalist culture, smacked of being an occupying force. In its relationships with other police agencies then, the SQ waved the nationalist flag and approached all points of contact with a desire to protect, preserve, and assert itself, the people of Quebec, and the French language, even at the expense of collegiality and, if necessary, of justice. All of which pissed off Cinq-Mars.

Still, times and troubles arose when anyone wearing any color uniform—the blue of city cops, the red of the Mounties, the muddy military green of the SQ—conceded that private grievances and agendas needed to be set aside, as doom, or, what was considered worse, public disgrace, might otherwise result. Good people abounded in every agency. Enlightened officers maintained personal, private, and often secret contact with one another, as a means to achieve consensus on matters of mutual concern without anyone's hierarchy finding out that the issues had been scrutinized and secretly negotiated by their own officers. Given his potential involvement in a case precipitated by the murder of two SQ officers, Cinq-Mars knew that it was not only expedient, but fundamentally necessary and wise, to call in an SQ colleague, in order for the two of them to bring each other up to speed and to short-circuit any potential, and most likely inevitable, antagonism.

"I just turned the heater off," Cinq-Mars groused. "How hot do you want it?"

"Give me Miami Bench to sit on," Borde ordained. "Or an island at the equator. Don't give me this air-conditioning-in-February bullshit."

"Fine. It's on. Don't blame me if you asphyxiate."

"Modern cars, hey? They don't kill you like they used to, Cinq-Mars. How the hell are you, anyway? How's your retirement going? Must be a bitch."

"Why do you think that?"

"You're investigating a quadruple murder. That's my first clue."

"What's your second?"

"You called me to this meeting."

He had to chuckle. "Right you are. Retirement's a bore. So I called you."

"First thing that happened is, the FBI got in touch. Don't play dumb with me, Émile. That never works with you. What's that about? FBI. Here? Why?"

Cinq-Mars started talking, and explained much of what he knew.

"Émile, we checked the attic."

"Did you? With a dog?"

"No mutts. Somebody thought about it, but none were available. The nearest K-9 mutt was searching for some Alzheimer's guy who wandered into the woods. He thought he was Robin Hood. Horny bastard was looking for his Maid Marion. He took his clothes off before the dogs found him, frozen stiff, so to speak. They say his dick shriveled up as skinny as a snow pea. Maid Marion would not have been impressed. But look, we found out for ourselves that our guy hid in the attic. We know that. Nobody in the SQ believes in magic carpets, I don't care what the papers say. Émile, we checked the fucking attic. We did it right away, too. I mean when the killer was still up there we did it. We checked up there again after he was gone, and that second time we found out where he had been hiding the first time, under the insulation. Okay, so you got me on that one. We were two days late. We didn't look close enough. We let him get away. Shoot me, okay?"

"Gabriel, I'm impressed. You checked the attic."

"But no sniffer mutts. Screwed that part up. Go ahead, spread the good word. Just remember, we got pig farms near here. A load of pig manure in your front yard, the stench stays on your skin for months. Your clothes? Burn them. Want me to drop a load of pig shit on your porch, Émile? Tell the world how we screwed up and after that you'll want to go drown yourself in perfume."

"Come on, Gabriel. Who would believe a rumor that the SQ screwed up?"

"Fly a kite. In a blizzard."

"Anyway, I'm retired. The media doesn't talk to me anymore."

"Is that why you miss it so much?"

In a way, Borde was asking a question so many cops wanted answered. What's up with retirement? Is it doable? Can you really walk away from the job and still feel that you have a life? *Will it be all right when my time comes?*

Cinq-Mars didn't feel that any of his answers readily applied to anyone else. He said, "I don't miss the media, no."

"People, they always said you were in it for the fame. The attention, anyway. I never believed that, Émile. Hell, *I* am in it for the fame, so I know the difference between me and you. You were in it for the money, don't deny it now."

They enjoyed another laugh. They both knew that Borde had never met a microphone he could resist. His penchant for PR probably made him less of a cop, but helped him rise to the top, and he was definitely a top cop now. A capable one, in Cinq-Mars's view. Unlike older detectives he knew, Borde, who was no athlete, a little short for a cop and more than a little rotund, kept in shape. Despite his form, dominated by a stomach with some girth, he lifted weights, and people were surprised when they discovered him to be as strong as the proverbial ox. When Cinq-Mars inquired about that one time, over a couple of whiskies in downtown Montreal, the detective reflected back upon a night in uniform in his twenties when he'd been beaten up. Surfacing from that disgrace, Borde vowed to never let it happen again and promptly hit the gym. "You want irony?" he asked back then.

"From you? Sure," Cinq-Mars said. "Hit me with some irony."

"Never been in a fight since. Not one. And I'm a cop! Call me a liar, but that's the truth."

"I don't think you're lying. Why would I?"

"Something happened in the gym though. I found out that I was strong. My old man was strong, too. It's in our genes. But still, you gotta work at it. A boy thinks that he can never measure up to his old man. For sure, that was me. Then I found out that maybe I could, with weights anyhow. I just had to be disciplined. I also found out that it got rid of a lot of tension, and anger sometimes, pumping iron. Did me a world of good, career-wise. Personal-wise, too. Yeah. Nothing like putting on some muscle to make you feel like God's gift, you know?"

Like Cinq-Mars, he lived off the island of Montreal, also to the west, although in his case in one of the rapidly expanding residential communities and not on a farm. He was a family man who lived a simple life, and Cinq-Mars liked to see that in someone who wielded considerable power in his day job, and with whom he shared confidences. He would not go so far as to say that he trusted the man outright, because he knew that Borde endured pressures in his position which meant that he might not always mean what he said and he might not always do what he promised or even what he himself wanted to do. The captain was subject to compromise and contradiction when solicitations mounted from various sides. In dealing with him, any man had to keep that in mind, but in understanding the complexity of modern life for a man with some power—within those bounds—Cinq-Mars considered him a relatively straight-up guy. If he was going to be snowed by him, he believed, at least this guy would have a good reason to do so. Fair enough.

"Were you on the scene yourself?" he asked him.

"Day two. Not day one. I was up in Quebec City breaking bread with the government. How's the wife?"

"She's fine. Sandra sends her love."

"She knows we're meeting?"

Cinq-Mars laughed.

"What?"

"She says my quota for secrets ran out a long time ago. New rules. I keep her informed."

"That true? I'm not going to retire if life's like that."

Cinq-Mars cut to the chase. "I'm heading to the Deep South, to investigate similar murders down there."

"Deep South? You mean like Huntingdon?"

"Not southern Quebec!" Cinq-Mars chortled. "I mean New Orleans. The southern U.S."

The SQ officer sat there with his mouth open a moment. "What, the FBI can't do their own job now, they need you? What's up with that?"

"I find it curious myself."

The comment carried weight, a gravity they had to acknowledge in silence. Something was going on that passed beyond the bounds of the ordinary. And possibly, beyond the bounds of what might normally be construed as safe.

"Who do you got to watch your back for you in this Deep South? Eh, Émile?" Borde's tone turned serious. "Think about it. The FBI is asking you to do their job. Does that sound right to you? Does it make any sense at all?"

"Gabriel, with your permission, I have to talk as you do for a second."

"Talk as I do? What the fuck does that mean?"

"Your kind of language, if you don't mind."

"My language? Go ahead. What's my language?" They were speaking only in French, so he really didn't know what he meant.

"You're the only Frenchman I know who swears only in English, even when you're speaking French. You're unique that way, Gabriel. But anyway. Me. Going down there. Working for the FBI for who knows what reason. There's only one way to put this and I can only say it in your language."

"Okay. Go ahead."

"It's fucking intriguing."

Borde understood what he was saying, but remained cautious. "Okay. So that's fine. Keep me informed. I'll keep you informed. Don't get your head blown off just because the case is fucking intriguing, all right? I don't want to read about it in *USA To-fucking-day.* I'll say all that in English if you want. Hell, for you, to keep you safe, I'll swear in French if you want."

Cinq-Mars appreciated the sentiment.

NINE

In a thick binder, a number of reports arrived at the farmhouse the following afternoon. Émile took care of the horses then sat down with a whiskey at hand to study the documents. He had reshoed a horse earlier that day and being bent over awkwardly out in the chill of the barn cost him. At such times, when the back started to protest, he knew what to do. Remain neither prone nor seated for too long, stop the pain with medication before it gained the advantage, and redouble his exercise regimen. So he performed his program, then settled in for his reading in a good mood. The ache felt shoeing the horse proved beneficial, for bent over and grunting Sandra entered the barn and something snapped between them. They were both instantly reminded of the first time they set eyes on one another, when she was the one slumped over a horse's shoe, scraping it clean of muck.

The memory refreshed them both.

Mathers had finally sent over FBI reports on the southern murders. Émile read them, ensconced on his sofa with his feet up at times, or seated on an exercise ball, or standing, and periodically he switched the three positions to keep his back supple. Each time he changed positions he poured another splash into his glass. After showering, Sandra joined him, and, given her new status as a confidante on the case, she perused the reports as well.

By the time they were both finished, Cinq-Mars was gently bouncing on his ball, while she curled up against the plush cushions.

"So," she invited him, "what does this tell you? What are you learning?"

He would rather take more time to process what he read, but this was a new regime and his marriage, apparently, remained at stake.

"What's curious," he speculated, "and I have to think about this a little more, is that the murders are less violent than they appear."

"Murder's not violent? Since when? These murders are violent, Émile."

The correction was warranted.

"Yes, but . . . each murder is meant to appear to be the result of a rampage. As if by design. But the victims died early—well, relatively early, as these things go—during the event. On the surface, we see some sick aspects. Before the woman is killed, for instance, she probably finds out that her husband is dead. Most likely, she watched him die. That's traumatic. Gruesome, I suppose. It's cruel. Hard on the psyche. All the more so knowing that she's likely to be next."

"But you don't consider it gruesome yourself?" Sandra spoke quietly. "I mean, you only *suppose* that it's gruesome?" She had asked to be included in the investigation, but was no longer certain that she wanted to be. "You're not that jaded, Émile. Surely not. Or should I be asking, how jaded are you?"

He tried to explain. "In every case, the cops on the scene believed the murders were gruesome. Odds are, some, if not all, of them were jaded cops. Such as the guys in New Orleans. Louisiana is the least safe state in the union."

"What's the safest? My New Hampshire, I bet."

"Sorry. Maine beats you out again."

"We always lose out to Maine. I hate that."

"You have better horses."

"True. Good. Otherwise, I'd have to move to Maine."

That was probably a slip, and Émile was careful not to slide off his gym ball as he stretched for his Highland Park. He let the comment go, as any reply might lead to trouble. He didn't want to think that she was considering moving.

"The point is," he analyzed, "the first cops on the scene always considered the murders particularly violent, but the facts of the case don't really bear that out. Violence is a relative term when it comes to murder. What I'm feeling is, they were meant to look pretty bad. But in truth they weren't, not really."

"Okay. Maybe I'm following you. The gruesome aspects were for effect?"

"Yes. Because there was never a rampage. Only the hint of a rampage. The murders were actually methodical and precise. Calculated, actually. Professional, in other words. At least . . . maybe. It's only a theory."

"Go on," she encouraged him. She knew that her husband was good at this sort of thing, yet she rarely had an opportunity to see him in action. "What's the theory?"

"First off, the victims seem to have died early in the rampage. So they were spared any prolonged physical and psychological agony. That suggests to me that the killer wasn't necessarily in it for his jollies. Rather, he had a job to do, but he wanted to make it look otherwise. Sick aspects show up, as I said, but the scenes were not prolonged, which is odd if the killer was driven by a desire for violent or warped sex, for example. Each victim loses his or her ring finger, and the rings on it, but in Alabama the medical examiner declared positively that the fingers were removed postmortem. So the victims didn't suffer that torture when they were alive. In Louisiana, the ME suggested that that might have been the case, but she seemed to lack confidence in her findings. I think she was just incompetent. In Connecticut, the ME raised the matter as a likely possibility. Here, for our murders, the coroner neglected to even ask the question. Most people have assumed the man's finger was snipped off when he was alive, but that's not necessarily true. And the killer might not have known the woman wasn't dead yet."

"Émile."

"Mmm?"

"Don't say *snipped*."

He pondered why she was strung out on the word, and concluded that it suggested that the act was somehow more *gruesome*.

"It just sounds so banal when, really, it's horrible," she explained.

"I won't say *snipped,*" he conceded. "Digging further," he went on, "theft as a common link is also odd. None of the victims were rich or likely to be carrying large amounts of cash, and the killer clearly left each house traveling light. Why rob these people? To risk a murder charge to steal trinkets is out of whack. It could happen once, maybe the thief expected more, but multiple times? As well, are the women of a certain type? No. Are the men? No. So why were the victims handpicked to be victims when nothing links them? Nothing fits a predetermined pattern or criteria for a calculating, methodical killer. The only real similarity, and it's intriguing, is that the murders followed in the wake of natural disasters, although in our case, it was only a big storm."

With that puzzle afloat in the air awhile, Émile chose to reload his Scotch.

He remained standing when he returned.

"And how did anyone link these crimes together?" he asked. "The ring-finger removal? That's a clue, for sure. But so easily missed given how these crimes are spread out across the continent. What was it that turned the FBI's crank on this?"

"Ask them."

"They're not talking. That's the other intriguing factor. The missing link, as it were. The FBI doesn't want me to know what they know. They want me to investigate in the dark. As if there's a way that that can ever work."

"But I know you, Émile. You never trust policemen. Except maybe Bill."

"Bill's naïve. Always will be."

"See what I mean?"

He smiled, and balanced on his exercise ball again.

"Sandra, here's the thing. If I'm to do this job properly, because I've got nothing to shake a stick at locally, I need to visit at least a few of the crime scenes in the United States and interview the local authorities there."

He sipped. Sandra nodded.

"Where, exactly?"

"First stop, New Orleans. Then I'll nip off to Alabama."

"Nip," she repeated. Sandra sighed. "If you have to go," she determined, "then you have to go. You're just interviewing people, right? Nothing dangerous."

"I'm not aware of any danger. So, do you think you can get your usual guy to look after the horses?"

She shrugged. "I can manage on my own."

"You're not taking my meaning."

She looked up at him. Saw a twinkle in his eyes.

"It's New Orleans, Sandra. You're on the case, right? So come with me."

She did a tiny double-take and saw that he was serious. "Oh, yes, I can get my usual guy. If not, I'll get some other guy. Émile! Isn't Mardi Gras coming up?"

"I believe so."

"Holy shit! New Orleans!"

She forgot for a moment that her husband was a religious man, that some swear words were more offensive to him than others, such as *holy* annexed to *shit*. She wanted to apologize, but their eyes locked then, for more than a few seconds, and both knew what the other was thinking. This was a chance, of sorts. To rediscover themselves. Or to fall apart. This was more than just a simple holiday. And certainly, not a simple investigation. They had a lot more riding on this case than the identity of a killer.

PART 2

TEN

Not knowing where to stay, they imagined a cool place on Canal Street, a converted brothel above a jazz bar where fragrant breezes wafted in off Lake Pontchartrain to mingle with a mournful, sexy, late-night sax, but neither Émile nor Sandra knew if a hotel on Canal Street really was the place to be, if it would be hip or merely a dive, or a place to get mugged in, or if jazz clubs were even located there at all, or hotels, or if opening a balcony door invited in the warm, humid air of the south or the muskiness of sour urine, or if the ambiance of a hastily booked room promised romance or might possibly instigate a near-death experience. So they booked the Hilton. From there, they could figure out the lay of the land and freely explore, and anyway, didn't it sound perfectly safe?

They so rarely traveled. Care for the horses took precedence, and usually if they managed a week away Sandra opted for the New Hampshire farmhouse where her mother resided on her own, now that her dad was deceased. Most of their travels were to horse fairs and competitions within a day or two's drive, trips that were pleasant enough and productive enough that they did not feel deprived of travel. And over the past two winters they had finally found their way south. Once for a week in Florida, then ten days in Barbados the following year. They appreciated the break from the cold and their bodies felt regenerated, but neither trip had been memorable and instead had left them oddly dissatisfied, so that in considering a southern excursion this year they had been unable to sufficiently rouse themselves to make a decision.

But now. By some miracle. New Orleans.

They hoped to find the city in revival mode after the devastation of Hurricane Katrina, but as they had not kept abreast of developments they really didn't know what to expect. Cinq-Mars was governed by a single tidbit of knowledge—serious crime abounded there—and knew also that Mardi Gras was on the horizon. He assumed that at such a legendary festival, bacchanalian and remotely quasi-religious at the same moment, he could find a niche and enjoy himself.

They'd have downtime with each other. Which created its own expectations and tension. Émile and Sandra aspired to connect again, to undertake a revival of some sort—quasi-romantic, perhaps, or even, who knows, bacchanalian. Rather than place their expectations at the risk of a crummy hotel room, they made peace with the likely dull security of the Hilton.

All that decision-making resulted in Sandra receiving a solid, undignified bump from a man in the lobby upon their arrival. A pair of men in their thirties were crossing each other's path as the couple entered. In sidestepping that collision, one tripped right into Sandra, giving her a jolt, then the other, stumbling himself, reached out to break her fall as well as his own. Émile reached for her also, flinging out his arms, but in that instinctive reaction he also caught the scene in his mind's eye and detected a foreign hand at his hip. Whether it was his police training, observations over a long career, or simply an impulsive intuitive notion, his right hand jumped to his rear pocket and his wallet there, and fell upon an uninvited paw. In the ensuing jumble, apologies were uttered by the men for their clumsiness and Sandra assured them to never mind and laughed the moment off. Émile Cinq-Mars, though, stood still and silent, arms crossed, certain that he had thwarted a carefully choreographed picking of his pocket.

Then he noticed that a clasp on Sandra's purse had been tripped.

He smiled at the fellow who had fallen into his wife, stretched out his hand ostensibly to thank him, then took the fellow's hand in his own and squeezed quite hard. He leaned into him, squeezing harder. He whispered in the man's ear, "Return my wife's wallet or I'll break your fingers in five, four, three seconds."

The man was small, casually well-dressed, with a smooth olive complexion and dark eyes. Under the pressure on his hand, his face was distorting rapidly and he involuntarily exhaled.

"Two," Cinq-Mars said, and squeezed even harder. He gave him another friendly, encouraging pat as the man's mouth stretched open in pain.

The other man among them appeared confused. He and Sandra were united in wondering what Émile had whispered.

"Oh! Look what fell," said the man in the ex-policeman's grip and knelt down even though Cinq-Mars still held his right hand. No one saw anything on the floor, but when the suave fellow popped back up again he held Sandra's wallet out to her.

Suddenly she understood. Her wallet had appeared out of thin air. She did a rapid check, then said, "It's okay. You can let him go, Émile."

"I'll be here for several days," Émile let the man know. "You won't be." He patted the fellow's wrist, then released him.

Supposedly, the two men were strangers passing in the lobby, but the jig was up and one gave an indication to the other with his chin. The pair departed out the front door together. One wore a pink sports shirt, elegant gray slacks, and kept his hair spot-on with gel. The other, tricked out in a spiffy lemony suit, used less gel. They could be brothers.

"Welcome to the safe Hilton," Cinq-Mars murmured as he watched them go.

"Welcome to New Orleans," Sandra tacked on.

They smiled at one another and carried on arm in arm. What might have been a huge annoyance at the outset of their time away had been thwarted. Perhaps good fortune shone on their side.

Émile was glad that the situation had stayed calm. Any altercation at that moment might have found him deficient. In the Big Easy, apparently, men with slippery fingers knew how to keep their cool. After the cramped flight—for him, most flights were cramped—he was sore, stiff, and needed to exercise, so after checking in they went up to their room on the seventeenth floor where he performed his diabolical stretches.

Sandra partially unpacked before busying herself in the washroom. She emerged wearing a black sports bra and panties and headed across the room to pull the drapes together and darken the room.

"We're staying in?" Cinq-Mars asked, now in shadow on the carpet.

"It's a night town, Émile." She pulled the bedcovers down. "I'm resting up for the action." Tongue-in-cheek, perhaps, but serious, too, she grinned.

Émile was just as happy to strip down and crawl into bed himself, ready for a snooze, and yet, after about ten minutes, they turned, and slid a little closer to each other, and that soon evolved into a snuggle. They tried napping in the spoons position but before sleep overtook them they both grew rowdy. Cinq-Mars honestly believed that he had not expected this, and yet he'd made an allowance for the possibility. To be on the safe side he took the time to ingest a Cialis while freshening up in the terminal after disembarking—in anticipation of the weekend, really, not this nap. Soon both were glad for his foresight.

Later they stirred. Somehow it seemed the right time to dip their toes, at least, into their mutual puddle. Émile was the first to wade in.

"We haven't seen much of this lately."

"Twice in the past week. I call that a major escalation. Or did you forget about that time at home already?"

"I meant further back than a week." He seemed petulant to her.

"No one's to blame, buddy. We've been at odds. I threw you for a loop."

"I'm not too old to have my heart broken, I found that out. I'm not saying it broke, but that's only because you haven't left yet. But it cracked some. It's getting ready to shatter."

"Oh God. The melodrama! You're holding up okay. For Pete's sake, here you are, out fighting crime for the FBI on the blue bayou."

"Leather-skinned on the outside. It's all for show."

She admitted quietly, "Yeah, I know. Mine cracked some just telling you that I might leave. More than I expected, I guess."

He tilted his head further toward her. "In that case, shouldn't we be trying to stay together?"

"We should. That's what we're doing, no?"

True, but it felt good to hear her say so. This was genuine encouragement. Rowing together in the same direction was so much easier than haphazardly flailing their oars. "Are you any closer," Émile started in, knowing that he had to be careful how he phrased this or he could pitch himself into hot water, "to identifying what the core problem is? For you, I mean?"

Sandra fluffed a pair of pillows and arranged them against the headboard. She then lay back, partially upright with the sheet pulled high up. The air-conditioning cycled on again and, naked, she felt a chill. Reaching around to the back of her neck, she pulled her hair forward to let it fall along her right shoulder. Cinq-Mars noticed that strands of gray he detected previously were no longer visible. She must be tinting. A vacation tint. He propped himself up higher as well.

"It's everything," she decided. A single hair strayed over an eye and she inhaled and blew out two big puffs to send it back into place. "You mentioned sex, so okay, put it on the list. But you and I both know that sex is an extension of other things."

"Including that I'm getting older."

She looked at him then. They didn't talk about this usually. "You take pills."

"And I'm grateful to live in an era when that's an option. But, also, you know, the libido. It's diminished. That makes everything different."

"How so?"

He really hadn't wanted the conversation to come around to this. Now the matter was on him when she had seemed on the verge of opening up herself. He continued to speak cautiously. "When you remove the need, and, you know, the indiscriminate want, from sex—lust, essentially—the equation is different. You have what's left, which is pleasure, intimacy, good things both." He studied the ceiling first before daring to carry on. "But it's not driven. That's what's hard to get used to. It's no longer hardwired. Perhaps I shouldn't use the word *hard*." That got her to grin a little. "It's as if I have to arouse myself by visiting old memories, knowing that I used to feel a certain way, or maybe project myself into old responses or somebody else's responses, but it's . . . an adjustment, let's say . . . it's an adjustment to make love to the woman you love when sex is no longer urgent or a necessity or a response to need or even desire. So it's—as it just was—fun. But the passion is on a different plane. I can't pretend to be in the same place I was years ago or even—and this is telling, because you're younger—even where you may *still* be."

"So you don't need sex anymore," Sandra summarized. "The passion is gone."

"Not gone. Transformed. And diminished. But I'm not going to lie."

"I'm not asking you to."

"It's like the joke I heard this older comedian say once. 'At my age, if a woman says yes, that's great! If she says no, that's okay, too!'"

Sandra laughed. Then she did more than laugh. She leaned across and kissed her husband. In their postcoital ease he found it as natural as breathing to cup her breast, then to run a thumb over and around the lovely large brown nipple. She pulled back, but not away. And looked at him. She placed a hand over his, as if to assist him in caressing her breast.

Then she fell away again and covered up against the cool temperature.

"So I'm younger than you," Sandra said. "This is not news. I'm not at that stage yet when desire is . . . diminished, or gone, whatever . . . and maybe it's different for women anyway. But if you're saying, as I think you're saying—are you saying that even if you're no longer driven by urge or desire or some rampant horniness you can, with pharmaceutical assistance, perhaps, still enjoy yourself? And enjoy me?"

"And appreciate the whole shebang more than ever," he added.

"Shebang—no pun intended, I suppose."

This time he was the one who laughed. "Okay, so, the pun was not intended, but it is appreciated, if you follow my drift. Like sex, it may no longer be *intended* as it once was, but it is enjoyed just as much. Same pattern."

She loved it when they could playfully joust with each other's intelligences. In the old days the sessions often proved preliminary, a kind of foreplay before foreplay, and now, were such times to be post-postcoital instead? A shift, but, in the overall scheme of things, a minor repositioning. One she could live with, in any case.

"What else, though," he asked, "because I agree with you, sex is a symptom here, not a cause—what else pushed us off the rails?"

She had to think about it, or perhaps her delayed response sheltered what she would prefer not to say. Sensing her reluctance, Cinq-Mars grew worried, feeling a cloud, a larger issue he might neither have anticipated nor necessarily desired to spring from its hiding place.

When finally she spoke, he understood that his premonition was accurate. In a millennia he'd never have anticipated this response, not from her, and he wasn't at all sure that, for once in his life, the truth was something he wanted to know. That the issue had nothing to do with him made it all the more perplexing.

Sandra said, "I think I'm done with horses."

Whoosh. A wind blew through them both. Cinq-Mars felt a seismic lurch.

The silence lingered, then she pressed, "You have to say something."

"I can't. I'm stunned."

"I know. I *know.* It doesn't seem possible."

But there it was. He had quit policing, but time had brought that on. A difficult end to a career integral to his being. Nonetheless, in the realm of personal choices, a necessary one given his age and physical condition. Retirement had always been an expectation, even a reward, and given the dangers inherent in what he did—and what *he* in particular had done had been dangerous, taking on the various mobs and the bikers and on occasion the police department itself—retirement had been a logical conclusion. But for Sandra, at forty-six, to relinquish her one abiding passion sounded an alarm. A condition of her marriage, of leaving New Hampshire to come and live in Quebec with Émile in a French milieu foreign to her had been this singular demand: they had to live on a farm and she had to have horses. Cinq-Mars knew now that he wasn't dealing with a mere malaise or a common marriage slump. This was serious. Life changing. The whole of her foundation was in upheaval, and her inner psyche could only be disheveled as a result.

"Then I'm not the only one in the family," he said, glad to be able to speak, to respond at all, "who's holding up under a strain."

Their talk dissolved into hunger, and with a renewed burst of energy the couple dressed for a night on the town. Émile paused at the concierge desk downstairs to ask how far it might be to the French Quarter. Did he require a cab? He was tempted to ask his questions in French, but resisted, and was both surprised and pleased to be informed that, "We're located in the French Quarter, sir. It's outside the door." The warmth of the black woman's smile allowed his humiliation to feel entirely worthwhile. So in the end the Hilton Garden Inn may have been somewhat safe and dull but not totally uncool.

They hit the streets.

The hunger jag kept their initial jaunt short, but after a stop for gumbo—the first item on Sandra's list, which proved delicious—they did a short walking tour of the area, spending time in Jackson Square at the St. Louis Cathedral. They strolled along St. Peter Street, and Royal, and came back down Bourbon. These narrow streets, with their muted colors and patina and old-world charm and balcony life, offering up an other-era sense of festivity, almost beckoned them to kick up their heels, though no band played. Cinq-Mars yearned to see a funeral march, for the music, and said so. "I hope somebody important dies."

"Émile!"

"Come on. You know it would be cool."

Palm fronds rattled as they walked. They liked that.

And the sudden warmth from their winter was amazing.

Reaching St. Peter and Bourbon, he noticed a man he had checked out earlier near the cathedral. A brown-skinned man with patches on one cheek where the pigment was blemished, easy to identify after spotting him twice. He believed he could distinguish tourists from locals, but this guy seemed out of place among either clan. For someone who had shown up in different locations, or perhaps had followed him around for several blocks, he seemed disinterested in his surroundings and rather preoccupied with doing absolutely nothing. Typical cop behavior, he noted.

"What's wrong?" Sandra asked, detecting the change in his mood.

He shrugged. "I'm being paranoid, I guess."

"Seriously? Nobody here knows you, Émile."

"Maybe that's it." His laughter seemed coy. "The total lack of notoriety."

At least he succeeded in getting her to take his mood lightly.

"What do you want to do?" she asked.

"Drinks?"

Up for that, she remembered a place she had read about that they passed earlier. Down a few doors on St. Peter Street they stepped into a tourist mecca called Pat O'Brien's, or more commonly, Pat O's. Cinq-Mars was skeptical. Five hundred beer steins hanging from the ceiling seemed too obvious an effort to make an impression, but the talk around them proved convivial and the house speciality, a rum concoction known as a Hurricane—"I guess living here you need to find ways to lessen your fear of the word"—hit the spot.

If he was being followed, the stalker did not tramp inside after him.

They enjoyed a second round, and these were not light drinks, but when Émile started scouring out a local's politics, Sandra hauled him away. On the streets again, their weariness felt sublime. After the long flight, the round of sex, their talk, the good food and feeling awash in liquor, their mood was bright and sad and a trifle sassy even as they turned contentedly bone-tired. A stray, sultry voice lured them into another bar and Émile was into the Scotch now. They each had a shot, not planning to stay long. The female blues singer with the soulful sound caught their attention, but when the piano player dipped in for a quiet riff they fell in love with New Orleans. He paid homage to the tune but altered the song, transforming a narcotic sadness to a homily on love, and when the woman returned to the lyrics she conveyed a more poignant nuance on life's travail. Simple and riveting in its way. Arm in arm, Sandra and Émile strolled back to the Hilton and, given his mood, Cinq-Mars might have forgiven himself had he missed the signs, but as it turned out he did not.

The man in the foyer who had tried to snatch his wallet earlier caught no more than a glimpse of him, then sent an elevator up empty. Seeing that he was identified, the fellow gave him a stern look, a virtual challenge, but Cinq-Mars didn't fall for the bait. Rather than chase him out the door again he summoned the next elevator, which opened for him almost immediately, and they ascended.

"Stay behind me when we get out," he warned his wife.

"Excuse me?"

"Well behind me."

"I heard you. Émile!"

The doors opened. Out he jumped and she chose to do as he asked. Close to their room she saw the problem. The door stood ajar with a wastebasket jammed in the gap to keep it open. An intruder wanted the rightful guests to identify themselves before entering. Instead, Cinq-Mars pulled the basket out to the hall and shut the door quietly. "Go downstairs," he whispered. "Get Hotel Security."

She was on her way when the door pitched open. Out flew the man who had previously pilfered her purse. He drove into Cinq-Mars like a running back, a shoulder ramming his chest, knocking him to the opposite wall, where he regained his footing, though many steps behind the fleeing intruder now. Sandra looked frozen and terrified as he appeared set to barrel right through her. But he tucked in a little feint to the left and burst to the right, racing past Sandra like an errant wind. Cinq-Mars was running after him and his wife tried to get in his way, to reason with him through gestures but managed only to slow him down a tad, giving the culprit time to stab the elevator buttons, then, when no door spontaneously opened, sprint to the stairway. Cinq-Mars chased him as far as the stairs, but at the top looked down. He heard the miscreant leaping down the stairs a half dozen at a time in an accelerated burst to freedom.

Cinq-Mars let him go. No use pretending that he could compete on the same athletic scale. Besides, he was supposed to be retired.

Sandra, in any case, was pleased to see that he discontinued his reckless pursuit. The elevator door called by the trespasser opened behind them. "Catch that," he said. When she hesitated just a second, he added, "We'll go see Security."

He insisted that the hotel staff call the police. When the Latino head of security suggested that they keep this "in-house," Cinq-Mars volunteered to call the cops himself.

"There's no need, sir, really," the man insisted. "We'll file a report with the police ourselves."

"This is not an in-house type of incident," Cinq-Mars told him.

"How so?"

He'd rather not tell him. "I'm a retired cop myself," he revealed.

"Which means what, exactly?" The hotel man was small and lean and in a way his body type was remarkably similar to that of the two men who had now accosted Cinq-Mars twice. Perhaps that's why he didn't trust him. But he realized that the man was only following an appropriate procedure. As a cop, he never appreciated hearing from hotels about every little break-in. They could afford their own security so they should use it. He only wanted to be let in on the big stuff and the repetitive crimes, otherwise, just submit a report. He saw that the man had his dander up. He knew what this looked like: an old cop looking down on a much younger security staffer because he represented the minor leagues of law enforcement, without ever considering the difficulties and responsibilities of his position. The hotel employee felt irritated.

Of course he did. Cinq-Mars lightened up.

"I'm sorry. I apologize. Look. A couple of guys attempted to rob us in the lobby. They tried to pick my pocket and her purse. They were good at it, too. Professional. Now those same two men—one downstairs to keep a lookout—break into my room. That's not coincidence. It's impossible for that to be coincidence. Pickpockets aren't burglars and vice versa. I just arrived in this city today. I'm being targeted. I've come to you first, of course, you need to be informed. But I also want to talk to the police about this because it is not simply a random incident."

Clearly, the man appreciated his manners.

"I'll call," he said. "They come in half the time than if you call yourself."

Cinq-Mars had no trouble believing that that was true.

Together, the head of security, Sandra, and Émile Cinq-Mars went upstairs to see what might have occurred in their room. The men formally introduced themselves on the ride up, and Everardo Flores offered an apology on behalf of the hotel for the incident.

"Do you think," Cinq-Mars asked him, "I could get another room and have it booked under another name? Given what's occurred?"

"I'll see to it, sir," Flores said. "I won't say half, but, this time of year, with Mardi Gras coming up, maybe twelve or fifteen percent of our clientele are here under assumed names anyhow, so what's the difference?"

"Why are they . . . ?" Sandra started to inquire, then changed her mind. "Never mind. Don't answer that."

"Mardi Gras," Everardo Flores explained anyway. "Strange things happen."

They disembarked on the seventeenth floor once again.

This time, no one was in their room.

As far as they could tell, nothing was stolen, which only deepened their concern. The thief, if that was his proper designation—and Cinq-Mars had his doubts about that—had proven himself to be considerate and tidy. Émile's clothes remained unpacked, and it was obvious that the intruder had searched through his gear without unduly disturbing anything. The edges of his shirts had been lifted. The smaller pockets in his suitcase unzipped. Drawers had been opened and Sandra's things mildly rearranged. One tidy crook, then, who had probably intended to leave the premises as he had found them, as if he had never been there at all.

"But if he stole something," Flores pointed out, "then sooner or later you'd know that you'd been robbed."

"Not if he was looking for information," Cinq-Mars contradicted him. "If that's what he came for, and found it, we might never have known he was here."

"What sort of information?" Flores's query was not skeptical, and Cinq-Mars gave him a glance. A lesser mind might have assumed by now that these hotel guests had panicked, perhaps mistaken room service for the mob. That they were bumpkins. But Everardo Flores apparently took Cinq-Mars at his word and was not treating the event lightly. Nothing stolen, no one hurt, and yet the intrusion felt serious. Even, perhaps, ominous.

Cinq-Mars was examining his suitcase again, trying to remember what he might have had in it. In the washroom, items had been removed from his toiletries bag and set aside, most likely to facilitate a more thorough examination of the contents, but what, indeed, could the man have been searching for?

"That I don't know," Cinq-Mars admitted. "Maybe whoever invaded my room didn't know either."

"I know what's missing," Sandra piped up.

Seated on the bed, she now stood to show them. She pointed to the front of Émile's suitcase, but he couldn't see what was gone.

"Your name tag's been torn off. *And* your baggage tag from the airline! My baggage tags are still on my luggage, and I know that you never take your tags off for months—not until your next trip."

Cinq-Mars concurred. He had a leather name-and-address tag attached to the handle, and a baggage tag from the airline, and both were now gone.

"You'd think, if he broke into the hotel room of people he previously tried to rob, he might already know your names," Flores remarked.

"Proof of the visit, maybe. Something to show a boss. Or he's a collector."

"Of name tags?" Sandra asked.

"Souvenirs."

"Or he failed to rob you the first time. So he came back."

The police knocked and announced themselves. Cinq-Mars opened the door and the two uniforms entered and shook hands with Flores first, whom they seemed to recognize. Cinq-Mars didn't bother to mention that he was a retired detective as the introductions were being made, but he noted that the officers were efficient, if somewhat disinterested. They obviously had no clue as to why they'd been called to this scene, and with some urgency, when nothing more than a couple of tags had been swiped. At least they were not being outwardly sarcastic, although they did give each other looks, as if to ask, What's next? Do we get called if a guest farts?

They showed more interest when Flores told them about the first incident, but again they came back to the relevant information. "So, nobody actually pinched your wallet?"

"No, sir."

"Nor your purse?" the other officer inquired of Sandra.

"No, but he had my wallet in his hand."

"Which he picked up off the floor, is that right?"

"He made it look that way. Before that it was in my purse."

"This is before they accidentally bumped into you."

"That was no accident," Sandra let him know, her temper flaring. "That's the point. The wallet may never have been on the floor."

"I see," the first officer said. He had an Italian name, which Cinq-Mars had instantly forgotten. D'Amato or D'Amico. Simple enough, but it slipped his mind.

"He was on the job," Flores said quietly, obviously feeling the need to defend the hotel's guest.

"Who? Him?" the Italian asked.

"Neither here nor there," Cinq-Mars told him.

"That true? You were a cop somewhere, sir?"

Conceding the point with a nod, Cinq-Mars admitted, "Detective. Montreal." Then he added, in case that was not enough information, "Canada."

The officer surprised him, this D'Amato or D'Amico. "You know what they say. New Orleans. San Francisco. Montreal. Those are the three most lively cities in North America."

Cinq-Mars knew that, but he was surprised that this man did, too. Then he remembered that the Internet filled people's heads with an abundance of useless information, particularly when it came to lists and to ranking places and products. "That is what they say."

"And your description of the intruders again?"

A hopeless cycle, so he indicated Flores with a jerk of his thumb. "Both of them, they looked like him."

"So two small Mexicans."

The hotel guy gave him a look.

"Fit," the officer added. "A couple of small-build, *fit* Mexicans. About his age, too?"

"I'd say so."

"All right. Not much we can do here, sir. The guy stole nothing—"

"My husband's name tags," Sandra interjected, and Émile wished that she hadn't brought them up again.

"Yeah. Well, let's be grateful he didn't grab the entire suitcase. Of course, then we'd have an actual crime."

"Hey, Aldo." The quieter of the two cops spoke up to get his partner's attention. He indicated the door, and Cinq-Mars recognized the instant change in the young officer's demeanor. He'd seen that look before, when a subordinate's unwarranted confidence yielded to dismay in the presence of a superior officer.

In the doorway stood a man of some heft, emboldened by a stomach that overlapped his belt, who dangled a gold shield from a packet stuck in his suit's chest pocket. The man had short, tightly curled hair, but his features and skin tone suggested a racial mix that was relatively rare. African and Asian DNA predominated a blend that might include Caucasian and American Indian, making identification of his ethnic origins a challenge. Half a dozen disparate peoples might be willing to claim him as their own. What struck Cinq-Mars though was that the atmosphere in the room had been transformed, in part because their non-crime inexplicably warranted a detective, and in part because the two officers in the room were obviously wary of this man. Possibly—likely, he gauged—they feared him.

"Sir," the one called Aldo sputtered. He damn nearly saluted.

"Big case?" the new arrival inquired. His presence was further amplified by an impressive baritone voice.

"No, sir," Aldo briefed him. "Nobody hurt. Nothing—nothing of substance taken, sir."

"Nothing of substance," the detective repeated as he came into the room. "Good evening, ma'am," he said to Sandra with a nod. He had a wide smile and teeth that gleamed. "Evening, sir," he said to Cinq-Mars. Abruptly, surprisingly, he dismissed the two men in uniform. "I'll take it from here," he let them know.

When the door closed behind them, the new man pointed to Flores and said, "I don't know you. You're Security, right?" Again he smiled brightly, invitingly, as if welcoming everyone into the fold.

"Head of, sir. Everardo Flores."

"Hmm. Yes. Sorry. We have met before. I'm—"

"Pascal Dupree," Flores said. "I know who you are, sir."

Dupree said nothing at first, expecting nothing less than recognition from Flores, yet seemed unimpressed by his own local fame. He grinned again and gestured to the tall retired detective. He asked Flores, "Do y'all know who he is?"

"Well," Flores hesitated. "I know his name. I know he was on the job."

Dupree nodded. He asked Flores to stay although the man had not shown any sign of leaving. Dupree stuck out his hand, "Sergeant-Detective Émile Cinq-Mars, I'm guessing. Honored to meet you, sir. Sergeant-Detective Pascal Dupree, New Orleans Police Department."

"How do you do? I wasn't expecting a detective for our little break-in."

"Soon enough, sir, I'll ask y'all what the hell you're doing in New Orleans. But before we get to that, fill in the blanks for me, if you don't mind, on what this kerfuffle is about."

Cinq-Mars did so, briefly and succinctly, while Dupree flipped through a series of expressions that denoted his interest and at times his amazement. When the visiting detective was done, he said only, "I take it that y'all don't know me?"

The Montreal cop was flummoxed. "I've never seen you before in my life."

Dupree nodded, grinned, and looked over at Sandra. To her he said, "I'm the guy he came here to see."

Suddenly, Cinq-Mars grasped the situation. He went to his suitcase again to dig out the notes he prepared from the FBI files that Bill Mathers had sent him, but even as he did so he was not expecting to find them. The wee notebook, especially purchased for the occasion, was gone.

"I can't verify that," Cinq-Mars told Dupree. "But your name rings a bell now. My notebook's been stolen."

"Is that significant?" the big man asked him.

"How do you mean?" He was thinking that the fellow's broad smile kept him off his game. He couldn't gauge why he was so happy and consequently couldn't figure him out at all.

"Well, sir," he said, although his inflection made it sound more like *whale suh*, "is there something in your notes that somebody who stole them from you will find significant?"

He thought about it, concluding, "Hard to say. I think most people would find my notes cryptic."

"Cryptic," Dupree repeated.

"I guess it would depend on who's looking."

The heavy black man changed the subject. "Are there many Duprees in your part of the world? You're a Frenchman, right? It's necessary to go back a ways, some would say a long ways, but there's a trace of Cajun in me. My grandma on my mom's side was a Filipina, about the only pure blood in me. But then my granddad, her husband, was a black-Cajun mix. My dad's half black, my mom also has a white mom and a black father. One of those. So I'm a mongrel, but contrary to popular opinion I'm not some junkyard dog. I don't inhale the breath of the dead. But I got enough of a trace of Cajun in my dancing shoes to earn the name Dupree. Some kind of French, no? Even though as you might tell from my accent, I hail from Mississippi. We all live complicated lives, don't we?"

Cinq-Mars sat on the bed beside his wife. This man was beginning to sound like he did himself during an interrogation. Go all over the map in a discussion in order to tie the person up in his head and deliberately confound him then slice through to the heart of the matter. He wished he'd get to the heart of the matter.

"No Duprees where I come from," Cinq-Mars told him. "But Dupuis. Dupree could easily be a corruption of that."

"Corruption," the detective repeated, and smiled.

"Like my name, Cinq-Mars, could be a corruption of Saint Marc, possibly. That's one explanation. Or it can mean the fifth of March for some reason. Nobody's one hundred percent sure."

"Oh I get you, Detective. It's just that that word—"

When he paused, Cinq-Mars repeated it for him, "Corruption."

"It's not a word nobody wants to say out loud in this town. Not in the company of a policeman."

Sandra posed the question. "Why not?"

That great white-toothed grin again. "A few of our officers recently got sixty-five years each. Now that'll be a good long stretch for them, don't you think? Should teach them a lesson, no?"

"What did they do?" she asked.

"Ever heard of Danziger Bridge?" He carried on when she shook her head no. "A few of our officers killed innocent citizens there, just a week after Katrina. The victims were poor people. Hungry people. Folks without their homes. They were in a desperate plight. So our boys went down there and shot them. Killed two. Wounded a bunch of others. Four others. One young man was shot and, as he lay dying, an officer of the law went about kicking him. Really made him suffer before he died. He was a mentally challenged boy but some would apply that distinction to the cop. A few of our boys, not enough of them if it was up to me, got sixty-five years for that."

Sandra had another question. "Why did the police shoot them?"

"Did I not explain that?" Before answering, Dupree shot a glance across at Everardo Flores, a look which Cinq-Mars interpreted as meaning, *I don't know you, but I'm going to say what I think in front of you anyway.* "Why, ma'am, my fellow officers shot those people because they were poor, hungry, homeless, and scared, but mostly they shot them because they were black. The cops said they were shot at, opinion contradicted by the evidence, and by witnesses, including police witnesses."

Everyone let the opinion settle in the room.

"I guess y'all don't have such problems up there in Montreal," Dupree said.

"I'm an American," Sandra said, but Cinq-Mars did not know why she bothered to say that, and he wasn't sure that Sandra knew why either.

Dupree was smiling, but with his mouth closed, the smile an effort now as he looked around at the other three. Then he said, "*Corruption* is not a word that sits well in a policeman's head these days. It's what they call the elephant in the room. Anytime you're sitting down with an officer of the New Orleans Police Department, it's the elephant in the room. But you, Cinq-Mars, y'all fought corruption in your own department. That's your reputation. Good on you."

"You have me at a disadvantage," Cinq-Mars told him. "I don't know how you do or why you do. How do you know anything about me? I was given your name, but I forgot it. At no time did I do a background check on you."

"I'm the one who's at a disadvantage, Detective Cinq-Mars."

"How so?"

"Because I may know who y'all are, but I have no clue why the hell y'all are here. You might not know who I am, but who cares about that? I'm of no account. But y'all know why you're here. I don't. I'm the one, see, who's wearing the disadvantage like shackles on his feet."

Cinq-Mars noticed the man's eyes shift as Sandra raised her fist in stifling a yawn. The day had been long and seemed endless. Detective Dupree released that buoyant, all-encompassing smile again. "Y'all traveled today, right?"

Sandra agreed with a nod.

"Y'all had a night on the town. Adventures! Beyond what you cared to experience. And yet, Detective, we have some things to talk about, no? Such as, what y'all are doing here. Why has your arrival set off a fireworks within the New Orleans Police Department?"

"What?" Cinq-Mars barked.

Dupree seemed surprised by his reaction. "Don't you know? Then we have things to talk about. That could be a dandy conversation. I only hope this has nothing to do with Danziger Bridge. I've had it up to my eyeballs with that mess."

"I've never heard of Danziger Bridge," Cinq-Mars assured him.

"Y'all don't watch the news? I thought you were retired. What else y'all got to do but watch the news? I guess New Orleans affairs are of no more interest in Montreal than Montreal is a concern to us. But the point is," he hurried on before Cinq-Mars could interrupt, "we could go out, me and you. Your wife can get some shut-eye. I won't keep him out all night, ma'am," he said to her. "But if him and me can cover some ground, we all might sleep better afterward."

Sandra and Émile glanced at each other, acknowledging that this was not the most romantic outcome to their evening. "I was going to change rooms," Émile said.

"Good idea," Dupree opined.

"The hotel can take care of that for you," Flores interjected. "Check in at the front desk when you return. Mrs. Cinq-Mars, you can be in bed in ten minutes in your new room."

He liked neither the cosiness of all this nor the hurry. The unknown aspect. But Cinq-Mars said, "Okay," and Sandra nodded to confirm the right decision.

"I'll show y'all a side of the real New Orleans," Dupree enthused.

"Which means you don't think I've seen it yet," Cinq-Mars noted. He meant something by that, floating the opinion that Dupree may have done some earlier recognizance on his evening. But Dupree breezed on through the comment.

"How could you have? Is this your first time here, Detective? Yes? Then how could you have?"

ELEVEN

A keyhole dive on Bourbon Street, Sinners Too, slumped near the corner of Bienville. Big black wood doors sealed off the premises during daylight hours, only to be turned back 180 degrees to admit patrons after dark. The name played off the marching saints of the famous song and the football team, but came across to many as cute. For that reason, or merely to be less inviting, no sign was visible on its faded brown façade. A patron had to know the joint to find it, and once inside, if he knew where to look, the name was located on a sticker affixed to a mirror. Dupree showed it to Cinq-Mars, proud as peach. The mirror reflected the bar, manned by a redheaded Irishman to whom Cinq-Mars was introduced and who seemed to be perpetually washing up as he worried who might be coming through the front door or returning out the rear toilet. The man grunted often and incessantly glanced around warily—and unnecessarily to Émile's mind—and he judged his problem to be a Tourette's tic.

The dark narrow space that the bar presented to the street kept tourists at bay and encouraged cautious locals to scorn the premises as well. Inside, the regular barflies were positioned on their familiar stools, calmly inebriated and somewhat intent but nothing serious. Solemn in their declarations, they exhibited only quiet, desultory affections for drink, for the air they breathed, and for the company they so faithfully embraced.

Cinq-Mars and Dupree settled into a side booth where no one, the former Montreal cop noted, could come up behind them. "A favorite haunt of yours? Or are you trying to psyche me out?"

Loud laughter burst from Detective Dupree. The sound struck Cinq-Mars as jolly and genuine, which gave credence to the detective's repertoire of smiles. A joyful soul. He still had no clue how to take him. At this early juncture to trust him was out of the question, but whether he should weigh the merits of his skepticism or let things ride until real evidence presented itself remained a puzzle.

"No psyche-out intended. I drink to modest excess, Émile." On the way over, they had agreed to use each other's given names, as opposed to their ranks or surnames. Émile could no longer abide being called sergeant-detective, and Dupree couldn't pronounce *Cinq-Mars* in any acceptable form. His accent made it sound like a muffled scream, and after Émile spelled it for him, his pronunciation worsened. For his part, Dupree confessed to hating the diminutive "Sarge," which he got all the time. "I like to stay afloat. Not that there's a man in here who couldn't put me to shame if we raced a bottle down, but I drink enough that I prefer to stay away from places where the righteous might find me. They're a bore. I don't know what attributes make up a child of God, but boring can't be one of them. Thing is, neither the boring nor the righteous are likely to find me in here."

Here, no drinks were called "Hurricanes." In honor of the city, Cinq-Mars ordered bourbon, and Dupree joined him in that choice, adding a beer chaser.

"Drinking on your shift is not a problem here in corrupt New Orleans?"

Cinq-Mars thought he was chiding him gently, relaxing into their pending talk, but Dupree took it differently.

"I don't taste the divine mistress when I'm working. Y'all can take that two ways."

"Can I? How so?"

"If I take a sip it means I just booked off. It's my way of saying so."

Cinq-Mars chuckled lightly. "Okay. What's the second way?"

"I don't drink and work. Period."

"You aren't working now? You were in my hotel room."

"No, sir, I was not. I was passing by. Just visiting. I came to your hotel room because the man flying in to see me about a cold case was reporting serious trouble to the police. That news got back to me. The man who has a rep for taking down his own police department called my police department to say his room had been invaded. That's a curiosity to me. Wouldn't it be to you, Émile?" He was speaking a lot, yet slowly, almost methodically, in deference to the music of the night and the calming effect of his drink. "I came to see you because people in my department, friends of mine, they know that I haven't been sleeping so well lately, on account of y'all being on your way here, and because I worry about why a man like you is coming down here wanting to talk to the likes of me for who knows what reason. So they informed me that your name was in the news, that it jumped across the wire. I like to be informed and they do have my back on occasion. Émile, this whiskey I'm sipping—here I go now . . . ain't that sweet?—this whiskey, sir, is going so smoothly down my gullet on my sweet time off. Don't think otherwise. Because if you do, you'll be wrong, and I got this feeling that you're not the type to cozy up to being dead wrong too often."

Cinq-Mars clinked the other man's glass as a way to concede and apologize. "Here's to free time and plain talk. Pascal, I don't get what's going on."

"Call me Dupree. Pascal is not a name I go by much. My mama calls me Pascal, as do people just getting to know me on a familiar basis. I'm jumping the gun, but a man whom I like and respect right off the bat, a man with whom I may feel a kinship, that man should call me Dupree. So what is it that y'all don't get? Why you were accosted?"

"That, too. But mainly why my presence registered with anybody down here, including with you."

"You wanted to show up incognito?"

"Why would I? I never felt the need."

"And if I say to you—Danziger Bridge—what do y'all say back?"

Cinq-Mars shrugged. "I'm ignorant. Only what you said. It's got nothing to do with me."

"Seriously? Maybe so. But appreciate that it has us all on edge around here. A public relations nightmare times ten." Seated, relaxing, his big head easing back, Dupree displayed multiple chins and a bull neck. "Cops who go around shooting people on account of their tragic circumstances and the color of their skin, and then those among us who made some objection to that particular practice and assisted in the investigation, both sides, are on edge. You see my circumstances. But a person like myself, who's gonna come out of the shadows and shoot me down on the streets now? It's not only that I'm a moving target, I'm an obvious target. Too obvious. So if I take my leave of absence from this world to go mingle with the saints and sinners who have gone before me, suspicions are going to be aroused before whatever dust I might disturb settles back over me, and who is going to think that my demise is anything but unjustified? A consequence of a situation. Folks of different stripes, some of whom have power, will want to know who pulled the trigger. On the other hand, if forces are aligned against me, if some folks want to take me down and some of those folks have power also, then they might seek another way, given everything that's afoot. So. I hear that a cop from another force—hell, from another *country*—is coming down here to inquire about some cold case murders that I investigated years ago without much success after a screw-up and I'm thinking to myself, *hold on, buddy, watch it now, this could be some strange-colored shit walking straight upright out of the john.* Y'all follow me?"

"I do now," Cinq-Mars assured him and sipped his whiskey. "I see your predicament. But I had no idea about all these preexisting circumstances."

"So why y'all here?" The query was forthright, but Dupree tacked on a smile in any case, and once again Cinq-Mars did not know how to take the man.

"I wish I could simplify it for you," he told him, "about as much as I wish I could simplify it for myself."

"Complicated, is it? Try me out."

Cinq-Mars leaned closer to him, not to make himself heard, as it was a quiet bar on a relatively quiet night. Nor was he indicating that his words were about to be shared in the strictest confidence. But he leaned in closer to indicate that what he had to say would need to be contemplated and managed on an intimate level, if his words were going to be understood at all. "If I knew why I was here, Dupree, I probably would not be here."

Cinq-Mars had expected that the New Orleans detective might request further clarification, that in thinking it through his mind might short-circuit and leave him stuck in a mental loop, in a maze, with no way out. That was his intention, perhaps. But the man cottoned on quickly. He understood how a dilemma could draw a man in and not let him escape with his skin still attached.

"So your lack of understanding, Émile, and mine, match up."

"I'll drink to that," Cinq-Mars remarked.

"Let's do so."

Cinq-Mars raised his glass to the Irish bartender for another round of bourbon, and this time added the beer chaser for himself. Dupree was still working on his in a contemplative fashion.

"So, what do you know," Dupree asked him, "about what y'all don't know?"

Cinq-Mars moved the glass in his hand around the table, then drank. He didn't like the bourbon as much as his favored Scotch, a mite harsh on the throat, but it possessed its own guile that he could appreciate. "You investigated the deaths of Dorsey and Gifford Lanos. The cold case you mentioned. An unsolved crime."

"I did. Who is it who cares?"

"The FBI, for starters."

"You're working for the FBI now?" He laughed that bright laugh and resolved the tempest with the widest grin.

"Apparently I am."

The grin vanished. "What, they're hiring out private now?"

"One of many puzzles."

When Dupree drank again it seemed it was less to slake a thirst or to savor his drink than to settle his nerves. "Okay," he said. "You got me. Where do we stand? What's going on?"

Cinq-Mars took a breath, and started in. "A similar killing occurred in my backyard, except that two cops on the scene were also gunned down. Several similar murders have occurred around the U.S., always in the aftermath of a natural disaster. I know what you're nervous about. You investigated the murders of Dorsey and Gifford Lanos when the killer was hanging out over your head. In the attic. I'm not down here to burn a detective for not looking in the attic. But those murders, how they all add up, including what doesn't add up, paint a picture. And it's that whole picture that gets interesting. Why me? The FBI will tell you they need someone on the ground in Canada who speaks French and is a Canadian. I don't buy it entirely, but for now I'm on the case. My being here is purely a background investigation, to see what your case, and others like it, tell me about mine."

Dupree waggled his head a little as he processed the news. "I was getting myself worked up. Shadows jump out at me these days, you know? I fingered y'all to be a man behind a shadow, you know?"

"I understand. Well, to a point, I do."

"He was in the attic all right. But we only learned that later. It's true I thought y'all might be here to rub my nose in it somehow. So, you said . . . let's take it back a step. Y'all were talking about what adds up, but also saying that this is about what doesn't add up. So tell me, what doesn't add up for you?"

The alcohol was buzzing in his veins now, and he could feel his body relaxing. Cinq-Mars sat back a little. "Why the victims?" he asked. "Why them in particular? Arriving in the aftermath of a storm, I can see that. The authorities are preoccupied. But how did he choose his people? Maybe some of his personal psychological headspace accounts for picking couples, but why *those* couples? Do they relate to one another in any way, and will that help us? That's one thing I'm after."

"My people, Dorsey and Giff, seemed pretty ordinary types."

"My dead couple, too. So there's that. But how does *ordinariness* help us?"

"Go figure. Do you want to go up there tomorrow, Émile?"

"Scene of the crime? I do."

"It's a date."

A man was moving closer to them, swaying, barely staying upright and now holding to a chair back. He had his eyes on Dupree, apparently with some intent, though he didn't get within ten yards before he toppled forward, caught himself, then fell backward. The Irishman came out from behind the bar in a shot. Rather than drag him out to the street he heaved him off in the opposite direction.

"What's back there?" Cinq-Mars asked.

Dupree smiled, then laughed at his own joke before he told it. "Triage, a recovery room, emergency. Whatever you want to call it. A patch of concrete next to the garbage cans. A place to puke, piss your pants. When the guy wakes up, he'll be no worse for wear. Probably he'll be left alone back there. Trouble-free for a night. No bust. Tomorrow evening, in the warm air, he'll find his way through the front door again. All in the name of peace and quiet, Émile."

"Dupree," Cinq-Mars said.

"Yes, Émile?"

"A man was following me—me and Sandra—outside tonight. A black man, brown-skinned with pale pigment patches on his cheeks. A good-sized middle-aged man who just naturally kept his eyes down. Was he one of yours?"

"You're figuring him for a cop? Not one of the bad guys coming out of the woodwork to check on you?"

"I figure him for one of yours. You had motive."

"Well, okay. Tell me about this patch on his skin. Looks like a continent? Darkest Africa with a splash of sunlight, let's say, with some islands lying off the coast to the south, down his neck some?"

"More or less. So he's yours?"

Dupree shook his head slowly. No smiles this time.

"A dick-for-hire. Ex-cop. But you were with your wife, so I don't know who'd hire him to tail you. Do you?"

"No clue," Cinq-Mars admitted. "That's all I've got no matter which way I look. No clue."

Dupree ran a hand under his chin and across his neck to dispatch the perspiration there.

"One more thing," Cinq-Mars broached.

"Go ahead."

"The two guys who tried picking my pocket and Sandra's purse. I find it very strange that they also broke into my room. So I'm wondering, do they ring any bells?"

Dupree nodded, to confirm that the question was a good one for this hour. "I know the pushers and pimps, the loan sharks and kneecap specialists, the backstreet hustlers, the dips and stalls, the gamblers and lenders. They all faithfully adhere to my parish, Émile. Others, too. So it's a strange tale you're telling me. They sound new, and since they sound pro, that makes them sound out-of-town. Maybe you brought them down with you? But you say they were of the Spanish persuasion, so maybe not. I'll check into them, but I'm saying at this point that they interest me for the same reasons they interest y'all and one more—their action and their description comes across as foreign to my town."

At first he declined, but under Dupree's steady heckling Cinq-Mars agreed to have another, and the two men talked about the weather in their respective centers, one stunned by the heat and humidity, the other by the cold. Then they discussed police pension funds before Cinq-Mars announced that he was packing it in.

He insisted on picking up the bill. Dupree agreed only after he was assured that all his expenses that week would be passed along to the FBI. After that, their good-byes were cordial and brief, and they set a time to meet up the next day.

The walk home informed Émile Cinq-Mars that he had probably had more to drink over the full course of the evening and night, first with Sandra, then with Detective Dupree, than he had intended, or had consumed for quite some time. He was walking straight enough but repeatedly lost his concentration, and once, captivated by the coloring of a series of old buildings, his direction. Tipsy, but upright, he knew that he'd feel rough come morning.

Scudding clouds cleared out, unveiling a few faint stars whenever he hit upon a dim stretch. They would never be so brilliant here as they appeared from the darkness of his farm, yet they bequeathed a sense of companionship this far south in this other land. Constant travelers. All part of his inebriated bloodstream, he surmised. Nonetheless, he welcomed their relative vicinity.

He was heading straight for the elevators when he arrived back at the Hilton, bypassing the front desk, and almost punched a button to take him up when he realized that he could not do that. He didn't know where to go. He returned to the front desk, explained his predicament, and soon exchanged his old keycard for a new one, this one passed to him in a sealed envelope.

"Which floor?" he asked.

"That information is in the envelope, sir. It's not in our system."

Security had intensified.

The eleventh floor this time. The elevator seemed swift, silent, and steady, yet Cinq-Mars detected himself wobbling. Excess Scotch usually spared him the morning headache, but he was less confident that the harsh bourbon would treat him as kindly. The cabin eased to the gentlest of stops and Émile exited.

He had to read the directions indicating which rooms were which way three times before he gathered that he must turn left. Left he turned, found his door, and skimmed the keycard through the gizmo. A green light blinked. In he entered.

Cinq-Mars undressed in the dark and performed his ablutions in the washroom with the door closed to protect his sleeping wife from the noise and light. Everything had been laid out as if he had never changed rooms. Blindly, he fished an undershirt from his bag and put it on to neutralize the air-conditioning, and a favorite pair of oversize Jockeys served as his traveling pajamas. He felt his way back through the dark and slipped in under the covers. His side of the bed was always the same, a stringent rule of his wife's.

She didn't stir, which pleased him.

Especially with so much drink in his system, he started out sleeping on his back, his head raised. As the liquids were processed, he could strike out upon his side, his preferred position. He attempted that position early, and yet he was in bed for as long as four minutes before he realized that he was alone.

He flicked on the light switch, anxious now, and confirmed that he was in the room by himself. Perhaps she stepped out for air? Went hunting for ice? He poked his head out to the corridor. She was certainly nowhere in view. Coming back into the room he saw a blood splotch on the wall and the doorjamb and felt his heart smash through his ribcage. He ran to his pants and almost ripped the pockets open to get at his wallet. He snatched up Dupree's card and called the man's cell on the hotel phone.

The New Orleans detective answered. "Hello?"

"My wife," Cinq-Mars barked. He gasped as the reality caught up to him. "Dupree. She's been abducted."

TWELVE

A swath of powder-blue uniforms flooded the eleventh floor. Émile Cinq-Mars received them in a daze. Shaky, desperate, he drew some solace seeing that Sergeant Pascal Dupree had pull. He had called out the city's finest in force.

"Okay, Émile, so, you come back to the room and Sandra's not here."

"I kept the lights off. I didn't want to wake her. I was in bed for a bit—three, four minutes—before I realized she was gone."

"You called me right away?"

"I did when I saw the blood."

"Maybe she injured herself, Émile. Took herself to the hospital."

"She'd call. Somebody downstairs would know."

"You can't be sure. Sometimes there's a logical explanation."

This was called grasping at straws and both men knew it.

Dupree told him what was being done. "We're interviewing everybody who's been downstairs or outside. If somebody saw her leave, on her own volition or not, we'll find that person. Doormen, cab drivers, bellhops. Patrons in the bar. We're asking the cab companies to list what drivers were here while you were gone. We'll talk to them. My guy, and he's pretty good, guesstimates that the blood smear is about an hour old, so the injury took place not so long after we left your room."

"No one could expect that I'd be leaving with you," Cinq-Mars pointed out to him, "or that she'd be staying behind. Us going out was spontaneous. Nobody could've counted on her being here alone or planned it that way."

"So maybe they planned to take you and took her instead. We don't know."

"This is insane."

Cinq-Mars stared out the window a moment. An officer whispered to Dupree, who nodded irritably before dismissing him with a backhand motion of his hand.

"Who's the man with splotches on his face?" Cinq-Mars demanded.

"I put out an order to pick him up."

"Who is he, Dupree?"

"I told you."

"Tell me more."

In rushing back here from his drive home and hurrying up to the room, Dupree had left his jacket in his vehicle. His shirt was short-sleeved, a pale yellow with faint sweat stains showing around his armpits and across his stomach. The two top buttons were undone, the tie slackened. Over the girth of his stomach he wore his beltline high, so that his service revolver hung above his hip. His shield had been left behind in the jacket, but in this environment everybody knew him anyway.

Dupree released a long breath. "He wasn't a good cop. Okay? He was a bad cop. Bad enough to get himself canned, and in this town, at that time, that's saying something. But we have our own peculiar ways down here, so he was still able to get his PI license. Mostly he sniffs the tails of rancid husbands, but it's my understanding that off and on he's a political hire. Come election time, there's people who shovel shit around here. He's one who can tolerate the stink, no problem, so he offers his services."

"You don't like him."

"I do not."

"Nor do you hire him."

"I do not. What are you trying to say? Just say it."

"You're the one who took me out of this room."

"But it wasn't this room, was it? And I only *invited* you out for a drink. I didn't drag you into the streets to intentionally put your wife in danger."

"Look, I'm—"

"Forget it," Dupree said, and waved both hands in front of him. "Y'all don't have your bearings down here. This is your wife we're talking about. I get that. This far into things I'm like you—equally suspicious of everybody. I only know one person for sure who's not involved and that's me. You're in the same boat, except you can only substitute yourself for me, perhaps."

"Perhaps?" Cinq-Mars drilled him with a look. "I know it wasn't me."

"I know it wasn't you *personally*," Dupree said, and he gave him a good hard look as well and yet smiled slightly at the same moment, "because weren't we hanging out together? But just like y'all hold to the possibility that I might be involved, so will I hold to the possibility that you could be involved. As much as I like y'all, Émile, I know nothing about you. The sad truth of the matter is, y'all would not be the first husband to get rid of his wife on a vacation in another country."

Cinq-Mars continued to gaze back at him, without returning the smile. He understood what Dupree was implying and objected to none of it, but that phrase—*get rid of*—overwhelmed him momentarily. Sensing that, Dupree gently placed a hand on his shoulder. "Keep a good thought, all right?"

Cinq-Mars nodded. Quietly, he demanded, "No stone unturned. So where's hotel security in all this?"

"They're around."

"I haven't seen Everardo Flores. Have you?"

Dupree yanked out a handkerchief and mopped droplets of perspiration from his brow. "I'm told he went home after helping your wife change rooms. End of shift."

"Then bring him back here."

"His staff is being helpful, Émile." He put the handkerchief away.

"Which means they're doing bugger all."

"They're staying out of my way. That counts right now."

"Dupree, come on. Who else knew that Sandra and me switched rooms and to which room? Him. Not many others."

Dupree ceded ground. "I'll notify Flores to get back here on the double. Meantime, why don't you take a seat? I'll get a uniform to fetch a glass of water. A lot of weird shit's walking upright today. Just sit here. Think about anything y'all might have missed."

"The guys in the lobby. The pickpockets. I gave you their descriptions."

"We're looking for them."

Cinq-Mars sat down. He even accepted water brought to him by an officer with forearms bigger than Popeye's. As Dupree departed to confer with his people, a considerable buzz occurred around him. Detectives and uniforms alike desired a consult, then lit out in various directions. Cinq-Mars hated that he had to trust someone he didn't know, but . . . that was all there was to it, he had to trust someone he didn't know, and this guy appeared to be more than competent. He was just getting up to address Dupree again—damn it, he had thought of something he should have realized earlier—when the man returned to check in with him.

"What do you got?" the detective asked. Something in Émile's eyes.

"Your killer in the attic. And mine."

"Is this about that?"

"What else could it be about? I have no other connection down here."

"Okay. I'll buy that. What does it give us?"

"He's in the attic."

Dupree understood the reference.

Cinq-Mars explained his thinking. "Nobody saw anyone take my wife—walking upright or wrapped in a carpet. Not out the front door, not down to the garage. Cameras in the lobby or the garage picked up nothing like that, right?"

"Sorry, we don't have cameras in the lobby or in the garage. On the front desk, but that's it."

That was a disappointment, but still, Dupree was getting this. He didn't have to explain himself.

"So let's stop thinking that my wife and her abductor or abductors left the building. Maybe they did—but remember the attics."

Dupree scratched the back of his neck with both hands, squeezing his eyes tight a moment to release a building pressure, then he let his arms relax. "We'll start by searching every empty room. And the rooftop. Everett!" he shouted.

A slight Caucasian who seemed to be behaving more like a secretary than a cop, who was sheltering Dupree from anyone who wanted a word, allowing only a privileged few through to him and giving pointed direction to others, came over. Dark-haired with sloping shoulders and a weak chin, he sported a ring in an earlobe, which surprised Cinq-Mars. He wondered if the man didn't pull undercover duty regularly to warrant the embellishment.

"Yeah, Sarge?" Everett asked.

"I want a man on every floor," Dupree advised him. "We'll be room-to-room and I don't want movement without our knowledge. Officers in each stairwell and make sure they stay alert. I'm sitting on the first man who yawns. Make sure they get the message."

"Yes, sir. Room-to-room, sir?"

"Matching teams. One starts at the bottom and works up, the other goes top down. Empty rooms first. Get a list. If nothing shows up, then we start waking up guests. I'll get that permission."

"Dupree," Cinq-Mars interrupted.

"Yeah?"

"Some people—anyone tailing me—might know that it's empty. But the daytime staff hasn't had time to make it up, so it definitely won't get rented out to a late arrival. Anyone who knew where I used to be knows that. My old room."

Detective Dupree agreed that it was worth checking on. "Everett, first thing, get me two uniforms and a security guy with a master key. Émile, y'all might as well come with us on this one."

He was hoping he'd say that, even though he knew that, in Dupree's eyes, he remained a possible perpetrator.

They ascended to the seventeenth floor.

The room was not far from the elevator doors and one uniform took up position on the far side and the other was preparing to knock when Dupree stopped him. "Don't knock," he said.

"Sir?"

"The room's supposed to be empty. We're with hotel staff. We're legal. They're just showing us an empty room."

Like his boss in Security, this guy was also Spanish-speaking. He unlocked the door with his master and held it open an inch for Dupree to proceed. Then he stepped back out of the way, afraid of possible flying bullets. Dupree went through, then the uniforms, and finally Émile Cinq-Mars.

An empty room. The bathroom was vacant. The bed remained as Émile had left it earlier, the sheets crumpled, the pillows indented from the nap he had taken with Sandra before dinner. Émile looked at the bed and wondered if he'd ever make love to his wife again.

"Okay, well," Dupree stated, "it wasn't a bad try."

A uniform opened a closet door. Then jumped back.

Out tumbled the body of a man, hands tied behind his back.

"Shit!" For a heavy man, Dupree was swift when it suited him. He jumped so fast that he almost caught the dead man, who'd been propped up in a seated position, before his shoulders hit the floor. Almost, but not quite. Cinq-Mars moved over him and the two senior cops looked at each other.

"Africa," Dupree said, "with islands to the south."

"Now will you tell me his name?" Cinq-Mars asked.

"Grant," Dupree told him. "Jefferson Grant."

"Tell me about his hands," Cinq-Mars asked.

Dupree had to pull him farther forward and lean over him to peer at his hands. "Tied," he said. Then he struggled back to his feet and looked at Cinq-Mars again. "With the ring finger of his left hand dismembered. No doubt missing."

"Was he a married man?"

"I'm not familiar with his personal life."

"Dupree," Cinq-Mars said, "listen to me. My wife is in the building."

"We'll do an all-room search," the New Orleans detective vowed. "Regardless of what's occupied."

"I don't know if we can allow that," the security man said.

"Okay. So why don't y'all try to stop me?" Dupree challenged, then said, "Give me that." He snatched the man's master door pass from his fingers. "Thanks."

Dupree called for his man Everett, who came over. Every request made of his subordinate had been taken care of, and perhaps he knew that, but he went through the list to make sure. They needed a forensics team for this murder. He wanted the victim's phone checked for calls, texts, and e-mails, "Find out if he tweets," and he wanted a warrant to visit his office, if he had one, and his home. "Find out about next of kin."

"On it, boss."

"Now get everybody out of this room who doesn't have to be here. Where the hell is Everardo Flores?"

"Who?"

"The Head of Security."

"On his way, so the story goes."

"When he gets here, make sure he finds me. Émile!" Dupree barked. "You're coming with me. Security!"

"Yes, sir?" one of the hotel guys responded.

"Do you got an empty room on this floor?"

"A few, yeah. There's this one."

"This one's a crime scene! Give me a number."

The man checked his list. "1712."

He told the man he called Everett, "That's where I'll be." He told the security guy, "Let me in there," And he repeated to Cinq-Mars, "With me. Come on along."

Émile was again impressed by how well this big man moved when he was possessed to do so. He carried his weight like a cartoon hippopotamus in ballet slippers. The two went into the vacant room and Dupree left the overhead lights off but clicked on a floor lamp, which cast a moody glow. Dupree sat down on one of the two beds, and Cinq-Mars, not really sure what this was all about, turned around a desk chair and sat on that. He welcomed the hardness of the chair's back.

"Understand," Dupree told him, his tone quiet, yet aggressive, "that this doesn't change a thing. Fact is, you're more a suspect than ever."

Cinq-Mars raised no objection. "I agree," he told him calmly. "It's like I knew where the body was. But it was deductive reasoning, Sergeant, though I can see where you might want to consider that I had prior knowledge."

"Take your deductive reasoning and shove it up your pink ass, all right? I have no choice here but to take you at your word. I am doing so for one reason only. Your wife's life may be at stake. So that's the premise I'm operating on. For now. Until we find her. And we will find her. If y'all know where she is, if y'all left her somewhere, might as well tell me now, because lying about it will surely piss me off something fierce sometime in the near future."

Cinq-Mars choose not to reply, and the question died in midair.

"All right, then. This spins around you. Pickpockets in the lobby. Pickpockets in your hotel room. Jefferson Grant tailing y'all. Jefferson Grant dead in your old room. So this spins around you, but I don't know why. If y'all do, you're not telling."

"You know what I know, Dupree."

"Don't call me Dupree. That's been rescinded. Y'all will address me as Sergeant Dupree or I will fucking have y'all arrested right now."

"Fine, Sergeant Dupree. But we don't have time for games. I don't care what you think of me or do with me, but find my wife. Please. Now."

The New Orleans detective relaxed a fraction. As he adjusted his considerable weight, the bedsprings squeaked. "As I was saying, this revolves around you. Y'all contend that you don't know much. So I want you to find out more. Call your man in the FBI. Tell him the story. Convince him to tell y'all anything further that might help. Get him to step up, Émile. Because we don't have much else to go on here."

True, they were foundering in the dark, and the slightest lead had to be followed to see if it led to light. Besides, it gave him something to do and that might help quell his high anxiety, undermine his imagination when it came to fearing the worst about Sandra. He knew it also took him out of Dupree's way, which might be the idea, but he understood the value in that as well. "All right, Sergeant Dupree," he said. "I'll do that."

"Report back to me if you get anything, Mr. Cinq-Mars."

So they were no longer on a first-name basis, and Dupree's pronunciation sounded more like *Saink Mart*. Close enough.

THIRTEEN

He had lived within a code. Both sides—multiple sides, at times—lived by that code. On occasion, a new group emerged and refused to be put down. Russian gangs came close to the top of the heap for a time, then the Jamaicans threatened the balance as the Mafia descended and the Irish West Enders persevered and the biker gangs fiercely held their turf. The old Mafia power slid away, then reinvigorated itself again, then remained a niche group, corrupting city officials and intimidating contractors to stay rich. Newer arrivals always spotted opportunity in abandoning the code. Power derived from proving themselves as more brutal, more terrifying. And yet, over time, they conformed. In violating an unwritten, unspoken code, all retribution brought down upon them was deemed justifiable. And so the code returned, and prevailed.

Certain strategies wandered off-limits. When the Hells Angels chose to kill prison guards, new money was allocated for law enforcement. More than a hundred and fifty Hells went to prison for a variety of crimes, and so the code was restored. Lay off prison guards became the most recent addition to the code. In his city, over the past century, killing a police officer brought out the hounds. No cop killer could expect a peaceable sleep as long as he remained at large. Hope for a good night's rest depended upon incarceration. Lay off cops, that had always been the first commandment of the code.

Other limits and observances applied. Cinq-Mars recalled the poor lad shot umpteen times behind the wheel of his Honda Accord. An ambulance arrived on the double and the young man survived, but how to secure his safety during his convalescence in the hospital? Cops guarded the operating room. As the matter turned out, there was no need. Before the young man was off the table a call came in from a gang spokesman. They had shot the wrong guy. Same kind of car, a blue two-door, but the wrong one. Owners of such cars laid low, but the boy was able to recuperate without fear of being hunted. The bad guys had simply admitted to their mistake, so life went on.

The code held to its own skewed sense of honor.

Back home, spouses and other family members of cops and of criminals, both, were off-limits.

True, Colombian thugs who were upping the ante of their underworld influence had to have it explained to them that threatening the wives and children of judges and top cops might gain them a momentary victory, but a simple truth remained: cops came into contact with very bad men everyday and negotiated with them every single day, and if a cornered killer was offered a deal—to blow up the family sedan of a Colombian associate, for instance, to retaliate for a cop's missing child—the proposition would be accepted in the wink of an eye. So through all times and all manner of malfeasance the code prevailed.

Once, that he could remember, Émile armed his wife with a rifle, although the actual count was twice if he thought about it more thoroughly. Sandra was a capable shot, which they both put down to her American upbringing, and yet she never needed to fire her weapon in anger. Just prepare to do so. Either good luck or the code prevailed, she was spared being a party to violence, but down here in New Orleans, what code existed? Even if one did exist, how did it include him? What pact had he made with local devils that he could call upon them to keep his wife alive and unharmed? In a city once ravaged by storms, where the destitute victimized by ferocious wind and rain and by the collapse of levees—which were inadequately engineered and no warning was given that they might not hold—and where the only crime attributed to those people was that they were too poor to flee and were consequently fired upon and two of them shot dead—not by looters, not by warring gangs, not by manic throngs of frightened or disoriented people like themselves, but by the very men charged to protect them—in an environment such as that, who would help him rescue his wife? Moreover, what criminal entity could be prevailed upon to spare the woman they held captive?

Back home, a bad guy might be convinced that he had good reason to do so. Certain countervailing threats might apply. In some circumstances, contacts and connections could be called upon, deals struck. But here?

Why would any killer bother to be merciful here?

Émile called back to Montreal, to his former partner, Bill Mathers. He still wasn't used to the technology that allowed people to know who was calling before they answered, even though he carried that technology in his own pocket.

"Are you out partying, Émile? I've been asleep awhile."

For a split second he wondered if the night's terror had affected the sound of his voice. Even his ability to speak. "Bill, Sandra's been taken."

"Taken?"

"Kidnapped."

"Émile! What! Why? How did this happen?"

He plowed through these and other demands for details, all perfectly natural, shaking them off, to get to the nub of the matter. "Listen, Bill, I don't have time right now—"

"I'm flying down there."

"The hell you are."

"I am! I'll be on the next flight out."

"No offense, Bill, but there's nothing you can do to help. There's nothing *I* can do. I'm calling for one reason only. I didn't bring his coordinates with me. I need to get in touch with Rand Dreher, ASAP."

"Do you have a pen? I'll dig up the number in a second. But I'm going to call him myself and get him to call you."

"Why do that, Bill? I'll call him. Save a step."

"And if he's not in? You'll end up calling him back endlessly. I'll do that. Okay, here's the number."

Cinq-Mars wrote it down and also agreed to allow Mathers to call

Agent Dreher first. He negotiated that agreement by first getting Mathers to forget about coming down to New Orleans himself.

"You know you're not my boss anymore, right?" Mathers argued.

"Maybe not, but I'm still the voice of reason. Stay put, Bill. Look, I may need you there. You might be able to run some things for me as they come up. Down here, you're just another tourist. Like me."

Mathers consented and urged Cinq-Mars to take care before he signed off.

Émile hated every second that ticked by, and yet was surprised when Agent Dreher called him back within two minutes.

"My God, Émile. I can't believe this."

"Believe it."

"I'm stunned. I'm just so sorry. I don't know what to say."

"You can start by telling me what you don't want to tell me." Cinq-Mars didn't expect an honest reply. Water torture. If he could maintain the drip, sooner or later Dreher might yield.

"There's nothing I can tell you, Émile, that will be of any use."

"Never ask yourself, Dreher, why people hate law enforcement." He could feel his instincts taking over. Old habits, old talents, intended to keep his counterpart off-guard and unstable. "Was he one of yours?"

"Who? What?" Like Mathers, he had probably just been roused from sleep.

"The man with the pale pigment splotches on his face. Jefferson Grant. Some kind of half-assed private eye. Was he one of yours?"

"Why? What did he do?"

"That sounds like an admission to me. Is it?"

"What did he do?"

"He's dead."

"Émile. God. What the hell's going on down there? How'd that happen?"

"Looks like a spike wound through the heart and a finger cut off. Ring any bells? Again with the missing finger. I don't want my wife's to be next, Dreher." The way he said the man's name carried threat and vitriol.

"Okay. Émile. Okay. Take it easy. He was working for me."

"So he was spying on us."

"Not spying. Protecting."

"Yeah, well, he just gave his life to the cause. But from what I hear he wasn't the type. Couldn't you post one of your own agents, instead of some shabby ex-cop?"

"I never thought it would come to this. If I had I wouldn't have let you go down there. But putting one of my own on the job—they'd ask too many questions. Émile, honest, I didn't think there was any real *danger.*"

"You were definitely wrong about that, Dreher."

"Call me Rand."

"I don't care what your name is! I'll call you Mr. Asshole if I'm in the mood. Your man is dead. How's that for danger? As for questions, I have a few. Who did I need to be protected from that you hired him in the first place? By itself, that shows you thought this was dangerous. What aren't you telling me, Dreher?"

He could hear the other man take a breath and sensed him formulating a response. "Émile, it's nothing sinister. You're unofficial. You went down there to ask questions about a cold case. Who might come out of the shadows for something like that? I just—if you got into trouble, I wanted to be alerted and to have somebody in place to help you out. That's all. Somebody who knows the ropes on both sides of the fence. New Orleans is not an easy jurisdiction to be working in."

So he was being thoughtful. At least, that's what he wanted him to believe. Cinq-Mars was standing now, gazing out the window at the peaceful city lights flickering below. He felt that yawning gap of darkness between himself, from this height, and the softly illuminated streets below, this black abyss, into which his wife had vanished. He felt the floor, the ground, the whole of the earth, side-slipping out from under his feet, himself falling into a despair, an oblivion, he'd never known.

"Apparently, Dreher, you know whom to call down here, to pull up a lowlife like Grant."

"I had advice."

"So make more calls. Kidnapping's a federal offense, no? The local police are doing a thorough job, I'm impressed so far, but we don't know where this leads."

"I'll get help to you, Émile."

"I want top people. Fuck the budget. Can you do that?"

"Consider them on their way."

"Send the cavalry."

"You're at the hotel? They'll be there."

"Yeah," Cinq-Mars said, "the hotel. Dreher, top people. Do you need an incentive? Think about this. I'm no longer a cop. I'm no longer bound by confidences and secrecy. My wife knows everything that I know about this case."

The pause at the other end felt weighted, even accusatory. Cinq-Mars knew why. One way to keep spouses safe was to make damn sure they knew nothing. In that sense, he had screwed up, but Dreher wasn't going to say so under these circumstances.

He spelled it out for him. "If the people who took her want to know what I know then it's reasonable to expect that they do so by now."

"I hear you, Émile. But they wouldn't expect her to know anything."

"Not unless they ask."

His voice was quiet, determined, when he said, "They won't harm her, Émile."

That suggested to Cinq-Mars that he was making an educated guess about who snatched her up. "And you're confident of that why? Isn't this whole thing a trail of dead bodies? Isn't that why I'm here? So why should Sandra be safe?"

"Because—" Dreher started, then stopped. He knew that he was traipsing closer to what he did not want to say and to what Émile Cinq-Mars was after. But he chose to forge on and told him, "Because they have no reason to."

"Whereas the others, someone had reason. What reason?"

But Agent Dreher knew his limits.

"Émile, I'm sending help right away. Let me get onto that. I know who I want on this."

"Yeah? You got somebody you trust to call? Who trusts you? This I gotta see."

Cinq-Mars turned away from the window, the city, as he punched off his phone. The night beckoned him into a free fall from which he might not surface. Sandra's finger, her life. He had to go hard until a positive outcome arrived. Otherwise he might just collapse.

He took a step and winced. Oh no, this he could not allow. Of course it had come upon him. The plane travel, all the sitting he'd been doing, then the stress bounding through his bloodstream. Another step and his left lower side ignited with pain. He wondered if he hadn't slipped a disc. He could not falter now. Sandra needed him. He could not avoid doing what was necessary, and so Cinq-Mars lay on his back upon the bed, breathed deeply into his belly, then into his lungs, and stretched his considerable length and held his breath before he slowly let the air out as if deflating an air mattress and brought his arms down to his waist. He did that once more before he permitted himself a few normal breaths to keep from hyperventilating. Then he repeated the procedure several more times until he lost count. When he stood up again, he was somewhat okay. Semi-normal. Out of pain with decent mobility. He was able to function.

As he stepped toward the corridor he acknowledged that the incident was both symbolic and fortuitous. In this crisis, he had to make sure to look after himself or be rendered useless.

FOURTEEN

Everardo Flores had arrived back at the hotel, his trip home interrupted in similar manner to Sergeant Dupree's. Unlike Dupree, he returned looking impeccable, as if to start a new day. Had he let the breeze catch his hair on the way out, had he slackened his tie, no such gesture toward ease and relaxation was apparent now. Reconfigured as a coiffed, groomed hotel representative before daring to return inside the Hilton, he struck the rather studied figure of a meticulous and composed individual.

The moment he entered, a subordinate informed him that on his watch a man in the hotel, neither guest nor employee, had been murdered in a vacant room.

Instead of going straight to Dupree as several officers asked him to do, he went off to find Émile Cinq-Mars. Flores was directed to the seventeenth floor, and as Émile stepped out into the corridor, the head of security rushed to greet him, his concern and loyalty going first to the welfare of a hotel guest rather than to the dictates of the local New Orleans detective.

He came at Émile in such a rush it appeared he might tackle him.

For his part, Émile suppressed a desire to fly off the handle. Before he could think of a single articulate word, he felt an inappropriate rant surging through his veins—"What kind of a hotel are you running here anyway?"—which would escalate into a diatribe against the Hilton chain and, in due course, possibly denounce the Hilton family and generations of their progeny—"Do you think I care one whit about Paris Hilton?" The lunacy of his rage alerted him to his own imbalance. He was so rarely off his centerline that this unwanted mental harangue was indicative of an impending collapse. He reined himself in, hard and fast.

"Mr. Cinq-Mars. My God! I'm so sorry."

"Mr. Flores, what do you know?"

"I'm sorry? Know? Nothing!"

"What have you heard? Do you know about the dead man?"

"Oh. Sorry. Yes. I believe I'm up to speed, sir. Are you all right? You don't look well. The shock. I understand. Your wife! But where are you going now?"

"Where've you been? Home?" Cinq-Mars stopped walking and turned so abruptly that Flores rammed into his chest. The former detective looked down on Flores in his policeman's practiced accusatory style. "Were you home?"

"Almost. I came the moment I got the call. I take it she's not answering."

Cinq-Mars gazed closely at Flores. So rarely was he behind in any conversation. He realized also that he felt light-headed, mildly faint, and he wasn't at all used to that. "Excuse me?" he asked.

"You've called her?"

"Are you—" He abbreviated that dormant rage again, in this case censoring a torrent of personal insults. Forcing himself to be calm, or calmer, he understood at least part of what the man meant. "As radical as this may seem to you, Mr. Flores, my wife did not bring a cell phone along on the trip. What would be the point in two of us paying for additional coverage in the USA? Do you have any idea how expensive that is?" He was offtrack again. "In any case, no, I can't call her."

Simultaneously, Flores appeared both enlightened and confused.

"What's the matter?" Cinq-Mars inquired.

"Then how do you know—" He stopped himself, probably because he didn't want to appear to be the ignorant hotel security man.

"Never mind," Cinq-Mars told him. "You've just given me an idea.

Come on. I need to get back to my room. Then we'll find Dupree. How can we find Dupree?"

As it turned out, Everardo Flores could assist him with that. He got in touch with his associates in Security and tracked down the man staying close to Dupree without letting him out of his sight. First, they rode an elevator to the eleventh floor.

"I'm confused," Flores mentioned as the car slid downward. "What idea did you get from me, sir?"

Cinq-Mars answered quietly. "You came back when we called. That's a clue."

"That's a clue? Asking stupid questions, that's another clue, I suppose?" he grumbled. Flores wanted, and yet didn't want, to press him for an explanation.

"Maybe. In this instance, it hasn't hurt." Cinq-Mars assured him, "You'll see."

In his room, he worked at a pace, sorting through his wife's things.

"What?" Flores asked, baffled. He stood at the door, holding it open.

"Hang on." When Cinq-Mars broke for the elevators again Flores hurried to catch up. This time they rode a car down to the eighth floor. As the elevator doors slid open, the pair hurried to find Dupree.

In the corridor it became clear that Everardo Flores was not totally up to speed. He had not been made aware that cops were waking up guests. He was stunned. They stepped into the room where Dupree was seated on a bed.

"What the hell is this?" Flores demanded.

"Keep your voice down," Sergeant Dupree told him. "Y'all don't want to distress your guests, do you?"

"You're waking them up!"

"Ah, but we speak very softly when we do so. I find it makes all the difference in the world when you drag somebody from a deep sleep, don't you?"

An empty room served as a temporary command post while his people were on that floor. If a guest wanted to complain, or worse—have a fit, or go into a feverish paroxysm at this interference with their carefree dreaming hours, or, as in a few cases, become belligerent about an interruption to their porn-watching and whatnot—then they knew where to find him and Dupree could talk them down. Flores saw the merit in that, but remained upset that guests were being disturbed.

"Better to have us rather than killers and kidnappers wake them up, no? But don't worry, Mr. Flores, we're not telling people that. Or would you rather they knew?"

Then Dupree saw Cinq-Mars standing behind Flores.

"Mr. Cinq-Mars. We're doing our groundwork. Nothing's turned up yet."

"We've erred," Cinq-Mars said. He stepped farther into the room. "I erred. She's not in the building."

"Say what? This was your idea. It's worth pursuing, no?"

"Your idea?" Flores flared.

"We missed the obvious."

"Okay," Dupree allowed. "How do you figure?"

"What's the first question you ask when someone goes missing?"

Thinking about it, Dupree was also busily scratching the back of his right elbow. He sat with his thick thighs splayed outward. The indentation on the bed went deep. "I'd ask, what does the individual look like?"

"Except that in this case you know what she looks like. You met her. So the next question would normally be—and I admit, this is not a normal situation—*What was she wearing*?"

"Okay," Dupree played along, remaining sceptical. "What was she wearing?"

"I went through her wardrobe. Blue jeans and a pale green top, a pullover type thing."

"We'll get that on the wire," Dupree assured him.

"You're not following me."

"Why am I not surprised? Talk me through it, Cinq-Mars."

Émile took a breath, still putting it together in his head and trying to grasp the ramifications. "Sandra walked out of here on her own accord. She willingly left the building. She wasn't abducted—initially—because she took the time to choose clothes buried in her suitcase. Nothing that was on top, easy to get at. If she was being abducted she's not going to go carefully looking through her luggage to put something on for the occasion or to select clothes that match."

Dupree remained confused. "Okay. I get it. But you're telling me that—*initially*—she was not abducted?"

"I'm saying that she was lured outside. It's the only explanation. Everardo gave me the idea. He came back here as soon as he was called. The *call* was important enough that he turned around and drove straight back. Sandra—she also must've received a call. Something that lured her into leaving the hotel, probably to meet me, maybe to meet you. Who knows? Since then, I'm guessing, she's been kept away."

Rising from the soft mattress was not easy for the large man, but Dupree heaved and puffed and made it up. "We still have a problem," he noted.

"The blood smear. I know. I was thinking about that. It's what gave us—gave me—the wrong thought. But it could have been after the fact, no? We didn't know about Mr. Grant then. You said it was an hour old, the blood? First off, Mr. Flores here is tight with his security. It would not have been easy for someone to find out my new room number. Possible, but not easy. I'm not in the computer at the front desk, for instance. Instead, Sandra was telephoned. She doesn't have a cell. So maybe the hotel switchboard found her and put the call through. Check with Flores on that. But that's why I still think that she was grabbed. Because after she was grabbed, she gave up the room number. And her key card. That makes the blood smear in the room possible, probably from a sheared-off finger—hopefully, Jefferson Grant's, no one else's—which all occurred after she left. They wanted to make it look as though she was abducted straight out of her room. Grant's troubles might have started in my new room, he might have been killed there, but I consider that highly unlikely. More likely, the finger was brought back to the room after he was killed—so much easier than dragging his body around, don't you think?—then the wall was smeared, both to alert us to an abduction—"

"Alert us?"

"Who kidnaps anybody in secret?"

"Okay. So what's the other thing?" Dupree wasn't smiling anymore, but looked both puzzled and attentive.

"They wanted to alert us to the abduction, to fool us about how it occurred. And they wanted to intimidate us, or maybe just me, with the sight of blood and of course, eventually, with the dead body. I bet that's why we haven't heard from them yet. They expect us to need a lot more time to find the corpse."

Dupree nodded briefly and paced the floor a little. His size astonished Cinq-Mars in this intimate environment. "I'm not calling off the door-to-door," he told him. "But I get you, Émile. I'm buying into your interpretation. We'll follow both theories. Say, for now, that she walked out the front door, unaccompanied, all on her own."

"Most likely unaccompanied. Somebody sold her a bill of goods."

Pausing, Dupree stared directly into Émile's eyes. "Just so we understand each other, this is a tough one. I'm looking for the same miracle you are, but until we hear from her abductors, assuming that she has abductors, this is a tough one."

"I know what you're saying, Sergeant."

The detective nodded, touched his hand a moment to Émile's biceps, and quietly said, "Call me Dupree."

"Dupree, there's one other theory to consider."

For the briefest moment, the detective flashed that glittering smile again. "Go ahead. I'm all ears."

"The dead man. He might have told my wife to leave. In that sense, in some kind of scenario like that, she wasn't abducted. She put on some clothes. Things that she can move around in comfortably. Then she hurried out. She escaped."

"Escaped? You think your wife might have escaped? The Hilton Garden Inn?"

Cinq-Mars himself didn't want to wave this flag with enthusiasm, only to be keenly disappointed further along. But it was possible. "I talked to my guy in the FBI, like you asked me to do. It turns out, he hired Grant to protect me."

"Really? If that's true, Jefferson Grant's come up in the world. Not that it's done him much good. So the FBI was protecting you. Okay, from what? From who?"

"That's where we reach an impasse. They just won't say."

"Do they know?"

"They won't say. I'm guessing they know."

"Damn. Probably one of their asinine conspiracies. They're the biggest conspiracy theorists on the planet."

"Part of their job description, I suppose."

Dupree folded his arms across his chest. "Anything else I need to know?"

Cinq-Mars took a deeper breath. "You won't like this part, Dupree."

"I don't like any part of this, Émile."

"They're coming."

"Great. The FBI? Great. You're right. I don't like it. This is New Orleans, Émile. Do you know what you get when you put a New Orleans cop in the same room with an agent from the FBI? Doesn't matter who the individuals might be."

"You tell me," Cinq-Mars invited him.

"Disdain," Dupree let him know, although he might have guessed. "Sheer disdain. It grows on you. Like mold. Anyway, thanks for the head's-up."

"I'm told they're sending in the cavalry. I suppose I insisted on it."

The two men looked away from one another.

"I don't know what the fuck is going on," Dupree said.

"Does that mean I have to go back to calling you Sergeant now?"

Someone in the hall was waving for Dupree. Without answering the question, he turned away and walked off to attend to that matter. Everardo Flores came up beside Cinq-Mars and the two men observed the activity in the corridor.

"Everardo, did you give my new room number to the switchboard operator?"

"To the operator, no. To the computer? Of course. The operator types a name, the caller gets connected to the room. But the operator never sees the number. Nobody found your room that way. Is that why you called me back here?"

"What? No. You were called back here, Everardo, because you're a suspect. We don't want our suspects out of sight. Don't you get that yet?"

He didn't and, being put out by the idea, scurried off in a huff to ease the distress of his other guests in the Hilton Garden Inn.

Over the next half hour, Cinq-Mars pinned his hopes on the arrival of Rand Dreher's cavalry. As he expected, no further evidence was derived from the hotel searches and no news came in from the streets. Sandra had vanished. He didn't know what another infusion of police could do, but he was having a difficult time maintaining his usual equilibrium, and since he could not rely upon himself he was relying upon numerical force. If he could he'd call out a multitude from the heavens, a legion from hell, mobs from their sodden lairs, armies from their barracks. He'd like to summon the minions from every continent to search and destroy, to query every living soul on earth until answers were revealed. His weariness, perhaps, or his abrupt and free-ranging fears had taken over, and he no longer felt himself. The severe ache in his brain could be an impending stroke, not that he had any experience in such matters, but the sensation felt menacing and strange. Émile had to will himself to be calm and suspected that at any other time in his life he could manage even a crisis this severe with a higher degree of control and calm were it not for two aspects that impinged upon his usual strengths: he was out of his territory, therefore surprisingly incapable of action, and he just felt *older*, more tired. Whereas in another era he might have been running on adrenaline, postponing an eventual crash, now he felt as if he had already *crashed*, and was waiting for someone, or some event, or some *thing*, to pick him up.

Dupree moved his so-called command center a floor higher, and Cinq-Mars followed along. He was alone in that room when he heard a knock on the open door. Cinq-Mars looked up and saw a woman in conservative attire suitable for an office, and for the tiniest fraction of an instant a thought zipped through his head that she was Sandra. But no. Sandra did not have longish, dark brunette tresses or blue eyes. His wife was much younger than him, but nowhere near thirty, which was the approximate age of his visitor.

"Detective Cinq-Mars?" the woman asked.

He chose to dispense with denying he was a detective. "Yes?"

"Vira Sivak," the woman replied. She strode forward and extended her hand. Cinq-Mars had seized upon a thought that terrified him—"Oh no, the press!"—when she added, "Special Agent, FBI."

In a fog, he shook the slender, soft hand. She sat down on the edge of the bed beside him. "I thought I called out the cavalry," he told her.

"I talked Agent Dreher out of it, sir. We agreed upon a limited presence. Me."

He looked at her as if she spoke a foreign language.

"You," he said—and he wanted to register a complaint, *are not the cavalry,* but instead he caught himself and spoke to the more surprising revelation—"talked him out of it?"

Seated for no more than six seconds she now popped back up, returned to the door, and shut it. Cinq-Mars noticed that before returning she scanned the washroom to make sure they were alone.

"Detective Cinq-Mars—"

"Do you mind calling me mister? I'm supposed to be retired."

"Mr. Cinq-Mars. Are you all right? You don't look well."

"I'm stressed, Agent Sivak. I'm used to stress, but not like this. I'm unaccustomed to being helpless. It's a new experience, so no, I'm not well. But nothing to be concerned about. Now, please tell me that you didn't come alone."

She sat again. A handsome woman, with little makeup. Despite the solidity of her facial features her look was not severe, and despite the businesslike aspect to her attire—a pants suit, sturdy shoes—she moved with a subtle grace. The long hair helped. She reminded him of his wife that way, although Sandra was prettier and more overtly and confidently feminine, even in her barn clothes.

"I'm here alone," she told him. "It's very possible, Detective—Mr. Cinq-Mars, that your wife was taken precisely to see who might show up. If it's just me, her abductors may relax some. No one needs to know that our mutual friend sent me. This might play out in our favor down the line."

"I keep asking Agent Dreher to tell me what I don't know."

"I know."

"You know?"

"I do. I'm not going to tell you what you don't know either. Imagine if you did know too much, and imagine if you had told your wife. I understand that you've been confiding in her." She raised her eyebrows to gently chide him.

"What are you saying?"

"Things might be far worse for her right now."

"Is it not possible, Agent Sivak, that things could not be any worse?"

"Let's hope that that's not true." She leaned in closer to him. "Let's proceed on that premise, okay?"

Although he really didn't know what he was agreeing to, for this felt more weighted than a mere wish for his wife to be safe, Cinq-Mars agreed. "Okay."

She leaned in still more closely and spoke more quietly, so that Cinq-Mars knew that she wanted something from him. "Have you gathered from our talk so far that I'm somewhat aware, somewhat *au courant*, of this file? For instance, that I know why you're here in New Orleans?"

"I've gathered that, yes."

"So can we proceed"—Cinq-Mars noted that this seemed to be a favorite phrase—"on the premise that this is true, but that such an opinion need not travel to anyone around us at any time?"

Cinq-Mars studied her eyes. She certainly carried an intensity there. "You want to be presented to the world as ignorant?"

"Let's just say," she demurred and continued with her eyes on his, permitting no diversion, "that it's in our best interests, and particularly your wife's, that we don't scare anybody."

"So no cavalry."

"Just me. And I'm ignorant of most things pertinent to you and your presence here, as far as anybody else who's here needs to be concerned."

Cinq-Mars held on a moment, but proceeded to nod. "Now I understand how," he ceded.

She waited with a curious expression for him to explain himself.

"How you convinced Agent Dreher. You're convincing."

She still did not break her penetrating gaze. "Mr. Cinq-Mars, it's not that I'm convincing. If I am it's irrelevant. What counts here is that this is important."

"All right," he said. "I believe you."

He didn't know any of the people around him, everyone in a flurry and working in a blur, but for once he felt better. That growing ache in his brain seemed to diminish, and he had some confidence now that he might make it through the night. He realized that that had been weighing on him. Relief from the fret of being incapacitated right when he was needed most released his mind to think more astutely about the matter at hand, about saving Sandra.

"So," Agent Vira Sivak inquired, "do you want to introduce me to the investigating officer?"

"Sure. He's on this floor somewhere."

He wasn't hard to find. As it turned out, an introduction was not necessary. "Pascal," she said, extending her hand to him, which told Cinq-Mars that although they had met, they weren't bosom buddies. The notion was reinforced when Dupree referred to her as Agent Sivak. Not buddies at all. Although he shook her hand.

"Is this the cavalry?" Dupree asked.

"Mr. Cinq-Mars may have been overly optimistic as far as that goes, but I assure you, Sergeant, the FBI takes a kidnapping very seriously."

"Alleged kidnapping," Dupree corrected her.

Cinq-Mars intuited what Dupree wanted to say, but wouldn't in his company. He explained, "He's holding out for her to be a runaway wife. Or that I bumped her off myself. In this case, I'm hoping he's right, at least as far as that first part goes. You two know each other?"

"We've had the pleasure," Sivak said.

"Danziger Bridge," Dupree revealed as he looked at the agent.

"Pascal wanted to keep an investigation of the New Orleans Police Department internal," Sivak elaborated. "Obviously, as the external agent assigned to the case, I thought otherwise. We had our fractious moments. But we found a way to get the job done. Of course, we don't only go back to Danziger Bridge," she reminded him.

Dupree released one of his bright grins and drew his thumb and forefinger down outside his mouth repeatedly. Irritated, he tried to shake it off.

"Agent Sivak," he explained, "is the one who pointed out to us that the investigation into the murder of Gifford and Dorsey Lanos was underway at the same time as the killer was snoozing in the attic. Of course, she not only pointed that out to us, she also let it be known to the *Times-Picayune*, thereby making me in particular, and the New Orleans Police Department in general, the laughingstock of the entire State of Louisiana. But, hey, water under the bridge. Or, if you like, water under Danziger Bridge."

Émile Cinq-Mars was rocked by curiosity. Separate events from the past that addled Detective Pascal Dupree were now loosely knitted together by the presence of FBI Agent Vira Sivak, who, in turn, was attending to the abduction of his wife. For the first time since discovering Sandra missing, he felt clearheaded, his thoughts bell-like, as if his faculties were finally being summoned to figure this one out.

He was on his own, he knew, down here, but for the first time he didn't regret that and grasped that he wouldn't have it any other way. He felt it coming on. He was back on his game.

He wanted to become more active, but first, he had something to do.

FIFTEEN

Cinq-Mars asked Everardo Flores to take him up to the roof.

He was still pouting. "I think they checked the roof. I'll find out for you."

"I'm not checking the roof. I'm *going* to the roof. There's a difference. I presume I need a key. I'm asking you because I'm pretty damn sure you can help me out with that." He wanted to add, "Stop pouting," but chose to let that pass.

The man remained sullen as they headed skyward.

"Mr. Flores," Cinq-Mars said. "There's something you need to understand."

"I'm a suspect. I understand. You don't trust me. Fine."

"Do you trust me? If you do, you're a foolish man, because you don't know me. Not at all."

"Fine. But you are not a suspect."

"Of course I am. Sergeant Dupree considers me a suspect. Men do bad things to their wives, Mr. Flores. You know that. Why should I, a stranger, be the exception to a known rule? In Dupree's mind, I'm a suspect, and I'll tell you something else, in my mind, so is he."

"You are patronizing me," Flores said, but he was protecting himself. He was taking the comments seriously.

"Why would I, Mr. Flores? Do I care about your *feelings*? Dupree took me away from my wife and out of the hotel. In my absence my wife went missing. I'd be an idiot not to think of him as *potentially* involved. Do I believe it? That doesn't matter. Investigations become corrupted when people lean too much on what they believe. But he knows and I know that neither of us is in the clear. So. Naturally. Neither are you. Do I believe that you killed a man tonight and abducted my wife? Again, it doesn't matter what I believe. But am I experienced enough to know that anything is possible? As it happens, I am. What was your background, Mr. Flores, prior to hotel security?"

"Military police."

"That's impressive," Cinq-Mars told him, and he was obviously sincere, making Flores feel better. "Which branch?"

"Air force."

"More impressive yet, in my mind. Good on you, Everardo."

The elevator jerked to a stop and they were let off on the uppermost floor. Flores had used a key on a particular elevator—the general public had no access to this level. Yet they still had to go higher and took the stairs. Up a short flight, Flores unlocked a door to the hotel's roof, which was flat and functional in the usual industrial manner, with a tar-and-stone surface and no amenities whatsoever for guests. Flores glanced around. "See? Nobody's here."

"Are you Catholic, Mr. Flores?"

The man shrugged. "I'm of Mexican extraction. What do you think?"

"Practicing?"

"I go to mass sometimes. My wife goes regular. I'm not saying I'm pious."

"Some would say I am," Cinq-Mars mused.

"Practicing, you mean?"

"Pious."

"You? A cop?"

"It's not against the law, Mr. Flores. A little unusual, I agree. Of course, if the pope was asked for an opinion, and let's hope that he never will be, he'd probably call me out as a heretic. If I'm one I'm also the other. A pious heretic, let's say."

"Okay," Flores said. He was not comfortable with the conversation.

"Okay. This is why I'm here. I want you to notify me if someone from your staff calls you with anything important. In the meantime, I'm going to take some quiet time on my own. Because you're Catholic I can say this to you—I'm also going to pray awhile, after my quiet time. My wife, Mr. Flores, has been kidnapped. That's what I believe. Her life is in danger and that's if I put a positive spin on things. So I'll take a few moments to pray and to remind myself that there is more to this than we think. Then I'm going to do a good hard study of everything, try to discover if I've missed something, if there's anything I can do. So, quiet time, then prayer, then a good hard think. I want you to know what I'm doing because I don't want you to interrupt me unless you consider it exceedingly important."

Solemnly, Everardo Flores nodded. "I will also pray," he said. "For you, and for your wife."

"Thank you," Cinq-Mars told him, then moved off to the far side of the rooftop to commence his quiet time.

In a way, this was his preparation for prayer. And yet, before he endeavored to communicate with the cosmos through prayer, he wanted to commune with Sandra. As he moved across the roof his eyes flooded with tears. Soon he could scarcely see. Raw emotion shook him. He had to slow down near the edge of the roof as he couldn't trust his blurry eyesight. The lights of the city were magnified and distorted by tears. His heartache was singular and vanquished the pale, pitying sorrow he'd experienced in recent times after Sandra had suggested that she might leave him. He gasped for breath, and as he went to his knees—safer, given the height, but also necessary given the tumult now breaking through him—he loosened himself and gave himself over to a blooming anguish.

Cinq-Mars wept, first with a burst and then quietly, his torso shaking so that he finally had to hug himself to hold in the ache, the sheer galvanizing pain washing through him like an unremitting turbulence. He spoke Sandra's name several times, but could not be certain if the word was uttered aloud or not. For the nonce he had become her name and little more, that was all that he knew or could experience.

He fought against the many imaginative interpretations of what she might be going through. He had to stick with the simple fact that he didn't know.

Although Everardo Flores had been forbidden to interrupt, the visitor's misery compelled him to go over to Cinq-Mars and place a comforting hand upon his shoulder. He had seen people in torment before, and perhaps he felt that he could determine when enough was too much, when a cessation to the suffering was warranted.

Saying nothing, Cinq-Mars thanked him with a nod, touched his hand to the hand upon his shoulder, and bolstered his inner resolve. Emerging from the pain, from his own wreckage, now was the time to move on to his prayer.

Flores gave him some distance again.

Cinq-Mars rose from his knees. Any deity, just or otherwise, would recognize that he had sufficiently humbled himself. He stood, as if to be transfigured, although inwardly he was wholly prostrate. To receive a new identity and energy, the very act of standing upright was meant to be an accomplishment of his prayer, as yet unspoken, and to be its ultimate prescription as well. He had to work through all this and survive his agony standing, so he started out that way, upright yet broken, presenting himself to the cosmos to have himself, and this juncture with the world, transformed.

He prayed.

Like detective work, he believed, prayer required the proper approach. Both activities had to be ingenious. Each engaged the unknown, demanded the whole of one's experience and intelligence, vitality and intuition. Ultimately, the detective or the supplicant had to go it alone, no matter how many colleagues were brought in to investigate a crime or how many penitents submitted upon their knees. Humility was key to both endeavors, patience a virtue, honesty a prerequisite that would inevitably become an ongoing adventure of self-discovery. Cinq-Mars was never convinced that one could be done without the other, for even in prayer one needed to investigate, stay attuned, struggle to unravel the secrets and deepest mysteries in order for the act to be increasingly more true to oneself, and therefore more viable. Conversely, in balancing his way through a difficult inquiry into a complex crime, he inevitably needed to stretch himself out and summon the intricacies of the cosmos to have a look, to suggest possibilities, probabilities, improbabilities, chaos and string theories galore to get his mind around fresh core discoveries. Just as the conditions that predated the beginning of time had engaged thinkers and cosmologists for centuries, and theories continue to unfold, any inquiry into a crime shared that mindset: *What was life like the instant before all hell broke loose?* And before that, what exactly? What particles free-floating in a cosmic stew had collided, and what was borne of that devastating blow: What matters formed? How was it possible for one event, the big bang, say, or a murder, to be triggered out of and within the previous morass? But to get there, to *engage,* whether it be cosmological speculation or the scrutiny of a crime, required a measured, serious approach, a discriminating evaluation, and a critical judgment of one's own talents, abilities, and even a catalog of one's own shortcomings. For Cinq-Mars, the study of the cosmos as an independent pursuit of knowledge or as a yearning for the godhead, or the study of a crime in order to extrapolate truth from lies and thereby render justice—both these practices—constituted forms of prayer.

The heretic in him: the edict in scripture to pray unceasingly he interpreted to mean that all thought, and all activity, became prayers when the proper attitude for the circumstance was both discovered and sustained. Prayer could mean going to your knees in a cathedral, abject and penitent, but equally it could mean reveling in a concert, or a hockey game, making love or frying your brains figuring out your taxes with a dollop of integrity. Being prostrate, or upon one's knees, undoubtedly had it's time and place, such as on a mountaintop or a rooftop in New Orleans, and yet that form of public humility or degredation might also be misplaced and sorely ill-timed. He was not here to denounce his height, but to extend the rooftop further, albeit microscopically, toward the heavens, simply by stretching himself higher, arms raised. Let there be humility in this, in stretching to stars so distant they existed only in another time that had passed by and ceased realms ago, so that that fleeting light on a voyage through the universe was merely being intercepted along its distant vast path, and the very futility of reaching out to the vanished skies exercised then a blatant humility akin to the more familiar crouch in an attitude of prayer. The approach: he stretched himself to his fullest, albeit merely incrementally, fully extended, and beseeched the whole of the universe and any other universes out there to spare his wife should that be possible, should that be a token that the apparent oneness of life in its cosmic and subatomic and its known and unknown aspect might favor, and he was praying yet without words for the God in all particles and some particle of God to deem this doable, plausible, to find it within the bounds of renewal and invigoration and change, denote it as a cosmic duty, in a way, and return to an undeserving but nonetheless rewarded servant his august due, for which he vowed eternal gratitude.

If his supplication could not be granted, he would understand that also.

He had words, as well:

God. Please. Help her. Please help Sandra. Help me help her. Use me. Help her through me if that's possible. Guide me.

Please help.

He did not necessarily believe in God in the way that others did, although his faith was strong and he believed that there was a place in the world for signs and wonders that pertained to the cosmos and that the cosmos was a part of God. His understanding maintained that nothing could exist or be outside of the All, the One, yet despite his faith he did not believe in a God who used a cellular phone or even that God was capable of using any telephone whatsoever, not even a landline. His God had limits. Had predetermined His limits. Nonetheless, he was hearing a phone, and out of his semi-trance Émile understood that his was ringing and that the darn thing was only going to get louder and louder unless he attended to it now.

The display identified the caller as his friend in the Sûreté du Québec, Captain Gabriel Borde. What would he want at this time of night?

"Hello?"

"Émile? Oh God, Émile, I've heard. I'm so sorry. I told you to watch your back down there. But I never expected anything like this. Is there any word on Sandra?"

"How," he wanted to know, "did you hear?"

"They called me."

"Who, Gabriel, called you?"

"Sandra's kidnappers."

Cinq-Mars stood upon the rooftop above the lights below, which, though relatively sedate, now seemed to become a dizzying and intoxicated carnival array, not dissimilar to the night sky.

“Émile,” Captain Borde explained, “they’ve told me their first demand.”

SIXTEEN

Covering the mouthpiece on his phone, Cinq-Mars waved Flores over and issued a terse instruction. "Get Dupree now." He returned his attention to the call as the head of Hotel Security bolted off to do his bidding.

Flores was back in no time with his catch, as Dupree had been waiting for the same elevator from which Flores burst in a panic. They went to the roof, Dupree panting after taking the jaunt up the short flight of stairs too rapidly, and they found Cinq-Mars standing near the edge, phone put away, hands on hips. They rushed over to him, then stood beside him, breathing heavily, and waited.

"I got my call," Cinq-Mars revealed.

Dupree had hoped for and expected that news. "From the kidnappers? Good. Then she's still alive, Émile. Let me have your phone. See if we can get a trace."

"No point. A colleague in the provincial police called me after they called him." Émile finally turned to face them, as if emerging from a trance. "At his home in Quebec."

"I don't get it. How? Why?"

"So you can't trace the call, for one thing. My friend was awakened from his bed. He didn't even know that Sandra was missing. He certainly didn't get a chance to do anything that might have traced the call. He'll look into it, of course, but understand this, these people are sophisticated."

"I still don't get it," Flores admitted.

He and the New Orleans detective waited for Cinq-Mars to explain further, but when he didn't bother, Dupree filled him in. "They want to prove to Émile that they know where he's from, that they know who he knows, that they can get to him if and when they choose. Even when he's back home."

"Oh," Flores said. "Oh." He looked at Cinq-Mars as if the man had just learned that he had terminal cancer.

"It's hopeful, actually," Cinq-Mars expanded. "If they want to take the trouble to show off their power, it's an indication they have nothing more lethal in mind."

"What do they want?" Dupree asked. "Demands?"

"They want us to check my old room."

"But we did that," Flores pointed out, looking from one man to the other, baffled again.

This time Cinq-Mars was willing to break it down. "They don't know that we did. In one sense, we're ahead of the game. One step ahead of their game, anyway."

"They want us to find Jefferson Grant dead," Dupree stated. Still winded, he stood stooped, hands low on his hips, drawing deep breaths but more slowly now.

"Another scare tactic. To put the fear of God into me."

Light that spilled through the open door to the rooftop at once outlined the silhouette of Agent Vira Sivak.

"Yeah, I left a message for her to come up," Dupree explained. "She was in the can when Everardo ran me over."

In low heels, Agent Sivak was finding the uneven surface awkward to negotiate in the semidark, yet she managed to stride forward with evident authority.

"I got the call," Cinq-Mars acknowledged.

"So what's up?" she asked. "Is it money?"

Perhaps a trifle too proud of his knowledge, Flores answered, "They want us to check his old room, but we did that already, so we're ahead of them that way."

"What else?" Sivak asked. She was forthright and brought an energy that Cinq-Mars appreciated. He sensed that she was someone who got things done.

"That's the thing," Cinq-Mars postulated. "They're doing this piecemeal. They put their first demand through an intermediary. I've got a hunch their next call will come through someone else. I arranged with Captain Borde—from back home, he transmitted the message to me—to trace the call if they ring him up again, but I doubt they will when they're being so cautious. Anyway, right now they think we're scrambling around finding a dead body in a hotel room, that that's going to horrify me, break me down. So I'm suggesting we do just that."

"Say what?" Flores asked.

"He's suggesting that we should go find the dead body," Dupree stipulated. He addressed Cinq-Mars, "Y'all think they're watching?"

"Just holding out on the possibility, Detective."

Dupree crossed his arms, standing fully upright now. Cinq-Mars realized that he hadn't shown that wild bright grin of his in a while. "I've noticed, Émile, that you have a knack for thinking like they do." Flores may have missed the inflection, but both Sivak and Cinq-Mars recognized that the line was not meant to be a compliment. He was voicing a deepening suspicion.

Sivak elected to intervene. "Detective Dupree, this may be my fault. I told Detective Cinq-Mars that I called off the cavalry because we have a suspicion inside the FBI that the bad guys may have wanted to see who would show up for this. They may have wanted to find out how deep this goes."

Dupree looked between the two of them, and Cinq-Mars bobbed his chin a tad to show that he concurred.

"So that's why you think they're watching us now."

"Like I said, I'm entertaining the possibility," Cinq-Mars said. "Look, I have no jurisdiction here. All I can do is suggest that we make it look good. They may or may not see us on the roof right now, but they might be watching the room where they stuffed Jefferson Grant. It's a possibility anyway."

Simple nods of agreement confirmed the strategy, but Cinq-Mars had to warn Flores not to look over his shoulder at other buildings in the vicinity. "Don't show them that we might think they're watching us, Everardo. Tell me, that room faces what direction? Which buildings?"

Cinq-Mars had only to share a glance with the local detective before Dupree was on the phone. If suspicious people were hanging out in buildings across the street or a couple of blocks over, his uniforms would check them out. They all traveled down to the seventeenth floor and Flores reopened the door to the scene of the crime where Jefferson Grant's life was taken. They turned on the lights to allow their presence to be known, but did not open the drapes. Assuming that they were finding a body, that they were entering that chaos for the first time, opening the drapes would not be a likely early response.

"Just in case," Cinq-Mars whispered to Dupree, "put some uniforms in here. Ask them to have a party. Conversation. Give them something to drink. Just make sure they mingle, keep moving around. Shadows on the curtains. As if they're investigating."

"Consider it done."

"If another call comes soon, that might tell us the bad guys are watching."

"What do they get out of this?" Flores asked, and the question was humble for once. He accepted that his comprehension lagged behind theirs.

"They might want to believe that they're softening me up," Cinq-Mars told him. "Keeping me off my game. I may let them think that way."

Flores pondered the suggestion, then as Sivak and Dupree moved off together to have their own intimate discussion, he asked tentatively, "But are you, for real?"

"Am I what?"

"Softening up?"

"Actually, Everardo," Cinq-Mars determined, "I'm not. If you're working for them—and I don't believe you are—tell them that. See if I care."

Flores managed to smile. He was more comfortable with being a suspect now, given that it meant he was in the same boat as everyone else. He placed a hand upon Émile's back as encouragement, then waited as if for further instructions, his hands dutifully folded in front of himself as a faithful servant's.

Noticing him, what occurred to Cinq-Mars was that the man had previously been on his way home at the end of a long shift. "You must be tired," he said.

Flores shook his head. "No," he stressed, as if this was important. "I'm not. Second wind."

Just then, the phone in the Montreal detective's pocket buzzed. Across the room, Agent Sivak and Detective Dupree also heard it, and came over. Before answering, Cinq-Mars told them all, "It's too soon for them to guess that we've come in here and found Mr. Grant. This means they're watching."

Then he took the call.

This time, Bill Mathers was calling.

"My God, Émile, what the hell is going on?"

"They called you."

"How do you know that? This is my home, Émile. My wife answered. I have kids asleep in their bedrooms. My home, Émile."

"I didn't give them your number. May I remind you, this is about Sandra right now. That's what's real right now."

Mathers paused a moment. Cinq-Mars could hear him taking a breath.

"He wants you out of town, Émile. Out of New Orleans. He says that now you know what he's capable of doing."

"He?"

"He didn't give me his name."

"I'm not going without Sandra."

"He said you'd say that. He's calling back in four minutes after the first call to get your answer. If you agree to leave town, he'll tell you where to find Sandra."

Each man listened to the electrical buzz of the continent between them.

"Come on, Émile," Mathers advised him. "This is a no-brainer."

"Tell them yes. Okay, you'd better get off the line now."

"I'm calling you on my cell. I'm keeping the landline free."

"Actually, Bill, you should keep both lines free."

The weight of that message sunk in. Mathers said good-bye and they both hung up.

Cinq-Mars conveyed the gist of the message.

"Hopeful," Dupree told him.

"Very positive," Sivak agreed.

"Let's wait for their call first," Cinq-Mars cautioned them both, but he, too, felt his spirits rising. His hands began to shake and he sat down on the bed. He rubbed them together, surprised to find his palms damp. Agent Sivak brought a towel in from the washroom. He didn't know what for. He looked up at her. Lightly, she tapped her brow. Cinq-Mars passed the towel across his forehead and was shocked that it was soon soaked. He touched his right temple, his hand quivering violently, and the fingertips felt stuck to the skin of his head as if he secreted glue rather than sweat. He brought his hands down and tried to stop each hand from trembling with the other, but he only shook more. Flores ran for water and Sivak opened his shirt collar down another button. She asked him to bend his head between his knees. He tried, but couldn't make it that far.

"Brown bag," Sivak ordered, and Flores raced off again. Dupree held the glass of water he'd brought in and offered it to Cinq-Mars.

"Damn," Émile said. "Damn."

The water just spluttered on his lips. He couldn't swallow.

"Head down," Sivak said gently, and she assisted him to bend lower this time, to get blood to his brain. Flores was amazingly quick, and Cinq-Mars steadily breathed into the brown bag to keep himself from hyperventilating. He thought he should be embarrassed by this bad turn, but really didn't care in the slightest. He was just happy to be recovering and getting his senses back. He had to take care of himself through this. Over and over again, that was the message. He had to watch it. Who knew what faced him yet?

His phone rang.

Everyone took a nervy breath.

He answered.

It wasn't Mathers again.

This time his wife's kidnapper was calling him directly.

He said, "Hello, Detective Cinq-Mars."

He was no expert, but he had been in the city long enough to call that a New Orleans accent. Somewhat Brooklyn-like, some what New Jersey–like. "Yes?" At least he didn't have to fake being upset, weary, distraught, defeated. His voice carried that spectrum across the phone lines.

"So, what's your answer? Only a yes or a no will do."

"I'll leave town. Where's my wife?"

"She's not been harmed. She will be—you will both be harmed—if you hang around or if you come back. We're giving y'all a break here. Let's call it southern hospitality. But don't press your luck. Just so we're clear on that."

He wanted to scream at him. Swear at him. Threaten him. He wanted to reach through the phone lines and strangle the bastard, watch the life eke out of him. Instead, he said, "We're clear. Where's Sandra?"

The man told him and Cinq-Mars shouted back, "Where?" because he wasn't in his right mind and he didn't know where the place was, but the kidnapper replied, "You heard me," and hung up.

Cinq-Mars, pale, wavering, but breathing more evenly, clicked off his phone.

Dupree asked the question he had last asked. "Where is she?"

Cinq-Mars told him.

"Danziger Bridge."

SEVENTEEN

They ran. Émile ended up in Agent Vira Sivak's car and Everardo Flores—in their haste, the New Orleans detective was the only one to notice that Flores came along—wound up in the backseat of Dupree's vehicle. Other squad cars raced away from the Hilton Garden Inn with them, both ahead and behind.

They sped through the streets, Sivak and Cinq-Mars in the fourth car in line. He pumped her for information on the bridge, about its infamous history. "What does this have to do with me? Was the shooting as bad as Dupree said?"

"None worse, Mr. Cinq-Mars. Inexplicable. Incomprehensible. White on black, we're used to that sort of thing, even with respect to unarmed civilians. But this was sick. Depraved, in a way. So unnecessary. What's worse, one of the dead men was mentally challenged. He was the one who got kicked while he lay dying. Added misery for his last breaths. At the scene, all he did was run from trouble on his brother's command."

"What was going on? What started it?"

"The hurricane." She shrugged. "The misery. The Superdome. The lot of it. The shame. Some people, and I mean cops here, maybe they reached their limit. That's a justification. I don't buy into it myself, but it's the only one around anybody can latch on to, you know? The shooting started on one side of the bridge, went up over it, and continued down the other side. Cops ran. In a panic. In fright. Later they said they were being shot at. Not true, but maybe they thought it was, but when a cop issued an order to stop firing and let them know the civilians were unarmed, some cops didn't stop. They kept firing. Shotgun blasts. Close range, too. Later they tried to cover up their mess. That was real bad. If it wasn't for being in the aftermath of Katrina the city would have rioted beyond anything we've seen in this country. I don't doubt that. I mean, because of the storm, an NBC camera was in the area. Fuel for that fire. But folks were too distressed with their own problems. The demonstrations got angry but stayed civil, as these things go. As if it was one horror too many."

Émile let all that settle. Nothing stood out for him to weigh, nothing to evaluate or compare, no terms of reference that were meant to include him. "I don't know what this has to do with me. Or with Sandra."

"Probably nothing," Sivak noted. Cinq-Mars shot a glance at her. "I mean," she backtracked, "I can't think of any connection myself."

"But it has something to do with you," he pointed out, for he needed something to go on here. He finally had a glimmer. "And with Dupree."

"We're the good guys," she declared. "The bad cops are in jail."

They raced on through the night, the lights of the squad cars flashing and the sirens wailing in and out. Cinq-Mars went quiet. His mind raced. He recalled Dupree mentioning that not enough officers had been put away to satisfy him. And he wished he'd brought that brown paper bag, then just by thinking about it located the bag in his jacket pocket. He was unsure if he should take it out, but a moment later he had no choice and breathed into it. Then he sat back in the seat, his arms splayed out beside him, his eyes closed, being jostled and bumped about, his seat belt banging undone at his shoulder.

"You all right?"

"Right as rain. How far is it?" he asked. Time seemed to float by before she answered, her eyes and hands intent on the high-speed drive.

"It's a hike," Agent Vira Sivak told him, then ordered, "Hang on!"

They cut a corner that made the tires squeal and threw Cinq-Mars against his door.

Prior to that infamous night, Danziger Bridge was known principally as the widest lift bridge in the world, although in the down position it accommodates most marine traffic on the Industrial Canal. An expressway leads onto and off the bridge and also sharply veers away from it, spawning circular ramps so that drivers may negotiate their choice of direction. Like other waterways in and around New Orleans, the canal overflowed its banks at the time of the hurricane that lay siege to the city. Cinq-Mars thought that he saw his wife on the hump of the bridge, but he was wrong, an optical illusion of the night or a nasty trick of the mind. Moments later he verified that she was indeed near the crest, but on the opposite side from where he'd been looking. Squad cars were with her now, having been dispatched from nearby through Dupree's initiative. When he spotted Sandra, still at a distance, and knew for sure that it was her, he felt the whole of his body slump and gyrate. He might nearly have lost control of his bodily functions, when a glee for which he was totally unprepared overtook him and virtually snatched him out of his skin.

He felt staggered by joy. She was standing! She was upright!

Sandra was alive. Blood spun loose in his head.

Sivak's car rocked with her sharp braking, and Cinq-Mars protected himself against the dash then bounded out before the vehicle came to a screeching halt. He banged his hip hard against the door and was off, running across the road with a pronounced limp. Not all the traffic had been stopped and on one side it was being funneled into a single lane. A delivery trucker gave him an annoyed honk and tapped the brakes as he dashed in front of his headlights. Sandra caught sight of him then. She was partially supported on her feet by a uniformed officer and twisted now in his careful grip and turned to lift herself into her husband's embrace. The two wound together, holding fast, as if instantaneously melding into one being. Émile couldn't breathe and Sandra hadn't taken a free breath in hours, and didn't think she could. When finally they separated a touch, so that they could look at each other, his tears instigated her own. Their joy mingled with a shock of nerves they had both suppressed, but which now boomeranged through their bones like a sonic thump.

Sandra's first words were, "I need to sit," and with that they both nearly collapsed. Dupree, with help from Flores, broke Cinq-Mars's fall. Sivak grabbed Sandra at the last instant. They let them sag down awkwardly onto the pavement of the bridge where they held each other's hands and kissed and cried and laughed and wiped away each other's tears. Those who milled around, including Sivak, Dupree, and Flores, turned their backs on them and let them have a private moment encircled by a forest of officers' legs.

An ambulance was pulling up to take Sandra away.

"Are you all right? Are you hurt?"

She nodded. She was all right. She couldn't say those words though. As though she could not believe in their veracity.

Dupree turned back to them and knelt down. He wanted to get in a word before the paramedics took them away. "This is a precaution. We'll get her checked out. We'll ride with her, Émile."

"My God. Oh my God, Émile," Sandra repeated several times. Then she said, "I thought I'd never see you again. They told me I would and I wanted to believe them, but I didn't think I could."

He wanted to say that he knew that he would see her again, but before the words came out he recognized that the statement would be a lie and he swallowed it whole. He, too, had dealt with a nagging doubt that she'd survive this, and just that thought caused him to weep again. Happy now, but weeping again.

"Come on," Dupree said, as the ambulance attendants rushed over with a gurney. He was guiding Émile to his feet so the men could do their job. They watched as Sandra was assisted into a proper sitting position on the gurney and then laid back. The gurney was cranked higher and as she rose from the pavement she managed a smile.

"We're not riding with her," Émile stated. He looked directly at Dupree by his side. "Only I am." His voice cracked slightly.

"There's such a thing as protocol, sir." He stretched out his arm and eased Flores away from their conversation. The man took the hint.

Cinq-Mars looked away when Dupree turned to confront him. Émile wet his lips and swallowed. He needed water. But he had to win this argument first. "You don't get to interrogate her before . . ." He stopped and looked down at the lovely face of his wife. "I'm talking to her first on my own." He cupped her cheek in one hand.

"Émile," Dupree objected.

"You'll get plenty of time, Detective," Cinq-Mars insisted. "But we're taking this ride without you."

Dupree never formally conceded, but said nothing further.

Having strapped her in, the paramedics lifted Sandra into the ambulance. Émile followed and found where he could sit. He did allow the paramedic to ask his questions and check her blood pressure, but as they moved off the bridge, picking their way through the gathering of cop cars, he hovered right over her and kissed her forehead. Sandra smiled, a timid, faint reflex, a ghost of a smile.

"I'm alive," she attested, practically grinning now, briefly.

"You sure are," he said.

"Are you okay?"

"Just between you and me," he whispered, "I'm a wreck. I've probably had three heart attacks tonight and at least a pair of strokes. I should be lying where you are—you should be sitting vigil." He roused a giggle out of her. "And I'm parched." He suddenly barked out, "Don't you guys have water?" All his pent-up rage came out in that surge. Sandra noticed. The man next to Émile passed him a bottle and Émile let Sandra sip before taking several gulps himself. Then he inhaled a few deep breaths. "But we can deal with my demise later. Tell me. Honestly. Were you harmed?"

She managed a light, soft laugh. "Is this part of my interrogation, Officer?"

He brushed the hair from around her temples, not knowing what to say.

"Sandra, I—I have to speak to you before they do."

"Oh you probably don't, Émile. You just think that way. You can't help it." She was right all around.

"What did they want?"

Sandra nodded, as if this was the very question that she most wanted to ask and have answered.

"I think they wanted to convince me that they're not the bad guys."

He was looking into her eyes, and the surprise of her reply caused his brow to constrict, the furrows deepening. "So, the men who abducted my wife and killed the man hired to keep me safe are misunderstood innocent lads, is that it?"

"Don't get sarcastic with me, Émile Cinq-Mars. I'm still in a shambles, you know. The point is, the men who nabbed me, stuffed me in the backseat of a van, blindfolded and gagged me—the gag came off when I promised to be still, and I kept my word—those men, they want you to know that they are not the bad guys. I know that it sounds crazy, but that's my impression. I think that was the whole point of this."

"They killed someone tonight."

"Did they?"

Her pointed response indicated that she knew something. "What?" he asked.

Sandra took a breath, abruptly coughed and accepted more water, then told him what she'd overheard. "I was in another room. They were trying to keep their voices down. I have to tell you, Émile, that gave me so much hope. If they were being quiet, careful not to let me overhear, that meant that they didn't plan to kill me. Didn't it? Otherwise, why would they care? I clung to that thought, Émile."

Tears ensued, and they kissed again and Émile put his head on the pillow beside hers. He started to sense himself descend from a distance, as if this reality, her salvation, was now feeling entirely real to him.

Sandra wanted to keep going. "Anyway, I heard something. The word *dead* and the word *him*, so I assumed it was a man and I worried that it was you. That was my worst moment of all. But they said something, about the *dirty side of the street* in reference to him and something else, *ditched from the force*, so I no longer thought it was you. Before all that I heard someone say, 'Oh shit.' Like this was not something they wanted to have happen at all, but also, I don't know, like it was a surprise to them. So no, I don't think they killed anybody."

"They kind of claimed they did."

"I heard someone say, 'Well, let's use it then.'"

Émile nodded. "Okay," he said.

"Émile, listen, they tried to convince me that I was kidnapped because it was necessary, not because they wanted to. They tried to get me to believe that I wasn't in any danger. They said that you cannot be here, that you threw in with the wrong people, so you have to go home. They wanted me to convince you to go home. I told them, Émile, if they released me, we were going home. I'd see to it. You'd have no say in the matter. I convinced them, I guess. Here I am."

Émile believed that he could look into those eyes until galaxies collided and the time would pass as if in a wink. Of course he was going home. Even if he didn't believe in that course of action—and he did anyway—he certainly wasn't going to contradict her. Her willfulness might have convinced her abductors, but only if they wanted to be convinced and only if they never intended her harm. She'd be set free only if that was part of their plan from the start. This was a messed-up world he'd entered, some kind of madness, where strangers abducted the wife of a visiting former police officer in order to demonstrate their inherent goodness in the overall picture. Going or staying was not up for discussion. He wanted out.

She squeezed his fingers. "Émile, I know you. You want to run after these guys. But you have to let this one go. Take me home."

He kissed her lips and she kissed him back.

"First flight," he promised. The easiest vow he'd ever made.

Sandra closed her eyes and the ambulance released itself from the knot of traffic their scene had created and speeded up. The siren wailed, forlorn in the warm night air. Cinq-Mars also shut his eyelids, to conclude a prayer he had begun some time awhile ago and to express his everlasting thanks in rhythm to the siren's outcry.

One thought stuck to him, refusing to let go. *This is some kind of madness.*

PART 3

EIGHTEEN

Sandra and Émile Cinq-Mars returned home to snows deeper than when they left. The farm appeared luminous under the fresh powder and a bright sun. With the shock of their misadventure lingering, they each stole private moments to appreciate the peacefulness of the countryside. Pristine in winter. Exquisitely unblemished.

The couple was invigorated by the landscape, yet that genuine connection could not realign their shaky sensibilities, which wavered and gyrated. Their inner lives felt storm-tossed. Latent grievances, nascent anger, perpetual confusion, and an inability to properly center themselves made the adjustment to being home again difficult, underscored by a compulsive need for privacy. Both Émile and Sandra wanted to be alone yet they frequently bumped together, to fix or share a meal, to cuddle, to accompany the other on a chore. As often, they flew apart, discovering themselves at opposite ends of the house, on different sides of the barn, indoors while the other was out, as if moments spent together satisfied them only temporarily before a centrifugal force pitched them away from whatever had compelled them to reconnect and flung them against some remote, invisible wall in both solitude and surprise, where they endured an abiding, restless disquiet.

Had they indulged an inclination to analyze their predicament, they might have detected the opposing forces at play. Émile was naturally inquisitive about what Sandra experienced, and he was boundlessly curious as to how the matter had played out. Yet his style of inquiry, and her expectations regarding the nature of his curiosity, bore sharp similarity to a police *interrogation,* and she could no more bear that nuance than he could modify his posture in a false, easygoing manner. He did not want to *interrogate* her, yet he needed and desired to ask questions. Any attempt to do so provoked them to hurriedly forsake each other's company.

Émile couldn't help himself. Although off the case, he could not dispel his questions or vanquish a need to figure out the confounding aspects to everything that transpired. He failed to quell his instinctive passion to *investigate*, so in approaching his wife with good intentions, wanting to comfort and console, he discovered himself undermined by tangents of inquiry that beat him off that simple foray. He retreated then and sensed himself hurled away from the very center of their lives, dismissed for his prurient, professional intent.

Similarly, in the midst of her ordeal in New Orleans, Sandra had called upon her deepest reserves of resilience to maintain her bearings. In the aftermath, she felt her psyche submerge to the base of a well that she had since drunk dry. She wanted sympathy and tenderness and a chance to unload her fears and slough off her delayed responses, but to do so felt treacherous, as if she might discover herself void of any basic resolve. She might come undone. Sometimes she broached her need for company only to do a complete spin and flee the very comfort she sought.

Coming together, then, invariably wrenched them apart.

Neither knew what this meant for them, or for their marriage, in the longer term. Both instinctively understood that now was not the time for that discussion, although they could not dismiss the issue either. That, too, pushed them away from each other, often at the very moment when they most desired to be close.

Under the cloud of their mutual surveillance, watching, noticing, and backing away to ponder, Sandra made an executive decision to retain the farmhand hired to mind the horses in their absence. He had animals to care for on his own farm twenty minutes down the road, but in winter he also had significant free time so that he could tend to her horses as well. His two teenaged children were available after school to help out. She explained as vaguely as possible that she and her husband had returned early due to "a bit of a shock," and would he mind dropping by mornings and afternoons—they'd still look after the animals in the evenings—for the foreseeable future? The helper, Noel Lambert, was fine with that, and both Sandra and Émile were happy with the reduced workload.

So they persevered, somewhat aimlessly, with ample time to sit alone and do nothing or very little. Except get on each other's nerves.

Sandra barred any discussions that might pertain to their malaise from the bedroom. "I declare it a problem-free zone." As a consequence of that edict, although it was never her plan, time spent in the bedroom passed in silence. Given their trouble communicating, a full week went by before Émile finally got the lowdown on her abduction. They met in the barn, on a warmish day, when Sandra was active at nothing more than patting a horse's snout, and Émile was sussing out a place to hang from the rafters to ease his ailing back. They took each other by surprise and sat down on low stall stools. Rather than wait for a question, which might get them off to a bad start yet again and undermine the moment, Sandra waded in, prompted only by the silence between them and perhaps by a rising need.

A woman, she related, ostensibly a police officer with the NOPD, phoned their hotel room and asked for Émile. When Sandra explained that her husband was out for the evening, the female officer told her that the two men who had broken into their room that day after first trying to pilfer their wallets had been apprehended. Could she come down to the lobby and make a quick identification, to confirm that they nabbed the right pair? Sandra interrupted her husband's censure and insisted that she did indeed protest, begging that the matter wait until her husband's return or, better yet, until morning. The officer successfully mollified her, promised that it would take no more than a minute, one which might spare the police the embarrassment of keeping the wrong men in custody all through the night if they weren't the guys. Sandra acquiesced. Cleverly, as it took careful choreography, one of her abductors, a stocky man, was already on the elevator when it stopped for her on the eleventh floor. The car stopped again at the sixth floor where a woman boarded and immediately slapped a chloroform pad to Sandra's face. The man behind her bound her in a bear hug. Sandra retained an impression of the elevator doors closing, although she wasn't sure. After that, she remembered nothing before waking up in a bare, dark room. How they got her out of the hotel, sight unseen, remained a puzzle.

Discussions with her captors ensued.

They insisted that she relax. They wanted her to feel safe, to understand that she would not be harmed. They spoke well. They were articulate and calm. Their talk soon evolved into a negotiation. No one would hear her if she screamed, they told her, but if she promised not to, her gag would be removed. The gag terrified her. She feared she might vomit into her mouth then choke to death. She had to concentrate to keep her food down. Her head ached, her heart raced erratically, and she believed she was going to upchuck her dinner merely because she feared doing so. She agreed, violently nodding, and the gag was removed. Sandra coughed and spit up fluids and dutifully remained quiet.

She heard no evidence of other people within shouting range, so she felt no particular temptation to scream. The prospect of being gagged again thwarted any outburst.

Her wrists were lashed behind her back to a chair and one ankle to a heavy table leg. Strange, she said, that one leg was left free and it was her impression that they just didn't bring enough rope. In any case, she could flex and twist about, but only with effort and without beneficial effect.

They had her. She was utterly under their control. So fierce was her fury, she was surprised when she was unable to burst the ropes apart and kick the chair and table into smithereens through sheer rampaging will.

Émile absorbed the narrative as it emerged, in bits and pieces, and held her hand. Then he wandered off to the edge of the barn, forced to flee by the return of his flagrant anger and by a desire to pummel her with questions. He knew he could readily cause an event the kidnappers successfully avoided and make her scream. So he walked it off, minded his tongue, and gave his tension a chance to expire.

To himself only, he mentally highlighted two aspects of her experience. First, her abductors knew about the pair of Latino pickpockets and knew that those gentlemen had attempted to strike against them not once, but twice. This fact was known to some people but was not common knowledge across New Orleans. That meant that her kidnappers had inside information at some level, either through contact with the pickpockets themselves or through contact with the police or hotel security. Second, they were clever and efficient in how they executed the abduction. A flawless operation. Anyone might think that they were experienced at such a gambit.

Also, their actions following Sandra's abduction were consistent with her claim that they wanted to be perceived as being the good guys.

Trouble was, that last thought did not compute.

"Interestingly," Cinq-Mars mused upon his return to where she was waiting, and moved his stool under a crossing beam so that he could hang himself from his hands, "if they didn't know that I was out of the room, they might have been planning to kidnap me. You were Plan B. If they'd snatched me up, I wonder what our discussions would've been like and on what subjects."

"If they already knew that you were out on the town, carousing with New Orleans' finest—"

"I wouldn't say carousing."

"Hobnobbing, then. Whatever." To kid and to be kidded felt good. Normal, even. "But if they did know you were out—" Sandra repeated.

"Then they knew that when I arrived back at the Hilton they'd have me dead to rights."

He stretched as high as he could and worked his gloved fingers over the rough beam. Managing a speck of purchase, he stretched further, then released himself to hang in suspension, his feet dangling, his back straightening against its will. Émile grimaced, looking down between his feet. Sandra observed her husband, looking less Christ-like than like a cartoon cat hanging above a cavern just clear of a rotating saw operated by devilish mice, the whole of the feline's body, but particularly the arms, elasticized and on the verge of snapping as the cat descended closer to the spinning steel blade. The image was striking enough, as he struggled to support himself with only his fingers, that she started laughing under her breath.

Grumpily, Émile called out, "What?" And again, when she only laughed harder, *"What?"*

The images, and the sight of her husband, took hold of her and brought on hysterics. She seemed out of control, so Émile, as if through a hangman's trapdoor, let himself drop.

They held each other, gently.

Needing a break, he drove into the city to visit Bill Mathers. A last minute arrangement, and he presumed that he was interrupting the detective's workday. So be it. A consultation between them was necessary.

Mathers knew that, too.

Cinq-Mars expected to find the detective still upset by the call to his home, when in fact his former protégé had managed a turnabout on that one. Time had shifted his perspective. The call from criminals continued to vex him, but he appreciated that Émile's predicament at the time had been far worse. His former partner had nothing to do with the call. Just bad news all around.

Cinq-Mars apologized anyway, but Bill was feeling sheepish about his reactions on that night and was having none of it. "Funny, we're calm and rational when other people's lives are at stake, even when it's our own lives, but when it's our family the mind runs amok. Mine did. Sorry, Émile. I wasn't much use that night."

"It worked out in the end. That's all that counts. So how's business?"

The retired cop had warned him that he was coming, but sought to avoid a meeting at the old precinct building. Too many hands to shake and useless remarks to repeat. Officers might haul out pictures of their grandkids to show how they'd grown, as if there was ever a chance they'd shrink. So the two met at a café they had frequented in the past whenever a spot was required for a private chat that was both relatively close to the station yet far enough away to spare them the intrusion of other officers.

"Isn't it the beauty of our profession, Émile?" Mathers remarked. "Put bad guys away, more arrive to take their place. I guess I'm getting older myself. I'm finding the common criminal more common and less interesting that he used to be. Like I say, maybe it's because I've put on a few years."

"We ran down a few doozies in our time."

"How's Sandra?"

Perhaps Mathers intended the question to be polite, casual, but it sucked the energy out of their nostalgia-speak in a hurry. Cinq-Mars told him that she was fine, and made a gratuitous comment that it would take awhile before she put everything behind her.

"What about you, Émile? Have you gotten past it?"

Cinq-Mars stared back at him. The fellow had learned a few things during his time on the force, and not only during the years before Émile retired. He knew how to sneak up on a point.

"You know, Bill, it was your friend who sent me down there."

"Émile. I'm sorry—"

"Sorry? We were set upon by pickpockets, our room was broken into, Sandra was kidnapped, yet I haven't heard boo from the man. I expected to hear from him."

Mathers nodded and sipped coffee. He accepted Cinq-Mars's apology but his own wasn't getting accepted in a hurry. "Émile, the only friend I have in all this is you. Buy that or not. My relationship with Rand Dreher is no different than my relationship to this table. Or to this cup. Or this—"

"I understood the first analogy."

"But I heard from him. He asked about calling you or seeing you. He wanted my advice. It's like being back in university and some guy asks you about a girl, if he should call her or not. Really, the guy was screwing up his courage."

"Don't compare me to a girl. That's an analogy I don't get. What did you say back then? In university, I mean?"

"I was all for it. Call the girl."

"And now?"

"Leave Cinq-Mars alone. Let the dust settle. Words to that effect. Wait until he's ready to deal with you. Then expect to be reamed out sideways with a rusty spear."

Cinq-Mars thought about that exchange, then suggested, "He should've called. You should've let him. You shouldn't deny me that satisfaction."

Mathers was feeling his oats. "I'm a newfangled cop, Émile. I believe police should prevent crimes, not just solve them. Are you still in the mood to rip his skin off or have you settled down yet?"

The older of the two also sipped coffee, mulling the question, which he considered legitimate. "That's the trouble," he said. "That's the nub of the matter."

"What is?"

"I don't know what mood I'm in."

Later they walked.

The temperature nudged above freezing in the city, mild for the season, though still a huge drop from New Orleans. The city was probably five degrees warmer than the countryside. Wherever the sun broke through the phalanx of office towers and condominiums a melt ensued. They sidestepped and hopped puddles and minded the splash whenever cars drove by. Yet they enjoyed the walk, and where it was convenient, the two stuck to the side streets of Old Montreal. Cobblestone pavement. Horse-drawn *calèche* with tourists bundled under blankets clip-clopping past them. To think that he was that person himself a short time ago, in another city and climate, carefree and delighted. Now he was part of the scenery, someone who conveyed the tone and ambiance of these streets in his stride. He recalled the piano player in the old town of New Orleans. In a way, he resembled him. Someone who conveyed the soul of the city just by breathing the air.

"He's disappointed," Mathers said.

Cinq-Mars delayed his response. He was thinking that in this town in which he'd worked for decades, he was now a tourist, too. Time and even a short distance could do that to a person, make him a stranger amid familiar digs. "Dreher?" he asked. "Why? Because I'm back alive or not still down there?"

"Both. What I mean is, he's sorry that you're off the case."

"Who says I'm off the case?"

"Émile."

"Bill, of course I'm off the case. I'm up against people who will kidnap my wife for no other reason than to teach me a lesson. Imagine if they actually got angry with me. And as I keep reminding myself, I'm retired. I don't need this garbage."

At a corner, they waited for a red light to change. When it did neither man reacted, as if their boots had seized in the water freezing back to ice.

"That's pretty much what Dreher expected, Émile. Nobody's blaming you. It's impossible to continue. So don't."

"I won't."

"Good."

"So tell him," Cinq-Mars instructed him.

"I don't have to. He already knows. Or guessed."

"But he still wants to talk to me. Chickenshit is waiting for me to call."

"He's expecting you to call to cut him a new one. That's it. That's all."

"That can't be it. That can't be all."

"Émile."

"Flying leap, Bill. All right?"

"All right." Mathers was stymied by a red light again. "Look, I can give you that one shot, for how I reacted after I got the call at home. But that's the last free pass you're getting from me. I'm not your rookie lackey anymore."

"You owe me a lot more than one free pass."

"Bullshit."

"Not just for ten, eleven days ago."

"I know what you meant."

"For all those old times."

"I know what you meant, Émile. My answer is still the same."

Oddly, Cinq-Mars felt lost. "Which is what?" he asked.

Mathers pursed his lips briefly, chuckled slightly, and summoned the courage to look at him. "Bullshit," he said.

"Fine," Cinq-Mars responded. Looking away, he felt no particular animosity. "At least that's settled."

"What are we going to do?" The traffic passed. They started across the street before the light changed to green, although it did before they reached the other side. "You know what I mean. About Dreher."

"I'm inclined to shoot him," Cinq-Mars stated, "but like I said, I have to keep reminding myself that I'm retired."

Mathers pointed out, "You're the one who decided to go down south."

"I took my wife on an excursion. A vacation, Bill. Mardi Gras. He never suggested that we were taking our lives in our hands by investigating the fringes of a cold case his own people undoubtedly bungled seven years ago."

Cinq-Mars stopped walking. Struck by a thought.

"Émile? What's up? What's going on?"

The retired detective studied a pile of dirty snow, as if a body was surfacing from the melt.

"Émile?"

"God, I'm out of practice," he said. "How long has this been staring me in the face? Hell, this makes going to New Orleans worthwhile." He glanced at Mathers, then at the melting snow again, then illustrated his thought with a finger in the air. "Sergeant Dupree is a New Orleans detective. Right? My old rank. Yours, now."

"I recall the name from the files. He investigated the case you were going to look into, the first murders."

"Right. That makes him the first detective to have egg on his face for allowing the killer to hang around in the attic instead of doing the decent thing that all bad guys are supposed to do, namely running away to hide."

"Okay. So?"

"So his mistake was revealed, he told me, by Agent Sivak of the FBI. She told the press."

"Okay," Mathers surmised, "so I guess we don't like her very much, whoever she is. I'm down for that."

"Follow me on this. That was the first of a series of murders, the one after Katrina, right?"

"That's true, yeah."

"So there was no *series* of murders back then, at that moment. At the time it was a one-off. As it turned out, the first of many, but no one knew that back then."

"Okay," Mathers said, expecting his former partner to continue. But a thought alighted. Cinq-Mars saw the light go on behind the younger man's eyes and waited for Mathers to articulate what he'd just put together.

"This Agent Sivak told the press. So she was investigating the murder along with the NOPD."

"Correct."

"But why?"

"Exactly. It was not their case," Cinq-Mars emphasized. "The FBI had no jurisdiction. Our Agent Dreher seems to readily flaunt his jurisdiction, doesn't he? Case in point, coming up here."

"Why would the NOPD let the FBI in on the case?" Mathers asked.

"Why would they?" Cinq-Mars asked him back.

"You tell me."

"All right. I will. Possibly, Katrina had them understaffed and in disarray. But I don't buy it. In all probability, this had to do with the victims. Why else? The FBI had some connection to the victims. That must have given them access to the case."

In nodding agreement, Mathers was also looking at Cinq-Mars. He had another idea to process.

"What?"

"This has to do with, you know," Bill Mathers assessed, "those FBI secrets you were accusing Dreher of. Forgive me, Émile, but I thought you were being paranoid that day. Or maybe just a little stuck in your ways. Now I'm not so sure."

"Stuck in my ways?"

"Oh," Bill defended, "don't go off half-cocked on me now. It's an expression."

"Stuck in my ways?" Cinq-Mars jutted out his chin. "How about this, Sergeant-Detective Mathers? Contact Randolph Dreher. Tell him you think that maybe I've calmed down enough for him to approach me. Suggest that maybe he should crawl up my driveway to my doorstep on his knees wearing only sackcloth and ashes. It's only a mile. Say that I might be cordial to him after that. Go ahead, make fun of me. Let him know that he's found the soft spot in the retired old fart—that I got a check for my time and expenses so all is forgiven. But secretly, Bill, secretly, rather than be your usual naïve boring self, for once in your life keep your eyes and ears open in the company of another officer of the law, in case that helps you and perhaps helps us."

Mathers bobbed his head from side to side. "You're supposed to be retired," he complained. "Too bad that doesn't apply to your sarcastic attitude. I'd like to retire that."

Cinq-Mars put a friendly hand upon the man's shoulder. "Good to see you again, Bill. Sure, for a second there, I forgot myself. This feels like old times."

"Before you go," Mathers said.

"Yeah?"

"We found the dog."

"Dog?"

"And the family cats. Their bodies were more or less holding together, not rotten yet, frozen in the snow."

Cinq-Mars cottoned on that he was talking about the family pets of the murdered couple out near his place. "Anything pertinent to the case?"

"Not that anybody can tell. A dog in one spot, two cats five feet away. That slight difference in location suggests two separate trips out to the field, which makes sense. No collars on any animal. So no prints. The dog was big, a shepherd, a load to carry, but sorry, no hunk of human DNA down its gizzard. That's all we got. At least we took care of the carcasses with some dignity."

"Cremated after an autopsy, you mean? Yeah, dignified enough. Beats a slow rot in the springtime. Or being mauled by crows. Anything else?"

"A lawyer came forward with the couple's wills."

"Are you serious? Do we have a next of kin?"

Mathers shook his head. "No such luck. They left the farm, everything, to a charity."

Cinq-Mars expelled a heavy gust of air. No break ever emerged in this mire. "What charity?"

"A children's hospital."

"Yet we think they're childless, no?"

"It gets more interesting than that. You remember we were told that Adele and Morris Lumen came to Quebec from the Maritimes? They may have. We haven't found anything to confirm or contradict that. They're still a mystery couple. But the hospital to which they left everything? St. Louis, Missouri."

Cinq-Mars seemed to relish the news. "That makes sense," he said.

"How so?"

"The FBI has no interest whatsoever in Canadians. Nor should they. You can take that to the grave. I'll bet you dollars to doughnuts they weren't always childless. They once had a kid treated in St. Lou. Hey, Bill. Where'd your good friend Dreher say he was from?"

"Why do you always ask me questions you already know the answer to?"

"To find out if you're keeping up. What's wrong with that?"

"The American Midwest."

"Isn't that where St. Louis is located?"

"You know the answer to that, too. But what does it prove? Not much."

"Yeah," Cinq-Mars concurred. "Not much. Still. It's *something*. All I've had so far is a tall stack of nothing. So, are they going to sell?"

"Who? What?"

"The hospital. The farm."

"I don't know. I suppose so. Why do you care?"

Cinq-Mars smiled. "I might want to make a deal for the barn. Didn't you notice? It's an admirable barn."

Going into the meeting with Mathers, Cinq-Mars had no prior expectation or result in mind. Coming away from the talk he realized that he knew all along exactly what he was looking for. He wanted a little company, a sympathetic ear, a kind word, and a chance to indulge himself a little, and even, perhaps, to mope. He could admit to all that on the drive home, if not before. Instead of caring about any of those things now he was coming away fired up, transformed. He did not have a clue what he was going to do next, but he appreciated the renewed energy pumping through his veins, and the return of his usual unrelenting combative spirit when it came to ferreting out the truth to arrive at a reasonable facsimile of justice. Just maybe, he was thinking, retired or not, that's what made his life worth living.

"Up justice," he told himself out loud. "I just want to get these guys."

Sandra noticed the change in him when he got home, which surprised him because he tried his best to conceal his new mood. He didn't want her getting her back up or to fret that he might again put them in danger. One thing he knew well: he was not heading back down to New Orleans as a tourist in a maelstrom without a compass or a roadmap. Enough of that. But perhaps he could do something from home. After all, the murders of the two police officers and the couple in Quebec had occurred on his home turf, and no one was suggesting, yet, that he disregard that crime. Indeed, that was the crime he was hired to solve.

So he wanted to get on it.

While Sandra was out of the house he set up a flip chart in the basement. The materials were at the ready from the summer she'd picked up some charcoal and attempted to try her hand at drawing. She took a class. Her favorite riding horse, a Paso Fino, turned out looking more like a donkey who had downed the bottle of Percocet Émile kept handy in case of back pain, and she quit the hobby. So he had an easel, a flip chart, charcoal, and pencils, although when he looked upstairs in the phone table drawer, he found Magic Markers that would do a better job.

Then, at once, he was stymied.

He just didn't know where to start.

Arriving home and seeing the basement door open, Sandra went down the stairs speaking his name.

"Yeah. Here," he replied.

At the bottom step she found him a-squat on a tall stool. The room was not accommodating. She did the laundry there but beyond such functional uses—the furnace, the hot water heater—the basement was not a welcoming venue except for spiders. Lighting was on the dim side. Cobwebs abounded. She always meant to get at those and every few years she did.

"What are you doing?" she asked him.

He could say that he was staring at a piece of paper. Or that he was back on the case. Instead, he shrugged, and told her, "I'm thinking about taking up art."

Émile was a little offended that laughter burst from her so easily, a judgment being passed.

"I'm not saying I have talent," he countered, miffed.

Arms folded under her breasts, she sauntered over to him and also examined the blank white page. Émile did his best to repress his own desire to chortle.

"You do have talent," she assured him. She placed a hand on his shoulder. "You've talked to Bill. And you're back on the case."

He couldn't deny it. "You should have been the detective," he told her.

"But I am, Émile." Moving behind him, she placed her arms around him, and kissed near the top of his head. She squeezed her man. "We agreed, remember? I'm to be let in on this case."

"Yeah, well, look where that got us."

She kissed his neck, laughing a touch. “I know. A bad start. And I’m not saying you’re allowed to go anywhere. Because you’re not. But tell me something. Is this it? Is this all you’ve got? A blank page?”

Émile bobbed his head a little. “I’m afraid if I start writing things down, it’ll be an alphabet soup. An unholy mess.”

“So you want tidy? Since when?”

“Since I got involved in this case, I guess.” He turned on his stool so that he could face her and took her hands in his. She saw that he wanted to be serious. “Let’s say I work this thing from here. I’ll need to have people elsewhere. I’ve met Dupree. Agent Sivak. I don’t know whose side they’re on. Anyway, they’ve got jobs, responsibilities, their own cases. Why would they bother to work with me?”

“So you still want to investigate New Orleans in order to investigate Quebec?”

Cinq-Mars was not positive that he needed to, but thought that he might. “Seems to me the people who went to the trouble of kidnapping you feel that way. I had a thought when I was out with Bill. Why was the FBI ever involved in the murder case in New Orleans? They had no business being on the scene. I’m thinking that it had to do with the victims. I’m not sure I can fact-check them adequately without having someone there.” He placed her hands on his neck to disarm any possible protest. “I’m not going there myself. So, what do I do?”

Initially she drew close to him, kissed his forehead, but then backed off a few feet. As she turned, it seemed to Cinq-Mars that something was on her mind.

“What?”

She shrugged. “Just a thought. You’ll think it’s crazy.”

“Try me. That’s my way of doing business. Anyway, this case is nothing but crazy.”

“Just don’t laugh. Promise me.”

“Sandra,” he said. A growing irritation was evident in his voice.

“You want someone to be your feet in New Orleans? Your contact on the ground type thing, just as you’re supposed to be the FBI’s man on the ground here?”

“That’s about the size of it, yeah.”

“Dupree must be a busy cop, given the New Orleans crime stats. Agent

Sivak, the same. Like you said. So what about Everardo Flores? I can tell you one thing about him. It's my impression that he'd jump at the chance."

"He's no cop. He's even, sort of, a suspect, although not really."

"If he's a suspect, so much the better. Keep your enemies closer, isn't that what they say? Anyway, who else do you have?"

A ludicrous idea. For that reason, more than any other, Cinq-Mars liked it. He liked it a lot.

NINETEEN

His first call was to Pascal Dupree of the New Orleans Police Department. The detective had slipped him his home phone number before Cinq-Mars left town, but Émile chose to call him at work. Doing so lent a professional air to his inquiry, even if nothing in the matter could be deemed official.

"Funny. I was planning to ring you," Dupree told him. "Swear to God. Got the note right here, written down in block letters and everything. CALL ÉMILE. I've been underwater, baby, swimming in the blue bayou. Y'all know how that goes."

"I know what it's like to be drowning in a swamp," Cinq-Mars agreed. "Just not swamps with crocodiles."

"Are you sure about that? You wrestled a few crocs in your day, Émile. Just not down here. This is alligator country, my friend. If you stayed on a spell y'all might've found that out firsthand."

"There's a difference?"

"Significant. I could go on all day." Dupree seemed to be warming to the subject. Cinq-Mars heard the rustle of paper and the murmur of assorted voices in the background. Images arose in his mind's eye of the detective at his desk, tie slackened, crooks and dealers being shuffled through to holding cells right before his eyes. "I'll stick to the bare essentials. Alligators flee, crocs attack."

Cinq-Mars released a chuckle. "That *is* a critical difference."

"Crocodiles always show their lower teeth, that's their best identifier."

"I'll remember that the next time I'm wading through a swamp."

"It's good to know. But here's the thing. Hard to believe, but Louisiana is too cold for crocs. They like to bask in the sun to warm up. They can't do that when it gets chilly in these parts. And it does go all the way down to chilly here, though not by your standards. Gators can live at the bottom of a swamp—in freshwater, by the way—even if the surface is being chopped up for ice-cubes. Crocs die in weather like that. They're strictly tropical. And strictly brackish water or salt. You got to travel down to the base tip of Florida to find a croc sunning itself anywhere in the whole of America."

"At least now I know where not to go looking."

"Gators are pussycats."

"If you don't mind, I still won't take one as a pet."

"That's advisable. Anyway, I'm not offering."

"Both of us, we've had our run-ins with gators and crocs."

"That's why you're calling, I suppose."

"What were you going to call me about?"

"To see how y'all were doing. To check on your wife. How's she doing?"

Cinq-Mars let him know that they were both on the mend. Then he said, "I need boots on the ground in New Orleans, Dupree."

"Just can't let it go. Is that wise?"

"Probably not very. But have you ever known a situation in this life where it makes sense to yield to intimidation?"

"Do you want me to answer that honestly?"

He had a point. "Never mind," Cinq-Mars said. "But I know you're busy."

"That's God's truth. I'd be lying if I said any different."

"So I figured I needed to come up with something else."

A momentary silence while Dupree did some thinking. "Well," he said finally, "Sivak might say yes, but I'm guessing that she's busy, too."

"So you're saying no."

"More or less. Depends. Your wife was kidnapped. That's an open file. I can pursue the case to a certain extent. But she was released with no ransom paid, so my superintendent won't expect me to devote my life to the cause. That she was found on Danziger Bridge intimidates the brass, that has to be stated."

"Within those parameters, maybe we can work something out. I was thinking about asking Everardo Flores."

Another moment's suggestive pause. "Y'all are joking, right? Or is that some kind of backhanded reverse psychobabble razzmatazz bullshit intended to change my mind? Won't work, Émile."

Sandra entered the room. Cinq-Mars tipped his hand up as though tilting a glass, mouthed the word "please," pulled a beggar's face, and she left to get him a glass of water.

"Do you know what he did before taking over hotel security?"

"Parked cars? Served drinks? Beats me. A bellhop?"

"Military police in the air force."

The silence seemed respectful this time. "All right," Dupree said. "I hear you."

"He'll need some hands-on supervision. A dose of semiofficial authority from time to time. Somebody who can debrief him face-to-face, a look-him-in-the-eye type scenario. I haven't asked him, by the way. Wanted to check with you first. I don't know if he'll be willing."

"Don't be a kidder, Émile. He'll jump through hoops at the chance."

"So my wife says. You'll think I'm kidding again, but she's the one who suggested it." Cinq-Mars accepted the glass from Sandra.

"She's a good woman, Émile. I'm sorry I didn't get the chance to know her better. To know you both better."

"We had to eat and run."

Dupree released a laugh. Then he said, "If you like, I can go over to the Hilton myself. Talk to him about this. Look him straight on, as you say, and see how that goes down. You know, just in case."

"Just in case he wants to do this too much, you mean."

"Something like that. We saw what happened to Sandra, Émile. Y'all want him talking to the common folk, but still, this is not without risk."

"Make sure he keeps his head down. Remind him. We don't want him to spook the wrong people. Here's the thing—he might be able to go over to that neighborhood and talk to the dead couple's old neighbors and arouse no particular suspicion. That's all I'm really talking about. All I'm looking for is a rehash of local opinion on the matter. Sandra suggested Flores, mostly because she thought he might be willing. Me, I'm thinking that he might be able to move around the scene and be invisible, not a presence to be feared. Set off no alarms. Obviously, my showing up got people agitated, including you, initially, for no damn reason. Flores shouldn't have any effect. That way, no offense, he's a better choice than you."

He could see Dupree nodding and signaling to a colleague about another matter entirely, sipping his coffee and putting his feet down on the floor as he thought this through. Or perhaps Cinq-Mars was merely nostalgic for life in a cop room again.

"Are your feet on the floor yet?" he asked him.

"Say what, Emile? Come again?" For the first time, Dupree sounded puzzled.

"Never mind. Just curious."

He imagined Dupree swinging around in his chair, planting his elbows on his desk. "Okily-dokily," he said from New Orleans. "We're agreed. I'll chat up Flores."

"Fine by me. I'll hear from you."

"ASAP. Good talking to you, Émile. Y'all take care now. Say hello to Sandra. What a fine woman she is. Don't forget to tell her I said so, now."

"Take care, Dupree."

"As always, Émile, that depends."

Cinq-Mars put the phone down and smiled at Sandra. "Thanks for the water. I felt I was back down south, parched. Detective Dupree sends his regards. He thinks you're a fine woman."

"I'm glad you didn't argue the point."

His next call went through to Agent Vira Sivak.

"Who this time?" Sandra asked, but he put a forefinger to his lips to request silence. The agent was answering.

"It's Émile Cinq-Mars calling," he said.

"I know," she replied.

"Modern devices, hey? More information than you can shake a stick at."

"How are you, Mr. Cinq-Mars?"

He didn't know if it was because she was a woman that they spent time on the niceties, but he was certainly equally to blame. When they fell to silence, having discussed their general health and the business of modern life, he piped up with another innocuous question, this time about the weather. They wound up chuckling, for despite living in decidedly different climates, they both described their current conditions as *mild.* Which pleased them both.

"Traveling much?" he asked her then.

A momentary pause to process the odd query.

"Not at all. Why do you ask?"

He might have answered, *because it's a technique, to wander all over the map so that the person you're talking to doesn't know where on the map you are.* Instead he said, "Idle curiosity. Just popped out. But to get back to my original thought . . ." He wondered if she could get back to that thought, notwithstanding that he had made it virtually impossible.

Agent Sivak gave up on the quiz and asked, "Which is?"

If nothing else, he had lulled her into believing that he was a tad dim, or at the very least, past it. A view that Sandra, listening in, seemed willing to validate.

"Modern devices, Agent Sivak, and the information they reveal. Aren't they something? I have a favor to ask, Agent."

"Anything at all, Mr. Cinq-Mars."

Perhaps he should not have insisted on being called *mister.* If she was addressing him as Sergeant-Detective he might feel less sensitive to being patronized.

"That's incredibly kind of you. I was talking to Detective Dupree recently."

"How is he?"

This time, she was the guilty party and he was not going to indulge the pleasantry. "Ah, he seemed fine. I could have asked this favor of him, but I'm not sure that he has the resources for me to trust the result."

"As I said, anything you'd like, Mr. Cinq-Mars."

He realized then that she pronounced his name remarkably well for an American. "Do you speak French, Agent Sivak?"

She laughed. "I'm sure you didn't call to find that out."

"I'll take that as a yes. As I was saying, isn't modern technology wonderful? A long-distance call used to be a big deal, *especially* if I was calling the States. Now, a penny a minute, or less than a penny, a fraction, I can't remember now. To my mind, it's virtually free. So I'm happy to talk all day."

"Except that you want a favor from me that has something to do with modern technology, and if you don't ask the question you won't get an answer."

She was on the ball, this one, he had to give her that.

"The night of my wife's abduction—"

"Yes?"

"Everardo Flores received a phone call, to his mobile device—I don't even know if we can call them phones anymore, they do so many things."

"And what about that call, Mr. Cinq-Mars?"

"Could you trace it for me?"

"I'm sorry. Trace it? Which call?"

"The one from the hotel to his mobile device asking him to return to work."

Her slow way of speaking suggested that she was doubting his intelligence or sanity again. "The call went from his hotel to his phone. What is there to trace?"

"Oh, you know what I mean."

She didn't.

"Not trace. Track. Or something. Can you find out for me where he was when he received that call? Where on a Google map we might stick a pin? He said he was on his way home. I will feel more comfortable knowing that that was the case."

"And not up to the mischief regarding your wife, in other words."

"It's a process of elimination."

"All right. I'll be happy to do that, Mr. Cinq-Mars. Is there anything else?"

"Possibly."

"What's that?"

"Alabama. Would you consider going? In my stead, as it were. Apparently, as you know, my wife and myself are to be harmed if we venture into the United States. Maybe we can go for a swim and a nosh just over the border, but we don't really know that, do we? I hope she can visit her family. But anything related to business, police business, I mean, supposedly will result in harm to Sandra and myself. I realize that you're busy. I understand."

"What's in Alabama?"

"The next of the storm murders in the series. I was hoping that you might poke around. But I know you're busy. It is an imposition."

With some reluctance, she agreed to consider his request. Something that Cinq-Mars was not expecting. Then she broached a matter of her own. "Sir?"

"Yes?"

"Do you mind, if, when I phone you, I call you *Émile?* I have reasons to ask."

"Reasons? You don't need a reason. May I then call you Vira?"

"Thank you. I just wanted you to understand that—" She paused. This might be one of the times she was talking about.

"On occasion, you may want the call to sound informal." Émile said what she was not free to explain at that moment. "In case someone is listening in from the desk next to yours. You want a colleague to think it's a personal call."

"That's more or less the size of it."

"No problem."

He said to Sandra, after hanging up, "She'll consider going. To Alabama. I can't believe it."

"Excuse me if I'm not as enthused as you," she said.

"What's wrong?"

"*We* were supposed to go, Émile. She's going on my holiday instead of me. I don't find that thrilling."

Point taken.

"Yeah, San, but we might've gotten ourselves killed."

That point was taken as well.

She pressed him on what had just transpired. "So, you have the NOPD work with Flores to help us, and then you cajole the FBI into investigating him. One department works with him, one works against him. Émile? What's up with that?"

He wished that he was drinking something other than water, but persevered with his glass. He did feel parched, possibly brought on by the recent changes in climate.

"It's complicated, and contradictory, I'll grant you that," he said. "The right and left hands of this operation won't know what I'm doing or if I'm progressing. I want people to find it hard to differentiate between up and down or left and right."

Sandra asked, "And this is important why?"

He decided that he had no good reason to deprive himself. He drank down the last of the water and headed for the liquor cabinet. So what if it was early.

"This is the only case I've ever worked or known about," he told her as he poured a Talisker, "where the only people I've interviewed have all been cops. I'm including hotel security in that group, but you know what I mean. Plus, it must be said, I'd know a whole lot more about this case if only half those officers weren't lying. So if cops want to keep me in the dark, then I'll give them a taste of their own medicine. Not to be mean, just to be cautious here. I've learned the value of caution on this case."

Sitting, listening, and observing him, Sandra Cinq-Mars hoped that he had.

TWENTY

At slow speed, Sergeant Pascal Dupree drove Everardo Flores away from the Hilton, where they'd met up, to St. Bernard Parish, a neighborhood heavily damaged by Hurricane Katrina that in its comeback retained a mere semblance of its former impoverished self. Grace on spindly legs.

He coached him along the way.

"Y'all comprehend that you're not on the job, right? Don't ever say so. I can't emphasize that strongly enough, Everardo. Where your ambitions lie is not a particular concern to me. What *is* a concern is this—y'all will not speak aloud to a single soul about doing police work, because nobody has your back. Not me, especially." With his hands low on the steering wheel where it swung over his belly, Dupree looked across at his new confederate. "I hope y'all are hearing me, Flores, because I'm not seeing the disposition of a man who appears to be listening."

Flores was happily gazing out the window in the opposite direction. He smiled and turned his head around to answer Dupree's challenge. "I'm not a cop, but you got to admit, I'm working *for* the cops."

"Don't go around saying that out loud! It's not like we're popular with folks."

"Dupree, you're hated less than you think. Chill. The time the force decked itself out in its powder blues—who can forget that day?—people on the street, they cheered."

After Katrina, the NOPD underwent a change of uniform. To present a fresh public image, beat cops adopted the dark blues familiar to other cities. A few years later, revamped, wiser now, they returned to their original, distinctive powder blues. They showed them off on the first day of Mardi Gras. People welcomed the reversion. As if the worst of the past was put behind them by bringing back the familiar.

"Don't anticipate nobody cheering you in the field. The contrary."

"Airmen don't throw flowers at the feet of military police neither. Been there. You know I found that out."

Dupree offered a conciliatory nod, but he wasn't finished. He had a way of emphasizing his words by squeezing the steering wheel, which highlighted the massive size and considerable strength of his hands. The action felt threatening, whether he meant it that way or not. "In the air force, Everardo, I take it y'all had genuine authority. Not make-believe like now. Some drunken flyboy gave lip, y'all whacked him over the head and took him in. Didn't you? Admit it, now."

"Or, I whacked him over the head some more and left him where he lay. Depends on what kind of night it was. How much trouble he was worth."

"There you go. See? That's no longer a consideration."

"I don't aim to pick a fight. Will you let up on me or what, Dupree?"

The detective was not about to do that. Flores had to endure his initiation or have the rug pulled out from under this scheme. His choice. At a red light, the detective stared at the thin, spiffy man in the gray suit and the blue tie and squeezed the wheel with his chubby fingers until Flores grimaced and pleaded for mercy. "All right, Dupree. I get you. I got you an hour ago. Chill, man."

"What I'm telling y'all now, Émile Cinq-Mars himself don't know."

"What's that?"

"This is a damn near impossible assignment."

He detailed why. Situated close to the 9th Ward and the district of Holy Cross, and similarly to those two forlorn neighborhoods, St. Bernard Parish had also been utterly ransacked by the storm. Hundreds of its former residents never came back. Countless others returned, saw that nothing awaited them there except ongoing misery, and decamped for good. For anyone to wander around the neighborhood and ask people to recall a double murder that happened shortly after the worst of that time—to even find someone who'd been through it who cared enough to share a memory—that was asking a lot, more than Émile Cinq-Mars realized. The Montreal detective didn't grasp the factors at play. He thought he could waltz into the parish and *parlez* his *français*, chat up the neighbors, draw down a few opinions, jumble them together, and find out what that concoction brewed. He didn't know that chatting up a neighbor required luck, for starters, diligence, more time than he'd imagined or allotted for himself, and the good graces of many. He might be diligent, but luck and a good attitude were in failing supply throughout the parish.

"So, you're saying," Flores countered, "that I'm just here to—"

"To *appease* that Montreal detective, to make it look good for us down here, or, if you're really lucky, stumble across a miracle. I hope you got miracles stuck up your crack 'cause otherwise this is a major waste of everybody's time, and I mean by that especially yours. Just so y'all know it."

Truth was, Dupree held higher hopes than that, but he wanted to douse Everardo Flores with Katrina floodwaters—to impress upon him that this was not an easy gig. If he expected otherwise, he might fold his tent before his first hour was up.

"I'll drive by to pick up your carcass later. If I see some sign of life, if I detect a pulse, I'll call for an ambulance. But next time y'all want to come out here, expect to drive your own vehicle in both directions. I'm revoking your limousine privileges."

"No problem, Detective. It's a pleasure riding with you though. More than that, it's an honor. Good times."

"This is business, you understand that, right? It's not peaches and cream."

"Listen, if I enjoy myself, you have to live with that. So brace yourself. I know this operation is not about making me a rich man."

"Operation. It's not an *operation*." He turned to confront Flores again. "Base expenses," he reminded him. "That's it."

"Like I said, life being what it is, wealth is bound to elude me in mine."

"Keep your head up. Eyes and ears open."

"That's my style, Detective. You just said it. I keep my head up and my eyes down and my ears crossed and I get by with all that. You'll see. Maybe you'll recommend me to the academy one day soon. Help me get a badge to call my own."

Dupree stopped the car. A squabble of men already were checking them out from across the street. Under ball caps and sunglasses, they moved their shoulders and limbs with a certain lassitude that claimed this block as indisputably their own. A young, obviously homeless woman checked the litter blown up against a car tire. "This is where I set you free."

"So no badge today, huh?"

He didn't know if Flores was deliberately trying to irritate him or was actually that naïve. Fortunately, the man chuckled happily as he disembarked.

"You have a good day, Detective," Flores remarked.

"You, too, Everardo. Try to stay alive, all right? I got enough to do."

As Dupree drove off, Flores looked around the moonscape of St. Bernard Parish. He double-checked the street sign against the address in his notebook. He never looked at the men across the street, who were keeping an eye on him, as that would only invite trouble, and instead went up to a door and knocked. Walking on the porch provoked a nest of ants to march on down through gaps in the floorboards. Flores showed his hotel security badge to the wisp of an old woman who appeared behind the screen. "New Orleans Police, ma'am. Do you mind if I have a word with you on a matter of some dire importance here today?"

"What's this about, Officer?" the diminutive frail dear inquired. Behind the thick lenses of her glasses she looked all but blind, the eyes magnified to saucer-size. Tiny, she flouted a tall stack of stiff hair dyed auburn and the brown skin of her arms hung loosely over skinny bones. Her shoulders poked up as raw, sharp nubs.

"Murder, ma'am. That plain, that simple, sorry to say. Don't we live in a hardened old world?"

She opened the screen door to let him inside. "I try my darnedest to keep the flies out, Officer," she told him.

Flores remarked, "Yes, ma'am. I will try not to admit any in myself."

"They're pesky."

"They are."

"What murder?" she asked, wide-eyed, trembling, as the door banged shut. She looked all around and above his head for flies.

"The killings next door, ma'am. Were y'all here for Katrina? Those ones. The killings next door."

Émile Cinq-Mars did a measure of homework before initiating a few strategic calls. As a result of that he was heading for a farmer's co-op some twenty kliks away. He telephoned the farmer who put in the actual work on Morris and Adele Lumen's fields—planting a crop each spring and reaping the harvest while the couple took back a modest percentage for themselves, a sweetheart deal all around. The man sounded cheerful and friendly and indicated that he'd be happy to meet him, but at that moment he was heading to the co-op, partly to shop, mainly to hang out with friends, a weekly confab at a set time, which was why he needed to embark right away. The ex-cop couldn't believe his luck. He wasn't planning to set up a meeting that day, but now begged to join the man at his, unable to pass on an opportunity to quiz a gaggle of nearby farmers all at once. So he was off to meet those men, to whittle away at opinions they may have formed over the years about the deceased couple or to hear of anything unusual someone may have noticed around the time of the murders. Typically, men of their background might prove reticent around an official—they were bound to be territorial and wary of an outsider—so as he drove Cinq-Mars devised a plan to help open things up.

The nondescript box store sat on the outskirts of a one-street hamlet, similar to other hardware stores across the continent except that it did not carry the name of a chain and was smaller than most of those that did. A cooperative, anyone was welcome to shop there, but the shareholders were local farmers who participated in the success of the enterprise.

Michel Chaloult was the fellow working the Lumens' farm, not quite a next-door neighbor to them, but close enough that he could take a back road onto their property on his bouncy tractor in about thirty minutes. "Ten minutes the long way around on the roads by car." His home was as far from the co-op as Émile's, but each man was traveling from a different direction, one from the east, the other from the southwest. Cinq-Mars frequently shopped at the store for bulk supplies and farm implements, but he could discern upon entering that the place was akin to home for a few patrons. At least in the wintertime. For them it held the ambiance of a local pub, and they made it so with their gentle gab and laughter.

In the corner farthest from the entrance, men pulled up chairs in a widening of the aisle just off the hardware section. A heavy curtain guarded against drafts from the rear storage area where they sat amid a modest collection of basic American Standard toilets, sinks, and tubs. As each farmer arrived he reached behind the curtain to lay claim to his personal chair, a Windsor or a bent metal folding contraption or an old hardback with peeling paint or worn varnish. A man motioned to Cinq-Mars after he introduced himself and selected a chair for him.

"Here, sit on old Henri's."

A folding type with a soft seat. Wobbly. "Henri?" Cinq-Mars asked.

"Hospital," the man murmured.

"Cancer," another man revealed.

"Terminal," added a third.

"Oh," Cinq-Mars said. "I'm sorry to hear that." He sat. His weight steadied it.

"Prostate," Michel Chaloult verified for him. Not a loquacious gang, initially. They seemed able to express themselves, and capably, with single words only.

The first farmer who had spoken remarked, "When it's your time it's your time," and the others nodded in philosophical unison.

Sanguine, Cinq-Mars considered, taking note that they kept the chair of the ill man around, perhaps holding out for his miraculous recovery.

Most of the men, including Michel Chaloult, were in their fifties, although any one of them could pass for sixty-five. They possessed the weathered look of farmers, muscled, leathery, a resignation in their facial expressions as well as a brittle tenacity. Stiff wind in the crevices on their cheeks and brows, the dust of the soil around their eyes. Although they readily fell into shared, prolonged silences, and Cinq-Mars followed them into those communal meditations, when they got going they jumped over each other to speak—about cows, snow, acquaintances, politics, hockey—everyone percolating at once so that it seemed to a rank outsider impossible for a single voice to be heard.

And yet, he perceived at one juncture, as they emerged from a brief flurry, they were willing to give him the floor. They wanted to know who he was and what he was doing there. Despite his big-city reputation, these fellows seemed not to know of him, although the youngest, in his early forties, believed that he had heard the name. His surname was rare enough that the farmer might well have caught it on the news one day, and he was correct to apply it to this former cop. That's all it took for Cinq-Mars to acquire significant status.

He explained his intentions in vague terms. His remarks were failing to provoke any outpouring of commentary, and when he was interrupted by a fresh arrival, he was obliged to begin again.

On this second go-round, he made sure to emphasize that, like them, he lived on a farm and that he raised horses.

"To eat?" Michel Chaloult teased him. The men chuckled to themselves.

"To race?" asked another man, perhaps more seriously, but perhaps not.

He knew better than to answer this challenge by saying *show jumping,* or worse, *dressage.* "I raise horses," Cinq-Mars stated, "for men with deep pockets to buy for their spoiled daughters."

They liked that. They laughed a lot.

"We don't have any at the moment, but from time to time we raise and train—and sell, of course—polo horses."

He was different from them, but he lived off the land, like them. They welcomed him into their rather squared-off circle.

They were now eight. The clumping of chairs formed more of a rectangle than a circle. A path remained free should an unsuspecting paying customer slip in at the wrong time to price a toilet. Cinq-Mars suspected that that seeker-of-toilets might then be blitzed with advice, if not become the recipient of a subtle and good-natured mockery. He, on the other hand, was actually seeking information, which was moderately suspicious to them all, so it would not be readily forthcoming. He tried a new tangent.

"Did you hear? The property is going up for sale."

"What property?"

"The couple who were shot. The Lumens. Their farm."

"You heard that?"

"Yeah. I did. Of course, I asked."

"Who'd you ask?"

"They left the farm to a charity."

"No relatives to inherit it?"

"Do you know of any?"

"No. Can't say—Nope. Never heard of any."

"Neither has anyone else," Cinq-Mars let them know. "They left the farm to a hospital in the States. I talked to them. The hospital plans to sell. What else would they do with a farm in Quebec, eh? They'll be cashing in sooner rather than later."

"We were wondering about that."

"I thought you might be. Do any of you expect to buy?"

The question instigated a renewed quiet, but this time it did not feel the same as one of their odd mute progressions. An uneasiness traipsed through and among the men, and they shot indiscriminate glances at one another.

Finally, a man spoke up. He was the only one among them who made a point of dressing in the role of a farmer, in coveralls and a heavy plaid shirt, with a pipe poking out from a pocket, and he was a man who possessed in spades the sharp features of nose and chin, cheekbones and forehead, associated with the Québécois. The look allowed for a smidgen of Indian blood, mixed as well with a generation of Irish settlers' blood at a time in history. This man, despite his clothing style, struck Cinq-Mars as being the sage one in their midst, the thoughtful man behind his plow. To emphasize what he wanted to say, he withdrew his unlit pipe from its dedicated pocket—they couldn't smoke in here—to utilize as a pointer.

"Think about this," he declared, and Cinq-Mars noticed that, for once, no one was speaking concurrently, that as long as this gentleman was pontificating on an issue everyone listened. "Michel Chaloult, he's been working that farm, so he has first dibs. We won't create a competition, taking money out of my mouth or his mouth or your mouth to drive up the price of the property. Farming does not pay so well these days that a poor man can afford fantastic prices for a mediocre patch."

Others were nodding, learning how the affair ought to be conducted. "If somebody comes from the outside—" and the sage cast a rather pointed glance at Cinq-Mars, "who wants the property, then we have a right to respond. Maybe four of us will chip in to bid the farm, split it into quarters later. But for now, if Michel wants it, he's earned the right to bid on it without the rest of us jacking up the price."

Émile Cinq-Mars was not concerned that the man had separated him out from the crowd and had voiced an underlying suspicion. He could work with that.

"That sounds like a good plan," he said. "I'm personally not interested in the farm, but I'll tell you something, I might be interested in the barn. So whoever buys the land, keep that in mind. If you already have a barn that's good enough for you, you might have a buyer for this other barn. It's not big, but I could use a well-built barn that's not too big. And if you rent out the house to somebody from the city, they probably won't need the barn either. So keep that in mind."

The slight bobbing of heads continued as Cinq-Mars was being received into their enclave. He was here on police business, they knew, but they had also found common ground to share with him, which made him, if not one of their own, then at least one with whom they could exchange a laugh, or a covert drink, or an understanding. That made the whole police business a less formidable barrier.

They were not heavy drinkers, but a flask was passed around and Cinq-Mars joined the others for a nip. A Canadian whisky, he judged, nothing to write home about, but acceptable. Considering the environment, better than expected. He had anticipated nothing more than cider or coffee-flavored mud.

He finally got down to brass tacks. "I was wondering about Adele and Morris Lumen. Obviously, we want justice. But the police have discovered that it's very hard to locate any information on them. They seem to have come out of nowhere. Is that your impression?"

"They left everything to a hospital, you said?" one guy asked. He struck Cinq-Mars as being a hale man, without a lazy bone in his body. He suspected that the man had endured some stresses over time, probably a few sad losses, although he could not readily define why he thought that way, just a look around and within the eyes. A hunch, maybe. His teeth were his oddest feature, notable for the width of the gaps between so many of them even though he was not missing any. "I mean, that makes a kind of sense in a way. We never saw no family. No kids. Or grandkids. No parties. Never nothing like that."

"They stuck to themselves, but they were friendly, too," another man recalled. "The wife never entered the contests for the fair, you know, for the pies and that, but she came out to see the ladies just the same, to find out how they did, that sort of thing. She cheered them on."

"The woman in particular, she liked to laugh."

"She did. She had a big belly laugh."

"She had a big belly."

"You could hear her laughing across a room."

"Across town."

"He was quiet though, the man. Morris, his name."

"Like a mouse."

"He never laughed much. Don't get me wrong. He smiled. Sometimes he even had a big grin on him. Like he was laughing on the inside. But he never came right out with it. He just kind of looked away when other people—or his wife herself—were laughing away."

Cinq-Mars had the impression that these men had discussed these matters previously, probably soon after the couple were killed, so in a way they were running down their remarks as if following a familiar script. He interrupted their loop. "So, you never saw people with them, other than folks from around here?"

They had to puzzle through the question.

"I wouldn't never say never," Michel Chaloult submitted. "When they first got here, you know we were checking them out. I was checking them out."

"Only natural," the sage man concurred.

"What did you see?" Cinq-Mars asked.

"At first, some men came around regular. Three guys once. A couple of guys quite a few times. Don't know who they were. Haven't seen them since."

"They weren't movers? Or tradesmen, fixing the place up?"

"In suits?" Chaloult asked, and he was pleased to draw a few chuckles from his pals.

"Okay, they were in suits," Cinq-Mars noted, and to make it official he wrote that down on his pad. *Suits.*

"They drove black cars. Not trucks or pickups. Newer cars. Fancy ones. The kind you don't see plumbers or electricians driving to work."

"Or movers," another added, getting less of a laugh than Chaloult.

Black cars, Cinq-Mars wrote down. "Only men. No women. Did you ever meet these guys?" he asked.

"Once," Michel Chaloult told him. "That's the time I started talking to him about working his farm. The wife—mine, I mean—she baked them a pie, and a dinner, some kind of casserole. New neighbors, we don't get those too often, so that's what you do. You bring over a casserole and you say hello."

"You were introduced to these other men?" Cinq-Mars asked, trying both to keep him on point and to moderate his own rising excitement.

"Don't ask me their names. But yeah, we were introduced. Nobody said what they were there for and I didn't ask. I'm polite that way. I just presumed they were friends. They smiled. They were friendly in a way, but they didn't stick around."

"French names? English?"

"English. But the Lumens were English."

"Could you describe the men?"

He could, and Cinq-Mars wrote the descriptions down, but he might as well have been describing any men on earth who had short hair, in one instance, or were bald, in the other. The bald guy had biggish ears, as Chaloult had noticed their size at the time. Big lips, too. Cinq-Mars worried that, over time, the image in his head had become a caricature or even a full-blown cartoon. The second man, the one with short hair, sounded remarkably indistinguishable from the majority of forty-year-old Caucasians on earth, but he looked rugged, he had a good stout chest.

"Anything at all that was unique?" Cinq-Mars pressed him.

Chaloult thought about it some more, rubbing the right side of his jaw and drawing his hand down over his Adam's apple. "One thing," he considered, and Cinq-Mars grew hopeful again. "He hadn't shaved in maybe a day." The former policeman fell back into a mild despair. "Oh!" the farmer chimed. Cinq-Mars looked up again, not wanting to become overly expectant, but not being able to help himself either. The man was poking at the side of his face. "He had this like—" He didn't know how to describe it or the word was eluding his lips.

Ever positive, Cinq-Mars asked, "Scar?"

"No."

"Wine-stain?" He knew that he was being excessively optimistic.

"What's that?" Chaloult asked.

"A kind of birthmark, purple. Never mind. What do you remember seeing?"

"I forgot the word for what you call it."

"Pimple?" someone in the group suggested.

Chaloult got upset with him. "I wouldn't tell him about a pimple a man had four years ago! What the hell good is that?"

"What the hell good is it saying he didn't shave for a day?"

Thank you, Cinq-Mars thought.

"Oh, shut up!"

"Describe it, Chaloult!"

The man didn't want to do that. He knew the word and he wanted to bring it to the surface on his own. The other farmers seemed as frustrated with him as the investigator in the room. Cinq-Mars counseled, "Take your time."

A man shot out, "Dimple!" and Chaloult just fumed.

"Relax," Cinq-Mars encouraged him quietly.

He was now squeezing his cheeks as if raising an idea flush to the surface.

Then he said, "I know what it was."

Everyone waited.

"Rosacea."

A few farmers were clueless.

"The curse of the Celts," Cinq-Mars explained. "It's called that sometimes. Red cheeks, as if the person has been drinking. But he hasn't been, necessarily."

"Splotchy skin, he had a case of it," Chaloult recalled.

Of course, the man could've been drinking the night before or had his skin reddened by the sun or the wind, but Cinq-Mars faithfully wrote down *rosacea* on his pad. He asked for the men's relative sizes and received back what he had already suspected, that they were of average height and build, although one was big through the chest.

"Okay," he said. "Thanks."

He sat there listening to the others discuss whatever came to mind. An exercise in random association. The couple came from the Maritimes, they all heard that, but no one heard either of the Lumens say it, yet one man was certain that they came from New Brunswick and another said Nova Scotia, which prompted a third to say that he was pretty damn sure they arrived from Prince Edward Island. One farmer's daughter who worked as a waitress reported that the couple tipped more generously than most people. That instigated a discussion on what constituted a fair tip and Cinq-Mars let it play out. The longer they talked the poorer their prospective tips became. He waited for the right moment before asking his next crucial question.

"They lived on a farm," he mentioned. "But Monsieur Chaloult, you did the work. Do you think they knew anything about farming? Or were they city folk who wanted to live in the countryside for a change?"

Michel Chaloult surprised him, and perhaps surprised them all, for the others seemed unaware that he held to this opinion. "They were farmers," he declared emphatically. "Morris Lumen knew crops. Morris knew corn, for sure. I'd say that Morris knew as much if not more about farming than I do. For some reason I don't understand, he decided not to do it anymore. Why does any man quit farming?"

Everyone proffered an answer to the question. "A physical infirmity, I suppose," the sage man said, as if this was occurring to him for the first time.

"Or a physical calamity."

"Stroke. Heart attack."

"I hate those."

"Doctor's orders," the man with the sadder eyes surmised. Then he issued a swift invective. "Fuck doctor's orders, I say! Up the arse!"

The passionate antipathy took Cinq-Mars by surprise, but the men gathered in the rectangle seemed to have anticipated the volley, as if it was inevitable or at least common. They laughed and those closest to the sadder-eyed man offered him a pat on the shoulder and others in his proximity reached across and lightly tapped his knee. He exchanged a glance with Cinq-Mars, and, ceremoniously, it seemed, rather than apologetically, he shrugged.

The oldest among them, the former policeman offered his thanks and departed. He came away with one more puzzling notation, namely that the murdered man who lived in the farmhouse had been a farmer who had chosen not to engage in his profession despite living on a farm. This case, if anyone could call it that, seemed increasingly strange no matter which way it turned.

witness protection

TWENTY-ONE

The road on which he departed the farmers' cooperative created an illusion of crossing flat land, yet frequent dips into river bottoms and nasty twists through various geographic contours made the trip a challenge. That he was speeding didn't help. He was negotiating a tricky section when his cell phone played a jingle in his overcoat. Émile slowed down, initially to check the caller ID, then to pull off to the side. By a frozen stream in a winding gulley, he stopped.

"Detective Dupree," he answered, "how's it going, sir?"

"I'm seriously pissed off with the universe, myself," the New Orleans cop stated. "You?"

The man had a knack for making him laugh. "I'm in a better mood than you are, Dupree. Who knows why? Mostly I'm spinning my wheels. What's up down there?"

Listening to his response, Cinq-Mars took time to appreciate his surroundings. Without the call, he might never have noticed this place. A quiet stream meandered through the gulley in the summer, water slipping under the road through twin culverts, the shaded indentation out of sight of farmland on the next level up. In winter the stream was iced over, the trees bare, and at the base of the embankment he found himself situated in his own little world. Cinq-Mars was grateful that the operator of a snowplow had taken the trouble to clear a small, safe parking spot. Skeptical of human impulses, he figured the plow's driver had wanted a quiet place out of sight where he could enjoy a snack and a smoke without seeing his paycheck docked.

I might come here again, Cinq-Mars considered, if only to be undisturbed.

Dupree was going on about a number of inconsequential inconveniences before he said, "Our man Everardo Flores. May I remind y'all that he was your idea."

"My wife's actually. What's he been up to?"

"Bugger goes around telling people he's a cop! I specifically told him, I warned him, 'Don't tell people you're a cop.' Bugger won't listen."

"How do you know?"

"What?"

"Did you debrief him already?"

"Me? What? I haven't talked to the prick. Y'all think I'd let him run around out there on his own? I got an undercover dolled up as a bag lady tracing his steps, to keep tabs on what damage he does."

"I hope she's a woman, your undercover. What damage is he doing?" A small flock of cedar waxwings descended onto a nearby limb. Cinq-Mars leaned over the steering wheel to observe them. Knowing that it wasn't cold out, he opened the front door with his opposite hand and held the phone in his left, and stepped out into the brisk, clear air. The birds flew up, but settled back down again.

"I won't call it havoc," Dupree related. "Not yet. But he's got no business telling people he's a cop. That's way against orders."

"I hear you, Dupree. But he's a volunteer, right? He's not really under orders. If he's not doing any damage maybe he's finding something out."

"Pisses me off, my man."

Cinq-Mars laughed a little. "I'd have his hide if he was working under me. Look, I appreciate your procedure, Dupree, keeping an eye on him and all that. How did you swing it?"

"Officially? My undercover's people assigned to drug-check the neighborhood. Won't be too hard to clock visible hours, bust a few. This way, neither my boss nor the neighborhood knows what's up. At least, they didn't until that bonehead Flores told folks he's a cop. Undermines the whole point of using him, you know?"

"I appreciate what you're doing."

"Let's see what he comes up with before anybody appreciates a damn thing. Sorry to take up your time, Émile. Needed to vent."

"Gotcha. You take good care, Dupree."

He was rushing the call as another one was coming in. His quiet roadside spot was an information highway. "Agent Sivak, how are you?"

"Fine, Émile! How are things up there at the North Pole?"

"So-so. Santa's grumpy. The elves are dipsomaniacs. Everyone's depressed, post-Christmas. Up here we believe in Santa Claus, but we have serious doubts about spring. And you, staying clear of crocodiles?"

"Only alligators in our swamps, Émile."

"I have a hard time keeping that straight."

"Think of Crocodile Dundee. What country?"

Cinq-Mars hesitated. He'd seen that movie. "Australia."

"There you go."

"Okay. Got it. So no alligators nibbling at your toes?"

"Oh, I wish," she said, which he didn't get for a moment. "So about your Mr. Flores."

A popular subject today, apparently. "What of him?"

"He never went home."

"What?"

"On the night of your wife's abduction—you asked me to check—he never made it home."

"No, but he was *heading* home, right?"

"Wrong. We ran down the hotel's call to him, per your request. That wasn't easy, by the way. We have procedures in the FBI to track the GPS on phone calls and I wasn't following them. What I'm saying is, you owe me, because this can reach back and bite me. But anyway, he never made it home, Émile. He never left a four-block radius of the Hilton."

"No shit. Excuse my, well, my English."

"That's what I said when I found out. No shit. What do you make of them apples?"

"I was thinking to myself this morning, Agent Sivak—"

"Vira is fine with me. We covered this, remember?"

"Sorry. Vira. Nothing in this matter is anything other than strange. Don't you find that?"

"I'm off to Alabama," she interjected out of the blue. "Shortly."

Something in her tone felt consequential. "Great. I appreciate it."

"No problem. It's not on my own time. I had a talk with Special Agent Dreher. He thinks I should go but I have to do it on the sly, an officially unofficial type thing. Still. Maybe we can figure something out."

"It's a long shot. I know that. But thanks. So, what do you make of this Flores thing? I'm still trying to process the news."

"I know, hey? Isn't that something? He's lying through his teeth. But who knows about what or why. Soon as I have a minute, I'll challenge him on that. I'll also track down the location where he was really at, see what that gives us."

Cinq-Mars thought about it and tromped the snow underfoot. "If you don't mind, Vira, can we hold the first part of that in our hip pocket? I'll ask him myself when the time seems opportune, or you can, but I'd like to feel him out more before we point out to him that he's a lying skunk."

"Fair enough. But only until I get back. After that, I treat him as a person-of-interest in your wife's kidnapping. You know how it goes, Émile. I'm obliged to at least make it look like I'm doing something. I'm even obliged to do something."

"I understand, Vira. Again, I appreciate the cooperation. It's splendid."

"So, Émile," Sivak began, then paused.

"Yeah?" She had given him vital information about Everardo Flores, but her tone suggested that what she said next constituted the real point of her call.

"Like I said, I was talking to Agent Rand Dreher."

"Right."

"He was thinking out loud, you know?'

"Not about me," Cinq-Mars said.

"Yeah, actually, about you. He's wondering if he can come out from under his desk now, give you a call."

"I've been trying to get that message to him."

"He knows. But he worries he's being baited."

"He should call me, Vira."

"I'll let him know. Expect a call. By the way, he's in Montreal."

"What?"

"Up there to see you, I think. Once he summons the courage."

"Thanks for the heads-up. And thanks for the word on Flores. That's nothing if not interesting."

"Something I thought you should know."

Before moving on, Émile stood in the winter grove, among the birds and rocks, the trees and the stream. This was what retirement was supposed to have looked like, no? Spending time in beautiful quiet places. He had never developed a clear plan for his senior years, so perhaps that was the problem. Here he was instead, now as ever, crime-fighting.

Everardo Flores worked diligently down one side of his designated street and back up the other, an investigation that took less time than anticipated as most people had nothing to say. No one remembered the Katrina murders in any worthwhile detail. Back then, they were all too busy trying to stay alive themselves, a response he had no reason not to accept at face value. A few folks, including the first woman he talked to, remembered the dead couple, although the principal component of everyone's collective memory was that they kept to themselves and said little. They rarely had visitors. No family came around that anyone could recall. One woman thought she heard that they were not from New Orleans originally, nor even Louisiana, that they came from somewhere "north of the Mississippi delta," which in Flores's view narrowed it down to roughly forty-nine states and the District of Columbia.

Having tramped up and down two blocks, he thought he might call Dupree for a lift back when he noticed that houses on the side of the street where the murder victims once lived backed onto those on the next street over. The space between them was composed of yards that bordered one another, separated by fences. The victims might as easily have shared conversation out back as off their front stoop. So he started knocking on doors the next street over.

In the house directly behind the victims' home, he met a man who remembered the dead couple well. He professed to knowing them, whereas everyone else, if they remembered them at all, did so in passing, as someone might recall a shade tree that once stood on a corner lot. The man took him out to the backyard, cracked open a beer for Everardo Flores, and told him all that popped to mind.

Flores scribbled down that the dead neighbor, the husband, claimed to be a farmer from Nebraska. "He had the calluses on his hands to show for it, too." But he chose to quit that hardscrabble life. "Don't know if he was blowin' smoke up the chimney stack," the neighbor mused. "'It's not like I owned the Ponderosa,' is what he said to me one time," and the neighbor mimicked the dead man's voice. "'Black dirt farmers, poor like me, work a dry patch of dirt without no promise of rain. If folks paid hard cash for rocks 'n' stones, I'd do plenty good for myself. Except I raised corn. Most years, it's dry rock land, hot as cinders at the end of a bonfire.'

"Here's where my confusion comes into it," the dead man's neighbor reported to Flores. "The man had some nostalgia in him for those harder times. He'd tell me how much trouble it been, how poor he been, how cruel his stone fields got to be to him some years not to mention untimely squirts of rain, too much or too little, but he missed those days, I could tell. He had the nostalgia in him for his scorched land."

"I guess," Flores opined, "that became more true when somebody stuck a knife into him down here."

"Sliced across his neck, actually. So the paper said. All the misery in this town in those bad days, you'd think no man would heap more upon a soul or cause a body to suffer. We think that way but he's a dead man now because that's not the truth of it. Always somebody has to go inflict more painfulness. They wanted his head cut off him, but I don't know why."

They seemed to be done, and Flores was finishing up the most welcomed of beers, when the wistful neighbor added, "Still, now."

"Hmm?"

"He had a house to live in, didn't he? And yet he had no, what they call, 'visible means of support.' So, what was his invisible means? He said the farm. That sale. So it must have been something, not nothing to support him. And then."

The neighbor shook his head as he reflected upon the vagaries of life.

"And then?" Flores encouraged him.

"I solemnly swear that his was the misfortune to die a sorry death at exactly the time when good luck turned its head to shine its own clear eye on him."

"What good luck? What eye? Not Katrina's."

The man looked at Flores as if he had a screw loose.

"No, okay, not Katrina's," Flores corrected himself. "But what good luck?"

"The insurance company's. That eye. A few of us had the insurance. I did, that poor dead couple did, but I had to wait myself, and most of us around here had to wait months, some years, before any insurance company took any good notice of our plight. Oh, they knew we were here all right, waiting on them, but they said they needed the time and more time to get around to everybody standing with an empty hat in their hand stuck out. Myself, I think they were waiting for us to die off in that meantime it took to get around to see if any of us were staying alive. Gifford was one who died. That's his name, I remember it now although I never said it often. Gifford, he had an adjustor on his doorstep before nobody could imagine such a thing."

The hotel security man considered the news. Life seemed unfair so often. Especially, perhaps, down here in St. Bernard Parish. "Too bad he never lived to collect on that insurance."

"Too bad. Me, I'm still waiting on mine, although they did give me some down on account."

"Did they?"

"Generous fuckers, hey? But they were expecting me to die sooner, not later."

Everardo Flores was led back through the musty house and was almost out the front door when a thought occurred. He was about to let it go, but then he supposed that if he was going to be telling people he was a cop he might as well behave like one. "Sir, this insurance claims adjustor who came around. The one on Gifford's doorstep. What did he look like? Do you remember that?"

"White guy," the neighbor declared. "That's about all I recall now. Not nothing about him to distinguish himself. Just another white man looking skittish in a black man's parish. He never knocked on my door, that much I can tell you for certain, without no word of a lie going on there."

Cinq-Mars arrived home to learn that Special Agent Rand Dreher finally had telephoned. That the man declined to leave a message maddened him.

"So he just called, said hello, then good-bye?"

"More or less," Sandra told him. "He asked how I was doing."

"Sweet of him."

"I'm sure it was nothing of the kind." She was amused by her husband's consternation. "He asked after me, said he was glad that things turned out okay in the end, in New Orleans. I asked him if he wanted to leave you a message—"

"But he just said no. I can't believe it. Is he going to call me back even?"

"He didn't say. He said—"

"*No.* What a twit. I'm going to call the bastard myself."

"If you will let me finish, Émile."

Émile looked across at her, realizing that he hadn't allowed her to complete her thought. He stooped down slightly and ruffled the ears of his dog, Merlin. Trickles, the house cat, who lived a privileged existence when compared to the lives of the barn cats, chose that moment to head upstairs. Nap time, Émile supposed.

"He said it was fine, no message was necessary, but he expected to meet up with you soon. He wished me a nice day. I wished him one also."

"Bastard."

"Why is he a bastard?"

"Because he's trying to get me to call him because he's too damn proud—and/or chickenshit—to call me." He stretched all the way up as he returned fully upright. The dog, satisfied for once, returned to its cushion and curled for a nap of his own.

"But he did call you. And who's too proud not to call whom?"

"He could've called me back on my cell. Why didn't he? He has the number. What's the good of these ridiculous things if people don't use them?"

Sandra laughed out loud this time, briefly. "You could—I know, this is a radical concept for you—but *you* could call him back on *his* cell phone. I did tell him, you know, that you were probably on the road. Driving. He may have deduced that it was not the best time to call."

"Bastard." He was tempted to call him back, too. Give him a bigger piece of his mind about New Orleans. Not that any of it was the FBI's fault, but could he not have forewarned him, at least, to leave his wife at home? Rather than make that call, fuming still, Cinq-Mars opted for a Highland Park.

Later, down in his basement, he confronted the easel set up with a large flip chart. He hadn't managed to put much on it. Today he added notes from his conversation at the co-op that included the general descriptions of the men noticed on the farm when the Lumens moved there. Doing so energized him, and Cinq-Mars flipped pages to inscribe other descriptions, in large print, of everyone associated with the case. Easiest were the facial blotches of Jefferson Grant, less satisfying were his attempts to describe the pickpockets—Latino, small, slick, well-dressed—as were the height and weight of the men on the Lumens' property: *average*. Every cop alive hated *average*. Still, he wrote down the dreaded word. And, although he had to check the spelling, he wrote the word that Michel Chaloult had summoned: *rosacea*.

Given he was using large print on the poster-sized pages, they were soon adding up. He considered that he was gathering more intelligence than he thought, and when committed to paper it looked more substantial than he previously imagined. In surveying his final effort, flipping the big sheets over, he also determined that he was arriving precisely nowhere in his investigation—he didn't even want to call it an investigation, for fear of disrespecting both the word and the activity—that nothing here gave him a snowball's chance in Hades of unravelling the case anytime soon. He was panning for gold and needed another ton of information to sift through to find the nugget worth saving. Mostly, he required suspects. Still, his handsome flowchart seemed to mark, at least, the suggestion of a start, and Cinq-Mars took solace in that.

Done, he could help Noel, their hired man, water the horses, groom one out of habit more than necessity now, then tuck into another afternoon Scotch with a renewed sense of accomplishment. He'd done something with his day. If anybody asked, he'd made headway.

Sergeant Pascal Dupree picked up Everardo Flores after his first foray into St. Bernard Parish and immediately excoriated him for daring to call himself a cop. They hadn't yet driven a single block. The hotel security officer was dutifully contrite, sheepish, and profusely apologetic for the next four blocks before he spoke up in defiance of his inquisitor. "Hey!"

"Hey, what?" Dupree asked him. "Don't *hey* me, you bastard."

"You never heard me say I was a cop. Who told you?"

Dupree didn't back down an inch. "I smell it on y'all. Stinking up my car! The one thing I asked y'all not to go do, y'all go do! First words out of your skinny mouth, y'all telling people you're wearing cop feathers. What did I tell y'all?"

"How do you know that?" Flores bellowed back. "Who said they were my first words? Did you stick a wire on me?"

"Don't be an idiot. I can't stick a wire on y'all without y'all knowing. I'd like a device like that. Know what? Good idea. I'm going to invent that device and make my fortune. Anyway, what do y'all care how I know? Y'already admitted it to me."

"I only admitted it because you already knew! How did you know?"

"Everardo, get with the program, it's an old cop trick. *Pretend* y'all know what is suspected, let the perp imagine that he's toast, then let him own up to the crime."

"I'm nobody's perp!" Everardo protested, sounding petulant now, although no less chagrined. "I didn't commit a crime!"

"Y'all were tricked. Get over it. Y'all were stupid enough to call yourself a cop. Written all over your face. That's why I warned y'all. Lot of good it did me."

"It helped *me* do the job, all right? If I say, 'Hey, I'm in security down at the Hilton? What do you know about those murders happened over six years ago? Yeah, yeah, like I said, hotel security. So talk to me about the Katrina murders. Excuse me? What does the Hilton care? That's a good question, ma'am. Y'see, the dead couple, they were customers of ours one time and we care about our customers, ma'am. Cradle to the grave, we look after you. Doesn't matter if you never come back to see us. Once a Hilton customer, you're under our protection for your whole lifetime.

Why? Because we consider you family. Now, about those murders.' Hey, Dupree, you ever stayed at a Hilton?"

"Up yours, Flores."

"'Cause if you ever stayed at a Hilton, then me and you, we're like brothers."

"Okay, so you're full of shit. What else is new?"

"*I'm* full of shit? How did you know I told people I was a cop?"

"I had y'all followed."

"What?"

"You think I'd let y'all go out on your own, first time? Listen, I probably saved your life today. Nobody's fond of cops in that neighborhood."

"Now I know why."

A stony silence ensued. They were merging with rush-hour downtown traffic when Dupree recalled the point of the exercise. "What did you find out—nothing?"

"Like I'd tell you."

"Y'all never learned diddly-squat."

"I learned plenty."

"Then tell me."

"Suck my dick willingly, Dupree."

"Will you get off the ramp?" A car was slow to get going.

"What?"

"I'm not talking to you. Come on, Flores, what did you find out?"

"Plenty! Like I said."

"Nothing, I bet."

"Think so? Tell Cinq-Mars to call me. I'll tell him a thing or two."

Dupree had to stop on a red. "This is how things work here. I debrief you."

"Does Cinq-Mars know?"

"Know what?"

"That you were following me in my footsteps."

"Not me personally. I don't think that much of y'all to follow you around. But yeah, actually, he knows."

"Fuckers. The both of you then."

"Flores, come on. It's your first time making the rounds. We have to protect our asses, putting a citizen in harm's way like that. Don't take it so personal. We got procedures, man. We got protocol!"

The comment helped him to cool a tad. "I found out they weren't from here."

"We knew that," Dupree commented.

"Do you want to hear this or not?"

"Sorry. We heard they were from St. Louis. Go on."

"Not St. Lou. Not even Missouri, if you want to know the facts of life. I got close to the only man who got close to the dead couple."

"Y'all didn't." In slow traffic, Dupree almost missed braking for the car in front of him. They lurched forward again.

"Don't kill us, Dupree."

"At this speed? A bump on the nose. Where they from?"

"Nebraska. They were poor black farmers. They quit the farm."

"Yeah?" Dupree asked him. He grabbed a chance to switch lanes and line up for a left turn and took it.

"Yeah," Flores said. They awaited a flashing green.

"That's good, Flores, that's good."

"I can take care of myself, Dupree."

"Flores, everybody says that until they wind up dead. Then they don't say a damn thing anymore. Don't like what I did? Fine. But I don't like it that y'all went around—"

"Saying I was a cop. Okay, I got that yesterday already."

"So we're even, more or less. All right?"

"Fine. But I got more."

"What else?"

"Tell Cinq-Mars to call me."

"Flores—"

"I don't consider us exactly even. We need an equal distribution of the overall punishment here. Tell Cinq-Mars to call me. That's it. That's all."

Dupree made the turn and they were in freer traffic now, not far from the Hilton. "Cinq-Mars knows protocol, Everardo. I'll tell him, but he might not call you."

"Then you better convince him, Dupree. Because he will want to know what I now know. And you don't get to find that out unless he's willing to tell you after I tell him. That's what you get for *protecting* me, as you call it. That's the price you got to pay."

"Fucking civilians," Dupree muttered under his breath.

"Yeah, well, that's what you do regularly, isn't it? That's if you don't just shoot us first for walking on a bridge."

They stopped at the Hilton, where Flores had left his car.

"Will y'all go back there again?" the detective inquired.

"Let Cinq-Mars decide. After I tell him what I found out, he might not see the purpose. Probably he'll ask me to do something bigger than this. Bump me up the ladder. Put me on a payroll. Don't bet against it, Dupree. You'll see."

Half the time Dupree thought the man was an ass, half the time a decent guy. Overall, he figured that that was a better evaluation than he gave most people.

"I just might help y'all get into the academy, Flores, if that's really what you're after," he said.

Although he remained suspicious, the small man lit up. "Really? They like my credentials they say, but they keep pointing out that I'm on the old side. I guess they'll keep saying it until it's true."

"They'll keep saying it until you cross a man's palm."

"What?"

"Grow up. Anyway, being slightly too old can be overcome with the right reference and without no heavy envelope."

"I was hoping so. To get this reference, I got to tell you what I know?"

Parked, Dupree thought about it, but only for a second. "That would be like bribery. I don't want to start y'all on the wrong foot. Cinq-Mars calls you a volunteer. Says I can't order you around. Y'all want to talk to Cinq-Mars? I'll see what I can do. But if I can get you on the force, then from that point forward I'll be free to ream your butt. I'll enjoy that, too. Won't be a thing y'all can do about it then. I might get you on the force purely for the pleasure of my own amusement."

Flores liked all that. He opened his door and had a foot on the pavement when he changed his mind about a few things.

"Look, I'll tell you what I found out, if you want," he said.

"Shove it back up you know where and keep it warm. I'll call Cinq-Mars."

"Thanks, Dupree."

"Fuck y'all." The detective seasoned his pronouncement with a convivial tone.

Flores, happy now, climbed out of the car.

The weather proved mild, but from inside the house the look of the setting sun in the western sky, the light, the particular angle, evoked the season at its nadir, the promise of snow and cold yet to come. The thing that Cinq-Mars enjoyed least about winter was the scarcity of sunlight. So many long hours of darkness. Now that he was retired he was noticing light more, or its absence, perhaps because he rarely visited the bright lights of the city. He was thinking that he should suggest to Sandra that, since New Orleans had been a vacation bust, they take a few days and nights in Montreal, eat and sleep in an atmosphere of luxury. If he got to talk to a few cops during the day, well, what could be the harm in that? He was wondering how best to work up to the suggestion. Be blunt, straightforward? Or set up a romantic interlude to preface the notion? That gentle meditation was interrupted by a ringing telephone.

Sandra raised an eyebrow. The dog cocked an ear. Cinq-Mars glanced over at each of them, then chose to be the one to answer.

"Cinq-Mars."

Sandra rolled her eyes. She didn't understand why he couldn't just say *hello*.

"Émile!" He recognized that voice.

"Agent Dreher," he answered dryly, testily. "How are you?"

"The barbarians are at the gate, Émile."

"Meaning what exactly?"

"Maybe not in droves. There's only me. I'm down the road from your house, ETA in about, oh, less than three minutes—if you let me in the door, that is."

Cinq-Mars hesitated. "How did you know I was here? I thought Sandra told you I was—"

"Out on the road. Heading home. I'm taking a chance and it's worked out. So far, anyway. May I presume to drive up to your house? Will you admit me?"

"See you soon," Cinq-Mars confirmed and hung up. He told Sandra, "We have an imminent guest."

"I'll put the coffee on," she said. Then hesitated. "Will he want dinner?"

"I'm not inviting the FBI to dinner. Not after New Orleans."

She compromised, of course, quickly preparing a veritable feast of hors d'oeuvres by the time the man from the FBI knocked on their front door. The agent had been optimistic with respect to his arrival time, as it took him a full twelve minutes. Time enough for Cinq-Mars to finish his Highland Park and put away the bottle. His hospitality in this instance labored under exacting limits, even if Sandra's did not.

Her presence, and her preparations, gave Dreher an opportunity to insinuate himself within the household for a considerable time, at least another dozen minutes, before having to share a direct word with Émile. When they did sit down alone, the foodstuffs and coffee a proper buffer between them, Special Agent Rand Dreher came across as suitably contrite.

"The case was supposed to be as cold as ice. As frigid as a whore's—I'll spare you. Why would I ever assume otherwise, Émile? I had no idea that trouble would befall you in New Orleans. Except that, you know, you might find some on your own volition. A bodyguard in the background seemed prudent. That's it, that's all. Really, I figured you'd get a taste for the problems in all this, pick up the flavor of the case. If I thought for a moment that you or Sandra were at serious risk, I'd never have asked you to go. Just because you have a great reputation as an investigator in your professional life doesn't make you anything more than a private citizen now. I don't know what happened down there, or why. No one does."

All this pleading. What did he really want from him? Cinq-Mars was quite certain that the man felt no need for forgiveness. With men such as Rand Dreher—not unlike himself—every discussion in life was strategic.

"The kidnappers know who," Cinq-Mars reminded him, "and what, and why. Apparently their only objective was to run me out of town. Why would that be?"

"I'm stumped, Émile. We all are. Everything that occurred was unforeseen."

Cinq-Mars nibbled coffee cake. Laying out the spread, Sandra had warned him not to spoil his supper. *Fat chance.* Smiling then at his silent pun. "We can't always anticipate trouble," he admitted.

"That's the truth. We cannot."

"But in this instance, trouble seems to have been alerted. For God's sake, the NOPD threw some kind of a hissy fit over my arrival. How'd they even know? I had felons waiting in the lobby of my hotel to pick my pocket. How the hell did *they* even know who I was? Let alone that I was there. That's all on your doorstep, Rand."

"Some of it might be. Good intentions, all around. You know how that goes. How the bad guys got wind, well, I myself, I look to the NOPD. If they knew you were coming, maybe one of them baked a cake. Between you and me, and I got nothing to go on, I'm not saying he's in any way involved, but Pascal Dupree? I can throw him farther than I can trust him, and I imagine he's a difficult man to shot put."

Some thought . . . some fleeting memory or reminder . . . crossed Cinq-Mars's face, and Dreher took an interest in whatever had just traipsed through his head.

"Émile? What did that thought provoke? I know you're thinking something."

He wasn't sure at first. Sometimes one thought connects to another yet the recipient of both ideas remains in the dark. Cinq-Mars had to concede that a light had gone on, probably down in the murky depths of his subconscious, and he had to wait a moment for the impulse to float up and acquire some articulation.

"Dreher," he began, taking it slowly, "there's no love lost between the NOPD and the FBI. That doesn't surprise me. Also, frankly, I find it quite boring. If you got along, oh, I don't know, like mature colleagues should, then I might get excited. But no. It's the same old pissing contest between rival cop gangs. But in this case there are specifics to the animosity. Specifics that reference this case. When Dupree investigated the murders of Gifford and Dorsey Lanos, after Katrina, why did the FBI charge along to investigate? How was it any of your business? Those were the first in your series, so at that point you possessed no prior interest. You had no series of murders. That's question one. Other people might propose their own answer but I want to hear your take in particular. A horse's mouth type thing. Answer that and I'll give you another question that's bugging me also."

The man patted down one of his excessively bushy eyebrows before replying. He seemed unperturbed by the query. "Émile, that whole zone was a nightmare's nightmare. Chaos times ten after Katrina. Do you know how many NOPD officers were dismissed for being derelict in their duty around that time?"

Cinq-Mars indicated that he had no clue.

"Guess. Take a wild stab."

Since he was asking, he figured there had to be a lot. "I don't know. Ten?"

"More."

"Twenty?"

"Two hundred."

"What? How many?"

"Sacked. Dismissed. Kicked out. For running away when the levies broke and for other offenses infinitely more vile than that. Two hundred. Every officer had to account for where he was and what he was doing during Katrina, and the runaways were chased off the force for good. So imagine being a cop in New Orleans at the time and you get called in on major crimes, murders included, about every half hour. Meanwhile, your department is in total chaos. Cops are missing. The few who are left are either disorganized or exhausted, usually both. Morale? Forget about it. Some are in shock. Some, as we would find out at Danziger Bridge, are prone to shoot the innocent. So you get called in to a bunch of cases and in the chaos you botch a few investigations. Who're you going to call? Not ghost busters. Even though it might rot your socks, you drop a dime for the FBI. See if they're willing to pitch in. Pull their weight for a change."

"All right," Cinq-Mars conceded. He was wishing now that he hadn't put away his Scotch. "I've heard this argument before but I'm beginning to understand the context. I can accept that it's valid. But here's my next question."

"Go on." Dreher sipped coffee, then placed an elbow on the arm of his chair and covered his mouth slightly with his hand, waiting.

"Especially given that environment, why would the FBI *out* the NOPD?"

"What do you mean, *out*?"

"The NOPD investigates the murders, but misses the killer in the attic. Why alert the press to that, if not to just kick a department, and I think some good cops, at least one good cop, when they're down? That strikes me as unprofessional."

This time, Dreher was objecting, waving the sentiment off. "Yes, yes, Émile, that was the result. But nobody's intention. The story went to the press because word on the street went around that cops had gone in and had a cup of tea with the killers. As if they were in cahoots. We had to get the word out that the killers *hid* in the attic. We let people know because it was the truth, but also—my God, those times were messy, Émile—people thought Dupree and other cops were in on it. Everybody found out that the killers were in the house. So what were the cops up to? Having a chat with them? Doing the tango? Cooking up a barbecue? We thought—it wasn't me but that's not the issue—we thought that if people knew what really happened, that the cops were merely outsmarted by a weird murderer who didn't want to leave the scene of the crime—who could ever anticipate a thing like that?—and so the cops were outwitted by someone who very cleverly hid in the attic—that he was prepared to piss up there in his hiding spot and shit and eat and sleep, everything—then the people would get it. And get off the cops' back. The whole thing got twisted thanks to the press, and the NOPD was made to look foolish. Dupree in particular, I suppose. That was an unfortunate development, an accident no one intended."

A bureaucratic screwup, in other words. A public relations fiasco. He'd been through his share of those and been liable for missteps himself in a couple of instances. Shit happens sometimes.

"Do you see?" Dreher pressed him.

"I do," Cinq-Mars admitted. He didn't really expect Dreher to convince him of anything, and now felt oddly dissatisfied. Dreher was a smart guy, politically astute, obviously, when it came to meeting everyone's concerns yet still pressing forward. A good guy to have in your corner, he believed. Still, he didn't like coming up on the short end of any discussion. "What, ah, what are you doing here anyway?"

"Here in Quebec, you mean?"

Cinq-Mars nodded.

"The SQ called me in," Dreher said, then quickly modified the statement. "They want to fill me in on recent developments. We might have done that over the phone, but frankly, I thought I should come up. To see you, as well as them. Two birds, as they say."

"Have you had that talk yet?"

"I did. With Gabriel Borde. I believe that you're in close contact with him. We discussed your high adventure in New Orleans, of course. It still bugs him that he was one of the people those bastards telephoned."

"Makes you wonder," Cinq-Mars interrupted, "how anybody knew that he and I stay in close contact."

"Leaks," Dreher summed up. "The world's a sieve now, Émile. You can probably ask the question on the Internet, 'Name an SQ officer in close contact with Émile Cinq-Mars.' Lo and behold, you'll get back an answer. The right one, too."

"It's a brave new world," Cinq-Mars mused, as if speaking only to himself. He was wondering though, if Dreher didn't eschew a telephone call with Borde in order to pick his brain in person about the secret caller from New Orleans. Yet he no sooner mulled it over than he realized that he was wrong to underestimate Captain Borde. Dreher was back in Canada because Borde insisted on him showing up for questioning. Dreher's response was all smokescreen.

"The principal point of our discussion," Dreher interjected, "has to do with the Quebec murders. Not much has been uncovered, I'm afraid. Noteworthy is this: the dead couple, they have no background. We don't know where they came from. We don't know who they are. As far as the official record goes, they don't exist. They've paid no taxes. They've made virtually no money, except from renting out their farm. It's like they're aliens. They're invisible to the world, and unlike you and Captain Borde, they're invisible even to the World Wide Web. Except in death. All they've done in life is to die badly and leave behind inexplicable wills."

"You've talked to the hospital in St. Louis?"

"They don't understand it. But they'll take the money."

Dreher, in his way, was inviting Cinq-Mars to marvel with him over this development, but that was not going to happen. Instead, he was met by his host's steady gaze and came under the influence of a silent accusation.

Finally, he asked, "What is it, Émile? What's on your mind?"

"It's time for the FBI to be straight with me. Bear in mind that I've seen my wife kidnapped for your cause, so I'm in no mood for any deflections, Agent Dreher."

"I really wish that you'd call me Rand all the time, rather than occasionally."

"Let's hear what you have to say first."

The special agent took a breath, issued a brief series of nods, pursed his lips, and permitted his expression to convey consent. "All right, Émile. It's true. Our victims are people living under secret identities. Within the FBI, it's a major calamity. It would seem that our security systems have been compromised somehow and those in witness protection are vulnerable. A few have been killed. We've got to find out what's going on and stop it or who knows how many will die. The consequences to all this, Émile, to say the least, are dire."

Cinq-Mars was first to break off their mutual stare. He stood and did a short pace in his living room. "So who were they really, the Lumens, Morris and Adele?"

Dreher separated his hands to indicate that he'd like to answer but could not.

"I presume this is really why Captain Borde had you up here. Not to share information but to have you on the carpet. To demand to know what you know. You're right that we keep in touch. So you can answer the question, but if you choose not to, I'll ask him to tell me whatever he got out of you."

The special agent acknowledged the likelihood of that, yet he did not seem chagrined or in any way concerned. "You're right, Émile. Of course. What I told him is the truth. I don't know anything about the Lumens—about the New Orleans couple, I know more—but perhaps, now that that cat is out of the bag, I can come up with something regarding the Lumens. Let me explain. Witness protection is a closed track even inside the FBI. Random officers can't just summon information. So I needed you, and you in particular, to get to the heart of the matter to force my hand, so that I could force the hand of my superiors. If other officers in other forces can find out that the victims are in our files, part of our calamity, as you've done, then perhaps myself and other agents can get a peek at the secret documents for ourselves. Without that push from the outside, you see, my hands are tied. I couldn't tip you off at all. If I did, I'd lose my badge. So thank you, Émile, you have already helped immeasurably on this case. Now, perhaps, we can get somewhere."

Still standing, pacing intermittently, Cinq-Mars considered this confession, of sorts, and pointed out to him, "You realize that I have succeeded at doing what I said I'd do, namely, demonstrate that the FBI was holding back secrets from me. This triggers a bonus for my services rendered. Just so we understand one another."

Dreher may have been surprised by the mercenary emphasis, but offered no resistance. "Of course, Émile. I'll see that that is executed. You have received your first payment then? Good. You see, I was rooting for you all along. In a way, you could say that I counted on you succeeding."

Just then, a cell phone jangled and both men checked their own. Cinq-Mars was the recipient of the call. "Excuse me a moment, Rand. I need to take this."

"Take your time," Dreher said. "I'm comfortable enough right here."

Cinq-Mars went through to the TV room to take the call from Sergeant Dupree. He was debriefed on what Everardo Flores had revealed, that the Lanos family in New Orleans hailed from Nebraska, and that he had uncovered more but wanted to say it directly to Cinq-Mars. "All part of his insecurity. The man has character flaws coming out the wazoo," Dupree touted. "I don't mind the guy though. He's growing on me."

Cinq-Mars told him what Agent Sivak found out, about Flores not going home the night of the kidnapping.

Dupree swore a blue streak. Then asked, "What do you want me to do?"

"Let me talk to him first, hear what he wants to say. Then we'll decide on a course of action. Sivak wants a piece of him, but she's lying low on that for now. I'm asking if you might do the same."

"Yeah, for now. God, this guy, I can't figure him."

"You don't have to, of course."

"Excuse me?"

"I'm asking you to lie low, just like I asked Agent Sivak to lie low, and I explained to you why, but I understand perfectly well that you don't have to. I'm not in charge of anything here."

"It's okay, Émile. I'm willing."

"You don't have to be."

"What?"

"Willing."

"What? I'm not following y'all."

Cinq-Mars let him mull it through silently.

"Oh." Dupree said. "Okay."

"I don't want Flores to know what we know just yet but that doesn't mean you have to agree with me."

"In other words—"

"I think you got it."

"I'll talk to him before Sivak does."

"I can't stop you from doing what I don't want you to do."

"No, y'all can't do that. Especially if ya'll really want me to do it."

"I didn't say that."

"Neither did I. So, Émile, playing favorites? Or just both ends against the middle?"

"I'm on everybody's side here."

The other man laughed.

"No, I am. But if you talk to Flores, you'll talk to Flores. I know what that's about. You'll get back to me on what he says, it'll be on the side. No documentation, no rap sheet, no lawyer involvement. But if the FBI talks to Flores, they'll take him in, maybe arrest him, he'll lawyer up, we'll never get our own chance to have a direct word and we'll never hear back on what Flores says even if by some miracle he does talk. Not verbatim anyway. Only a filtered version and only if we're lucky."

"That's nothing but true," Dupree concurred.

"Listen," Cinq-Mars told him, "I've got the FBI in the other room."

"Not Sivak!" He sounded shocked.

"No, not Sivak. She's off to Alabama, I hear. I got Randolph Dreher. Know him?"

"To know him is not to like him so much."

"I hear the feeling's more or less mutual."

"No surprises there."

"I'll let you go, Dupree. Thanks for this report."

"Back at you, Émile. Talk soon."

Realizing that their guest was left temporarily abandoned, Sandra had joined Agent Dreher in the living room in Émile's absence. Their chit-chat never passed beyond life on the farm, the dog, and of course the weather. She was pleased that her husband, upon his return, seemed unperturbed that she was engaging the agent in small talk, but then he shocked her. "Rand, my good man!" he exclaimed. "My God, where're my manners? Please, say that you'll stay for dinner. I insist!"

Sandra might have fallen off her ottoman if she wasn't suddenly paralyzed in place.

"Émile," Dreher responded, a polite falseness inherent to his protest. "I can't possibly impose." He looked to Sandra, for he required her endorsement of the suggestion before acceptance.

"Please," Sandra stammered. "I also insist. You must stay."

"Rand, stay. I'll pour my best Scotch."

And so, it was agreed.

Sandra shot her husband a look as he seated himself and put his feet up on the ottoman she now abandoned. Whatever that phone call did to him, he had oscillated through a radical change of mood. He learned a few things that day, confirming that both the Lumens and the Lanos families were farmers who didn't farm. Finally, a connection. What it could mean, he did not know, but for the first time in this whole sordid business a line was drawn, two dots were successfully connected, and after repeated failures and much floundering in the dark he inhaled the intoxicating whiff of progress. Indeed, the victims—the Lumens in Quebec and the Lanos couple in New Orleans—adopted secret identities concocted by the FBI. No matter how anybody swung this cat—multiple ways existed to skin a feline—the FBI knew stuff. No way was he going to allow an agent to just walk out of his house without first delving into the depths of the man's being.

So let the games begin.

TWENTY-TWO

Special Agent Vira Sivak believed herself wired to fail. Born that way. Part of her genetic code. Despite this, through oversight or some cosmic flub, she still managed to spend a significant portion of her life contradicting that innate impression. Never did success run in her family, nor was she gung-ho on dreaming, which in America was relentlessly touted as the principle ingredient toward achievement. This was the land where anyone and everyone was free to not only follow their dreams, but to rampage after them in manic pursuit, but where oh where did the person go who didn't dream so much? Wither the dreamless light sleeper devoid of ambition? What on the green earth became of an individual who only fantasized in miniature? Her countrymen gave much tenor to the notion of the Great American Dream, and perhaps she was merely envious when she chose to decipher the rhetoric as meaning to get rich on the backs of others. She thought of it as the Great American Crapshoot, and not being a gambler, Vira was not particularly interested in that roll of the dice.

Nonetheless, contradicting her own expectations, she excelled.

Emerging from university, the brainy young woman was courted by IBM, Microsoft, and a pair of Fortune 500 companies she'd never previously heard mentioned which, nonetheless, held impressive balance sheets. The latter struck her, perhaps unfairly, as being remnants of an old world economy, to whom she conveyed her disinterest. She really wanted to be at Apple—in her shoes, who didn't?—but Steve Jobs never called, not even after she submitted her résumé twice, something she did not need to do once for any other company. Her sense of failure properly restored, she chose to shuffle off to IBM, preferring the opportunity in product development they dangled over a generic pitch from Microsoft. Before signing—she liked the idea of keeping IBM on the hook if only to verify that their interest was genuine—Vira filtered through a few additional opportunities that were slowly drifting in. Cisco got her attention. Google, not so much. As she confided to a friend, her shilly-shally was not to determine if she could do better elsewhere, but to see if she could not find a way to screw the whole thing up.

By *the whole thing*, she meant her future. She meant *life*.

FedEx delivered an inquiry from the FBI. Would she be interested?

A laughable notion, really.

Imagine, *packing a weapon. Shooting people! Me!*

Hilarious. Downright ludicrous when you thought about it, and she thought about it, had a few drinks with pals and made jokes. And yet, upon quieter reflection, Vira grew curious, enough to at least check out what they had to say. A few days after an interview with the Bureau, FedEx rang her buzzer with another message in an envelope: the job at IBM had evaporated. Had she delayed too long? At least they were demonstrating that their level of interest was never all that strong and were courteous in saying so. Saddened, Vira did not dwell on her misfortune. She deserved it for procrastinating, and, as she perpetually anticipated and perhaps encouraged failure, this was a perfect example of how things were meant to be. *So it begins, the downhill slide. What a shambles.* She joined the FBI as if to put an exclamation mark on this blight she was obliged to call a career, which, given her sense of doom, she would also frame as being her pathetic life.

Only after she was hunkered down as an agent for eight months did the thought finally dawn on her that she'd been snookered. A colleague whispered the suggestion over lunch—IBM stepped aside from competing for her services only because they were asked to do so. By this time she was losing the shine off her innocence. She gleaned that the Bureau did not always play fair. Indeed, the Bureau played fair only when that strategy favored a positive outcome. Otherwise, the FBI did exactly what was necessary to achieve an objective.

She was an objective. They wanted her.

She got that now.

Something to do with her outside-the-box, peculiar, yet spectacularly analytical and computer-savant mind intrigued them. As she advised a colleague at the time, "Either that or my retarded social skills, one of the two."

Nonplussed. Her failure, as inevitable as she always supposed, someday would morph into dust around the heels of those who recruited her. Given that the FBI resorted to dirty tricks in acquiring her services, she took pleasure in knowing that her eventual comeuppance—their oversight, their error, her shortcomings and eventual failure—served them right.

Vira evaluated her professional life as she drove solo through the state of Alabama in a rented SUV. She had no need for a vehicle this large or anywhere near this luxurious, but landing at Birmingham International in a downpour she opted for an upgrade in case the roads were flooded. She wanted to ride above the slosh and an all-wheel drive might prove to be the ticket. More than a size upgrade, the Acura was the only such vehicle available and, what the hell, later she could explain to Agent Dreher that it was the last black car on the lot. He wouldn't know if that was true. Neither did she. She presumed it was a lie. But Dreher suffered from a foible: he preferred his agents to drive black cars.

That was not his only peccadillo, although in all honesty she did not find the list of his peculiarities long. What intrigued her about him the most was that he reached out across a great breadth of humanity to bring her aboard his team. She was obliged to do a few years in the field before being eligible to move up through the ranks in D.C., at 935 Pennsylvania Avenue, and he wanted her for that time. The Bureau wanted her at headquarters and, on the day her superiors found out that the CIA had their bloodhounds out and were taking an interest, rapid promotions were promised. Yet time in the field remained an obligation to fulfill, then up the ladder addressing national security and international crime issues through the use of technologies that in all likelihood had not been invented yet, possibly because she hadn't imagined them yet. She was destined to foster a slew of high-tech developments, and in due course to administer their use. Still, a few years in the field came first, in part for the experience, in large measure to meet the requirements of a massive bureaucracy.

Dreher delved into the bounty of that bureaucracy to snag her. "Out of thin air." She voiced that thought in that way to him. Secretly, a question.

He explained, "I take on the difficult tasks, Agent Sivak, the cases few can figure out. I'm not that bright myself so I put brilliant people to work and succeed that way." Of course, he arranged things so that she had no choice. Being assigned to him over the chagrin and vocal objections of others, even from those who outranked him, demonstrated to Vira Sivak that he was neither "not that bright," as he was fond of claiming, nor someone who failed to succeed on his own merit.

Despite the phony modesty, Dreher made no false assertion. He worked the difficult cases and very bright people stood dutifully in tow. She was happy to serve her apprenticeship under him and with his team. If the day came that she outranked him, which was everyone's expectation, she might bring him onto her own team, who knew?

Driving, the young agent revelled in the Acura at speed out in the rain, appreciating the road clearance, the smooth acceleration, and having the whole of her ruffled life ahead of her. She laughed once to herself, thinking of how Dreher would fume on the day the invoice arrived. She was meant to be in Alabama semi-incognito—unknown to outsiders, scarcely known even to the FBI. Renting an Acura was not going to help that aspect once her expenses landed on a desk at HQ.

Poor Rand. She could hear him blustering already.

That was another of his peccadilloes: his adoration of budgetary restraint.

Torrential as the plane landed, the downpour persisted but was diminishing. Rain fell steadily and Vira enjoyed the rhythmic swish under her tires. Small town lights periodically reflected off the shimmering black asphalt, then all was dark again for long stretches. Vehicular traffic on the highway was not heavy, but constant, with an annoying number of tractor trailers. She was on her way to Marshall County, to the town of Albertville where she'd booked a room, then on to Geraldine in the morning. Marshall was one county over from DeKalb, which had its heart ripped out by a tornado two years earlier, but in Geraldine a couple had been murdered in the storm's aftermath in similar fashion to the man and woman slaughtered in New Orleans. She had issues with her boss, but he consistently delivered on this one account—he drew down the complex assignments. Indeed, her boss reached across and steered the tough ones into his orbit as effectively as he selected her. Strange, that ability, yet Vira reveled in the challenges it provided.

The storm murders were especially perplexing.

She chose accommodation in Albertville for her own specific reasons. She preferred not to sleep and wake up in the same neighborhood where she was conducting an investigation. She preferred to keep her quiet time to herself across a physical boundary where people were unlikely to identify her as a special agent. Albertville was also significantly larger than Geraldine, which might permit her to go out at night and still stand a half decent chance of meeting people, men in particular, with whom she might converse and share a drink. Perhaps a liaison. She was not the first lady to whom men gravitated when she sat alone in a bar, so her odds improved when the bars were both plentiful and pleasantly populated. In a city as large as Albertville, should she find herself in company that pleased her, she might then venture an invitation back to her room without churning a small town's rumor mill. Long before she arrived she was feeling that that's how she wanted the evening to go, and Vira was pleased to be greeted by an abundance of twinkling lights along the strip where her motel was located.

Good. Promising.

First, a shower, a change of clothes, makeup that was apparent, yet subtle—she could manage that contradiction—then dinner.

Over honey-mustard chicken and roast potatoes, Émile Cinq-Mars and Agent Rand Dreher were discussing slime, and the biological stew in the earliest days of the fledging planet. Sandra objected to the subject matter. "Gentlemen, please! We're eating!" Into their drinks—white wine, the Scotch put away—they cheerfully carried on.

"Here's the thing, this is the thing," Dreher was saying, in pursuit of a notion that kept slipping off his tongue. He couldn't seem to get his head around his own thesis. "It's been proven, I mean not *proven*, *per se*, but there's been experiments—*experiments!* yes—to show that slime—pure simple slime, single cell slime, brainless heartless revolting slime—slippery gooey pungent—"

"Okay, thanks, I think we got it," Sandra intoned.

"Slime thinks for itself. No, no," Dreher protested to objections he only imagined as none were spoken in this room, and, indeed, Cinq-Mars knew of the experiments he referenced, "it's true. I swear on my mother's grave. Slime thinks."

Sandra did not know what he was talking about and expressed curiosity and perhaps disbelief with a simple expression.

Cinq-Mars explained. "Slime, living slime, can follow a path to food. To sugar, let's say. In an experiment, scientists blocked the path of slime, made it difficult, then let the slime try again. Even if its old trail was masked to a certain extent, slime figured out the route to food more quickly the second time than the first. Similar experiments have indicated—well, it depends on one's analysis I'm sure—that slime thinks. I like the idea, although perhaps for different reasons than Rand here."

"Slime thinks!" Rand postulated with inebriated enthusiasm. "That's such a sublime thought! I'm in awe of that thought. Single-cell slime thinks! No wonder that the detritus of the earth, the bottom feeders, the night crawlers, and the slimiest of human specimens also think, enough to make things difficult for those of us charged with cleaning up their god-awful messes."

Seconds were dished out. The chicken had been consumed, but Vira had plenty of roast spuds, caramelized onions, and Brussels sprouts drizzled with a secret sweet sauce, popular dishes all. Perhaps the presentation instigated Dreher to discuss life in a primordial slough. He attached himself to the subject with relish.

"This is the thing!" he sang out. "Organisms way back then in that fetid slush interchanged their cells and their DNA willy-nilly."

"Meaning what?" Sandra asked, scooping.

"Meaning exactly that!" he enthused. "I'm talking about microorganisms, you understand, but if Polly wanted Molly's mouth or Ralph thought that he might strike a more impressive figure in a bathing suit if only he had Harold's pectorals, they'd just switch off. Just like that. None of this reproductive morass we're subjected to."

"Microorganisms have pecs? Cool." They laughed, and drank, and dug in again. Sandra was alert to the possibilities. "Just think, Émile, you could've have had a new nose, on a daily basis if you wanted."

"I'd probably wander the swamp looking for the culprit who made off with my perfectly good one."

"Surely it wouldn't be that hard to find," she put in, which scored a second chuckle from Dreher.

"But seriously, this is the thing. The thing!"

Apparently tipsy as well, Émile enjoyed a laugh at his guest's expense. Sometimes, as he already cautioned himself, folks who normally embraced decorum, yet who easily succumbed to the influence of the grape, needed to be watched. And encouraged. "What, dear Rand, is the thing now? Pray tell."

Cinq-Mars couldn't be certain if the drink or the subject matter was the cause, but the fellow was having trouble lining up his words. "What life used to do on this planet was comparable to one massive, messy, all consuming, wet, slurping, unrepentant *orgy*. A ram's horns on a monkey's arse, that was the way of our fledgling planet. Difficult to sit, I agree, ha ha. But it was a free-for-all in those days! Cells and DNA were traded like penny stocks. You don't like your skin? Try scales. Don't like your monkey face? Become a goat. Metamorphically speaking, of course."

"Of course. But metaphorically."

"Of course. Metamor. No. Metaphor. Phic." He gently burped and excused himself. "But this is where it gets interesting."

"It's all fascinating, Rand."

"This is the moment, Émile," Dreher insisted.

"The moment and the thing," Émile emphasized, yet nothing in his tone indicated that he was having one over on him.

"One species."

"Yes."

"Nay. One individual within a species. One ego, perhaps. One jerk. Or one inspired and enlightened soul, who knows? But one specimen in that great global petri dish, decided, all on his own, or should I say, on *its* own, I mean we're not talking people here—my god we're probably talking fecal matter or what swam in and chewed on the fecal matter of the planet—"

"A fine meal. What else was there?"

"Gentlemen," Sandra chastised them both.

Rand looked at him to ascertain Émile's level of seriousness.

"Go on," Émile encouraged.

"One specimen—perhaps thoughtful slime, but check that, the scientists would disagree—one primordial *slug*, say, put an end to this beautiful mucky orgy of life, and declared that he—sorry, *it*—was keeping its DNA and cells to *it*self, and henceforth—"

"Henceforth?" Émile egged him on when Dreher paused unexpectedly. Sandra could keep it in no longer, her giggles erupting into laughter at the two of them in concert.

"Henceforth, yes, henceforth—"

"This is the thing."

"It *is* the thing. Henceforth that specimen, and consequently, that species, was keeping its—"

"You said that. Go on, Rand."

"I said that? Okay. Henceforth, he—it, whatever—would only share it's cell structure through copulation, that is, consequently, through procreation. I've got nothing against procreation, the way we do it, but once that selfishness, shall we say—shall we say that? Once that selfishness was observed, all the other species of the world cottoned on and they all, henceforth, kept their DNA to themselves and moved it along only to their offspring. All other species could suck lemons. That is, if they left themselves a mouth to suck lemons with when all their trading of orifices was completed, when their game of musical limbs came to a fast close."

"Assuming they found a lemon," Cinq-Mars added, and Dreher, confused for only a moment, concurred.

Émile poured but the bottle was dry.

"Dessert is still to come," Sandra mentioned, "but first, I'll get a new bottle."

"I can go!" Cinq-Mars intoned.

"Sit. I'm already up."

"Thank you, sweetheart," chirped Cinq-Mars.

"Don't mean to impose," Dreher lamented.

"Rand, I may be living on a cop's pension, but it's not so bad, and anyway, my wine cellar is all but bottomless."

"Émile," Sandra chastised him. To hear him boasting sounded strange. She slipped free from her chair and the table, beckoned to Merlin, and went through to open the front door to let him romp outside. Then she headed for the basement door. The men observed her go, then gazed back drunkenly at each other.

"She's right," Cinq-Mars agreed, apropos nothing whatsoever. "I'm a rooster's fetid ass. Rand, you've been drinking. You must stay the night."

Dreher resisted the idea, but added, "Here's the thing." He whispered for emphasis, *"this is the thing!"*

He was working toward a point he wished to convey, although he still had to muddle through significant mental flotsam to find its articulation. Finally, he broached his principal concern. "Before the dawn of our time, Émile, the worst and the best of swamp-dwellers commingled and exchanged their cells, their very DNA. After eons, millions of years, someone or something decided that that was a bad idea, or at least that he had enough. Perhaps he simply wanted to keep his own *nose*, even though no one else could comprehend why. Back then, we couldn't talk about the best and the worst of things, because really we were all one thick soup. Interchanging our body parts and not necessarily trading up either. Just—everything goes. And that's what's persisted, it's my belief. More evident in some than in others. That the best and worst of surviving cell material was passed along to us all. We're a mishmash, Émile. And now, it's becoming possible to take human embryos, different embryos, and mix them up in a petri dish. In a way, it's going to be just like the old days, Émile. One big stew, except that it's all being cooked in a lab instead of simmering out there in the orgy swamp. We'll exchange DNA and cells and we'll have no need to procreate. Why risk it? And this is my point, Émile."

He seemed to be drawn to a serious moment, even a teary-eyed one.

"What's your point, Rand?"

"Who will we reproduce? And who won't we? The money people will have their preferences, which they may be able to bully through. Politicians will have their say, and let's not forget the mad scientist, who might artfully trick us all. In the old days, the best and the worst commingled and thought nothing of it. I wonder what beasts such an impossible treaty will engender now, when people—*people*, that wretched tribe of mongoose—presume to *think* about it."

"I know you're drunk," Émile stated. "So am I." He paused to gather the gist of his unease. "But what is it that worries you, Rand?"

Dreher elected to mull it over awhile. "What happens," he pondered at last, "to all the wonderful bad guys in this brave new world? What happens to us when there are no more of them? Does it not seem to you, Émile, a man of your intellectual pursuits and investigations, a man of your acumen and genius, that all of human life has been about striving and achieving amid a myriad of accidents and conflicts? We're all about discovering. Awakening. Carrying on. And what are we to do when we mix our progeny up in a dish in a lab? Will we not pursue mediocrity with a passion? Here's the thing. Rule out the bad guys, the villains, and without them, will we not rule out our better selves at the same time? For whose finger will be on the pulse? It's all going to hell—may I resort to cliché, Émile? Will you allow me this one?"

His host gave him a nod of compliance.

"Émile, it's all going to hell in a handbasket."

They clinked glasses, before they realized again that they were still empty.

In the silence, they waited, forgetting for whom or why, perhaps. Then Émile asked, "What the hell is a handbasket anyway and why is it always hell-bound?"

Sergeant Pascal Dupree called ahead, putting on a professionally friendly voice over the phone to book an appointment with Everardo Flores when the man had an hour free. He waited for him at the taxi stand in front of the Hilton, half sitting on the rear bumper of his cruiser with his porkpie hat pushed back and small beads of perspiration spotting his brow in the warmth of the evening. Earlier, a cool rain tramped through New Orleans. Lamplights were reflected in the puddles left behind. Palm fronds caught by the breezes sashayed and rattled, then went limp once more, dormant before repeating the dance. Dupree desired a drink. He considered that he should have met the man on a barstool inside and, if it turned out that Flores could run up a bill on the Hilton's tab, cadged a whisky. But the spry man appeared in the front entrance patting the shoulder of a doorman who possessed the appropriate regal bearing for the task. Spotting Dupree, he jogged down the steps to greet him. Flores wore a quirky grin, as if any chance to talk cop business gave him such a thrill. Dupree felt himself weakening. He needed to boost his own resolve in order to take the man down a peg.

"Get in," he ordered, a partial growl. "We're going for a ride."

"Cool," Flores consented.

"Think that way," Dupree warned him, "see what good it does you."

"What's wrong with you?"

"Me?" Dupree asked him. "Something's wrong with me now? If something's wrong with anybody around here it's totally with you."

"I didn't meant to—What's going on, Dupree?"

"More questions out of your shit canal. But I want answers. Just get in."

Less fond of the meeting now, Flores succumbed and got in the car.

Dupree still wanted that drink and wondered where he might go. His eyes scanned his passenger—the gelled hair, the mauve silk tie, the suit cut to a perfection that Dupree's own slumping, big-bellied body would never permit—and hit upon the ideal spot. He had taken Cinq-Mars there for a different reason. Such a spiffy man wouldn't feel at ease inside Sinners Too where only the tawdry and the smelly lamented their shabby lives. In there, Dupree would have him at a disadvantage, while the additional benefit of easy proximity to the back alley, what he liked to call *triage*, remained at his disposal.

"Don't tell me that y'all don't drink on duty," Dupree warned him, "or I'll pound the living crap out of your bones right now, squeeze whatever mush you got left in your hanging balls to secrete out your ears."

Flores was silent as he leaned his body into a turn, then straightened up again. "Christ," he murmured under his breath. "Get a grip, will you?"

"Me?" Dupree challenged him again. "Me, get a grip?"

Flores wanted the man to be both civil and reasonable, but gathered that any such desire was not realistic tonight. He yielded to a burning premonition that matters were not destined to go well.

The worry redoubled as they entered Sinners Too at the same moment that a local drunk fell into a psychotic episode. Kicking, flailing, and bellowing straight out of his diaphragm, so rambunctious and out-of-whack was the tall, thin man's behavior that his companion dipsomaniacs chipped in to help subdue him, assisting the bartender by grabbing an arm or an ankle, a fury that closed out only when Sergeant Pascal Dupree lent his significant bulk to the fray. This would seem to be a case for an ambulance, but the cops had already been summoned and they arrived first, surprised to find a top-drawer detective sitting on the afflicted man.

"We got this," an officer told him, in one sense a complaint.

"Take him away," Dupree allowed, and they did, although with difficulty and some violence.

The detective then nonchalantly settled into his favorite seat.

Adjusting his tie, not the least pinch out of place, skimming back the sides of his hair, which lay perfectly flat to his scalp, and pulling back the lapels of his suit jacket, which did not require attention either, Everardo Flores examined the seat presented to him to ascertain that no cockroach or chameleon had pitched a tent upon it first and built a nest, that no crusty aged puke preceded him.

Finally, tentatively, he sat.

Dupree leaned in to release his initial volley, even as he simultaneously raised a finger to signal the Irish barman over. "We've got a private patio out back where we lay the drunks down to sleep it off. Sometimes, Everardo, we lay them down out there to their eternal rest."

"Why are you talking to me like this, Dupree? What did I do wrong?"

Despite his evident flaws, Flores demonstrated backbone.

"Because I have a mind to speak to y'all this way, Everardo. That's why. It's the only reason I require. I don't need a good excuse. Anyway, you're to blame. You're the one who put me into this frame of mind."

"What did *I* do?" That he did anything to disturb his alliance with Dupree seemed preposterous to him.

First, Dupree addressed the Irishman. "Bourbon and my usual chaser, times two."

"I *am* supposed to be working again tonight," Flores protested. The comfort of work was appealing to him at the moment.

"Why did I tell y'all before? Don't you listen?"

"Don't get your damn back up," Flores conceded.

"It's up."

"I got that part. Why?"

"First, I want y'all to understand the evening, how it's going to go."

"What evening?"

Dupree nodded, slowly, emphatically. "I intend to sit here and enjoy my bourbon and my beer after a torturous day. It's not my wish to be disturbed. If y'all disturb me, with lies, with falsehoods, with untruths, with innuendo, with ripe dog shit in this heat, I will be furious, Everardo Flores. Maybe I'll take y'all into the back alley to be introduced to my volatile temper. Though I like to keep it a secret, y'all will discover that side of my nature. It ain't noble. I'm advising y'all as a friend right now, to spare the surprise to your small body later on. I will leave my badge with the bartender, but not necessarily my gun, while I go whale on y'all in a haphazard fashion. It'll be impossible to predict, but most likely I will bruise your fine bones. Am I being understood? Let me know if at any time y'all require an interpreter."

Flores gazed back into the intent eyes of Pascal Dupree and did not doubt his fury. Finally, he said, swallowing once in mid-sentence, "I don't need any interpretation, Dupree, but—no offense—I sure could use an explanation."

The detective slid a hand up from under the table and gripped a single lapel of the man's spiffy jacket and crushed the fabric, drawing Flores's head down closer to him and to the tabletop. "On the night that Mrs. Cinq-Mars was kidnapped, y'all claimed to be heading home. But the good ol' boys in the FBI, they have their methods, they have their fancy electronic toys to play with. They say that Everardo Flores never left the vicinity. The hotel, maybe. The vicinity, not at all. That he did not go home. That he did not even head home. So answer me this, are we going to have a polite conversation here so I can enjoy my drinks, or do I pass the bartender my badge for safekeeping so we can go out to the alley and talk this over like a couple of white-assed Neanderthals? Flores? It's been a long time since I seen myself this pissed off with somebody. That last guy is still recovering. Mind, he has the time to do so. First we made him wobbly on his feet, then we put him away for a good long stretch."

Flores thought it over. Dupree let him. He was serious about wanting to do this in as polite a manner as possible.

"Some things about me you don't know," Flores said, and Dupree let him go.

He sat back in his chair as their drinks arrived. He took a sip of the bourbon and enjoyed it and the barman departed. "I'm listening," the policeman said.

"I'm gay," Flores said.

Dupree's eyes went sideways once, then back upon the hotel security man. "So?" he said.

"I'm also married," Flores said.

"That's what I thought."

"So I was at my boyfriend's place. We were having sex. All right? I can be more specific, but I doubt you want to hear it. Why would you?"

"I'll have to talk to him."

"Just don't hit him. And don't talk to my wife about this, that's what I'm asking for and that's all."

Dupree kept his gaze on the man, but he already believed him. "Don't ask, don't tell, huh?"

The question, he supposed, was an invitation to discuss all this, but Flores didn't bite. "I wasn't so gay in the military."

"*So* gay? What the hell is that?"

"I'm just saying. It is what it is now. I didn't think it would be this way when I got older and got married and started having kids. But I work long nights. Things happen. I got to understand some things about myself. For the record, since you're asking, I'm bi, but I used to be less gay. That's just how I talk. What I used to need less of once upon a time I need more of now for some reason. I don't know why."

"I see."

"I'm not asking you to understand it. You think I do? I'm just saying, I had nothing to do with the kidnapping. But I was in no position to explain my whereabouts."

"I'll make sure of all this—"

"Up yours, all right?"

"Hear me out, you little shit. I'll investigate what you say, but just between y'all and me, for now, I believe you."

That seemed to mollify Everardo Flores, and he sat back, then took his bourbon as a shot, wiped his mouth, grabbed his beer bottle, and poured it into a glass. A regular, Dupree had never been delivered a glass and took a good long swig from his bottle.

"Holy shit," Dupree said, and wiped his mouth.

"What else do you want to know?" Flores asked him.

"Is this why nobody's letting y'all be a real cop?"

Flores had never considered that before, but as the seconds ticked by the possibility took hold. "Crap," he agreed. "Did the cat get out of that bag?"

"Yeah," Dupree said. "Maybe. But this helps. At least it's not because y'all got flat feet or no big flaw like that."

Sandra Cinq-Mars had hesitated selecting a wine in the basement. Her hand rested first on a bottle that she thought they might enjoy, but then she remembered the price, which was high, and questioned whether the evening might not be too far along, and the men too inebriated, to appreciate it. She mulled through a number of cheaper bottles, which had their place, but none appealed. Then she noticed a pair of bottles tucked away in a corner that weren't so cheap, but she didn't like them very much and this might be the occasion to get rid of one. She doubted that either man would notice. She might not be able to distinguish flavors either, and anyway she wasn't planning on imbibing for much longer. She chose one. She had recently discovered a number of decent Ontario wines from Prince Edward County—this was not one of them, but came from there. Now would be as good a time as any to put it out of its misery.

She hesitated again before departing the makeshift room they used as a wine cellar. Émile had been working down there lately, adding data to his flip chart. Perhaps her own level of inebriation caused her to take a moment, reading absently what was written on the facing page, heedless of the time. After further study, she began to flip pages. Soon though, she was feeling quite sober and returned upstairs with her head abuzz from what she learned.

Vira noticed him long before he ever laid eyes on her. She hadn't been looking around and was just starting her dinner, when she spotted him. The gentleman was eating alone, his back to her, yet somehow, in some mysterious way, she liked the cut of his jib. *Oh damn, I'm projecting again.* The usual indicators: broad of shoulder, nice threads, well-groomed hair and a healthy crop, too. Between courses, and he was ahead of her in this regard, he put his cloth napkin down and pushed himself up from the table to use the washroom. An assessment in a glance: muscle-tone unexceptional, yet he passed muster with a standard-issue paunch, nothing egregious, no facial hair, a lined brow, a decent jaw and a favorable overall look to him. An apparent pleasantness and a measure of confidence. He might have had fifteen years on her, or twelve, but that was not a road she hadn't traveled numerous times.

On the negative side, he failed to notice her as he went by.

On the plus side, he *was* dining alone.

If this was Vegas, she'd bet that he was a traveler, too.

Married? Unmarried? This was of no consequence. More importantly, he did not make a point of looking gay nor did he advertise the preference.

Although she remained alert for his return, he slipped up behind her unnoticed, and his only negative washed away the instant he accorded her an appraising look.

Vira regretted being on her main course as his desert and coffee had arrived.

Damn!

A somewhat upscale restaurant was not a great meeting ground. No elegant way was ever devised to uproot an interested party from one table to attach him or her to another across the room. When he departed ahead of her, speaking cordially to the waitress, she figured that his ship just sailed.

And so Vira took her time with dinner before heading out. Had she known that he was waiting in the restaurant's adjacent bar, she'd have masticated her food more vigorously. Said no to coffee. Passing the small room, she paused, needing to ascertain that her reading of the situation was appropriate and not mere wishful thinking. He smiled, the only encouragement she needed to step inside the room for a nightcap. A gentlemen, he took over from there.

The guy was confident, smooth, and interested, and Vira was well pleased.

Sandra Cinq-Mars was well acquainted with her husband's ideas on intuition. A religious man in his own idiosyncratic fashion, in mind and at heart a spiritual man, he might properly be described as a mystic. Yet he was nobody's space cadet. Émile preferred ideas to be well grounded. If the facts did not readily align, then he preferred a reasoned hypothesis, not some wide-eyed claim descending from the ether. Intuition, he postulated—and he quoted the science to bolster his claim—was a cognitive sense. Every brain possessed a supercharged thought process at least eight to ten thousand times faster than conscious human thought. At that speed, the individual who was unknowingly doing the thinking on a subject was kept unaware of the thought process or the rationale as it was all too swift for his conscious mind to process. When a light dawned, that beacon seemed to shine out of nowhere, or descend from the heavens on a beam, spun from gossamer threads and knit in another dimension, or, at least, that was the illusion. In reality, according to recent theory, the thought owed its brilliance to mere rapid computation. What people termed *intuition*, then, could be considered a thoroughly processed thought accomplished at warp speed.

Sandra had been flummoxed by an intuitive notion of her own upon returning with her chosen bottle of wine from the cellar and letting the dog back in. She noticed her husband check the label, then glance at her quizzically. That surprised her. She was equally intrigued when he took his first sip, stifled a critical grimace, and carried on with his chat. That's when she knew—intuition just told her so, but in a trice she was aware of the evidence, that he never poured as much for himself as for his guest—that Émile was not nearly so drunk as he appeared. A moment later, she elaborated on the notion, tracing an obvious deduction. Appearances be damned! Her husband, Émile Cinq-Mars, the eminent detective, was not nearly as drunk as he *pretended* to be. Given that he was putting on an act for his guest—surely not for her benefit, as she was not amused—for whatever reason, she chose to keep her most recent discovery, until such time as she could speak to Émile alone, secret.

Their guest really did seem to be under the impression that the wine was wonderful, so she supposed that his intoxication, at least, was genuine.

Merlin went over and nudged his thigh, deciding that it was high time the dinner guest earned his keep by giving him a pet. "Dear Sandra," Rand Dreher intoned, "I do hope that my gluttonous self has not ruined my reputation with you for life, that in the circle of time you may find it in your heart to forgive me."

"Don't be silly, Rand—" He was sounding such a fool and she really did wish he'd stop.

"Is he trained?" he asked.

"Merlin?" Cinq-Mars replied. "He has his tricks. Farm life demands it. If one of us is unresponsive, say, from a horse kick or a heart attack, he knows to run to get the other. If no one else is about he'll charge off to the next farm. That's his best trick. And, you know, I lived the life of a cop with enemies. Sandra was often alone on the farm. So she keeps a weapon and, yes, even in his old age, Merlin will refuse entry to an intruder and defend San if given the command. He's a sweet old dog, but his bark and growl are still impressive. I heard him giving it to a racoon up a tree not so long ago."

The agent had a silly grin on his face, and had forgotten his original question. He raised his right arm over his head and pronounced, "I am not a man with any great capacity for alcohol. Although I do enjoy it. I have a theory, namely that my parents never drank. Somehow my body developed little tolerance. Nonetheless, I have enough sense left in me to know that I will not be driving home tonight, or anywhere else—where would I go?—and so your kind invitation, your so kind, really so kind invitation, is accepted. With whatever flourish I can muster. Now if I may bring to a close what is possibly an endless string of embarrassments, I believe that the hour has arrived for me to retire for the evening."

Sandra showed him to his room, having to endure more babble despite his vow otherwise. Returning downstairs, she found Émile sipping Scotch again. He was hovering a little off the ground, but seemed under control.

"How can you drink that stuff?" he asked, indicating the last wine bottle, still half full.

"Not me. It's all down Agent Dreher's throat. Émile, I saw something in the basement."

"Mice? Not a rat."

"I was reading your flip chart."

"Oh that. I'm under the impression that I don't remember things as well as I used to. No big deal. So I'm keeping a record that's easy to reference. I know, I know, please don't start, I should be using a computer by now."

"Émile, I saw descriptions of two men. If I understood your notes properly, they were associated with the Lumens. Is that right?"

Cinq-Mars lingered over another sip. "If you were on that page, yes. Description is overstating what the local farmers told me. A bald guy with biggish ears and a short-haired man with a stout build and maybe a touch of rosacea only narrows it down to, oh, I don't know, half the general population in that age group."

He seemed to be interested in his own thoughts, and Sandra waited until he noticed her.

"What?" Cinq-Mars asked.

"A bald guy with biggish ears and a short-haired man with rosacea doesn't narrow it down, unless they show up in each other's company a second time."

"Meaning?"

"Émile, for heaven's sake. You should write *everything* down."

"I'm trying. Why?"

"Those two descriptions, as vague and as general as they may be, also fit two of the men from New Orleans."

"What two men?" Then he went wholly attentive. "You don't mean—?"

"The ones who abducted me, yes."

He looked at her and then his right hand rose to his forehead. He left it there as if holding a cap in place.

"I don't recall you mentioning rosacea."

"Ruddy-cheeked, I think I said."

Now he remembered her phrase. In a moment, his hand traveled over the top of his head and down the back of his neck before returning to the tabletop. He gripped his glass of whisky. Sipped. Gazed at Sandra again, and smiled.

"My God," he said. "Good work."

She laughed a little. "Yeah. Work. These dishes, this mess—"

"I can take care of it."

"I know you can, and you may. But not tonight, Detective. We're leaving it all until the morning. You're coming to bed."

He was not disinclined to go. As they went through the lower floor turning out lights, Merlin padding along behind them, they did so arm-in-arm and bound together. Even though the fit was tight, they maintained close contact on up the stairs where they turned off the last pair of overheads.

TWENTY-THREE

She could arouse a eunuch before breakfast. Cause a neutered dog to moan. Play spin-the-bottle with an octogenarian on life-support and, between wheezing and pleading for his oxygen mask, watch him grow playful again. A dying man might wink.

All tomfoolery, she knew, but still, if she was not the first woman a man might notice in a bar she'd be the last one he forgot. She'd make a point of it. This one didn't think he was God's gift exactly, he was humble enough in his way and a kindly sort, nonetheless he initially gave off an air that he was doing her a favor. With half his scrotum in her right fist and her left thumb down his throat and words more enticingly whispered in his ear than he could bear, he was half-bent backward and groaning and crying out and they'd barely gotten started. She even spoke her mind. "Doing me a favor there, bud? Think so? By the time I'm done, there won't be much left of you." Maybe so, but he was up for the challenge, and she wouldn't have to do all the work either. She let him rummage around and did a little writhing and gasping of her own. Whatever spot he neglected she attended to herself, so that it felt at times that a dozen wanton hands were on her flesh at once and six slippery tongues. The man had game that surprised her.

Vira Sivak wanted men to abdicate thrones, if not for her than for the sex she provided them. She made it a point of pride. She wanted to return married men to their lairs feeling disinterred, vampire-like, scoured, and replenished, glad to inhabit the sanctity of their own rooms once more, too petrified to ever emerge at night again. She fixed them. She wanted to vanquish the wannabe Lotharios, cause them to feel the absence of their own skins, their nerve-endings denuded. For the scarce, genuine hot-to-trot testosterone-macho blood-rush studs out there, oh God bless them, the tender ones especially, let the walls fall down when they collided with her, both of them having gleefully met their match.

This guy was working out for her. Limited in his gymnastics, but she got to relax and just enjoy herself at times, too. Perfect for her mood.

A decent enough guy that he attended to her gratification before his own.

After they were done, and the return to a steady heartbeat was gradual and sweet, she accepted his compliments and dished out a few of her own. He was honorably depleted, she could tell, but he didn't seem intent on sleep right away and perhaps was seeking an elegant way out the door.

"I have a decent Irish whiskey in the car," he proposed. Surprising her.

The offer told her that he had his doubts at the outset, otherwise he'd have brought the bottle up with him when they first arrived, she in her rental, he in his.

"Jameson?" She named a whisky, but had to think twice to remember his. Blake, something? The sex had been good enough for her mind to still be fuzzy.

"Tyrconnell," he corrected her. "My choice of poison on the road. Something I started years ago, just stuck with it."

"So you're in sales."

"Somebody has to make the world go 'round. The sun won't come up in the morning without somebody somewhere making a pitch."

"I prefer my whisky on ice. Would you mind taking the bucket with you? The machine's straight below us, between the outer stairs and the office."

He didn't mind and snatched up the plastic bucket after dressing. Would he be back? She didn't know and clothed herself in loungewear. Either way she'd be awake for some time before retiring. Having taken the trouble to put his clothes on, she assumed that his easy exit was to enjoy a nightcap and then be gone. Vira Sivak was fine with that. She lured the animal out of him, and now he was a gentlemen. Could she ask for better on a stormy night in Alabama?

She admitted to herself though that, when he knocked, she was pleased. Perhaps he'd be up for a quieter second round.

Out of habit she checked the keyhole first. He held the ice bucket in view. She opened up.

The bucket and ice struck her face with the force of a sledgehammer and Vira Sivak reeled backward, struck the jamb to the bathroom door, and landed hard on the floor. By the time she yelped for the first time the door to her room was already shut and her assailant was twisting her around and—*no! damnit!*—taping her mouth. She had never done well with her self-defense training, and her wrists were buckled behind her back before she could even see what method he was using. The bindings bit into her skin and by now she was kicking, furiously kicking, but the man in the room didn't seem to mind.

She looked at him and he looked back at her. He was not the man with whom she just made love. Perhaps that man—*Blake!*—would return. Perhaps he would save her yet. She needed to buy time. To depend on him. She had to hope that more animal was left in him. She kicked again, but this time her assailant objected. He pulled out a pistol and so she stopped. She was breathing heavily, and trying to quell her panic. He leered over her.

"Do what you're told," he ordered. He aimed the barrel of the gun just to the left of her eyeball and she nodded in compliance. "Good," he said.

He hauled her up so aggressively her loungewear tore and he dropped her into the chair that served the small writing desk. She heard the tape pulled sharply free of its roll and momentarily her arms were bound to the chair. He put the gun down. For good measure he wrapped the sticky tape around her body and around the chair and then he held her chin in his hands and made her look up at him.

The fire in her eyes amused him.

"Do I need to wrap up your legs, too? Seriously. Do I?"

She couldn't believe the question, but she understood it. She shook her head. She calmed down again.

He ripped her thin lounging frock further to expose her breasts and thighs. She did not know why. He did not look at her after that, nor did he touch her.

"Settle down," he told her. "Be a good girl. There's something I want to show you."

Not for the first time she wanted to scream, *What? What?* But nothing she intended to say sounded any different from a muted groan.

The man was barrel-chested, not tall but weighing well over two hundred pounds with excess weight around the middle, but his arms, she'd found out, were like steel and he could snap her, she knew, with just one hand. The man wore a sports jacket wet from the rain, and he was reaching into a side pocket and pulling out something from a brown bag that was wrapped as well in cellophane. She started pushing herself away from him as the wrappings were undone, and she hit back against the bed, able to push herself no farther. The last of the cellophane was removed, and she tried to turn her head away, as much from the consequences now as from the horror of the thing itself.

"Recognize it?" the man taunted her. She didn't like his voice, the onion smell of him, the garlicky breath, the venomous tone. She tried to keep her eyes steered off him but he made her look. "Your lover's," he said. "Bet it was just inside you. Was it? Hey? Was it?"

Her evening lover's ring finger. Well bloodied. He had been a married man. The ring still on it.

Her attacker carefully wrapped the finger up again and placed it in the bag and the bag in his pocket.

"I'm sure you're wondering how the rest of him is. Well, that depends. Do you believe in life after death? For his sake, I hope so and I hope you're right, because that's all he's got going for him now." The man started a low staccato laughter, as if his pleasure was a craven secret. "I stuffed him in a laundry hamper. Ha! Unless somebody goes looking for dirty sheets, nobody finds him before dawn. Maybe not 'til he starts to stink. So, you know, we got all night."

She tasted blood on the inside of her upper lip from the smash of the ice, and she had bitten her tongue also. She was vitally scared now, worried about choking, asphyxiation. What he yet might do hadn't yet occurred to her, or she was pushing it out of her mind.

"Calm down. Take it easy. We have to get through the hard part first. I'm not going to drag this out. Then it'll all be over."

He extracted the knife from under his jacket at his back, and her eyes rolled at the sight of it and she started kicking again and kicked some more and then she directed her kicks at him, but, shoeless, she was nothing to him, a mere flea he smacked once, hard, across the top of her head, and she ceased her paroxysm. Then he spun her around in the chair on wheels, and now she knew his intentions and did not know if this depravity or what was yet to come frightened her more, but she was screaming into her gag now even before the knife was wedged against her left hand ring finger and he isolated the finger next and cut it off. Only it dangled, still attached, and she bucked in her chair and he had to put a foot right on her naked lap to stop her thrashing and wiggling. Leaning over awkwardly balancing on one foot, he seized the finger out of the fountain of blood and at first tried to rip it the rest of the way off, but when he failed, he hacked at it, cutting up the rest of her hand in the process until the bone and tendons and tissue gave way and he had his second prize for the evening.

Blood was pumping from her hand. He was swearing angrily. She groaned and battled her restraints, and he went into the washroom to clean himself up. When he came back, still wiping his hands, he said, "I don't get this part, do you? Why does he want a finger? Fuck's sake, what kind of sick puppy needs that? Makes a mess, too. Guess you did some dirty shit to him. He must want you to suffer."

The man returned to the washroom to package his trophy, then he returned and her eyes now were sinking into her brain and he could tell that she knew. She had no hope left in her, and they both knew that. Now was the time, and they both knew that also. Vira was convinced that what was coming was coming, and he had never seen anyone lose all hope like that before, which he supposed meant that she was intelligent, and he said, as if in sympathy, "Okay. Okay? I'll make it easy on you. We'll do this real fast." He didn't like that she didn't seem to care, as if she'd already left the room. She just seemed gone. Or maybe the blood loss or the shock was dropping her into an abyss, but whatever it was made him inexplicably angry, so that he killed her in a fury, ending her life with a deep rough stroke across her throat. Blood sprouted across the bed and carpet.

"One holy fucking mess!" he yelled, as if it was her fault for bleeding. He had to clean himself up in the washroom a second time and blustered whenever he found more blood on his clothes. Somewhat satisfied at last, he switched off the lights and departed the room, taking her key and locking the door behind him.

TWENTY-FOUR

They slept in.

Émile Cinq-Mars stirred as his wife awoke to her inner clock and dutifully embarked to the barn for the care of the horses. Their man came later to exercise them, but she still got the feeding shift before morning light. Merlin tramped along beside her, but only after gazing longingly at his master snug beneath the covers as though to ask how he got to evade the chore. Dutifully, he did not disturb him, but a few gentle guttural noises indicated that an act of disobedience was tempting.

Cinq-Mars was awakened early enough himself as it turned out, startled by the jarring exclamation of his bedside telephone. Vengeful memories of his old days on the job returned, of when his phone would crow across the countryside more stridently than any alarm, a rooster up with the sun, and he, just in from pulling an all-nighter of dreary investigative legwork, was obliged to answer.

Still dark out. In this land in winter that could mean just about any hour. He didn't bother to consult his clock before answering.

"Cinq-Mars," he said. Then coughed. His free hand rubbed his eyelids.

"I know it's early."

He recognized the voice, but never before had it sounded so dull, so somber.

"Even earlier where you are."

"Good that y'all know that. Your brain is functioning."

"You're at work, Dupree?"

"Bad news."

"Hang on," Cinq-Mars told him. "Bad news can wait. I need a minute."

"Émile—"

"Don't argue."

Cinq-Mars was less convinced than Dupree about the capability of his brain, but after all the wine and Scotch his bladder was indeed on the job. He got up, left the room to use the washroom, did his business, and snuck a peek through the half-open door into the guest bedroom as he returned. Dreher was still down for the count. When he picked up the phone again, just as sleepy, but more convincingly awake, he remained standing in his pajamas. "All right," he said. "Tell me."

"I got the call from my department because they heard the news. It's already a big deal in this town, even in the middle of the night. A night watchman or a night manager, somebody like that, noticed a cart out of place at a motel in Alabama."

Cinq-Mars took a breath at the mention of the state. Dupree paused. "Alabama," Cinq-Mars repeated.

"Yeah. So y'all know what this means."

"Tell me."

"It's bad, Émile. Vira Sivak, she's dead. Cut up. Some other guy, too. The night manager or whatever was moving a cart out of the way when he noticed it was too heavy. This other guy was in the cart."

"And Vira? Tell me about Vira."

"Upstairs in her room. Émile, her ring finger was cut off, even though she didn't have a ring on it. Same as our killings. The guy, too. He had been a visitor in her room, the local detectives think, because he left a tie and jacket behind. His finger was also cut off, and he was on the downstairs level. She was a flight up."

The news seemed to be more than he could process so early in the day.

He recognized that his head was in a dull throb and blamed the tiny sip of incredibly bad wine that Sandra served.

"I know," Dupree commiserated, as if speaking for him. "It's incredible. I'm going there."

"To Alabama?"

"With a banjo on my knee if I have to. She's FBI, but she was stationed in New Orleans and she was working a couple of our cases. Easy to imagine that the killer came from here. The FBI will never share a word on this so I need to be on-site, hear what the local cops are willing to reveal."

"This is incredible," Cinq-Mars managed to articulate. "I'm stunned."

"Yeah. Me, too. She and me, we had our quarrels, truth be known, but I figured she was straight up."

"I'll tell her boss."

"I'm sure he knows by now."

"I don't think so. He's asleep in my house."

"No fuck."

"Talk to you later, Dupree. Soon."

Dreher's eyes were still adjusting to the light when Cinq-Mars knocked and stepped into the room through the open door.

"Good morning, Émile. I heard you talking."

"You better sit up for this."

He told him the tragic news and Dreher hardly responded. What he was saying was incomprehensible. Then he held his face in this hands for a whole minute before he got busy. He discovered that his cell phone's battery had run down. Cinq-Mars carried over his suit jacket, and Dreher fished out the charger. Seated on the bed in his underwear, he plugged the phone in and made three calls to have the news confirmed. During the last call, Cinq-Mars excused himself and got dressed and went out to the barn to tell Sandra, and they walked back together. She started preparing breakfast, guessing that Rand Dreher would soon be off. She brought up coffee to the two men.

The American guest was still on the phone. His voice and manner remained thoroughly professional, but when he signed off they could see that he was emotionally wrung out. "I can't believe it," he said.

"I'm so sorry," Sandra said.

Dreher became conscious of his state of undress and moved to reclaim his clothes. Sandra left the room, but Cinq-Mars stayed. They hadn't had a chance to talk yet.

"What do you make of it?"

"She must've been followed. Somehow it was planned. I don't know who the dead guy is. I mean, we have a name, we're contacting his family, but it doesn't relate, you know? I knew she was going to Alabama, and you knew, that's about it."

"Dupree knew."

"What?"

"I believe I mentioned it to him."

Dreher was tucking his shirttails into his trousers. "Perhaps there's been too much fraternization, generally speaking, among police departments."

Cinq-Mars wanted to remind him that he was the one who brought him onto the case in the first place after first contacting Mathers, but he let it go. Instead, he asked, "Where're you off to?"

"Alabama, I guess. Where else would I go?"

He let that pass as well.

Dreher apologized. "I didn't mean to snap. You've been kind. I'm just—I've never lost a colleague before."

"Sandra has breakfast ready. There's no point leaving before you have a bite. You can arrange flights from here if you want."

Dreher thanked him and accepted breakfast, but argued that he needed to think things through and would do that on the drive to the airport. "I have choices with respect to flights that aren't available to folks, but only when I show up in person. Thanks, Émile. I'm sorry to have dragged so much trouble into your home."

Breakfast was both quiet and brief, then Dreher was on his way just as the first signs of dawn appeared beyond a distant horizon. The special agent stood by his rental and observed the faint glimmer.

"That's east?" he asked at last. He seemed confused. Discombobulated. Turned around.

"This time of year, there's a lot of south in our sunrise."

He nodded. He seemed to understand. "Thanks, Émile. I'll be in touch."

"Take care, Rand. You and your colleagues, and of course her family, you have my sympathies. I liked her. I thought she was strong and clever."

The former detective was underdressed and as the car pulled away he rushed back inside. Sandra was holding his mobile phone out to him. "Dupree," she said.

Émile took the phone and, shivering a little, asked, "What's up?"

"One thing that might be significant, Émile," Dupree told him. "I worked a few connections that got me through to an Alabama trooper who's up to speed."

"And?"

"It's about the fingers that were cut off. Both victims had their throats slit, but the guy had his ring finger cut off *postmortem*. Here's the thing—Vira was not so lucky. Her finger was cut off *before* she died."

"That's not the MO." The words were off Cinq-Mars's lips before he could even think about them.

"Made to look like, maybe, or maybe the killer didn't get all his facts straight. Hard to say. Maybe he wanted to make it worse on a cop. Who knows?"

"Do I have to ask? Did they check the attic?"

That may have been a partial chuckle out of Dupree that he heard. "A flat roof, apparently. And they checked the roof. I believe someone from here made a point of telling them. They checked the entire motel. No sign of the killer. Émile, I'm told it's a bloody mess. That's also not the MO at all, not the same style. One more thing."

"Go ahead."

"Not related to this, but Flores, he told me what he wanted to tell y'all. I guess he just couldn't wait for your call."

"Okay."

"The deceased couple here in New Orleans had a visitor before they were killed. Someone who claimed to be their insurance adjustor. That struck me as interesting, because each of these killings, until now, happened after a storm. After damage was done. So that could explain how the killer gained access to all those places. Not yours, maybe. But the other ones."

Cinq-Mars remained silent, processing the news.

"Émile?"

"Interesting, Dupree. Makes me wonder. You're going to Alabama?"

"I've already made a connection there, so it might be worthwhile."

"Maybe you can do what Vira Sivak was going to do. Interview the previous victims' neighbors out there. Ask that one question."

"Was there an adjustor?"

"That's the question."

"I'm on it, Émile. We'll talk soon."

TWENTY-FIVE

Émile and Sandra Cinq-Mars spent the morning tidying up the house after their festive dining and imbibing with Dreher the previous evening. They were both particularly quiet, saddened by the death of someone they knew only in passing. Her death held a deeper pang given that Special Agent Vira Sivak had served in law enforcement.

Although tired, Émile declined to nap and resorted to more coffee. Sandra, weary also, snuggled up on the living room sofa for some midmorning shut-eye. Merlin wanted up, but had to settle for the carpet below her. Another call came in from Dupree which Émile took right away, not to disturb her rest too much. He spoke standing in the kitchen. Dupree's travel plans had been denied. Yet he was able to make contact again with the state trooper known to a friend of his, and so managed access to the file on the Geraldine murders. According to that record, a neighbor stated that in the aftermath of the tornado the couple was visited by an insurance adjustor shortly before the murders. No one followed up on that, presumably because thousands of people across several counties were being visited by adjustors at the time.

"But if it's in the file," Cinq-Mars objected, "why in God's name did that information not get around to anyone investigating the other cases? Dreher never mentioned it to me."

"We're only attaching significance," Dupree pointed out, "on account of what Flores told us. The other investigators—no, okay, forget it. I won't make excuses."

"Don't. Consider this. Flores heard it and considered it significant. The cops in Alabama, and I daresay the FBI, heard it and let it drop. What does that tell you?"

"Good on Flores, for one thing. He wants a cop job. I might get him one."

"Hold back on that for now. We're not trusting anybody just yet."

"Except each other." The man paused before he released a big belly laugh. "Don't worry, Émile, we both know that that's got limits, too."

"Dupree, look," Cinq-Mars carried on without commenting on their mutual level of engagement, but he was very much inclined to trust this guy, "if your superiors won't allow you out of the state, why not see what you can come up with about the insurance company instead, the one that sent an adjustor to your town? Usually after a disaster, adjustors are outsiders, partly because so many are needed, but also because expertise in disasters is a specialty job. So they go to the disaster, since disasters tend to be all over the map, rather than living where a disaster comes to them only once in a lifetime. See if you can't find out who he was and where he came from."

"Already on it, Émile. I had to lie about why I needed two detectives, but I've got them working that file."

"Good on you, Dupree."

"Y'all realize the alternative?"

"You mean that the adjustor's not an adjustor, that he only says he is? But it's still good to know if that's the case. Dupree, don't take any offense to what I'm about to say to you, all right?"

"Why am I not going to like this?"

"Take it as a compliment that I'm asking you a question straight-up and not slinking around behind your back for the answer."

"I'm really not going to like this, am I?"

"I told you that Vira Sivak was going to Alabama. Think now. Did you tell anyone else?"

"What're y'all accusing me of?"

"You knew, I knew, and Rand Dreher knew that she was going. Plus anyone she told. I'm just trying to find out how wide a field that might be."

"Why should I take offense if y'all accuse me of shoddy police work and/or murder?" He laughed, and really quite heartily. "No offense taken, Émile. I had no reason to tell anyone. I'm trying to think if I might've done so off the cuff for one reason or another or maybe I was talking in my sleep. But no. Definitely not. Any leaks, they never came from me."

"Okay. I figured that. Dreher's on his way to Alabama himself. Maybe he'll let us in on anything interesting."

"Wishful thinking, no?"

"True enough. Thanks, Dupree. Now I'm wondering if I can press you for one more item on my shopping list. I've been doing some thinking."

"You're the pearl oyster, Émile."

"Excuse me?" The man from New Orleans did have a few sayings that might be common enough, but they were new to Cinq-Mars.

"Some men say to me, 'I've been thinking,' and I say back to them, 'Spare me that pain.' Know what I mean? It's not what I most want to hear, the deepest opinion of a dumb-arsed man. But what's on your mind is of interest to me, Émile, no matter what it is, because there's always a chance a pearl's in that oyster. You're the pearl oyster, Émile, that's not just a glob inside y'all, tasty as it may be."

"All right, if that's a compliment, thanks." Cinq-Mars figured he might as well throw in a few exercises while he was talking, to make the most of his time. Tucking the phone between his neck and shoulder, he stretched that arm to the moon.

"Let me in on those thoughts, Émile." Somehow, Dupree said that as he chuckled.

"I was casting my mind back to the pickpockets in New Orleans. I can't seem to get them out of my head."

"Okay. What do they do for your pondering?"

"For one thing, I can't release them from being involved in all this in some way. All they took from me was a notebook."

"One strange theft, grant you that."

Cinq-Mars switched ears for the phone and stretched his other arm high, trying to extend the muscles the long way down to his hips. "They were professional, Dupree, yet they don't come up on your radar. So let's say they were outsiders. Let's give them that designation because it feels more than possible, it feels likely. So if we say they flew in from elsewhere, such as Miami, or maybe L.A. or New York, what does that give us?"

"Drawing a blank. But I can see how a question like that can obsess a man."

"Who would make that flight to nick a wallet or pinch a notebook?"

"Nobody I know well."

"The only outsiders—and not one guy, but two—who would do that, would be outsiders who were hired. Money up front and expenses paid."

"Then the question raising up its head out of the sand is who hired them?"

"That's it, Dupree. The answer, I'll bet you the cash in a bank, is found on somebody's ledger somewhere." He put his arm back down. "Whoever paid that bill."

"Who? Are you stringing me along or do you have that answer, too, or just the question?"

"Only the question, Dupree. But is there anywhere you can think to look where such a ledger exists, which might show a strange and inexplicable entry?"

"Not offhand, no. What're y'all accusing me of now, Émile? Just when we were getting along so well. I don't have access to the books of any crime syndicates."

"Are you sure? Maybe if you think about it some more."

Émile took the silence as being respectful, a willingness to meet him halfway.

"Yeah, well, now, yes, something's come up in my head."

"Danziger Bridge, Dupree. Danziger Bridge. I do recall that my arrival had your knickers in a twist over something I knew nothing about."

"My what? In a what?"

So Cinq-Mars had his own expressions new to Pascal Dupree.

"You've got a couple of detectives," he reminded him, "checking on insurance adjustors. If they get that done, maybe they can move on this."

Émile felt that he could almost hear the other man shaking his head.

"No way," Dupree let him know, "this one, I will do myself."

"I understand. Thanks again. For everything."

"No promises, Émile. But you're welcome."

"Take good care, Dupree. Stay cool."

"Y'all stay warm."

Sandra came away from his flip chart with so much success that Émile retired to the basement to give it further study himself. The aggravating issue for him was to posit how her abductors in New Orleans could also have been involved in installing the Lumens on their property in Quebec years earlier. By any stretch of the imagination, how could those two circumstances be linked, and what flowed between them, over time, across borders, and amid disparate lives?

He tried to get at it from any and every possible direction through a series of rash suppositions, including the blatantly ridiculous, anything that might trigger a possibility. He considered that the men were indiscriminate killers, but showing up in two locales in two countries and both incidents being connected to Cinq-Mars remained a more extraordinary coincidence than he could swallow. If they were not, then, *indiscriminate* killers, did that make them *discriminating*? And presuming that that was the case, what targets attracted them and for what purpose? *Or,* the men could be police, but what game were they playing and to what possible end? The Lumens were in witness protection, so the men who established them on their farm could easily be, and were likely to be, FBI. And in New Orleans, Sandra's abductors wanted to make a point of being considered the good guys in all of this. Your garden variety benevolent kidnappers. Of all the scenarios that came to mind, this was the most promising. But if they were indeed the good guys, who were the bad? *Or,* maybe they were not the good guys at all and were really international criminals whose activity involved the Lumens somehow. Émile's own investigation of the Lumens' murders meant that he had shown up on their welcome mat, hence their actions down south. Such men wanted him to return to mucking out stalls in the Canadian countryside, not to muck about dives in New Orleans. *Or,* they were international terrorists hellbent on world domination and somehow, some way, he had interfered with a master plan. That thought provoked a smile. Given what he knew about the case, one crazy idea just might be as valid as the next, although he conceded that he was barking up trees that might not exist.

Nothing worked for him wholly or succinctly. Nothing at all. He could not see through the maze. But he sensed FBI involvement where perhaps it did not belong.

Already dressed for the outdoors, Sandra skipped downstairs to kiss him good-bye and offer up a summary of leftovers lurking in their refrigerator should he want lunch. She was off to the village for an outing and a little food shopping. She didn't expect to be gone for more than three or four hours and did he need anything? He requested that she stop at the pharmacy for his monthly medications and she happily added them to her list. He detected that she was glad to be off on her own—now that she'd hired a man to look after the horses during the day, such an excursion was a pleasant indulgence. She didn't have to rush. Émile could tell that she was not canvassing for company, so he didn't ask. Individual forays were a break from being stuck together constantly, so had merit apart from the practical purposes served.

"The roads are dry. I'll take the Nissan. Leave you the Jeep."

"Don't need it."

"Whatever."

When she bent to kiss him, Émile ran a hand up her back, then down.

"Don't spend the day in the basement," she commanded, and was soon gone.

In her absence as the house went still, he acknowledged that the space was dark, despite the bare lightbulbs, and dreary, so before long he abandoned the easel and returned to the company of Merlin and the sunlit rooms on the first floor. The dog greeted him and wholeheartedly concurred when Émile suggested a walk.

Despite a nip in the air, he became ambitious, hoping the walk might clear his synapses and provoke a good thought or two. He slipped one leg then the other over a wood fence, one that the aged Merlin leapt through, and headed off across the fields of snow. The wind still had bite, picking up the snow's coolness, but if the day was this breezy going out the wind would be behind him on the home trek and easy to bear. The walk took about twenty minutes down a riding path to a lone pine at an intersection of split-rail fences, and it seemed obvious to Merlin before it occurred to Émile that they were achieving their destination for the day. The retriever waited for his master, who leaned against the tree out of the wind when he arrived, and they both took in the vista, then trudged on home again.

The hired man's pickup was in the yard by the time he got back, but Émile decided against going into the barn for a chat. For the nonce, he was taking the measure of his solitude and enjoying it. Inside the house, he started up a fire in the wood stove, more for the ambiance than the extra heat, and looked through his CD collection for something, really anything, neglected over the last while. He decided on the Rachmaninoff Concerto No. 3, performed by Horowitz, when the telephone rang again. His home phone this time.

Émile was torn, but finally put the CD down and crossed the room to the side table to take the call. No screen to identify the caller here, and he began as usual with his own identification.

"Cinq-Mars."

"Émile, it's Bill. Have you heard?"

"About Vira Sivak. Yeah, it's very sad."

Mathers was quiet a moment. "Ah, who's that again? What happened?"

Realizing his error, that Mathers didn't know her, that he'd only mentioned her name in passing, Cinq-Mars relayed a short version of the morning's news, adding, "I hope you have something better."

"Only marginally, Émile. Morris Lumen's farm is on fire."

Once again, he could scarcely believe what was being relayed. "What? Who told you that? On fire? How can a farm be on fire in the winter?"

"Not the farm. You know what I mean. The house, the barn, maybe both. I'm heading out there to have a look."

"Why?" Émile asked.

"Why what? Why is it burning? I'm not there yet. How am I supposed to know? I don't have the particulars."

He wanted to yell at him, but instead took a couple of seconds to calm himself. "Bill, I mean, why are you going out there? You're a city cop, remember? The Lumens' property is not in your jurisdiction and anyway, you're not a fireman. You don't have the muscle mass."

"Ha ha ha. Captain Borde called me. Just now. He's on his way himself, but since it's connected to our case, he gave me a call. What's wrong with that, Émile?"

"Nothing. I'm sorry, Bill, I'm just—"

"That's okay. Listen, Borde called me as a courtesy. Now I'm calling you, same courtesy. Borde knows I'm calling. So if you want to come out and see it for yourself, he said to say that you're welcome. We don't know what's going on. Could be kids. Could be an electrical short. Could be nothing. Could be interesting. We don't know."

He was on his own anyway. He might as well do something with his day. "Yeah, I'll go up. I hope it's not the barn. It's a well-built barn."

"Then you've got a good reason to go. To look after your interests."

Merlin wanted to come to, and Cinq-Mars considered it. He could run around the other property, help the fire department do their work. But sometimes one thing led to another and who knows when he might get back home. The dog might starve. So he filled up his water bowl and left him on-site, with a stern warning to protect the premises.

The drive took him across rolling countryside, then through a lengthy corridor of spruce for about two kilometers, then onto a plateau of farmland. The moment he emerged from the woods the smoke and flames were evident. Departments from several towns must have been called, as so much equipment was on the scene. Volunteers all, so among the hook 'n' ladder trucks and the pumpers were personal vehicles, mostly large pickups and four-wheel-drive SUVs. Cinq-Mars already knew what he'd find before arriving all the way up the long drive. The pumpers had no water to pump, as hydrants didn't exist out there. A nearby pond probably took time to locate as it was frozen over and under several feet of snow. The trucks couldn't reach it easily, but men were cracking ice, though that was mostly for show. Whatever was burning was going to burn to the ground. As he neared the farmhouse he saw that everything was ablaze—house, barn, tractor, and truck.

The fire on the tractor had been doused by shoveling snow onto it, but so far everything else was being allowed to incinerate.

Cinq-Mars drove up the long road and climbed out of his Jeep. Borde and Mathers were nearby, behind a line of firemen who gazed at the flames.

"We think it was set," Borde told him.

"Really? You think that?"

"You know, Émile, it's not a sin to state the obvious. It's just a way that people communicate sometimes. You should try it. It's called being friendly."

"Great to see you, too, Gabriel. How's the family?" Then he acknowledged Mathers. "What kind of a greeting do you require to make your day, Bill? Will an everyday cordial comment do for you?"

"Be more effusive than that, thanks."

"He requires a hug," Cinq-Mars said to Borde and all three men smiled. "What do we have, really?"

Borde blew his nose into his handkerchief first. "According to our lovely volunteer firefighters, it's too early to tell if this was set. They'll have to bring in an investigative team."

"But—" Cinq-Mars started to object.

"Exactly. No way did the cars catch fire from the buildings. They're all separate fires."

"Plus," Bill Mathers said. He seemed coy.

"Plus?" Cinq-Mars asked him.

"We found the packaging for the accelerant. Can't say why they didn't let the packaging burn. And—"

Cinq-Mars waited, then finally had to ask. They were obviously yanking his chain.

Borde answered. "We found the gas can. Thrown away in the field. Nobody was trying to hide that this was an arson. But the fire department, they'll have to send in an investigative team."

Cinq-Mars listened to the fire crackle and snap and gazed skyward as the plumes of gray-and-white smoke ascended to the clouds.

"I'm brokenhearted," he attested a minute later. "I wanted that barn."

"Why?" Borde asked him. "You don't need another barn, do you?"

"That's what I thought," Mathers said, although only after he spoke did he realize that he had been too intimidated to ask the question himself.

The retired detective shrugged. "If for no other reason," he admitted, "than to see who would show up to try and sell it to me. Now, I'll never find that out. But, yeah, I was serious. I can use another barn."

They had to move aside for a vehicle to back up to the burning pickup. The firefighters wanted that flame out to prevent an explosion, although the charred metal suggested that the gas tank had already been compromised. Probably not a lot of gas had been left in it.

The three men reformed their circle with a slightly different viewing angle of the twin fires to barn and home.

"So what do you think, Émile? We've been scratching our heads trying to figure how this could have anything to do with our murders. We've fired off nothing but blanks so far."

"Did they make any noise, your blanks? I wouldn't think so. A hospital owns the property now. To suggest that they might burn their holdings to the ground to collect on the insurance strikes me as ludicrous. I know it's not a great market in agriculture right now, but the death knell hasn't been sounded. The property has to be worth more with two sound buildings on it than with none. So you know who that implicates."

Borde appeared to be nodding in agreement so Mathers asked the question.

"Who?"

Borde answered. "Buyers."

"The property is worth less now," Cinq-Mars concurred, "and the seller might be even more motivated than before. So I hate to implicate our local farmers, but that's the first place I'd go looking. I let them know that I'd be willing to buy the barn, but that wasn't enough to save it, I guess."

"I'll pass that on to whomever gets the case. It won't be me."

"The arsonist got away with it. Your only hope is an eyewitness. The odds on that? Finding a winning lottery ticket in a snowbank is easier."

With no dispute of the argument, they permitted themselves to observe the blaze. The robustness of the flames would shift from one section of each building to the next, sprout here and appear to diminish there, then be fanned to a new brightness and rage all over again. Fortunately, the smoke dissipated in a constant direction, they didn't have to duck it, although sometimes it did gather itself and strike for the ground well beyond where they were standing, only to billow up again. With no other buildings within two kilometers, and with the owners already long in the grave, the fire was almost a peaceful thing, a sound and a fury quite fascinating in its evolution and slow demise.

Sergeant Detective Bill Mathers was the first to turn impatient. "So," he inquired, "nothing for us here, I guess."

"Guess not," Borde acknowledged.

Cinq-Mars hesitated. "Bill, you said that the dogs and the cat were found. Or the cats and the dog, whatever it was. Do you know where, precisely?"

"That would be my people who located them, Émile," Captain Borde interjected. Unlike the other two, he was in uniform, and his overcoat was the same grim green as the SQ tunic. "I could find that out soon enough."

"Why?" Mathers wanted to know.

"All part of the killer's mindset. Granted, we don't have much to go on. If he dropped them a short distance away that indicates one set of parameters. Perhaps that he was hurrying. Or just didn't care. But if he dropped them into the snow a long way off, then he really was trying to keep them concealed forever. If he thought that way it gives us a different set of mental parameters." He looked over at Mathers. "If he dropped the animals and the accelerant in the same spot, is that coincidence or is that the same person doing it? Good question, no? In a case like this, when we have nothing, I want to keep looking for something, anything. I found out today that the people killed in Geraldine, Alabama, and in New Orleans, Louisiana, were both visited prior to their deaths by an insurance adjustor, who presumably was there to assay the value of the destruction to their property. Cops dismissed the information and never took it a step further. So that's what I'm looking for, Bill. The evidence we're missing not because it's not there, but because it's been overlooked." Émile shot a glance at him, then chose to apologize. "Sorry. I'm in a mood today. I didn't mean to lecture." To Borde, he explained, "An agent for the FBI, someone I worked with down south, was found murdered this morning."

"Sorry to hear that. The adjustor thing is an interesting angle though."

"Why's that?"

"This place. It didn't need one before the Lumens were murdered. But it's going to need one now. I'm not serious, but I'm pointing that out. Maybe he's in the neighborhood. Might be interesting to see who shows."

"I see. You want our killer to just appear on our doorstep."

"Admit it, Émile. That would be nice." The three enjoyed a brief chuckle, but they were moving to go their separate ways. "Bill," Borde said to Mathers, "if you don't mind, I'll get my people to send the answer on Émile's request to you. That way, I don't have to explain sending information off to a civilian."

"No problem. I'll pass it along."

"Gentlemen, next time, let's bring marshmallows. Have a great day."

Each man returned to his vehicle, and Émile Cinq-Mars, last in, was positioned to be the first out, and led them back to the highway where they split up, Émile going one way, the Montreal and SQ policemen the other.

TWENTY-SIX

Where farmland yielded to a spruce forest, at the crest of a rise, Émile Cinq-Mars pulled over. He didn't know why. Not a hunch or the need for a quiet moment, yet he felt that he was responding to an inner notion that, although amorphous, was somehow compelling. Stepping out, looking back over the plateau under its snow blanket, he observed the buildings still spewing smoke onto the breeze and the gathering gloom of dusk. The sun was setting behind him and behind the spruce, the darkness gaining upon a land that remained shot through with a ruddy glow of light. He felt, if anything, nostalgic, but had trouble putting a finger on his mood.

Nostalgic? he pondered. *For what?*

That was the question.

Not for the day, as it was just another one on the cusp of spring, soon to be over. Better weather, if nothing else, was promised for the coming weeks, and he felt no nostalgia for winter. Although the hour and the red sun suggested a finality, the expiration of an allotted moment—he acknowledged that the day brought the news of Vira Sivak's death and that was likely part of this—but something else, vaguely mysterious and quaint, was taking a tentative hold on his sensibilities.

Cinq-Mars tried to scratch away at his mood. The day was ending, and the grand epic that is winter in the north was terminating as well, so there was that, and in following that line he soon realized where his nostalgic thread was guiding him. Way in the distance, mere pinpricks now, the taillights from Borde's and Mathers's cars shone. Then even those infinitesimal dots vanished as Venus and the first stars of the evening emerged. So was that it then? He was going home, and those two might be heading home to their wives also, and in Mathers's case to his kids as well, but the men remained on the job, and in the morning they'd wake up to their responsibilities to investigate and to protect. Whereas he would not. Cinq-Mars recognized that he was pleased to be working this case despite it's sluggish and even nonexistent progress, but for the first time since retiring he was truly missing both his badge and his duties, even his Glockmeister. In the months that passed since retirement, he'd been too distracted by cracked ribs and pneumonia, and the announcement by his wife that she might be done with him, to take any time to simply say good-bye to his long and eventful career, to reassess, and to get on with something new. This case yanked him right out of his new life and dropped him into a time warp among aliens. Thanks to the case he could almost believe that he was a legitimate policeman again. On a hillock at dusk, observing the fire diminish to smoke, Émile Cinq-Mars understood, really for the first time, that he was a detective no more, and for the first time, with an appropriate level of honesty, he was saying good-bye to his long career, and more importantly, to the life he'd led and even to the person he understood himself to be.

All that wasn't so bad, he considered. Sandra had shocked him more, perhaps, by saying that she was done with horses than she did when she let him know that she might be finished with him. Without horses, whatever came next for her would be a complete rebuild, a transformation. Surely the same held true for him. His change had been thrust upon him, partly by circumstance, but primarily by time, whereas Sandra wanted to reshape her outlook, redistribute her priorities, develop alternate routines and charter unknown territory if for no other reason than to do so. She honored change over routine or familiarity. Given his own situation he saw the virtue in that, both for her, and by extension, for himself. So this wasn't so bad. If she was willing to let him be a part of her next move in life, then he was at a juncture when he could thoroughly accommodate whatever she might choose.

Down in his coat pocket, his fingers discovered an old stick of gum. He took it out and studied it in the gloaming to ascertain that the wrapper hadn't been compromised, then removed it from the sheath, folded it in half, and dropped it into his mouth. Cinq-Mars chewed on that as he mulled his life.

As the day's last light vanished and the smoky fire was close to being extinguished, he considered the lives of the four who died on that farm. Morris and Adele Lumen, Officers Ron Bouvard and Marc Casgrain. A sorry, wretched business. Had it been him in similar circumstances dispatched to answer a call as a young policeman in uniform, his own life might have been snuffed out as quickly. Those boys would never know the blessings of a long and honorable career, or have families, or grow, like him, old. And the Lumens, what threshold had they crossed during their sojourn on earth to warrant such a swift, brutal demise? What linked them to the violent deaths of others? What developments brought them from who knows where—Nebraska, he was told, via Everardo Flores, although some said the Maritimes, but really nobody knew—from who knows where, then, to land on a farm in Quebec now reduced to cinders and ash? And why, he asked himself point-blank, couldn't he solve this one?

Maybe if he was still a cop, able to tap into available resources and personnel, maybe then he could solve this. Stuck on his own on a farm, he had given it the old college try, but he felt much like a collegian suddenly thrust into a workforce and out of his element. In any case, excuses aside, he'd failed.

Cinq-Mars considered his situation comparable to one of those impossible crosswords that so flummoxed him these days. When he peeked at the answers, he understood the clues, but when the next crossword came in, once again he could not comprehend what on earth was being asked. He didn't really want to think this way, yet Émile was convinced that persons less intelligent than himself (although he was beginning to have his doubts about that), less well read, who possessed inferior vocabularies to his own were far more astute at the game. He didn't get that. He supposed that if he was ever going to get the knack of these infernal things he would have to learn the logic behind the clues. That's what he didn't grasp now, and so he was deeply frustrated.

He decided that he wasn't enjoying the stale stick of gum so much, spit it out, and climbed back into his Jeep. He turned the motor on, let the heat blast him, and tipped the toggle switch to warm his seat. So what if the damn car burst into flames and scorched his rear end? One more fire on the evening air, big deal. He put the vehicle into drive and moved it about a foot when he clamped down on the brake pedal again and backed up that same short distance off the road.

What had he been telling himself?

An unprovoked excitement drifted across the pores of his forearms, all the way under his down coat and shirt.

To do crosswords, he'd have to learn the particular language of the clues.

One more thing: once he read the answers, he understood the clues.

He was not convinced that he could turn around his success at crossword puzzles, but was his inner self not speaking to him across a widening chasm?

He had to find the answers to understand the clues.

He'd been going at this the wrong way around! He was hoping for clues to lead him to answers, as they did in every other case he'd ever investigated. This one, though, was different, and required a different approach. Cheat. Go straight to the answers. Figure out the clues later.

But how to do that?

As exciting as the possibility seemed, it also appeared unfathomable.

Émile checked his watch. The correct time was available to him on the car's dash, but he wanted the old familiar comfort of looking at the hands of a watch to tell him what he needed to know. Yet that time check became protracted, and he took a moment to admire, once again, his elegant timepiece.

What, he wondered, am I doing wearing such a thing? All that money on his wrist. A gift, but a gift from people who hated him, admired him, resented him, loved him, dismissed him, revered him, some of whom were so glad that he was leaving his job they'd chipped in to buy him the watch. What did he care for all that sentiment worn on his wrist? Next to nothing. But he admired the timepiece. The real question, though, wasn't what was he doing by wearing an instrument of such obvious value on his wrist, but what was he doing *enjoying* it so much.

Times, if he could permit himself the pun, change.

So did he.

He started the drive home, feeling cautious, alert, awaiting bright answers.

He didn't need to assess more clues. They weren't going to help much. He only needed answers. Thinking that way, he soon felt freer, brighter, more attuned to himself and, as a consequence, to his case. He felt that if he didn't solve the puzzle by the time he went to bed that night, he would most likely wake up in the morning with the whole thing figured out. Just like that. Like magic.

Answers first. His new mantra. Then the clues.

Solve it first. Understand it later.

Little did he know that he was destined to figure it out much sooner than expected. He had barely walked through the front door to his farmhouse when he understood everything.

TWENTY-SEVEN

As Merlin padded through to the vestibule to greet him, lacking, it seemed, his customary enthusiasm, Émile heard Sandra preparing dinner in the kitchen. He removed and hung up his winter coat, kicked off his boots, and leaned down from his significant height to stroke the dog's brow and snout. Merlin carried on as curiously cheerless although he managed a faint tail-wag on his way back to rejoin Sandra. Émile kept his eyes on him. He often sought her company—or her protection, or to protect her—when distressed. Cinq-Mars returned his coat to the rack a second time, it had slid off a hook encumbered with jackets, then wandered through to the kitchen. Hands in the sink, Sandra tilted her lips to him, they kissed, and before he could fill her in about the fire or inquire about her day, the phone rang.

Émile answered the wall-mount. "Cinq-Mars."

Sandra rolled her eyes. Clearly, reforming his salutation was a lost cause.

"Émile, hi, it's Bill."

"Sergeant-Detective," Cinq-Mars said, "how goes the battle?"

"Still driving home, of course, but Borde's people just called him. Then he called me. We have the answer you were looking for."

"I don't recall the question, but go ahead."

"The dead pets, gas can, and empty packs of accelerant, as near as Borde could figure out over the phone while he was driving, were dumped in more or less the same spot. What's your best guess, Émile? Coincidence? Or the same guy?"

Clues were not going to help him, he already decided that. He needed to start thinking from the perspective of the answers.

"Hang on," he said. He processed Mathers's news, but something else was bugging him. Merlin went over to his food bowl and somewhat disinterestedly helped himself, then slurped water, then moved off again. Cinq-Mars continued to study the dog's bowl. Holding the phone to his chest, he asked Sandra, "You fed Merl?"

She looked up. "No. Why? It's not time." The geriatric dog was on a strict diet and feeding schedule. They never altered it. Yet he had more food in his bowl, by far, than when Cinq-Mars left the house for the day.

He got back on with Mathers. "Bill? Where are you exactly?"

He had stopped for a doughnut. He mentioned that without a shred of embarrassment. "Near the Île aux Tourtes right now. Still on the west side."

He was referring to the bridge to take him back onto the Island of Montreal.

"I know an excellent shortcut from there, Bill. Saves time. You can skip a ton of traffic."

"Excuse me?"

"Take the turn-off to go east of Aldgate, Bill. Cut your time in half."

Privy to only one side of the conversation, Sandra, who was busy at the sink and running water to wash lettuce, knew that what he said made no sense. Or made sense in an alarming way. She turned off the tap and stared at him.

A grim fright reared up.

Émile was waiting for Mathers to respond. He understood that the man needed a moment to process his code. His silence meant that he grasped that it was code, but he needed him to not only understand it but to do so at lightning speed. His life might depend on Bill Mathers getting this, and fast.

"Yeah," Mathers said. "You're right. That's a timesaver. Thanks."

"No problem." He meant it the other way around. He had a problem. "You owe me." He meant that the other way around as well.

"You're right about that." He meant that he understood. "Take care, Émile." He meant exactly that, for Émile to take care.

Émile put the phone back in its cradle. He whispered, "Of course," to himself, then turned to face Sandra. Their eyes locked. "Us, too," he told her quietly, redoubling her trenchant fear.

By the way her eyes shifted to the bottom cupboard next to the pantry he could tell that she understood him. Then she looked back at him, and Émile tilted his head in such a way that she looked over at Merlin's food bowl. She dried her hands on a dish towel. Sandra was a good American girl. She had no qualms about crossing the kitchen at that moment, even though her knees felt like jelly, to open the undercounter cupboard to take out her shotgun. Her weapon, not Émile's. She pulled out a box of shells and inserted one in each barrel and dropped more shells into the side pockets of her blue cardigan with the rope-like weave that hung extra-low on her hips. She looked back at Émile.

"Rather than go out again later," he said in a normal voice, "why don't we feed and water the horses now? Then relax for the evening."

That voice of his. He was telling her that someone might be listening. Although she already guessed as much.

"Good idea," she said.

He moved across to the gas range and turned the flames under two pots off. He checked that the oven wasn't on, turned, and indicated the front door. A finger to his lips curtailed further discussion. Sandra tapped her thigh to invite Merlin along and the old dog fell into step behind her, though he seemed reluctant.

In the front vestibule, they discreetly took turns holding the shotgun. They dressed for the out-of-doors and a cold barn, then went out with the weapon, which was cracked, concealed under Émile's down coat. They crossed the yard between the two buildings, Sandra going on ahead, Merlin at her heels. The side door intended as a convenience for humans was still heavy and more broad than any normal one, mainly to facilitate the passage of wheelbarrows and wagons, though nothing the size of the barn door for horses. Sandra heaved it open without any help as Émile's hands were occupied. Inside, he removed the shotgun from under his arm. Sandra swung the door shut and turned on him in an instant.

"What the hell is going on!"

"Sshhh!" he urged her.

She quieted instantly. "Nobody can hear us in here." Her statement carried the inflection of a question.

"We don't know that." She was about to object when he put two fingers on her lips. He whispered, "Don't assume this isn't sophisticated."

She urgently wanted to ask what the hell that could even mean, but she didn't. Not so hard to imagine. Listening devices. Bugs. Wireless this and remote that. Even out here on the lone prairie they had satellite TV, for heaven's sake, so who knew what toys bad guys might be playing with?

Whoever they were, they might have satellites, too.

Émile was walking past the horse stalls to the rear of the barn and Sandra scurried after him. She didn't appreciate being left alone. Merlin chose not to follow. Émile checked the latch at the rear—it was closed—then stuck a peg through the bolt. The peg hung by the side of the door permanently for those rare times when they wanted to lock that door to extreme weather. He returned to the front and the big barn doors that, apart from their latch, could be bound together and shut by fitting a six-foot-long two-by-ten plank, through four pad eyes. Which he did.

Émile then returned to the door they had entered and looked out the window. The old cracked glass was barely opaque after a winter's dirty abuse. The house stood as they left it, with a few lights on, but no movement within could be detected.

Indeed, the whole of the farm seemed serene and quiet.

Just as he loved it.

He motioned his wife over to his side and whispered directly into her ear, as quietly as he possibly could and still be heard. "The Lumens' barn burned. If somebody tries that here—only a remote chance—we shoot our way out."

She looked into his eyes then. She'd given herself barely a moment to be scared, but fright took hold now, simmering. She breathed in deeply. No time for histrionics. Explanations could come later. She'd been through enough with Émile before to know that she had to be brave, smart, expectant, and decisive. She nodded.

Merlin whimpered. They didn't know why. The cold and damp of the barn? He never liked it, but he was used to it. Their inactivity? He was staring away from them as he did whenever a horse put him on his guard with unsettled behavior.

But no horses were out.

In a stall, one lone mare whinnied.

Émile let Sandra carry the weapon. She grew up shooting grouse, gophers, and wild fowl. She could hit targets with that thing better than he could and fire and reload more rapidly than he could, and anyway her life was the one he most wanted to protect.

He checked his mobile phone. No communication from Mathers or Borde. He had to hope and pray that their silence derived from intention, not neglect. *Some trap I laid here.* He considered smiling. But self-mockery could not help him now.

Then Émile thought to look up. He scanned the rafters, but his vision was limited, as the floor for the hay loft above him covered most of the barn's footprint. The ceiling was low, one reason he was hoping to buy a new barn.

Sandra followed his gaze. A barn cat poked its head out from the loft, staring back. "You don't think?" she asked. Right inside her coat, against her skin, she felt a chill that held her as if by a human's grip.

Émile whispered, "Let's get in the Jeep. I didn't think. I'm supposed to think. I was being a cop, wanting to catch him. But I don't have to do that anymore."

He was legitimately cross with himself and breathing heavier. Sandra was watching him, breathing more rapidly as well. She wanted to comfort him, but wasn't in any shape to do so.

"He knew we'd come out here sooner or later. Or one of us would. To look after the horses."

"Who? What've you brought on us, Émile?"

"Burning the Lumens' barn was a distraction. To get me away from here. That would leave you home alone except he might've known you were gone, too."

"Émile. No."

"The Jeep."

"The horses, Émile."

"What?"

"I can't leave the horses."

"No one has any reason to harm them."

"He burns barns, you said."

True. Perhaps that's why, subconsciously, he came in here. To protect the horses as well as themselves. He hadn't realized that he was evacuating a two-story house for a two-story barn. Same difference. Same modus operandi.

But he forsook that idea. He came in here because his instincts to run were nonexistent. He wanted to catch the guy.

"Who, Émile?" Sandra asked him again, whispering still. Although she knew.

"Someone who might expect us to come out here to check on the horses."

He didn't want to say in case he was being foolish. Ridiculous, even.

"Any chance you're just paranoid?"

"Hope so. I pray that I am."

She considered all that. "Let's put them in the paddock. Then leave."

"Eight horses. Can we do that in one trip? Four each?"

"Are you crazy? We'll lose them!"

"That doesn't matter. Not really. We'll get them back."

"No, Émile. Four trips. One horse each. If this person knows anything about horses, if he's watching us, that will be a lot less suspicious. Four horses at once, even two each, will look like we're panicking."

"Which we are." A joke. He smiled. She did, too, finally. Briefly.

"Four trips," she said. "We'll look relaxed. Like we don't have a care in the world. Leave the shotgun behind. Take our time. Anybody watching will think we're heading back into the house after that. Only we jump in the Jeep instead. Oh, God, Émile, do you even have your keys?"

Even in a crisis a husband and wife were still husband and wife.

He felt through his coat pockets and nodded that he had them.

"We'll do it your way," he decided.

First he returned to the barn door that he'd just secured and pulled the locking brace back out from the pad eyes. He tripped the latch and swung each door wide open. Then he and Sandra each took a lead-chain down from where a dozen dangled on a wall and returned to the aisle of horse stalls.

They had done this in totally benign circumstances countless times before and so fell into an established routine. Émile went to a stall at the back of the aisle. Sandra chose the one second from the front. A halter for each horse hung on a hook outside its stall and they entered and kept each animal calm and slipped its halter on, then snapped on the lead-chain. They exited the stalls at the same moment, the two horses well separated, and Sandra led the way out.

At the paddock she unhooked a loop of rope that secured that gate, which was persnickety sometimes, but she succeeded in pulling the gate free with one hand and walked her horse inside. Émile followed with their only mare. They unclipped the lead chains and the two horses trotted off a short distance to enjoy the novelty of evening air. Émile closed the gate and secured it, and they returned to the barn to repeat the ritual. Cinq-Mars was beginning to believe that he was nothing if not paranoid. This was going to be a difficult one to explain to Mathers if ever he showed up and a difficult one to explain to Sandra once they were done and he was wrong about everything. But who fed Merlin? He had that to hang his hat on.

Outside, he whispered, "Your helper. Noel Lambert. Does he come into the house ever? When we're not here?"

"Why would he? Maybe for a pee, but he'd do his business outside if we weren't around, no?"

"He wouldn't bother to feed Merlin though."

"Why would he? But he might've. You never know. Do you think he might've?" She had a thought. "Where's Merl?"

The dog never left the barn. Unheard of. Inside, they found him moping on a bed of straw. Barely able to lift his head now.

"My God," Sandra said.

Émile so wished that he was merely paranoid. That he could drum up some other explanation for the extra feeding and subsequent demise of his dog.

"The horses first," he said. "We'll carry Merlin out with us."

He forgot to whisper. Sandra was the one to put a forefinger to her lips.

This time Sandra entered the first stall, Émile the third.

They repeated the process without a blemish, then started on the opposite side of the aisle. They finally did appear relaxed, as if this was old routine and not frightening.

Then the last two horses were escorted out to the paddock to run under the light of the rising quarter moon.

Émile swung the paddock gate shut and secured it.

Sandra was already hurrying back to the barn.

She went straight for the dog, Émile to the shotgun where it rested upright against a stall. Sandra slumped onto her knees over the animal. "Merl," she said. "Merl." Émile joined her and she asked, "What's wrong with him?"

"He's been drugged," Émile said. He could have said more. That he believed the dog inadvertently had saved their lives with his lethargic behavior, which had shown him the food in his bowl, but this was no time for explanations.

"Why? Who? Where?"

Émile supposed that the last question meant *Where is he now?* But he did not have to answer. Another voice spoke up.

"Yes, Émile. Why? Who? Answer the little lady."

Cinq-Mars swung around and aimed the shotgun, ready to fire.

"Don't bother," Rand Dreher advised him. "I took the liberty of removing the shells."

Not one to fall for a bluff, Cinq-Mars aimed the gun to the side and pulled one of the twin triggers. The hammer impotently clicked on nothing. Husband and wife remained shock-still after that, Sandra kneeling, Émile at her side, the gun raised.

"Take it easy," Dreher said. "I'm not going to shoot you. Not right now. Although I should, after that stunt."

Cinq-Mars aimed the gun at him and tried the other trigger.

Click!

He felt his life expire like air evacuating his lungs.

"Told you."

They were surprised that they didn't see a weapon, that his arms were folded comfortably across his chest. They couldn't see his hands.

"What's going on?" Cinq-Mars asked him.

"You're the famous, brilliant detective, Émile. Why don't you tell me? I'd be interested to hear what you've discovered."

"Until now, not a thing."

"No? Is that why you're out here hiding behind your wife's skirts? Why you put the horses outside? Why you carried in a loaded shotgun? You aimed it at me and tried to fire the damned thing! Not friendly! Is that because you haven't figured anything out? Or—were you venting your frustrations? Emile, don't take me for a fool, it won't help you at all."

"What've you done to Merlin?" Sandra beseeched him. All three looked over at the dog.

"He'll die slowly," Dreher said. "But he's an old dog and he won't feel much pain. He's getting groggy. I was hoping to delay his sleepiness, but it's hard to get the dosage right. So, you two, haven't you messed up my plans! I considered burning the barn with the horses in it. But you went and saved them. Pity you didn't think to save yourselves."

"We were working on that, actually."

Dreher raised his left hand to make a point, which is when his pistol came out from the folds of his overcoat in his right hand. Probably not government issue, Cinq-Mars analyzed, too expensive a weapon. Although he was not an expert on firearms, his best judgment told him that he was staring at a Glock 21, a high-capacity, forty-five caliber pistol. He perceived no benefit to any quick rush.

Dreher wore surgical gloves. No prints.

His free left hand motioned Sandra to stand and close ranks with her husband. She rose slowly and stood beside him, their clothing touching. "This is what I'm asking you," Dreher emphasized. "What tipped you off? How did you know I was on the farm? You must tell me. I want to improve my practice."

Sandra didn't give her husband a chance to answer, asking a question instead. "Why, why would you want to harm the horses?"

Dreher smiled. "Nothing personal. I have no particular dislike for horses, although lately I'm finding that I'm mildly allergic to their dander. Or maybe it's hay. Strange, for a farm boy like me. But no, if you didn't come out of the house on your own, I was going to draw you out. I was counting on you rushing out to save the horses as the barn started to burn and before you thought to phone for help. But it would be all right, if you phoned first. You might've saved the horses in that case as well, so there you go, I wasn't being mean. Merely . . . pragmatic. But you helped me out. You came out here on your own."

"Not the best plan in the world."

"Mine or yours?"

"Yours. We might've gotten in the car and left."

That simpering, disagreeable smile again. "Not to worry. I fixed your cars. Simple little thing. Squirt Crazy Glue in the ignition. Big headache after that. *Sorry!* So your flight to the barn was a good one. If you tried to run away, I would've been so disappointed, Cinq-Mars. Honestly, you don't want to disappoint me right now."

"What do you want, Dreher?"

"Oh, you know, Émile, what I've always wanted. Your humiliation. Complete and utter. Thank you so much for obliging me so very well up until this minute. But first, let the shotgun drop. It's not of any use to you anyway and I want to rule out the temptation to swing it around."

Émile put the stock to the floor of the barn, then let the gun topple over.

"Now your cell, please. At your feet. Then kick it over."

He did as instructed, although the phone plowed through hay and didn't travel far.

"Do you have one, too, Sandra? It's best to be honest."

She shook her head.

"Back away. Both of you." They did so until ordered to stop. Dreher went over and picked up the phone, gave it a glance, then put it in his pocket. "I've been listening in anyway. I'll need to delete that app. Wouldn't you like to know when I put it on? Charming device. Our Vira Sivak—yes, the very same—she invented it. Now, shall we go inside? The house, I mean. Barns are so cold, don't you find? And damp. As well, I've got this little allergy thing going on. The sniffles. Red eyes. Nothing serious though."

"Why'd you want us in the barn? You had access to the house."

"A mystery, isn't it? I was going to connect this barn burning to the other one, which directs suspicion from me onto the man I'll convict for this dire crime. But not to worry. No fire. Plan B. We'll go back to the house now."

"Merlin—" Sandra started to say.

"Let him die in peace. There's nothing you can do for him now."

"I can carry him."

"Don't be ridiculous."

"No! Please! I'm not leaving him."

Dreher measured her resolve, his eyes narrowing intently, yet looking vacant. His voice adopted a flat, low staccato beat, and a tinny, mechanical timbre. "Have it your way. I can never say no to a pretty dame. But Émile, you do the carrying. Help the little lady out."

And so they moved, from the barn to the house, Cinq-Mars carrying the heavy weight of Merlin, a considerable strain on his lower back. He hesitated before attempting the steps up to the front door.

"Come on, Cinq-Mars. In exceptional circumstances, any man can discover extraordinary strength. Isn't that what they say? Don't give me that old man's pose."

He hated that this was true, but being baited that way compelled him to gather his strength again. He remembered his osteopath's instructions, clenched his sphincter and tummy muscles to take up the strain, then climbed up.

Sandra opened the door and they went inside.

She helped her husband lower the retriever to the sofa.

Merlin's head lolled forward.

"Almost gone," Dreher said. "It'll be peaceful. You'll see. Ah! Of course! You might not live long enough to see him go. But I give you my word. It's an easygoing, gentle death. I have nothing against old dogs."

He wore an insidious grin.

Émile rose to his feet. His wife remained seated on the sofa, petting the head of her dog. "All right," he said. He had but one purpose here. To delay. "What do you want?"

"Initially, your compliance. Please don't ask me to make any specific threats, Émile. That would be so unbecoming, you know? Just do as I say and know that it's for the best."

Holding his weapon with one hand he was shaking an arm free of its coat sleeve. Then he switched hands and did the same for his other arm until the coat fell off his back. He retrieved it off the floor and placed it over the arm of the nearest chair. "Take your own coats off, and please, kick those boots away. I'll tidy up later, but we don't want to be tracking snow through the house. Sandra, your cardigan, please, remove it. Throw it over here."

Perhaps he was being weird for the sake of weirdness, but the detective doubted that. Whatever his plans, he wanted them to adhere to a certain look and protocol. If he had their executions in mind, and Cinq-Mars assumed that he did, then he also planned to stage them, either to assist with an exit strategy or to obfuscate the circumstances to foil future investigators. Cinq-Mars took his coat off, pulled one boot off with the toe of the other, then the second boot was similarly peeled away. Sandra let her coat fall back behind her on the sofa.

She threw her sweater his way, and a shotgun shell tumbled from a pocket onto the rug. Dreher stooped to pick it up, and smirked. "What *will* the IO think of these, I wonder," he said, and put it back in the cardigan's pocket.

He was not yet satisfied.

"Okay now," Dreher determined. "Let's get comfortable. Émile, pour us each a fine Scotch, will you? And don't be stingy."

"I'm good," Cinq-Mars told him. "But I'll get you one."

"Ah, that's not a request, Émile. I was merely trying to be polite, to keep this pleasant. So pour yourself a fucking Scotch, as well as one for me, please and thank you. Sandra? I'll give you a choice."

"Fuck sake," she said.

"Whoa. There's a mouth on that one. Suit yourself. You might regret that later—declining a drink. But life is full of regrets, isn't it? I'm sure you must be running through a whole catalog of them right about now. Such as, why did I feed this bastard dinner? Don't deny it now. Émile? The Scotch. And please, you know better. Don't throw the bottle at me or do anything silly. The matter won't go well if you do."

He moved over to the liquor cabinet. "Will the matter go well if I cooperate?" he asked.

"As you know, Émile, everything in life, and in death, is a matter of degree."

He poured into two snifters, and if this was to be his last drink on earth, he was not being stingy, just as Dreher requested. Bringing a glass over to his captor, he obeyed Dreher's gesture with the pistol to place it on a side table.

"Now sit," Dreher said. Apparently, he didn't care exactly where. Once Émile was seated in a hardbacked extra chair, Dreher made himself comfortable in a deep cushioned armchair and inhaled the scent of his single malt before imbibing. "It's been a day," he said.

"A dead field officer. Then burning barns," Cinq-Mars concurred. "Yeah. That's a busy day."

"Only one barn, Émile. Could've been two. The second won't be necessary."

"That's good news."

"Always have a backup to your backup plan," Dreher opined. "That's how you do it."

"And what is what you're doing all about, Rand?" The man always wanted him to be familiar, to use first names. Now might be the time for that.

"Émile, honestly, trust me. I'm sorry that it became necessary that you, or someone like you—but of course, there is no one quite like you, is there? At a certain point it became evident that a person of your reputation needed to become part of this. Geography was a factor, for sure. But I also required someone with impeccable credentials, and honestly—congratulations—you fit that criteria to a tee."

"To what end?"

Dreher chuckled lightly to himself.

"What's so funny?"

"You are. Stalling like this. Thinking that time is on your side. That time will be your friend and help you."

"What else would you have me do?"

Their captor waved his pistol in the air. "You're right. It's desperation. Your last resort. So, good. We can have a conversation, as futile as your hope for this talk may be."

Émile and Sandra exchanged glances. Nerves caused her elbows to jump, and she returned to giving comfort to, and in return, perhaps being comforted by, the dying retriever. "So, tell me—"

"No!" Dreher stopped him, his voice sharp but not raised. "That's not how this is going to go down. You will guide me through what you know, and then and only then, *if I am satisfied,* and if I'm still in the mood, only then will I fill in the blanks for you. So, you first, Émile. Talk."

He flicked the barrel of his pistol to urge him on.

"All right," Cinq-Mars said. "I'll talk. You want to know what I know. The killing in Alabama was botched."

"How so?" Dreher, his eyes darting between his two captives under his bushy eyebrows, appeared bemused.

Cinq-Mars knew that he had to engage him. He had to prolong his curiosity, in order to extend his own and his wife's lives.

"First, there's the botched business with the finger. Whoever amputated Agent Sivak's finger didn't do it right. She was still alive. In all other cases, including with the Lumens up here, the fingers were removed post-mortem."

"Oh, but aren't you the brilliant detective!" No admiration underlay his words. Only derision.

"I said 'first.' There's more."

"Okay, Detective, show me what you've got. So far, not much."

"So, a lesser detective, shall we say, could look upon that killing and think that it was a copycat. But even a lesser detective wouldn't hold that thought for long, because the previous killings were not public. There's been no public suggestion of a series of deaths, and the business of the fingers being cut off may not even be known publicly. So the inferior detective would have to assume that a surrogate was brought into all this to execute Agent Sivak and to make it look as though he was part of that series, if only to provide the initial killer with an alibi because he was elsewhere for the latest crime. The inferior detective would conclude that the murders were botched."

Dreher was holding Émile's gaze, less dismissive of him now. "What do you mean," he asked finally, "by *inferior* detective?"

"Because a superior detective would get it. That the surrogate was intentionally provided with improper instructions. That the whole point of those two murders was to make them look botched. They were meant to appear botched."

Dreher looked over at Sandra and smiled. "Your husband," he said. "I find him interesting. You must enjoy having him around the house. How do you figure all this, Émile? I'm curious."

"Up until now, all the murders have been meticulous. Almost perfect."

"Why only almost perfect? Who's been caught?"

"*Touché*. But I'm saying *almost perfect* because the cases are still being investigated. If they were perfect they would've disappeared off everyone's radar screen by now."

"They're being investigated," Dreher objected, "because I'm investigating them."

"And that's why they're almost perfect. Because you couldn't let them go. You created these perfect little murders, but you admire them so much you have to keep involving other police, and to keep even famous retired detectives from Canada investigating them, to show off how brilliant they all were and how devious you are."

"That would be an indulgence," Dreher contended. "Here's a tip, Émile. Not that it can do you any good now. One does not *indulge* in murder. The proper killer needs a sound reason, a logical strategy, a platform."

"Of course," Cinq-Mars agreed, and allowed a note of derision to enter his own tone, "I was getting to that. But let's not lose sight of the fact—the *fact*—that ego was involved in your gambit. The killer did not hide in attics merely to get a handle on police procedure. The killer could have walked in the front door and shown his badge to manage that. The killer hid in attics in order to expose police departments as incompetent. And that was done, largely, out of ego."

"Marginally," Dreher protested. "Marginally for ego. A pattern had to be created, for the simple reason that it could be repeated, for *repetition* has strategic value. That police reputations were damaged in the process was a bonus. Mind you, an ingenious bonus, even if I do say so myself. Ego was not being served, Émile. You've got that wrong. Everything, everything, is purely strategic."

"Bullshit."

"Émile. Please. There's a lady present. Besides, I'm the one holding the gun, remember?"

The conversation was allowing time to slide by, and that was all he cared about. He could tell, though, that Dreher was enjoying himself. For the killer, prolonging the inevitable was a pleasure. He imagined that the man had conducted these conversations with each of his victims, explaining himself, pontificating, exulting in his genius for subterfuge and strategy, the whole time listening to their desperate pleas and laments. Taking his time to inflict the highest degree of psychological anguish, rather than physical pain, was a critical aspect pertaining to his style for murder.

"Vira was killed," Cinq-Mars explained, "in the way that she was killed, because she was getting close."

"That's your fault, Cinq-Mars. Her blood is on *your* hands. Take that to the grave. Anything that happens to you today may be unfortunate, but it is well-deserved. You must agree."

"My fault?" Cinq-Mars repeated.

"You and that fucker assistant of yours. Everardo Flores. Who is he anyway?"

He understood. "Had she interviewed people in Alabama, Vira would have gleaned more information about a self-appointed claims adjustor who promptly showed up on the doorsteps of storm victims who just happened to be in the FBI witness protection program. He then assassinated them. That's all the pattern required. Staying behind in the attic was done for two reasons. Ego, which took pleasure from damaging the reputations of legitimate and solid officers of the law, and danger, a joy in itself."

"Don't forget now, hiding in the attic extends the pleasure of the kill."

"Okay. Also, our killer is drawn to high-risk like the proverbial moth to the flame. Why else are you here today? You could have sent your Alabama killer, used him one more time. I assume that your plan is to eliminate him soon enough?"

Dreher mulled it over. "Actually," he revealed, "that is the plan. And won't I be the hero for that one? In a gun battle, most likely. I'll kill the man responsible for slaying an FBI agent in Alabama and shooting the husband-and-wife team of Émile and Sandra Cinq-Mars all the way up in Canada. Such a shame. For the world to lose their revered detective. Are you surprised? It's true. He's here now. Not *here* here. But in the environment. Lives close by, actually. I hired a somewhat local. Upper New York State. So you see, as you may have guessed—"

"I have guessed. It's Exit Strategy 101."

"Oh, come on, give me a little more credit than that!"

"I won't. I'm sorry. It's too basic. Create a foil—"

"Over years! For years I had him waiting in the wings! It's brilliant, Émile! Give me that much credit, at least! If you don't, then I'll know that you're too ego-obsessed yourself to speak the truth where and when the truth is warranted."

"So, now you want the truth." Cinq-Mars shook his head. And looked over at Sandra. To her, he said, "He wants the truth." And back at Dreher. "You know what they say about the truth."

Merlin took that moment to pull his head up a little, and he struggled on the cushions to push his front end upright. Sandra comforted him and kept him still. The movement, though, interested Rand Dreher.

"Did that dog eat all his food?"

"He doesn't chow down as rapidly as some big dogs do. Anyway, you fed him early."

"Then he might not expire. Too bad your own prognosis is decidedly more bleak. As for the truth, Émile, don't kid yourself, I can take anything you can dish out. You, on the other hand, will melt if you hear what I know. But we don't have all day. The time has come to get on with it."

Cinq-Mars thought fast, to keep him interested in talking. "Didn't you want to know how I knew that you were here when I got home?"

Briefly, he pointed with his free hand at him. "You're right. I'm curious. What tipped you off? Educate me. I won't want to make the same mistake twice."

"Merlin tipped me off. That was your error. He left more food in his bowl than was there before I left the house. That told me that somebody visited. Also, his temperament seemed decidedly subdued. So, Rand, you were outwitted by a dog."

Dreher chortled. "I suppose you expect me to be mortified by that insult? I'm far more mortified by your response. Look what you did. You took your wife and ran out to the barn. Why? That seems so stupid to me. Even when you thought someone was on the premises, you thought you'd be safe in the barn. Or is it because, like most people, you were too proud to act on your basic animal instinct? You needed proof before you were willing to run."

"Something like that, I suppose," Cinq-Mars conceded. "Unlike you, I don't aspire to perfection in what I do. I just take what comes."

"Émile! God! Don't give me that humble-jumble crap! You're a goddamn power-hungry, fear-mongering, asshole-reaming *cunt* of a detective and the vast majority of your peers say so. I checked you out, don't forget, before this all began. There's your public reputation, and then there's your reputation according to those who *know* you. So don't spoon-feed me any of your hyper-ego in the form of humility horse manure—no offense to horses—because I'm not buying it."

"Fine. I didn't run because—" He hesitated.

"Because why, Émile? Don't be so damn proud. Share your ignorance with us lesser mortals."

"Because I didn't want to catch you. I wanted to outwit you."

Popping back out of his chair, Rand Dreher waved his gun around, as if consumed by a rant and intending to theatrically deliver more upon the stage of their living room. But he stopped short, as if he understood in a trice that he was being baited.

Interpreting the change in him that way, Cinq-Mars switched tacks.

"I'll grant you," Émile said. "This is not about hating cops, although that's at least a small part of it, and this is not about your ego, although that is a part of it, too. Has to be. But I'll grant you, Rand, that neither of those things is compelling enough for a man like yourself. They are only the side benefits you've picked up over time, similar to getting an extra week's vacation after putting in twenty years on the job, that sort of thing. So the real question here is, what's your angle? Because—grant me this much intelligence, Rand, this much investigative acumen—you're no bottom-feeder. I recall our talk about the swamp. That was a good talk. You were defending the intelligence of sludge—"

"Slime, actually," Dreher corrected him.

"Slime. You indicated your sympathy for slime, and by osmosis for all beings bent to a criminal or warped mentality, yet you are not a bottom-feeder yourself. Don't get me wrong. I'm in a difficult situation here, but I'm not sucking up to you. I'm too proud for that. So I'm telling you, I do not number you among the elite intelligentsia and certainly not among the angels. You have your horrific attributes—you're a killer, Rand—but you don't dwell in slime. You may be sympathetic to their plight but you do not live among the swamp bugs. You're in this for your own benefit.

If I'm to die today, the least you can do is let me in on that part. What's in it for you? What do you get out of all this?"

Standing above them both, the gun at his side, Rand Dreher gazed from one to the other. For the first time, his victims saw the killer in him. He had a finger on the trigger of his gun, but now, and really for the first time, he had his mind on the trigger of his intent. He was contemplating killing them soon, they could tell.

"Don't overestimate me, Émile. Do you know why I kill couples the way I do? Hatred. It's that simple. I hate couples. I hate that you don't share your DNA, that you keep it in-house, so to speak. I hate that you presume to rise up out of the morass and swamp-muck to live behind your white picket fences and tidy wee homes. We should all be down in the swamp, Cinq-Mars, down low in the muck and mire, slurping each other's shit. I *hate* all you shithead couples who presume to adapt to civility. Who have manners when you screw. It's against fucking nature. I protest."

He paced before them, and Sandra began to tremble.

"Out of respect for our fine chats, Émile," Dreher went on, "I might grant you that dying wish. Why not? But first, let's take care of business. Sandra, I'm going to ask you to stand and to face your husband. Let's see if you can do so without making a fuss or falling over. It'll be better that way, I promise."

She did so reluctantly, feeling dizzy now, transported, as if this was not a real moment. Not a dream, but not a real time or place, either. What allowed her to remain upright, for she was surprised that she could, was Dreher moving away from her, not toward her, which gave her a measure of relief. But after he visited his coat he returned. Blocked by his wife's body, Émile was not able to observe what the man extracted from a pocket, then he and his wife held to one another's gaze, silently beseeching one another to be brave and to have faith. His gaze was meant to remind her that he had summoned help.

Dreher told Sandra, "Clasp a wrist behind your back with the other hand."

She dreaded doing so, but he poked her with the pistol and she obeyed. He then bound her wrists tightly with what felt like thin strong cord—the treasure seized from his coat pocket—and she was ordered to remain standing.

"Émile. Your turn. Stand up."

Doing so, he exhibited the posture of an older man with a failing back. He slowly straightened. Dreher ordered Sandra to sit in the hardbacked chair Émile abandoned, and she did so and he knotted Émile's wrists behind him. Told to remain standing, he was relieved, given the cramping just above his hips.

Dreher chose to sit again.

"There's something you must understand. I'll tell you now so that you can deal with it, get over the shock, then make an informed decision. I know what your decision will be. How do I know, you ask?"

Not having a clue what he was driving at, Émile shrugged.

"Because everyone else has made exactly the same decision when offered the same identical choice."

By everyone else, he presumed the man meant everyone he had slaughtered.

"What's that?" Émile asked.

"When it comes time to cut off your ring finger—we'll do it the old-fashioned way, not like in Alabama, so you will be dead first—yes, you may thank me for that—you're welcome—when it comes time to slice and dice, Sandra will do it."

"What?"

"What's he talking about?" Sandra asked. A tremor entered her voice.

"Sorry, dear," Dreher explained, "but you're going to have to cut off Émile's ring finger. End this fucking marriage once and for all."

"I won't. Émile!"

"Actually, you will. And don't ask Émile to help. He'll be dead by then. And anyway, he's tied up at the moment."

"You fucking bag of crap."

"The mouth on this girl, Émile. And you, some sort of good Catholic man. Do you know that your former colleagues call you the Pope? The ones who like you, anyway. The other ones call you the Fucking Pope."

"I'm not going to cut off his finger," Sandra declared, finding her strength again.

Dreher smiled and returned to his feet again and paced in front of them, staying out of Émile's kicking range. He allowed his calmness, his quietude, to parlay his menace. "I can understand how you might feel that way. And you do have a choice. Listen to your options first. Option number one, after I shoot him, you cut off his ring finger. After I shoot you, I'll cut off yours. Then I'll bury your two fingers together with your wedding rings in this sweet little graveyard I've got going. Down by a riverbank. Only the ring fingers of couples are buried there. Quite romantic, actually. The river flows by, day by day."

"Oh God," Sandra said. That he was monstrous and murderous had seeped through at the onset of their ordeal, but the breadth of his depravity struck home.

"That's option one, which you say you won't accept. It's your choice, but that leaves us with option two. In this scenario, while he's still alive, I saw off Émile's head. You watch, and then, I saw off yours. Again, we'll keep you alive for that."

The couple gazed at each other. Tears flooded Sandra's eyes that she couldn't wipe away, and her shoulders and torso quivered violently now. She shook her head, though, to try to persevere through this.

"Perhaps you understand now why option one has been the preferred choice, one hundred percent of the time. Should you renege on option one and refuse to honor your commitment after I shoot your husband, then we revert to hacking off your head. Hacking, of course, is the operative word. It's not like I'm walking around with my own private guillotine. It's a slow and difficult operation with second-rate tools. Whatever I can find in your kitchen, actually. Do either of you doubt my resolve in this matter?"

Reeling, Émile found it hard to think in any cogent way. "Yeah, actually," he challenged Dreher. He had to keep him talking, keep him boasting, if necessary. "I do. In the past you've only cut off the fingers of dead people. That's easier, I should think, than if someone's alive and the blood is spurting everywhere. A neck, more difficult still. You might not have it in you, Rand. As I pointed out, you're not a bottom-feeder. Don't you agree with me?"

"But I dream about it, Émile. I can't tell you how much. Anyway you're wrong. Adele Lumen was still alive when I amputated her finger. I should have known she was still alive. Just didn't believe it. But her hand bled more. I liked that. I still see it in my dreams. Émile, I will carry through on you and your wife's decapitations if you want to test me. So go ahead. I'm begging you. Test me."

Both Émile and Sandra endeavored to hold their heads up, Sandra weeping, Émile trying to remember to breathe. He struggled for a deeper breath, felt his lungs collapsing. He remembered his episode in New Orleans, when a panic attack had overwhelmed him, but here he needed to maintain, through all this madness, his composure. Even unto death. His hope, dissipating, still clung to that necessity.

"She'll do option one," he managed to say, his voice garbled.

Sandra nodded when Dreher looked to her for confirmation.

"Good. Good. This is important to me, actually, that you accept your roles as coconspirators in one another's removals. I don't know why, I just prefer it that way."

Removals.

Émile took another shaky breath, his lungs like twin spikes inside him as they expanded. "So, Rand. If you're not going to spare us, at least tell us, what's your angle? You said you would."

Dreher placed his right hand, which held the pistol, over his heart. "Happy to, Émile. Some criminals, I believe, and I'm sure you've seen this throughout your career, some criminals are only too happy to get caught. Why do you suppose that is, Émile?"

"I'm not a psychiatrist. I can't say."

"Take a wild stab at it. Entertain me and your life is extended for those few minutes. People like doing that, I've found, extending their pathetic lives that last little speck. Gives them hope, I suppose, even though it's fleeting. People want to believe that rescue is on the way when so clearly it isn't. They want to think that God will strike me down. Or that, miracle of miracles, I'll change my mind. By the way, your wrists are tied, but I've left your fingers free. Do you want your prayer beads?"

He waited for Cinq-Mars to reply.

"It's possible," Émile began slowly, "that some men can't really keep a secret. That they need for other people to know what it is they've done. In their minds, I suppose, they think of it as what they've accomplished. Even, in some cases, they want people to know who they are. Sometimes, men are proud of their crimes, and want other people to know that they were the ones who pulled them off. Later, they'll regret being caught, but that's just how things go."

"I believe you're onto something, Émile. I want people to know who I am. And what I've done. But confession, that's out of the question. Incarceration? Let's just say that I'm not going there. Still, I do experience a need for people to know. So, I tell them. I get it off my chest. Afterward, of course, I kill them."

They waited. What they did know, between them, was that death was not imminent, not as long as he had a story to relate or a boast to advance.

"Émile, trust me, you're going to love this." He waved his gun with his rising excitement. "It's just so cool. Inside the FBI, we have found a way, incrementally, but impressively, to augment our budget. At least, to circumvent certain budgetary constraints. The consensus being, if criminals' funds are confiscated, why not use them to further our pressure against crime? But this is where it gets interesting. Within that program, a few have found ways for their personal aggrandizement. I'll leave the rationalizing to them. Now that's a big word I'm using but I prefer it to greed. But it's true. Some people who walk this earth are atrociously greedy. I'm not naming names, you understand. By our own careful accounting," and Dreher spoke ponderously now, as though his excitement required him to linger over his words to fully satisfy his impending pleasure, "we participate in, oh, nearly eight percent—" He shifted his attention to Sandra to augment his point, his eyes opening wide. "That might not sound like a lot, but trust me, it's huge. Or, as you would say with that mouth of yours, it's *fucking* huge!" Then his attention reverted primarily to Émile again. "Eight percent of the entire marijuana trade in the continental United Sates of America. We control. The supply end. Like you say, I'm not a bottom-feeder getting my hands dirty with distribution. But we grow weed, baby. In the cornfields of Nebraska. And Kansas. As far east as Kentucky. As far north as Idaho and Montana. We've got Mormons growing our pot amid their corn in Utah." He laughed at that tidbit. "We've proven that it's less dangerous to grow pot under my auspices than for the mob, and we can protect the honest farmer against the mob. Not that anybody knows its for the Bureau, only that somebody seems to have power and the ability to move mountains. Even the mountains of Utah. So it's a win-win-win situation all around. If I benefit to a certain extent, then so be it, mere humble servant that I am. I come from that milieu, you understand. We're talking about my people. I was recruited into the FBI while my daddy was growing corn. But that wasn't his only cash crop, if you know what I mean. He had a cash crop that essentially wasn't very different from growing cash. Instead of threshing corn, although we did that, too, for the sake of appearances, we were mainly into plucking greenbacks from the stem. So you see, it's all good."

He observed them, shifting his gaze from one to the other, anticipating their praise.

"Of course," he continued, "from time to time we have to protect our growers. So-called honest cops might arrest them, so we take them into witness protection. Or we have to show that we're doing our job. We get our people to inform on their neighbors, who the mob controls, then we have to take them out of the operation even as our operation increases, because we've now taken over new fields from the mob. But you see my problem. It's a chess game, that's one thing. And some of that comes back on me. I have to play it five moves ahead or I'll be behind. So I have people in witness protection who know me as a special agent in the FBI who has, shall we say, complicated ethics. So that leaves me with no choice but to go back through that field and cull the chaff from the wheat, so to speak. I know that sounds ass backward, but that's what has to be done on occasion. It's safer."

Émile could tell that Sandra was disinterested and losing hope. He could not allow that to happen. He had to buoy her up with his own enthusiasm for Dreher's story.

"But the Lumens, Rand? Did they fit into that scheme? Up here in Canada?"

Dreher clicked his fingers. "You're right, Émile. Different scenario entirely. By this point, somebody is noticing inside the Bureau that not only are we losing informants—usually they think our witness protection people are informants, and usually we do manipulate things to make it look that way—but we're losing informants who were attached to me. We're losing *my* informants. So I get to investigate, but also I have to find a way to take this off my shoulders."

"It's a tangled web we weave, Rand," Émile encouraged him.

"Call it a web," Dreher said, as if missing the familiarity of the remark entirely, "but for sure my operations created a pattern and that pattern was growing visible, for those with eyes to see. People associated with my work in the war against drugs and in my geographic concentration were being eliminated. One by one, spread out over time. Oh, I was clever in creating the storm motif, this wandering serial killer who struck in the aftermath of a strong wind or a quaking earth, but, nonetheless, the idea persisted that a pattern was forming that revolved around me. So, guess what I did?"

Cinq-Mars obliged him. "You struck outside your parameters."

"Precisely. I blurred the pattern. That's where you fit in. Lovely of you to come down to New Orleans, for example. To give yourself that exposure. Meet the troops. Too bad about Vira. She was an up-and-comer, but the connection, the bond that she was forming with you, and you guys finding out that the killer was a claims adjustor—" He performed a pantomime of shivering. "Too close for comfort. She had to go. And now you. Then I'll solve these murders, Vira's and yours, and dear Sandra's, and that won't be difficult, it just means shooting the killer before he gets to talk to anybody, then we'll trace his movements after the fact to prove his guilt. Brilliant, all around. Puts me in the clear inside the Bureau. Our market share continues. Life goes on. Everything is put behind us. Hell, even your dog lives to die a natural death. What more can anyone ask for?"

That Émile managed, somehow, an incomprehensible smile, transfixed Dreher's attention.

"Do you know what I enjoy the most about killing people?" he asked them. "There are many aspects I relish, but do you know what gives me the deepest, most gratifying satisfaction?"

"Of that, I have no clue," Cinq-Mars whispered.

"You should know killers, Émile, if you want to be a cop when you grow up. Allow me to educate you. To be honest, there are many moments I love. I can't tell you how much I enjoy it when the wife cuts her husband's ring finger off. So much for that marriage! Ha ha. That's what I say. It's nearly orgasmic. But the moment I love, though, is when I see hope dissipate, when hope leaves the eyes to be replaced by despair. When I see them die before they are dead. I just so get off on that." He resorted to his Scotch and that seemed to elicit a quieter, more philosophical moment. "You know, the phenomena has been studied. In a Russian movie theater, for instance, many hostages looked like they were dead already. But some didn't, they clung to hope. Those who survived remarked on this. Once the shooting started and the bombs went off, it was those who looked dead ahead of time who ended up dead. Those who did not, did not. It's an amazing phenomena about life and death, how one informs the other. Those who were going to die *knew* they were going to die. I love to see my people die before I've even touched them."

In a way, Cinq-Mars noticed, Dreher had accomplished what he himself was trying to do, sparking Sandra back to life. She was not willing to yield her spirit to this madman.

"But you two. Look at you. Go on! The two of you. Look at each other!"

Émile and Sandra did as they were instructed. They each noticed the other's pain, which instantly intensified their own suffering, as if that was even possible, and yet they each took strength and solace one from the other.

"Do you see what I see?" Dreher demanded.

They looked back at him.

"Neither one of you is dead yet. Why not?"

This time, when Émile and Sandra shared a look, they smiled. The gesture was faint and unremarkable, and not meant to be provocative, but it was there, perhaps only in the other's eyes, perhaps only for themselves to see.

"So how come? You are both about to die. You have no hope. Stop dreaming in Technicolor. No god and no angel and no flying hero from any police department anywhere is about to rescue you. So forget about it."

"We'll get there. We'll lose hope. But first, explain New Orleans to me."

"What about it?"

"The kidnapping."

Dreher was only too happy to gloat. "The other side, Émile. Blame them. The people who are after me who don't know it's me they're after, just an amorphous ghost—but maybe they were thinking it's me, I can't be sure—they're the ones. They kidnapped your girl. You tell me what they got out of that. Nothing, it would appear, because both of you are about to die and I'm still up to no good! So say your prayers and let's get on with this. If you're not going to give me the satisfaction I'm looking for, fuck it, I'll do without. But sorry, guys, I must be on my way. Émile. You first."

And just like that, he aimed his pistol at his head.

"Oh!" Sandra called out. Then yelled another desperate sound.

"There's things you don't know!" Émile bellowed. "You won't be getting away soon."

"Sorry, Émile. Can't talk your way out of this one. Don't disappoint me. Take it like a man. If you insist on being optimistic, grant me that at last. Your integrity. Let me blow that away with your brains."

"Help is on the way! That's why I've been stalling you! That's why we have hope! Everything you've told us is theory, so who can convict you? You're still in the clear, Rand. But this, this you can't walk away from."

"Nice try, but you lie, and now you die."

"My husband doesn't lie!" Sandra shouted out.

"Lovely sentiment, my dear. But sentiment holds no water with me. Is that a surprise to you?"

"Were you recording us?"

He looked at her. "Recording?"

"Could you hear what we were saying?"

"Oh yeah."

"She's right," Émile said, catching on.

"About what?"

"I used code," Émile said. "Bill Mathers is my old partner. He knows my language."

Dreher released a plaintive sigh, then rubbed his eyes. "As much as I love to see the light go out early, I really hate it when people start this relentless, useless pleading."

"I can prove it to you," Sandra told him.

"How? Prove what?"

"Do you know what Émile told Bill? You were listening?"

"He gave him instructions on a shortcut home. So?"

"Bill Mathers," Émile answered, "has lived here all his life. He doesn't need directions home. And the directions I gave him are bogus."

"You're pathetic. You're making that up."

Sandra yelled, she screamed near the top of her lungs: *"I can prove it!"*

He was shocked for a moment, but that insidious grin arose again. "Okay, lady. Go ahead."

"I'll tell you what Émile said means. In a different room. In the kitchen. Then we'll come back here and he'll explain it himself. You'll see. It'll be exactly the same thing."

They stared each other down a few moments before Dreher addressed Émile. "I got to say, you married a lady with guts. That's good to see. All right. Sandra, get up. Into the kitchen we go. Émile, I'm going to tie you to that chair. If this is some sort of pathetic plan, just remember that I'm under no obligation to stick to a script today. I can make you pay before you die, and you won't want that. If your wife pisses me off, then she pays, and I'll let you live to see all that in its fullest glory."

He put down the pistol briefly and lashed Émile's wrists to the hard-back chair, yet neither of them could do a blessed thing. Dreher then clutched Sandra's forearm so forcibly that she gasped. He yanked her forward. He pulled her with him into the kitchen to listen to her explanation with the door closed.

But instead she pleaded for a bathroom visit.

She squeezed her thighs together and hopped on one foot, then the other.

"Please don't humiliate me. Let me pee."

"Fuck!" he hollered.

"I'm scared! It's the excitement. Let me pee!"

He opened the door to the living room again. "Don't move, Émile! I'll be checking on you."

Cinq-Mars didn't bother pointing out that he was unable to move, not while attached to his chair.

Roughly, Dreher pushed Sandra ahead of him down to the powder room. He went in first, did a quick scan of the medicine cabinet. Pills, floss, ointments, gauze, Band-Aids. No razors, no scissors, nothing to be construed as lethal. He stepped out of the room.

"You're not closing the door," he told her.

"You're not watching," she told him.

"Of course not. I'm a gentleman."

"Undo my hands."

He studied her. He saw her predicament. She had to undress. She hopped some more.

"Turn around," he instructed her, and when she did so he untied her wrists.

He then retired to a spot in the kitchen where he could keep an eye on the door and on Cinq-Mars by shifting his glance. He heard the tinkle, and when the toilet flushed he went back to the room, gave it a visual inspection as Sandra adjusted her clothing and checked her hands and pockets.

He pulled Sandra back into the kitchen and checked that Cinq-Mars had remained still. Then he closed the door and told her to quietly say what she wanted to say, and after telling him he tied her wrists again in front of her.

His eyes bore into her. Then he opened the door and signaled for her to go through. In the living room, he shoved Sandra back down into a chair.

Despite the roughhouse handling, Émile could tell that he had changed. Worry had crept in. A darkness behind the eyes, perhaps a premonition of the very same darkness that he'd been waiting for, and not seeing, in their eyes, was now evident in his.

"Talk, Émile. Explain your code. Not that you don't die either way."

Sandra's gambit was his last prevailing hope. "I told Bill to go east of Aldgate. In the old days, that's what I told him when it was time to draw our weapons. It comes from a Sherlock Holmes teleplay—"

"Yeah, yeah, I heard that already." Dreher drew a hand through his hair and down the back of his neck, in distress.

"'Always carry a firearm east of Aldgate, Watson,' Sherlock said. Bill took it to be code. I can pretty much guarantee that. So you see, we haven't given up hope because we know the cops are coming and probably in force. Your best bet, your only bet, is to get out now, then you'll only have our stories to defend against in court. Otherwise, you kill us now, and you're the dead man."

He seemed to be considering his options. He went to the front door and looked out. He sprung the lock. He crossed to a side window and checked that it was locked. But it would be in winter. He walked though the living room, checking on his captors, warned them with a wave of his gun, and went through the kitchen to the back door and locked that. He searched in that direction. Nothing alarmed him out there. He returned to the living room.

"This does change things a little," he agreed. "Sandra, you're getting out of the finger-cutting, you'll be pleased to know. If you don't mind, I'm going to borrow riding tack from the stables and mount one of your horses. I'm an old kid cowboy from Missouri, you know. Riding a horse can't be much different than riding a bicycle, once you know how. That gets me as far as the riding trails out back. My GPS will guide me out of there. Then I take the redeye to Birmingham. Technically, I'm already on a flight to Jacksonville, but that's not really me, as you can see. Either way, I get to investigate Vira's murder tomorrow morning, and I guess that's when I'll hear about yours. So. Short and sweet. It's been nice knowing you."

Sandra emitted a sound, one that Émile had never heard, and both men looked across at her. "There, Émile," Dreher said, "do you see? There it goes. All hope. We're back in the swamp. I love the swamp. You see? Her light's gone out. She's already dead and I haven't even touched her yet."

But Sandra was not going to tolerate that verdict or at least not give him the satisfaction. *"Fuck you, you fucker!"*

"That mouth!"

Cinq-Mars tried to kick him. A futile effort. Dreher went around behind him. Cinq-Mars tried to twist around but there was no point. He felt the barrel of the gun against the back of his head.

Dreher leaned in and whispered in Émile's ear. "Personal aggrandizement, Émile. That's why you're dying today. But I like you. So I'll tell you something else. It's also political. So many of us have plans. For those plans, we do a little fund-raising on the side. So you see, you're dying for a cause. My cause. You're not dying in vain. Oh, just wanted you to know."

"You bastard."

"You fucked up," Dreher said, as if wanting to console him. "I know, it's hard to stomach. But look, don't feel bad. So did I. Today is but one example. Shall I let you in on a touch of irony, Émile? I never counted on that big snowfall. When I arrived at the Lumens' place, one footprint was the same as any other. When the snow covered everything, that's when I knew I was in trouble."

"The cops would think you were still in the house," Cinq-Mars whispered.

"That's right. Adele Lumen not dying instantly was one mistake, but I didn't count on the implications of the storm. Normally, they'd never think to look for me. They'd just call it in. So you see, I'm always trying to improve my practice. I learned new things today. So, thanks. I promise, Émile, I'll do better next time."

He straightened up. Shoved Émile's head forward with the gun's muzzle.

"Ready, lady?" Dreher said to Sandra, although he wasn't looking in her direction. "Say good-bye, then watch him die."

The shot was fired. Sandra released an unholy scream to drown out that noise, to explode that final terror.

TWENTY-EIGHT

Funereal, grim, the procession of five black cars turned off the county highway to traverse the pockmarked road on up to the farmhouse. A thaw transformed the drive into a series of puddles and ponds and made it particularly bumpy where frost heaves rippled the surface. Sandra Cinq-Mars stepped out onto her front porch to watch the cars and SUVs arrive. She was surprised, although only briefly, that she recognized one of the first men to emerge from his vehicle. The fellow buttoned up his black suit jacket and exchanged a glance and a nod with her. He stood out as strikingly familiar.

She'd know that face anywhere. She just never expected to see it again and not in a million years on her own property. He was one of two men, both in their fifties, who approached the porch and came up the steps.

Not him, but the other man, extended his hand and said, "Mrs. Cinq-Mars, on behalf of the Federal Bureau of Investigation, may I convey to you our sincere regret for all that has transpired."

Her eyes remained reddened from crying jags that in the last day were finally becoming less frequent. She replied cordially, "Thank you. Won't you come inside?" Taking note of her front yard, where more and more men stepped out of the vehicles, she added, "My goodness, so many of you!"

"Don't be alarmed," the man assured her with a smile, "we won't all come in."

"Perhaps what you mean to say is," she contradicted him, "not all at once."

"Ma'am," the man said, which she thought a meaningless response.

The two agents from the lead car stepped inside the front door. They'd already dispensed with their overcoats, left behind on the vehicle's front seat given the unexpected warmth, and once inside slipped off their rubbers, leaving their shoes on. Spit and polish from head to toe. They came through to the living room, where they found Émile Cinq-Mars, also dressed in a suit and tie, lying in state on the sofa, hands folded across his chest in at attitude of peaceful, eternal rest.

They stood respectfully in silence, hands crossed solemnly at their waists.

"Gentlemen," the retired Montreal detective decreed, without opening either eye, "the last of my osteopath's exercises. My back's been acting up in light of all this. The stress, he says. I don't have a clue what he's talking about. I blame the change in the weather."

"Don't let him kid you," Sandra chided. "He's been practicing lying in a coffin since the moment he came within a hairsbreadth of one. Coffee?" she inquired of her guests.

"Thank you, yes. Much appreciated," an agent said. They'd not been introduced as yet. "But, really. Just the two of us. The minions outside can wait."

"Minions?" Cinq-Mars asked, eyes still shut. He had just returned from mass.

"They brought an army," Sandra let him know.

He at last opened his eyes, to see the agent indicate with a facial expression that her observation was abundantly true. "Sorry about that," he said. "We had nowhere to leave them, so we brought them along."

Departing for the kitchen, Sandra pointed to the man she recognized. "That one," she informed her husband, "kidnapped me in New Orleans."

Cinq-Mars spun up onto his derrière.

"Gentlemen," he announced and rose from being prone with an

evident flexibility unbecoming a man who supposedly was smitten with a sore back, "Émile Cinq-Mars. How do you do?"

Quietly, Special Agents Pettibone and Hartopp agreed that they were doing quite well, thank you, and having introduced themselves went on to repeat their regret concerning recent events. They apologized again on behalf of the Bureau.

Cinq-Mars was not ready to accept their words of contrition. "You do realize," he pointed out to both of them, "that Special Agent Dreher's blood and brains were spread across my wife's face and throughout her hair? I had his blood all over me."

The two men stood in silent acceptance of that horrific moment.

"Better his than mine, I suppose, but still. Not to mention Sandra's abduction in New Orleans. What the hell has the FBI come to, gentlemen?"

"With all due respect, sir," Pettibone remarked, "that's more or less what we're here to find out. We're hoping that you can help us with that."

Crossing his arms, Cinq-Mars took a deeper breath. He relaxed his combativeness a notch. "I agree. We have a deal. Please, take a seat. Sandra and I are both consoled by the fact that we're alive today when at one point we didn't particularly expect to be. I apologize if you find me on the edgy side."

"No apologies necessary, sir," Michael Hartopp said as he located the soft chair behind him, hoisted the cuffs of his trousers a notch, and sat down. Darren Pettibone seated himself as well and Cinq-Mars followed suit, although he remained forward in his chair and folded his hands together between his knees.

"Actually," Cinq-Mars agreed, "I know that."

Émile's posture caused Hartopp to ease himself forward as well, either consciously or unconsciously needing to assume a position that conveyed a sense of urgency. "Out of respect, sir, I'd like permission to call you by your former rank."

Surprised by the request, Cinq-Mars nodded agreement.

"Sergeant-Detective, we've read the transcript of your debriefing, and you and I have discussed this over the phone. As you say, we've made a deal. Inside the FBI, to say that we are alarmed about recent events is a gross understatement. I won't kid you. I don't think I can overstate our concern. The seriousness of this situation, I'm sure, has not escaped your attention either."

He rubbed his hands together, which gave Cinq-Mars the feeling that he was releasing pent-up stress of his own. He did not doubt that the pressure was on inside the Bureau, probably to an extreme degree.

"So I want to begin by asking if there is anything else, in light of the passage of a few days, regarding your exchange with Randolph Dreher that has come to mind. No matter how seemingly insignificant, we would be glad to hear it."

Cinq-Mars had indeed been through the debriefing mill. As had Sergeant-Detective Bill Mathers, for he had shot FBI Special Agent Randolph Dreher to death. Nodding, Émile resisted an urge to rub his own hands together, simulating Hartopp's gesture. The agent was a slim man who clipped his hair high around his ears, an odd preference, and his facial features were narrow and bony looking, the nose thin except that the nostrils took a wide flare, as if he had a bit of the dragon in his genes. The eyes, though, were relaxed and nicely set apart, a soft gray, and somehow initiated the primary impression that he gave off to others, for he exhibited a cautious openness that Cinq-Mars, along with most everyone else, picked up on.

The other man, Pettibone, had the physique, and also the nature, of a stevedore, a rare FBI agent in that he came across as a tough guy, even a wise guy, an overt physical bully rather than being someone who found his way through mental acumen or even subterfuge. Cinq-Mars didn't mind him, though, as he carried himself with the demeanor of a mean-streets cop, and he was deeply familiar with the brand. Pettibone, though, had suffered a transformative flaw: he had once abducted his wife. He realized firsthand how frightened his wife must have been in his unwanted and unwarranted company.

"I learned something last night in a conversation with Sergeant-Detective Bill Mathers," Cinq-Mars began. "I know that you've talked to him. We've not had much time to chat, he and I, until last night, given that we've both been subjected to nearly continuous interrogation."

"We apologize also for our part in that," Hartopp said. "Necessary."

"And the beat goes on," Cinq-Mars pointed out to him. "Of course I understand. Bill and I enjoyed a lovely talk over whisky—the lad doesn't drink much and I may have overlubricated his tongue. I do owe him my life. More importantly, I owe him my wife's life. He asked me not to repeat what he had to say, but I rather gently told him to go to hell, so you can see how far that owing-him-my-life thing goes."

Hartopp smiled, asked, "How did he react when you told him to go to hell?"

"He grinned, actually. Which I interpreted as his way of saying that he expected nothing less from me."

"What did he tell you?" Pettibone inquired, which, in Cinq-Mars's mind, marked him as the less patient and more abrasive of the two. No surprise there.

"If I may, I'd like to frame this for you. We're sitting right here last night. The lights are down. We're listening to Coltrane, I'm introducing Bill to the experience, and we're drinking my best Scotch. As *A Love Supreme* comes to a close, I'm waiting to hear what he thinks. Bill leans into me and speaks in quite a subdued tone."

"He was sharing a secret," Hartopp surmised.

"That's what I thought, too, at first, but it was more than that. He was sharing a secret that he did not intend to share and didn't particularly want to. That amounts to more than sharing, it verges on confession. Trouble is, confession or secret, he needed to confide, for it was nagging at him. What's difficult for Bill is that he's not certain that he believes his own suspicions. But here's the rub: I do."

"Suspicions?" Hartopp asked.

Cinq-Mars shifted his weight and lowered his voice, hoping to emulate Mathers's tone and mood. "Bill told me that when he peeped around the doorjamb and saw a gun to my head with Dreher about to blow my brains out, that he looked at him."

He paused. Pettibone asked, "Mathers looked at Dreher. And?"

"No," Cinq-Mars corrected him. "Of course Bill saw Dreher, and the gun, and me. But it's Bill's recollection that Dreher looked back *at him*. Right back at him. And we're not talking about an amount of time that anyone can measure, but as Bill said, he needed a split second to take aim, whereas Dreher already had a gun to my head. And Bill had to take another split second to decide whether or not to shout out that he was there or that he was the police and demand that Dreher put the gun down, for

I'd be a dead man by his first syllable. He had to fire, and in the nick of time, but with those milliseconds ticking by, or whatever milliseconds do, Rand Dreher was holding his gun to my head and in Mathers's mind—and this is the part that Bill is having a hard time admitting to, and therefore doesn't want to say, or at least, not say to just anybody—in his memory bank, Dreher was staring at him and *waiting*, in Bill's mind, during those milliseconds, for Bill to shoot."

The three men considered that report in silence.

Hartopp ventured, "Even if Dreher did hesitate, he may have done so out of surprise—"

"True enough."

"Or out of fear, frozen there for, as you say, a millisecond or so."

"Also true," Cinq-Mars concurred. "As well, he may have realized that he had something to think about, a choice to make. Such as, Do I pull the trigger, kill this guy, then get shot myself? Or, he may have been thinking, 'Oh-oh, before my next heartbeat I'm dead.' Before he got to complete that thought, he was."

They let the news settle in the air another moment. Hartopp again was the first to break the silence. "Yet you believe that Dreher saw what was about to happen, and—? And what, Sergeant-Detective?"

"Rather than duck, spin, and try to shoot Mathers first, he waited for Bill's bullet to kill him. He knew that the gig was up, but he did not want what we enjoy today, a chance to talk about it. In that *fraction* of a millisecond, and this is partly coming from Bill except that he doesn't believe it, but I'm inclined to believe it, he *chose* death. He chose to take the last of his secrets to the grave with him. He chose, gentlemen, to protect his colleagues inside and outside the Bureau who are involved in this unholy mess with him."

He initiated eye contact with each agent and held that connection long enough to communicate what the three of them understood, that as far as Cinq-Mars knew or was concerned these two agents and anyone waiting outside in the yard for a chance to question him, some for the umpteenth time, could be in cahoots with Randolph Dreher, that every conversation needed to be conducted with that thought or at least that distinct possibility, in mind.

Special Agents Hartopp and Pettibone hadn't arrived with knowledge of Bill Mathers's story or the implications that Cinq-Mars ascribed to it, but the account and his opinion dovetailed perfectly with what they had come to ask about. As the FBI processed two potential scenarios, they took comfort in neither, but feared one exponentially more. One limited Dreher's schemes to himself and perhaps a cohort or two, a cerebral madness that any bureaucracy needed to cut out on occasion. The other delved deep into the heart of the FBI and uncovered core tissue that was infected, cancerous, terminally ill. Even should the former hold true after a thorough internal investigation, and even if doubts lingered if and when that opinion became accepted, the damage affected and likely infected the whole of the enterprise. What the consequences would be should the second opinion win the day remained a matter no one wanted to even contemplate, let alone discuss.

Dread remained prevalent.

They were considering all this as Sandra returned with coffee and biscuits.

Perhaps due to her husband's graphic description of her ordeal leading to Dreher being shot in her home, the agents were solicitous to her presence, and profuse with their thanks as she departed again. She left plenty of coffee behind. The two men drank as if desperate for a buzz to lift them out of the gloom they'd carried into the house. An impression vexed Cinq-Mars: the agents seemed to be in mourning, they had that vibe, but he didn't want to ask if their sadness was for Dreher, who had been a colleague at one time, or for the swift demise in Bureau self-confidence. Even, perhaps, although it seemed an incongruous word to ascribe to them, their own innocence. Either way, their supreme lack of cockiness today felt put-on, something of a performance, but in their shoes he'd probably present the same dollop of shamefaced sobriety to the world.

In the wake of Sandra's departure from the room, Cinq-Mars asked Pettibone if he knew that she had identified him.

He was confused. "You mean, recognizing me from New Orleans?"

"And, sir, recognizing you from the Lumens's farm. She never saw you there, that's true, but a local farmer mentioned that when Morris and Adele first arrived, men in black cars helped them settle in. Sandra made the connection that the rosacea of a man on the Lumens's farm matched the rosacea of the man who kidnapped her in New Orleans. That would be you."

"So you understood you were dealing with FBI involvement," Hartopp noted.

"You kidnapped my wife, sir. I could use a word other than *involvement*."

Cinq-Mars, though, kept his eyes on Pettibone, until that man responded.

The agent surmised what Cinq-Mars was asking him. "Okay. Yes, I was here then. But what you need to understand is that the repositioning of Morris Lumen had nothing to do with Rand Dreher. We feel that Dreher was on the lookout for someone in witness protection not connected to him, to take the heat off him, as it was coming on and he knew it. It's precisely because Morris Lumen was not connected to him that he came here looking for him. And killed him."

"Why didn't you just take Dreher out of the field if he was a suspect?"

Clearly, the question landed in Hartopp's purview. "Sergeant-Detective, we ask some of our special agents to do grim work. We know there's dirt under their fingernails. They're trusted, and that's what allows them to get their jobs done and it allows us to give them some scope. If one goes bad, as we've just found out, or if a bad one works himself into a significant position, which would seem to be what's happened here, then we're in trouble. This is a hot button issue inside the Bureau right now. We need to reevaluate."

His response gave Cinq-Mars a thought. "So, in your opinion, Dreher was bad to start with. He wasn't corrupted over the course of time."

Hartopp slipped in a grin.

Cinq-Mars called him on that. "What?"

"We're supposed to be debriefing you, sir, at least at the start, as per our agreement, not the other way around."

He was having none of that. "Would you like me to ask Sandra to come back into the room, so that she can provide the intimate details of the horrors you put her through?"

Once again, the FBI yielded. First Pettibone spoke. "We're working night and day on the file, but the suspicion has been broached that from his earliest days Rand Dreher was involved with marijuana production. We've concluded that it was, in fact, a family business for as many as three generations, going back to the days of corn whisky. They also grew mustard seed. Entering the FBI afforded him special opportunities in that regard. We didn't know."

Then Hartopp had his say. "Sergeant-Detective, we confess that we weren't suspicious of Dreher. We should have been. But we trusted him. He brought very smart people onto his team, and our suspicions of his work were deposited there. Someone in his group. Procedure required us to keep him out of it, in case he was indeed the problem, but we weren't actually thinking that way. His team was under surveillance, more than he ever was. I only say this with regret."

Cinq-Mars had been around the block in his long career. He knew about cops and robbers often being the flip side of the same coin, that there but for fortune . . . As someone who had considered first the priesthood and then veterinary medicine in his youth, he was an exception among cops. More than a few he'd known had chosen crime-fighting over a life of crime, if not one it might as well have been the other. Moths to the flame. They'd done a good job, too. A rare few, one always supposed, right from the outset, pretended to do one but concentrated on the other.

Pettibone offered a further insight. "We think that one of the reasons he was so successful is that from the get-go his knowledge of that soft-drug world was paramount. That made him impossible to spot."

He saw where this was going. "Not to rain on your parade, gentlemen," Cinq-Mars parried, although he meant to do just that, "but it's not good practice to excuse police failure to successfully discharge their duties by crediting the bad guys with otherworldly brilliance. Just putting that out there."

He liked that they were in no mood, and in no position, to argue.

"Here's something else that came up since that day," Cinq-Mars told them, carrying on with his advantage. "I asked Dreher to place funds in escrow, which were to be paid to me if I proved that he was withholding evidence from the investigation into the Lumens's murders. I did prove that, and he paid up. The check arrived in the mail yesterday."

"You're kidding," Hartopp reacted.

"That makes no sense," Pettibone added.

"Sure looks like an FBI check to me. I deposited it, too. I guess it'll be a few days to find out if the bank clears it."

"I don't get this," Pettibone reiterated.

"Actually, it makes perfect sense," Cinq-Mars postulated. "This whole Quebec thing for Dreher was about deflecting suspicion. So why have a check issued for a man he expected to kill before he got a chance to receive it? Answer, it's the same as everything else. It deflects suspicion. He was expecting to still be alive, of course. But what's interesting is that Dreher could put his hands on extra funds like that."

Hartopp broke from his flatline disposition. He grimaced, put his head back, and ran both hands through his thin hair. Resurfacing, he acknowledged that he had nowhere to go with that line of inquiry, except to the admission of a problem. Cinq-Mars had received an FBI check. He already expected that they would find out that the money was not exactly FBI money and told Cinq-Mars so.

"Not exactly? You suffer from strange accounting practices, do you?"

"Sometimes we move bad money, confiscated money, normally drug money, inside the Bureau to serve special purposes. Funds to pay off kidnappers, for instance. Funds to pay informants. Special situations. We now have reason to suspect that Dreher became a master of moving that kind of money around. But to pitch it around, it still has to exist. We think, now, in light of everything, that he knew how to bring money in from his own illicit activities to make it look like the FBI was funding this or that operation—this also made him look good, you understand, look effective—and he was able to redistribute that cash back into the field again. That's what I suspect happened with your funds."

"He was using the FBI to launder his own dirty money?"

"That's a way of looking at it," Hartopp admitted. "I'm waiting on an official verdict on that one. We're trying to track his ways and means."

"Do you have any idea how much pleasure this gives him in his grave?"

"Ah . . . an inkling, I suppose."

"I'm keeping it," Cinq-Mars let him know. "The cash."

Hartopp remained undisturbed. "I see no reason for you to do otherwise." He was left, he knew, with a problem that went straight to the financial center of his universe, one that might take a lifetime to unravel.

Cinq-Mars could see a dilemma unfold behind his eyes. The man cared. And he was worried.

All three indulged in the coffee briefly and enjoyed a few bites of the biscuits. They were store-bought, as Sandra, who loved to bake, was outside her routines of late. The phone rang, and they heard her picking up behind the kitchen door. She spoke in bright yet murmured tones before hanging up again.

Having given them a few matters to think about, Cinq-Mars was not shy to ask his own questions and to expect answers. "Here's one for you, Agent Pettibone. Why Danziger Bridge? It's not a landmark without significance in New Orleans, particularly with respect to police business. So what was that about? Why release my wife on that bridge?"

A slight rocking of his head indicated that the query was legitimate. "Code," he acknowledged. "We didn't know who we were dealing with. We wanted to find out. Was it the NOPD? Always a possibility. But we thought we might be circling forces within the Bureau, so we wanted to put the fear of God into anyone and everyone. Since we didn't know the culprits, and we didn't even know if there were any culprits, we were chasing ghosts, really, ghosts and shadows. If they did exist we wanted to communicate with them, to let them know that our involvement was precipitated by an interest in what police were doing. We chose Danziger Bridge as an example of what perpetrators might face, to remind them of what happens to cops who do bad things. We didn't care if you, the Montreal visitor, understood or not, obviously the bridge didn't carry much weight with you, but officers in New Orleans who were walking on the dark side might get it. Someone like Rand Dreher, if it was him, or anyone in his group, might get it."

More questions followed, and answers and speculations, ground plowed before. Yet going at it face-to-face this time, rather than through the filter of written reports, had value. Cinq-Mars was weary of it all, but as a cop he'd been a lifer, so he appreciated repetition and honored repeated surveys of the same terrain. When they finally let up and were about to give him what they'd agreed to give him, he said, "You guys revealed yourselves, you know."

"How so?" Hartopp asked.

"Agent Pettibone mentioned, and I quote, 'circling forces within the

Bureau.' That tells me something. The use of the word *forces*. You know this isn't scant."

That admission was not going to be made, but these men were not going to deny it either. "Now, Sergeant-Detective, we have an agreement. We have vowed to answer your questions. You're right, it's not the normal way we conduct our business, we find ourselves adrift. And we owe you. The least we can do as recompense is to tell you what you want to know."

Cinq-Mars tugged on an earlobe. "I'm going to ask Sandra back into the room. Two reasons for that. One, she wanted to be part of this from the outset. And two, I want you to explain things to her knowing that she had an FBI agent's brains on her face and in her hair. For more than a moment she thought they were my brain bits. She had to leave it all there, too, let forensics do their thing. So anytime you want to renege on our agreement, or curtail the truth or dress it up a little, look at her, know what she has gone through, and for the sake of her recovery from this trauma, for the love of Mike, speak the truth. We've agreed to this over the phone, but face-to-face, I'll ask you again. Are we in agreement?"

"Certainly," Pettibone informed him.

Hartopp tacked on, "Absolutely."

Sandra returned to the room and curled up comfortably on the sofa, a pillow in her lap as though for protection, to hear what the men had learned. Hartopp began. "The man's name is Orritt. Alexander Orritt. He goes by Alley, and he told us that he was known as Alley O for a time but that naturally evolved to Alley Oop. Whether he's named after the old cartoon character or the basketball move, even he's not sure, probably neither. But he's Alley Oop."

"Sorry," Sandra said. "Who?"

"This is the man," Émile said quietly, "who killed Agent Sivak in Alabama. Dreher told him to cut her finger off before she died, to make it look like he wanted it to be a carbon copy murder, but not really. He is also the man who the FBI arrested near here, who Dreher intended to kill, to then claim that he had solved our murders and Agent Sivak's."

"Okay. Him. Alley Oop."

"Has he been cooperative?" Cinq-Mars inquired.

Pettibone separated his hands then brought them together again.

Hartopp was deferring to him in this aspect, so clearly he was the one with firsthand knowledge. "That depends, sir, on your definition of cooperative. He has not been inclined to be friendly. But with dead agents involved, we are not accepting reluctance from anybody, especially given Agent Sivak's luster within the Bureau and given the gravity of the overall situation. Besides, we're on foreign soil. We're willing to take advantage of different rules."

"What different rules?" Sandra asked.

"There are none," Pettibone told her.

She nodded, accepting that.

"What we've learned is that he killed Agent Sivak in Alabama, the man that she was with that evening, and also a former New Orleans police officer."

"Jefferson Grant?" Cinq-Mars piped up.

"The same," Pettibone let him know.

"So what happened," Sandra wanted to know, "in New Orleans?"

"Your husband, ma'am, asked Detective Dupree of the NOPD to investigate police records, to see what payments may have been made to informants or to outsiders to conduct investigations. What surfaced showed that two Latino men were imported from Miami, ostensibly to give information to help convict a criminal, and they did that, but normally if a detective has a chance to slip out to another city to gather testimony, he'll go on his own if only for the time away, the fun, he won't ask the witness to come to him. Especially when there are two witnesses who need to travel. Perhaps your husband has figured out why."

Cinq-Mars was willing. "Jefferson Grant was an ex-cop with shadowy ties, now a lowlife so-called private eye. Dreher hired him. Not merely to follow us around in New Orleans, but primarily to slip to certain bad officers inside the NOPD that an outside cop was coming down from Montreal, a former officer with a reputation for cleaning up police departments."

Hartopp and Pettibone took turns in outlining the sequence of events.

"Cops with something to worry about got themselves riled up about it."

"They wondered what was going on. When a good cop, Pascal Dupree, heard that your husband wanted to speak specifically to him, he was also riled up."

"Policemen, good or bad, don't want outsiders investigating them. Outsiders are never likely to understand the environment."

"Basically," Pettibone explained, "Dreher wanted your husband's life in New Orleans to be difficult and chaotic."

"He achieved that," Sandra mentioned.

"But then Dreher had a problem," Pettibone went on. "One that he most likely perceived ahead of time. Jefferson Grant had done what he wanted, and he was useful as a very visible tracking dog. Dreher guessed that your husband would notice him, due to your husband's experience and the identifying pale pigment patches on Grant's skin—he'd be easy to spot."

"According to Ally Oop, Dreher now needed Jefferson Grant out of the picture. Probably his thinking was that Grant was unreliable, that sooner or later he'd let slip what he'd been hired to do. That would shine a light back on Dreher."

"But you were the guys," Cinq-Mars pointed out to the Agents, "who told us, through your call to Captain Borde of the SQ, to check my old room."

"Because we had that room wired," Hartopp said. "You were on the town with Dupree. Your wife wasn't there, we'd picked her up. But something happened in that room when it was supposed to be empty. Not knowing what went down, we checked the room and found Jefferson Grant. I admit, we used the murder to our advantage and smeared blood from the scene onto a wall in your new room. Even through we didn't know who we were after, we were sending confusion back through the pipeline. To Dreher, as it turned out. We had to. We needed to add to the confusion, to help gain some leverage in all the developments."

"The pickpockets?" Sandra asked. She was thinking that if these men wired their room, they had listened to their lovemaking. She didn't want them here any longer.

"They were working for detectives in the NOPD. The bad ones. They wanted to know what Sergeant-Detective Cinq-Mars was up to. Like the NOPD, we also wanted to know what was going on. We found out about the pickpockets, but who was conducting that operation? We wanted a word with your husband." Hartopp looked sheepish a moment, then forged on. "Sergeant-Detective Cinq-Mars had gone off with Dupree. We found out about Jefferson Grant before that, that he was tracking you, just like we were. That worried us. Then he's murdered. We thought to take your husband out of the picture by having a word with you."

"I was kidnapped. I wasn't invited out for a cup of coffee. For a *word*."

Both agents let their heads drop, mulling that over. They glanced at each other before responding. "I apologize for the euphemism. We justified that action by telling ourselves that we would treat you very well. We just felt that your husband was involved with the wrong person or persons. Yes, we were investigating Dreher's group, and whatever it was he had up his sleeve. We didn't know it was him, didn't think it was him either, but whoever that guy on the dark side was, we wanted to eliminate the activity. We didn't grasp that we were being played."

"So Alley Oop kills Jefferson Grant—"

"Which instigates chaos on every side. It puts Dreher back in charge, pulling our strings. I can't say what a certain segment of the NOPD was feeling—I don't mean Pascal Dupree, but his foes in the department—but I can only imagine they found themselves in brackish waters. I know we did. We were swimming among the alligators. But we had to play our hand."

"At the very least," Hartopp said, "we needed to get the two of you to leave town. Everything was getting out of hand fast."

"Meanwhile," Cinq-Mars summed up, "Dreher is enjoying himself. Having a laugh a minute. Loving what he's put in motion. Reveling in the incompetence of every other cop in Christendom but him."

Hartopp deliberately, gravely nodded, "Pretty much the size of it."

Pettibone added, "Dreher had his Achilles' heel though. He involved other people at various points in his enterprises, be they weed or murder, but then he couldn't allow those confederates to live for long. He feared betrayal more than anything. So he always had to plan his next execution. Killing Agent Sivak, who was not a confederate of his in crime, definitely not a suspect, prevented her from asking questions around the Alabama tornado murders, which would have verified the existence of an adjustor. Not his identity, but his method. Dreher could not permit that. She got too close. So he went after her first. And now Alley Oop was also too involved. He'd killed Grant and Sivak for him. He was brought up to Canada for one more job, but really that job was supposed to be his own death. He gets that now. That still doesn't make him fully cooperative, but his overall disposition is improving day by day."

A quiet pervaded the room for several minutes.

Cinq-Mars said, "I don't disagree with you, but I'm struck by your confidence in Agent Sivak."

That remark was met by an intriguing disquiet between the two agents.

Interpreting their mood, Émile said, "I see." When Sandra exhibited a questioning expression, he explained, "She was working with these two."

Hartopp conceded with a shrug. "We needed someone in that group, on that team. This goes way back, even before the murders. We flaunted Agent Sivak's credentials, knowing that Dreher could never resist lassoing the latest brainiac to join the Bureau. So she was charged with the duties that Dreher brought to her, but also to be our person inside his group. And, I have to say, once we made contact with you, her job was to make sure she kept your confidence going forward. So we could figure out your role in all this. Which wasn't so strange to us, you understand. That was Dreher's thing. Find the brightest and bring them onto his team. But, I guess he had other intentions with respect to you."

Émile let that sink in. "Might that be why he killed her then? Not the matter of her investigation in Alabama, but he got wind of her involvement with you? Remember, gentlemen, that we know he was in a defensive mode. This whole Quebec escapade was part of that. He may have found out, or deduced, that Vira was working with you."

Perhaps that had not occurred to the men previously, but in any case they chose not to respond to the possibility.

Émile reached across and touched Sandra's knee, and she looked up at him. If she had any more questions of her own, now was the time to ask them.

"Why," Sandra wondered, "did Dreher bring Émile into this in the first place? Not just because he's smart, surely. It turned out to be Dreher's biggest mistake. Why didn't he leave well enough alone, for his own sake?"

Her query seemed to arise from the center of her being, as if this one mystery so vexed her that no piece of the puzzle could settle onto the board without this locking mechanism being in place. Émile noticed that the two agents were studying him with equal intent, indicating they'd rather hear his take on the matter than postulate one of their own.

"I hate to be the one to say this," Cinq-Mars admitted, "but partly—only partly—it's accidental. As these two men indicated, Sandra, Dreher needed his hired killer, his adjustor, which is to say his evil twin, to descend upon FBI business, which had to be business not connected to him. He probably had very few options. He would've *wanted* access to everybody in witness protection, to make an informed choice, but he'd take whatever he could find."

Sandra nodded, absorbing that. She said, "So he found out about Morris and Adele Lumen by accident?"

"I'm guessing yes. Probably through a personal contact with a loose tongue, he got an address somehow and went with it. In a way it turned out to be perfect for him. Not only out of sight and out of mind, totally unconnected to him, but also out of the country. That was a bonus. After killing them, he wouldn't have to say it himself or point it out to anyone. It would just be so obvious that neither he nor his team were connected. He'd know that others would think that any relation between the storm murders and Rand Dreher was coincidental now, because it obviously extended well out of his reach and even beyond the American border, which is to say, way beyond his working territory."

The men were nodding in agreement, and Sandra did as well.

"Was he sent here officially?" Cinq-Mars asked the agents.

"He was never sent here. But Dreher had scope," Hartopp explained. "He could latch onto things if he gave himself, and the Bureau, a good reason."

"As for bringing me onto the case," Cinq-Mars speculated, "he essentially could not trust local investigators. I told him that at the start, even though I didn't understand the ramifications then. Local authorities would not include him in what they were learning, if anything. He couldn't have that. He couldn't speak the language. He needed someone on the ground to keep him informed. So I was duped. When that errand took me on to New Orleans, he was probably surprised by that, but he wasn't in any position to fight against it. So he took advantage of it instead. He could make life difficult for me, and he did. So that's how it came about, except for one thing. This is where I'm in slight disagreement, Sandra, with our new friends in the FBI. As to what constitutes his Achilles' heel. Yes, he feared betrayal. But his undoing, gentlemen, which we find in every crime he committed, has to do with his disdain for the police, and his conviction that he was smarter than any of us. He may have been smarter, but that character flaw, that need to be in the attic when the cops investigated, that need to phone in this crime while he was in the attic and couldn't get out because of the snow, that need to publicly humiliate investigating detectives, and the need to choose me—I have a reputation, I'm ethical, I've been a success—all that derives from his compulsion to prove the universe wrong. In his own head, he was the most cunning, the one and only wicked witch of the Midwest, so he had to take on the wicked witch of the North to prove his own greatness. That's why he chose me even before he killed the Lumens. So he could better a foe some might consider worthy then brag about it before putting a bullet through my head."

"Don't be graphic," Sandra whispered, and he would have obeyed, but he was done. She looked satisfied though; she'd heard enough.

Cinq-Mars looked across then at Hartopp and silently they accepted that their mutual agreement had also been fulfilled. They were finished here.

At the door, the agents shook hands with Cinq-Mars, only to have Sandra swish by them to pour coffee for the other men and to feed them cookies. They weren't going to get out of here without experiencing hospitality on Canadian soil, even if she was a born and bred American herself. Everyone seemed quite grateful. When she was done—and only when she was done—the caravan prepared to move out, and Sandra joined her husband on the porch to watch it go.

"We got the call," she said. She looked at him and smiled. "From the vet. Merlin's ready to come home. We pick him up at four."

He released a deep, slow breath, and smiled back at her.

Waiting, Cinq-Mars let his eyes cross the paddock, observing the horses in an early spring frolic. Merlin was coming home to carry through on his old age, but the horses, what of them? Would they be staying? Would he and Sandra be saying good-bye to all this and letting them go? Now was no time for such a major decision, but he knew that it weighed on Sandra as much as it did on him, and events of the last weeks might have reached a tipping point, precipitating a crucial change in their lives.

If he held to Sandra, and she to him, then he'd adapt to whatever came next.

The final car made the turn in the mud of their yard and headed out, and the couple turned back inside. They collapsed on the sofa, then napped sitting up for twenty minutes before Cinq-Mars extricated himself to make a phone call from his den.

"Dupree," he said when the New Orleans detective answered.

"How're they hanging, Émile?" That wasn't quite how Cinq-Mars understood the phrase and it made him laugh. Dupree had that knack.

"I called to fill you in and give you that advice you were looking for. Go ahead, Dupree. Hire Everardo. It's always a decent thing to give a good man a good job."

This time, Dupree was the one who seemed most amused.

"What's so funny?"

"I already set it up, Émile. You must be slipping. For the first time in our brief history together, I'm ahead of you."

"Good man," Cinq-Mars said, and he laughed, too.

"So I guess you've heard about our Miami boys by now. We're bringing them back here for a chat."

"That'll make you more popular than ever within your department."

"Oh, it might. Or make the department a little smaller. Open up a spot for Flores. So how are you, Émile? Heard y'all been defying death. And how's Sandra holding up? You've been putting her through it, my man."

"Sandra and I are both counting on her resilience, but it's being tested. As for me, I cut it a little close this time. This retirement of mine is more dangerous than being on the job ever was."

"I hear that."

"Do you know what she did, my lovely wife? She saved our lives."

"I didn't hear. Tell me."

"When Rand Dreher was in the house, ranting away, getting set to kill us, she coaxed him into letting her use the bathroom. In there, she took the lock off the small window, opened it for a second and stuck out a long flag of toilet paper to blow in the breeze. Grace under pressure. She closed the window again with the paper jammed in it. The powder room window has opaque glass, of course. Dreher couldn't see her flag.

But our rescuer, my old partner, didn't have to waste time finding access into our home. Otherwise, I'm a dead man now."

"Émile," Dupree said, and he whistled. He marveled at Sandra's acumen. "Do you know what y'all should do, after she goes and saves your shabby life?"

Cinq-Mars chuckled again. He liked this guy. "What should we do, Dupree?"

"Take a vacation. Y'all allowed back now. Come on down to New Orleans. We'll warm you up. Feed your bones good food. Get y'all out chasing alligators, something easy like that for a change."

"That might be the best advice I've heard lately. I may bring that up."

"Do it, Émile. I'm serious. I bet our friend Everardo can get the Hilton to donate a room. After what happened last time, they should be willing. And after what you put her through, how she saved you, your wife, she deserves it. Big-time."

Cinq-Mars mulled it over. The idea had its appeal. "I may go for something a little more *interesting* next time, with respect to accommodations. Now that I have someone to guide me to a good spot, why not?"

"You found the Hilton boring? I personally had a great time."

"I'm glad you were entertained, Dupree."

"Sounds like a plan, Émile. Y'all should make it happen."

Émile spun his head around to thinking that he might do just that. This conversation alone felt good. More than cheerful, it felt lively and restorative. As though time, which had taken a breather, which had been standing still for him for days while his heart, so he felt, was stopped, might again begin to tick away the minutes, bring on new days and nights, and resume once more its own familiar sure rhythm. Besides, he could have a drink with his new pal Pascal Dupree, although not at Sinners Too, and be shown around the town. That sounded not only beneficial, but necessary.

"Come to think of it," Émile suggested, "I could go down and identify those Miami boys for you. If you say it's necessary, that might be best."

"Ah? Y'all fishing for a good excuse? All right then, Émile. I can hand that out. We need y'all down here lickety-split, all right? Get your ass in gear."

He could detect the other man's smile and presumed it matched his own.

"All right," Émile told him. "If you insist, we'll both go down there. If I have to discharge my duty as an ordinary citizen, Sandra might as well come along."

"That's the stuff, Émile. Y'all talking now. Anyway, you're safer with her than without her. That much is clear."

Cinq-Mars responded in kind to the other man's jibes. "If I get down there, Dupree, I might as well clean up the NOPD. What do you think?"

"Bring a mop and a bucket, Émile, and get to work. Why not?"

The two men heard each other chuckle. That felt good. By the time he put the phone down, the retired detective was doing what retired people are supposed to do, dreaming of his next journey, the adventure oncoming.